BEYOND
THE
SHADOW
OF
NIGHT

OTHER TITLES BY RAY KINGFISHER:

Historical Fiction

The Sugar Men
Rosa's Gold

General Fiction

Matchbox Memories
Tales of Loss and Guilt

Writing as Rachel Quinn

An Ocean Between Us

Writing as Ray Backley

Bad and Badder
Slow Burning Lies

Writing as Ray Fripp

I, Smith (with Harry Dewulf)
Easy Money
E.T. the Extra Tortilla

BEYOND
THE
SHADOW
OF
NIGHT

RAY KINGFISHER

LAKE UNION

PUBLISHING

Published by Lake Union Publishing, Seattle

www.apub.com

Amazon, the Amazon logo, and Lake Union Publishing are trademarks of Amazon.com, Inc., or its affiliates.

ISBN-13: 9781542041768 (hardcover)
ISBN-10: 1542041767 (hardcover)
ISBN-13: 9781612189345 (paperback)
ISBN-10: 1612189342 (paperback)

Cover design by Ghost Design

Printed in the United States of America

To Maria

Prologue

Hartmann Way, Pittsburgh, July 2001

Diane Peterson was returning home after a great night out with Brad. Well, perhaps more average than great. Enjoyable, but about as good as it ever got for a middle-aged woman who still lived with her father, and for whom the phrase "boyfriend and girlfriend" was stretched to the limit and should have snapped a long time ago. Like a lot of things.

Nevertheless, she *had* enjoyed the evening: bowling followed by a meal with Em'n'Dave, who for once didn't mention their upcoming fifteenth wedding anniversary and didn't yammer on endlessly about how well their two kids were doing. That was good. For both Diane and Brad. Kids—and probably marriage too—were ships that had long since drifted over the horizon for them.

She pulled her keys from her purse and opened the front door of number 38 before turning to wave goodnight to Brad, who returned the gesture discreetly from the cab window.

She waited until the cab's brake lights told her it had reached the end of Hartmann Way before stepping inside the front door and shutting out the rest of the world.

"Dad?" she shouted. Not aggressively or even stridently. She'd been told off for that thirty years ago and had never forgotten. He'd said something about harsh shouting unnerving him, which had puzzled her at the time, and still did just a little. But she knew not to question.

But her call was greeted with silence, so for once perhaps a measured increase in volume was appropriate.

"Dad?"

Still nothing. Nothing but cool air.

"You upstairs?" she hollered, now fearful of both a sore reaction and no reaction at all.

A step to the side. A strange, almost metallic smell. Stickiness at the back of her throat. Three paces forward. A glance into the kitchen. And then she saw.

Her keys and purse dropped from her limp hands onto the floor. She nearly followed, summoning up just enough energy to stop her knees buckling.

There was something she should be doing.

The phone.

A call.

Her face felt hot, her breath unnaturally cold.

The number 911 flew into her head and straight out again, as she turned and staggered back to the door. She opened it, and then her knees gave out. No energy. No control. A scrabble to her feet. A stumble into the road. The rest was blurred. It wasn't real. It couldn't be.

Chapter 1

The two boys were born within days of each other on the same farm, during a warm and dusty June week.

Like any farm in the breadbasket of the burgeoning Soviet Empire, it had a big responsibility to its citizens. A crop failure some years before had caused widespread famine, so work took priority and the boys' papas didn't see much of them in the days and weeks that followed their births.

One of the boys, the firstborn of Mr. and Mrs. Petrenko, was given the name Mykhail, a traditional Ukrainian name. The other was the third born in his family, but the first boy. His parents had prayed for a boy—someone to manage the farm when Mr. Kogan got old—so they called him Asher, a traditional Jewish name meaning "blessed," because they felt they were, and he should be.

Asher's family had owned and operated the farm for decades, living through the First World War, the Russian Revolution, the Polish-Ukrainian War, and even the Ukrainian Civil War. That was a lot to survive, but as the farm was nestled deep in the rural heart of the country, most of it seemed to pass them by. The only remnant of those days the boys got to know about was that Mykhail's parents had fled the more troublesome areas three or four years before, and had been taken in by Asher's family. In return for much-needed labor, Mykhail's parents were given the smaller of two farmhouses on the land and a share of the produce—eggs, grain, milk, chickens, and occasionally some goat meat.

In the first seven years of their lives, Mykhail and Asher became inseparable—closer than brothers. Of course, there were chores—gathering hay for the horses, mucking them out, feeding leftovers to the chickens, fetching water from the well. But they also found time to play together, to fish in one of the many rivers threading through the terrain, and, yes, occasionally to fight each other. They played with children from the surrounding farms too, often games of hide-and-seek in the woods and long grasses, but they always remained each other's best friend. And when the weather kept them indoors, they were also taught to read and write together.

One day, when climbing one of the few trees around the farm, Mykhail fell and was unconscious for a few seconds. Asher helped him home, but the large vertical gash and subsequent scar just below his left eye would be a lasting reminder of the dangers of climbing trees. At least, that was what Asher's papa told them. Mykhail's papa didn't seem so worried, and the boys still climbed trees occasionally.

But during the 1930s many changes took place—changes that the boys weren't old enough to understand. All they knew was that they went hungry more often, and that they were forever being encouraged to go fishing.

One typical summer's day in 1932, the boys took a leather bottle full of fresh milk and a small bag of pumpkin seeds, and headed out for what they knew to be the best river for fishing.

The walk seemed longer than usual, and the crops sparser and unhealthier. They'd both heard their parents talking about "the situation," but whenever they asked what this situation was they were shown a forced smile and told it was nothing for them to worry about.

So they didn't worry.

On this trip, they each had three rods to keep an eye on, but the fish were less inclined to bite than usual, and after an hour they'd caught nothing. Mykhail left his fishing rods to fate and flopped onto his back, soaking up the sun's rays. Then Asher did the same.

"My papa says it's the Russians' fault," Mykhail said.

"What is?"

"The situation. The hunger. Papa says the Russians are trying to starve us all."

"Why would they do that?"

"I don't know. He says they hate Ukrainians. He also says . . ."

"Says what?"

"He says the Jews don't help."

Asher frowned. "What does he mean by that?"

"Oh, not you. Not the Kogans. I'm sure he's talking about the other ones—the bad ones."

"Good. Because I can't remember doing anything wrong. Except I don't let my sisters tell me what to do. And anyway, we're Jewish *and* Ukrainian."

"Of course. Perhaps I didn't hear him properly. I don't think I was supposed to be listening."

Asher nodded. "I hear my papa talking sometimes too. He says these lands have been chopped up so many times that most Ukrainians don't know who they should be fighting, so they usually end up fighting each other."

"Perhaps we shouldn't talk about it," Mykhail said. "It doesn't matter."

Something caught Asher's eye: one of the lines twitching violently. "Fish matter," he said, tapping Mykhail.

Mykhail lifted his head, noticed the bite, and grabbed his rod. "You're right," he said. "And we've just caught one."

The fishing carried on with mixed success for the rest of that summer, and whenever they fished together the two boys spoke of what food they'd eaten recently, what tricks Asher's sisters had played on him, even the weather—anything apart from "the situation."

By the summer of 1933, however, "the situation" had clearly become more serious. A heavy atmosphere clung on to the whole farm like a curse, and the boys' parents were having a lot more whispered conversations.

The boys had been attending school for a few years, but still managed to make time for fishing trips. Their parents had always encouraged the trips, but now they were being *told* to go, and to stay longer, and to bring back more fish. At least, they were told that by their papas; their mamas usually said nothing.

And most of the time there were no seeds or bottles of milk to take with them on their fishing trips.

On one occasion, Mykhail's mama was sweeping the dust from the kitchen as he was preparing to leave.

"I'm sorry," she said, "I've nothing for you to take. We're just so short of food."

Mykhail knew; he'd heard it many times before. "Yes, Mama," he said, much as he had all year.

"Things will get better, have a little faith. But for now you'll have to drink river water instead of milk, and make sure you bring back anything you catch."

"Yes, Mama."

"Even the small fish. Don't throw anything back in, will you?"

"No, Mama."

Then Mykhail saw that worried frown on his mama's face again—the one he'd seen more often lately. She laid down the broom, drew the back of her hand across her brow, and rushed over to him so quickly he was frightened for a moment.

"And please God, take care of yourself," she said, and kissed him on the head.

Mykhail, slightly confused, left the farmhouse and crossed the yard to his friend's farmhouse.

"He's in the barn," Asher's mama said as she pummeled the dirty water out of a soaking-wet shirt. "Helping his papa sort out the seeds."

"Thank you, Mrs. Kogan."

In the barn, Asher and his papa were sitting on the ground, sifting through the seeds, discarding the rotten ones. Mykhail's papa was there too, grooming the two horses. As Mykhail entered, his papa glanced at him, but held a blank expression and turned away.

"Are you coming fishing?" Mykhail said to Asher.

Asher looked over to his papa, who nodded. The boy stood up, wiped the dust from his hands, and headed for the door.

"They were arguing again," Asher said when they were well away from the barn.

"What about?"

Asher shrugged. "I don't know. But your papa is a nice man."

"Yours too."

"So why do they argue so much?"

"They don't agree about the Russians," Mykhail said. "I don't know what it means, all this talk of the state and food production. They said the authorities take what food they want and don't provide enough seed."

"What's that got to do with the Russians?"

"I don't know, but they say that's why everyone's hungry."

The fishing hadn't been good recently, so the boys walked upstream, to somewhere they'd never fished before. They found a calm, deep section of water their lines could reach, and sat down on the riverbank facing the sun.

Their rods were the usual long sticks with string tied onto the ends; their floats were rough chunks of wood. They found grubs to impale on the bent nails tied to the ends of the string, then tossed the lines into the river and settled back.

"Is your papa angry?" Mykhail said after a few minutes' silence.

Asher shook his head. "Not angry. Just very serious. As if I've done something wrong."

"My papa shouts a lot about seeds and crops and things, usually when he's complaining about the Russians."

"My papa says we should be grateful, that many people are dying in the towns and cities."

Mykhail shook his head. "My papa says we should fight the Russians, that they're deliberately destroying our country and our people. He says we're Ukrainians and will never be Russians."

Asher said nothing to that, and the boys turned their attentions back to fishing, watching the slow-drifting river, flinching every time a rod twitched.

A lot of time passed by—perhaps three hours, judging by the movement of the sun. And they were good hours by recent standards: seven fish were now wrapped up in one of Asher's threadbare old shirts.

"Shall we go?" Asher said, getting to his feet. "I'm so hungry."

Mykhail shook his head. "We need another fish. One for each person. Papa will be upset if we go home with less." He showed Asher a serious frown. "That's only fair."

Asher sat down again.

A few minutes later, they saw figures approaching from the direction of the sun, and then heard voices breaking through the burbling of the river.

They exchanged glances.

Their parents had told them to be careful—and not just today. People were desperate in these times.

"We should go," Asher said.

Mykhail grabbed the rods, leaving Asher to pick up the shirt and the fish wrapped inside it. They turned and started walking.

"Not too fast," Mykhail said. "And don't keep looking behind."

They walked on casually, and a few minutes later heard a shout from behind: "Hey you!"

"Ignore it," Mykhail said.

They quickened their pace despite Mykhail's words.

"Hey! You two boys!"

Mykhail cursed and turned back; Asher too.

There were three of them—all grown men, all bony and sunken-chested, one much older than the other two. They must have been walking quickly to have gotten so close.

"Do we run?" Asher whispered to Mykhail.

Mykhail squinted at the men, then turned to Asher. "We could outrun the old one, but . . ."

Asher gulped. "They might just be lost, wanting directions."

"Yes. That's probably it."

They waited while the men sauntered over to them. Asher hid his hands—and the day's catch—behind him.

"How long have you been fishing?" the biggest man asked.

"Not long," Mykhail said. "They aren't biting today."

"You didn't catch anything?"

Mykhail shook his head.

The man stepped toward Asher. It was man to boy, but nevertheless the man stretched himself up to his full height. "You," he said, his lips smiling but his eyes too focused to join in. "What have you got behind your back?"

"Just my shirt."

"Let me see."

"No!" Mykhail shouted, pulling Asher away. "Go away. Catch your own fish."

The man laughed, then turned to the other two men, who grinned like cats. He looked directly at Asher again, then stopped laughing, his face suddenly taking on a grim appearance. "Come on." He fluttered an upturned hand toward the boy. "Let me see."

Asher shook his head.

The man took a step closer. Asher stood firm, but saw a flash, heard a crack, then his world spun around and his head thumped the earth. He felt grainy dirt on his face and smelled blood. He turned and looked up to see the man wiping the blood from the back of his hand. Then he saw a blur, and after that, nothing.

As the man bent down to pick up the shirt, Mykhail took a run and barged into him.

The man stumbled, but still picked up the shirt, glancing at the fish inside.

Mykhail tried again, but the man held him at bay with his free hand and shoved him down onto the ground. "And stay there, you little scarface," he said. "Or I'll knock you out too."

Mykhail stayed.

"Good catch," the man shouted back to his friends. He gathered the corners of the bundle up so no fish would fall out, then joined them. They left, walking away slowly with an occasional glance back at the boys.

Mykhail sneered as he watched them leave, then scurried over and knelt down next to his friend.

Asher was motionless, the lower half of his face now encrusted with dirt turned red.

"Asher!" Mykhail shook him. "Wake up, Asher!"

Nothing.

He tried again and looked back toward the men, briefly considering asking for their help getting Asher home. "Don't be stupid," he muttered to himself.

He lifted Asher's head off the ground, and held his ear to his friend's mouth.

Yes, there was a rhythmic rush of air.

He lifted Asher's arms up, grabbed his torso as best he could, then heaved him over his shoulder. With two long grunts, he pushed himself up onto one foot, then the other, thanking God he was a little bigger and stronger than his friend.

But bigger than Asher or not, it was a struggle, each step a wild stamp, each breath a gasp. Ten yards became twenty, but a few staggers later he lurched and stopped, exhausted, and stared ahead. They were still some way from home, and he would collapse if he tried it all in one go, injuring them both, so he laid his friend's body down on a grassy mound.

"Only a rest," he whispered. "Only a rest."

He rubbed some feeling back into his shoulder, took a few deep breaths, then grabbed Asher's arm again.

This time Asher resisted, and with a cough and a few blinks he was conscious. He spat out blood, but his lips were numb and swollen, so it merely dribbled off his chin and onto his clothes. He looked up. "Mykhail?" he said. "Where are we? My head hurts."

"Can you walk?" Mykhail asked.

Asher staggered to his feet like a newborn foal. "What happened?"

"We were fishing. Some men came."

Asher cast a glance back at the riverbank.

"A man hit you."

Asher held his head, grimacing. "Now I remember. Did they get the fish?"

Mykhail nodded.

"Did you carry me over here?"

"Of course. I was going to carry you home."

"Really? All the way?"

Mykhail shrugged. "You're my best friend. You helped me get home when I fell from that tree, remember?"

Asher tried to smile, but only half of his face responded, the other half numb. "They'll be expecting fish," he said.

"We can only tell them the truth," Mykhail said. "Papa says good Ukrainian boys always tell the truth."

They started walking.

◆ ◆ ◆

Once the cluster of thatched, whitewashed shacks came into sight, the boys' pace slowed, as if each was trying to be the last one to arrive.

Eventually, Mykhail took the lead and strode into the farmyard.

His papa was busy grooming one of the horses, but stopped and flashed a smile when he saw his son. He hurried over, rubbing his hands on his overalls and chewing on nothing, as though priming his digestive system. His eyes darted around his own son, then Asher. "Where are the fish?" He struggled to hold his smile, which turned sickly before falling.

Asher looked to Mykhail, who shook his head.

"You didn't catch any? None at all?"

"We were robbed," Mykhail said.

His papa dropped the brush and grabbed him by the shoulders. "Robbed? Are you okay?"

"They stole all our catch."

Mykhail's papa cursed but didn't take his eyes off his son. "Did you fight them?" he said.

"They were much bigger than us."

"But you put up a fight, yes?"

Mykhail looked at Asher, and so did his papa.

Asher patted the dried blood on his chin and clothes. "We tried, Mr. Petrenko. Mykhail punched one of them and I kicked the other."

Mykhail's papa turned his attentions to Asher, peering at his face, holding his jaw and turning it left and right. "You have a split lip there, Asher. And a nasty bruise. Any loose teeth?"

Asher shook his head.

"And you . . ." Now he spoke to his son. "Did you take any blows?"

Mykhail made to speak but instead just stared at his papa.

"He's a better fighter than I am," Asher said. "So he didn't get hurt."

"But I gave one of them a black eye," Mykhail added, with that same straight expression.

His papa's gaze hopped between one boy and the other for a few seconds, before the man gave a well-considered nod. "Good," he said, and gave his son a slap on the back. "You didn't give up without a fight. You're good Ukrainian boys."

That evening, the two families ate together. As usual, the talk was more plentiful than the food.

The eight of them thanked God that they had some food at all when so many didn't, then ate in silence for a few minutes. There was potato soup with matzos, a little cream, a few raisins, and water.

"I'm sorry," Mykhail said.

"What for?" Asher's sister, Rina, said.

"Well, I . . ." Mykhail stopped and looked across to his papa for approval.

"Mykhail and Asher caught some fish today," Mykhail's papa said, sullen-faced. "But they were robbed."

"These are desperate times," Asher's papa said.

Mykhail's papa harrumphed. "And we all know whose fault it is. If the—"

"Never mind that," Asher's mama said. She looked at her husband. "Hirsch, tell me what happened with the boys today. You told me the fish weren't biting."

"I'm sorry, Golda. I didn't want to worry you."

"*Worry me?*" She stared at her son. "I *thought* your face looked a little swollen, and I was right. Well, that's it. No more fishing trips for my son—not without one of the men."

Asher and Mykhail stopped chewing for a moment and looked at each other.

"We can discuss it later," Asher's papa said to his wife. "Let's eat, not talk."

For a few minutes, the only sounds were clinks of spoon on bowl and a few slurps.

Then Asher's mama let her spoon rest on the bowl and wiped a tear from her face. "This is our only son, and we need him to risk his life to feed us?"

"Later, Golda."

"No, we won't talk about it later. He's not going anywhere without an adult."

Mykhail's mama, silent until now, cleared her throat and said quietly, "I agree." She looked at her husband. "The same goes for our son. It's no use pretending, Dmytro. We've all heard the stories."

"What stories?" Asher's eldest sister, Keren, said.

"Please, Iryna, no," Asher's papa said before the question could be answered. "Not at the dinner table."

She stared defiantly at him. "But everyone needs to know, Hirsch. My sister on the other side of the village has a friend. Her daughter was sent to fetch water from the well, but on the way there she was killed and . . . so they say . . . eaten."

Her husband shot her a stiff glance. "Hirsch is right," he said. "We are all eating, Iryna. *Eating!* Stop talking like this."

"Yes, well . . . Yes, you're right, I'm sorry."

Asher's mama picked up her spoon and pointed it at her husband. "I kept telling you. We should have gone to Warsaw with my sister."

"Well, we can't go now. The borders are sealed and people are shot for trying to leave the country."

Mykhail's papa slammed the palm of his hand down onto the table. "Damn the Russians! They stop us leaving, but when we stay they take our produce, give us so little in return, stop us buying and selling. Did you know that my cousin was arrested for trying to sell some of his hay?"

"The Russian people are suffering too," Asher's papa said.

"So we are *told*. But in Ukraine, we *know*. We only see a little but we all know. Whoever we talk to, the stories are the same: thousands of dead bodies lying in the cities—probably hundreds of thousands."

"But not us. We're surviving."

"But for how long?" Asher's mama said.

"Not very long if we don't eat what we have." Asher's papa pointed a finger down at the table. "Now, please. Everyone. What's happening is terrible. But let's eat, not talk."

They nodded, and soon they were all eating in silence.

Mykhail was first to finish, and sat with his arms folded. He coughed. Then again.

"Yes, you can leave the table," his mama said wearily.

He jumped to the floor and ran around the table. "Papa, can I sit on the tractor?"

"Of course." Mr. Petrenko patted his son on the head. "Perhaps one day you can show me how to use it." He forced a laugh.

Mykhail left, and Asher started to eat more quickly, eyeing the door every so often.

"At least the tractor is free," Mykhail's mama said. "And the fuel too."

"Free?" Mykhail's papa said. "*Free?* Pah! Nothing under the Russians is free."

"What do you mean?"

"He means we pay in other ways," Asher's papa said. "In return for the tractor we'll have to give most of our crops to the state."

"Oh, yes," Mykhail's papa said. "Also we have to produce the crops they tell us to, not what we need. And then they have the nerve to tell us it's all for the greater good of our beloved Soviet comrades."

Asher placed his empty bowl down on the table, making as much noise as he could.

"Oh, go on," his mama said before he had the chance to ask to be excused from the table.

He scurried out and ran all the way to the barn where they kept the tractor, and found Mykhail sitting on the seat, making his best engine noises.

Asher clambered up, and the boys were shoulder to shoulder.

"Can't you see?" Mykhail shouted above the imagined noise. "I'm driving."

"I'll drive with you," Asher shouted back.

Ten minutes later, they were still making noises, smoothing their hands around the huge steering wheel, and leaning left and right as they imagined the tractor turning. They both stopped when their papas came into the barn.

"Papa," Mykhail asked, "when are we going to use the tractor?"

His papa looked at Asher's papa. "It's your farm, Hirsch. What do you think?"

Asher's papa took his cap off and scratched his head. "This new contraption? I'm not sure what to do with it."

"So why have we got it?" Asher asked.

"Because we're told we have to use it," Mykhail's papa said. "The Russians don't think we can make our own decisions."

Asher's papa wandered over to the rear of the contraption and rubbed his chin, pondering. "It's a worry. Our horses are underweight. Perhaps this could help. It doesn't need feeding."

"And the horses?" Mykhail's papa said. "We let them die?"

But Asher's papa was still looking at the tractor. "I still don't understand how it works. It pulls equipment just like a horse would. But what makes it move?"

"You put gasoline in it," Asher said.

Mykhail pointed to the filler cap. "In there."

"Children," Mykhail's papa said. "What do they know?"

"More than us by the sounds of it," Asher's papa said. "One year at school and they can run the farm better than us."

"Tractors," Mykhail's papa said. "What nonsense."

Chapter 2

Dyovsta, Ukraine, 1936

The men's laughter turned out to be hollow. By their teenage years, Asher and Mykhail had worked out all there was to know about running a tractor. Air filters, carburetors, oil changes—Asher and Mykhail read the sheaf of papers that constituted a manual, asked questions at school, and read more books. The men eventually gave up trying to figure out how this modern metal horse worked, and just let their boys get on with it. The boys sometimes even drove the tractor, and between them they carried out most of the basic maintenance tasks, even giving advice to other farmers who had been encouraged by the state to use this new technology.

The Petrenkos and the Kogans had jointly developed the farm, introducing new crops and improving yields, and there was now more food for the families, so the pain of empty stomachs was gone. Mykhail's papa, however, never allowed anyone to forget the time of great famine, nor how some desperate people had coped with it, nor—most importantly—who was to blame for it.

For a year or more, food had been sufficient, arguments rare, and smiles easy to come by, but now both boys sensed something else was around the corner. Their parents' faces became sullen, there were whispered discussions, and there were silent meals. The boys talked on their fishing expeditions, or when tinkering with the tractor, but neither had any answers.

One day, after breakfast, Asher's papa ushered everyone out of the house.

Except one.

"Not you, Asher. Come over here."

As Asher's sisters, Keren and Rina, passed by, they patted his shoulder and showed him pitying smiles.

His papa pulled two chairs over to the stove and they sat together.

"My son, there's something I have to tell you."

Asher knew already that this would be no trivial matter, but his papa wore a frown and his voice was deep, his speech slow and staccato, which made Asher even more nervous.

"I know you won't like this, but . . ."

"What? What's wrong, Papa?" Asher wanted to smile, but it wouldn't come.

"We're leaving the farm."

"All of us?"

"Just the Kogans. The Petrenkos are staying."

"Including Mykhail?"

"Mykhail has to stay with his parents. I'm sorry, Asher. We're going to Warsaw."

"For how long?"

Now Asher saw his papa's eyes turn glassy. "I don't know."

"But . . . what about the farm?"

"Mr. Petrenko will look after it. In time, Mykhail will help more."

"And we'll be coming back, won't we?"

Asher's papa took a long breath and held his son by the shoulders. "Asher, I promise you. I give you my word. We will come back here one day, when things are better."

"Better?"

"You're a clever boy, Asher. You must have heard how the authorities are closing down Jewish schools and discouraging the use of Yiddish. But politicians change like the tides, and one day the situation will improve for us."

"I don't want to go, Papa."

"I know, Asher, but try to be positive. I can get a factory job in Warsaw. So can Keren and Rina. You'll probably end up at a better school." A crooked smile played on his lips. "You might be able to study tractors—even those new motor car contraptions."

"But I want to stay here."

"Asher. Listen to me. Your mama misses your Aunt Freida; she's wanted to go to Warsaw for some time now, but we couldn't afford it. Now we've saved up a little money to get there and we think it's for the best."

"You mean it's best *for Mama*."

"Don't be like that, Asher. She's . . ." His papa struggled to carry on. As he took a breath, Asher jumped off the chair and ran for the door.

"No! Asher! Wait!"

But the boy was gone.

A few seconds later, Asher wiped the tears from his face as he rounded the corner of the farmhouse, where Mama and Rina were hanging out the washing.

His mama smiled sadly. "So, your papa's told you."

"I don't want to go, Mama. I'll be lonely and I want to stay here."

"Oh, Asher. I know you'll miss Mykhail, but Warsaw is a big city with so many things to see and do. You'll make new friends, just like your sisters will."

"But why can't Aunt Freida come here instead? Why do we have to go there? Why, Mama, why?"

"It's . . . safer."

"Safer?"

Rina handed the washing basket to her mama and crouched down in front of Asher, her brown eyes large and warm looking up at him. "Asher. Listen to me. I promise that you won't be lonely."

"But why do we have to go?"

"Well . . ." She looked up to the clear sky, using her hand to shield her eyes from the brightness. It wasn't long before she pointed into the distance. "Look over there, Asher."

"You mean the birds?"

"Yes. Have you ever wondered why they flock together—why each one doesn't just fly off wherever it pleases?"

Asher stared at the cloud of dark spots constantly changing shape.

"You see, they do that because they feel safer when there are lots of them together."

Asher nodded, although he didn't really understand. But perhaps life in Warsaw wouldn't be so bad after all, not with a sister like Rina.

At the same time, in the smaller farmhouse, Mr. Petrenko was breaking the same news to his son.

"But we get the farm," he said. "Isn't that good?"

"I don't want the farm," Mykhail said. "I want the Kogans. I want everything to stay the same. Why can't everything stay the same?"

Pain briefly flashed across his papa's face. "Nothing can stay the same, Mykhail. They want to be with their own kind. You'll learn to accept it, and eventually you'll make more friends. The harvests are getting bigger. And now the laws have changed to allow us to sell some of what we produce, so we can pay people to work."

"But I don't want other friends."

"Trust me, Mykhail. Be a good Ukrainian boy and be strong. Things will get better from now on. I promise." His fist playfully nudged his son's chest. "And when you make more friends you can go fishing with them, yes?"

Mykhail looked down at his feet and nodded slowly.

"Are you crying?"

Mykhail sniffed and shook his head. A moment later, he sensed a rare closeness as his papa put an arm around his shoulder. He smelled the stale earth and sweat, then heard the words, whispered with coarse passion: "Good boy. You're nearly a man now. Be strong. Strong Ukrainian boys don't cry."

For days after the Kogans left the farm both boys felt numb inside, and each had their own way of dealing with the problem.

Asher kept asking his parents about Warsaw—whether they had motor cars there, whether there were rivers to fish in, whether he would have his own room to sleep in, how many people lived in the city—and eventually his mama told him to wait and see, to just enjoy the train journey.

In truth, he really wanted to ask when they would be going back to the farm.

Back on the farm, Mykhail coped with his best friend being taken away from him by going fishing whenever he could. Alone.

It didn't seem right.

And the fish stayed away.

The boys had lived next to each other on the farm since birth, and had seen each other every day of their lives. They were brothers in all but blood.

Warsaw, Poland, 1936

To Asher, the noisy, bustling city of Warsaw was such a different world that it might as well have been another planet. He hadn't even visited the big towns and cities of Ukraine, although he'd heard stories and seen photographs of the huge buildings and wide streets. But now he was on a sidewalk in a city that was, according to his papa, bigger than any in Ukraine.

Yes, he'd asked questions on the journey, but now he was too absorbed by the sights and sounds to even speak. When he looked up he saw so many buildings—some taller than the tallest tree he'd ever seen. And the number of people . . . well, there were just so many of them he was almost dancing left and right to avoid them.

Then there was the noise. People were talking and laughing, shoes cracked and scraped against concrete, doors squealed open and slammed shut, musicians played on street corners. The sound of a horn made him jump, and he turned to see a car. Yes, it was a car—a real motor car. Asher had only ever seen one in pictures before, and knew it worked a little like a tractor.

And when they eventually reached their destination the noise didn't stop; it was always there in the background, as if it would be there forever.

"You'll get used to it," his papa said.

The apartment, one floor up, was basic and less roomy than the farmhouse, but felt warmer. The main room had a kitchen area on one side and a table and chairs in the other. There were two small bedrooms, one for the parents and one for the children—although they were hardly children anymore. The window of the main room looked out over a large square. Asher was mesmerized by the view at first; he'd never seen so many people in one place before, all rushing in every direction. *Where are they all going, and why?* he would ask himself.

Asher's mama placed a few pictures and ornaments around the apartment, and Aunt Freida came over from the north of the city to welcome the family.

The day after that, Asher was enrolled in a school.

For the first week, his instinct was to run for cover whenever he heard a car approach, and he felt the tall buildings all around closing in on him, squeezing his spirit. He wondered why there were no fields or wide-open meadows, only buildings and concrete.

And he missed the fishing.

But he went to school and learned Polish, mathematics, and some science. The latter turned out to be his favorite subject. Every day he would return home enthused by a new fact about electricity or magnetism or how metals react to changes in temperature.

His mama would usually reply with something like, "That's very interesting, Asher, but did you make any new friends?"

On the first few occasions Asher simply ignored the question, but then he started replying that of course he'd made friends. A few random names would pass his lips, and that would do the trick; his mama would smile and say she was pleased for him.

A few weeks after their arrival, his papa's words—that he would get used to living in Warsaw—were starting to come true. Yes, he was getting used to it, but he was getting used to *being away from home*.

One day, in class, a fellow schoolboy asked him where he was from.

"A farm," he replied. "In Dyovsta."

The boy shook his head. "Never heard of it. But I went to a farm once, it was like paradise. You must miss it."

Asher had to think for a few seconds to remember, but yes, he did miss it. He wondered whether Mykhail had gone fishing that day, and pictured him resting on a riverbank in the Ukrainian countryside with only sweet birdsong and the babbling of water to disturb the peace.

That evening, while his mama was cooking, Asher lingered in the kitchen end of the main room, occasionally glancing at her.

"What is it?" she said. "You want to eat before everyone else?"

"When will we be visiting the farm again, Mama?"

"In time," she said. "I promise."

"Can Mykhail come visit us?"

She wiped her hands and pulled a chair out from the table. "Why don't you write and ask him?"

"Write?"

"We can buy paper and envelopes. You can tell him what this place is like, and ask him to write back and tell you what's happening on the farm."

Asher thought for a moment, his mouth twitching into a nervous smile. "I'd like that."

"Good boy." She hugged him, and held him close for longer than he really expected.

Asher wrote many letters in the months that followed, but also kept asking his parents when they would be returning to the farm.

He never got the answer he wanted, and eventually stopped asking.

He also gave up asking his mama whether there were any letters for him. Perhaps Mykhail didn't miss him. Yes, that was it. He'd probably made new friends in Dyovsta.

So Asher stopped writing, and, in time, strangers became friends, the apartment became a home of sorts, and the noise, bustle, and traffic of Warsaw belonged to Asher as much as anyone else. His papa got a job hauling flour around on a cart for the local bakery, Keren and Rina got jobs in factories, and Asher got on with his schooling.

Also, there was money. Paying for anything—but especially food—felt strange to young Asher, but his parents kept saying that even after paying for food, there was still money left over. And with that came visits to the theater, books, occasionally a toy—even a soccer ball for Asher and his new friends to play with.

Perhaps he had found a new home after all.

Chapter 3

Diane Peterson tried to summon up a little fury to inject into her voice. It wasn't something she was accustomed to doing, but this wasn't a normal situation. She'd asked Detective Durwood twice already, and although he hadn't reacted negatively to her request, he hadn't really reacted positively either. She was used to these obfuscating, delaying, and damned irritating tactics from her father—by God she was used to that. But that would no longer happen, which was the point. So she leaned forward across the table, took a wavering breath, and put the words out there with a deliberate emphasis on every syllable.

"I need to see him," she said.

Detective Durwood looked up from his folder of notes and flicked his eyes across to the clock on the wall, an action that made Diane say, "Well?"

He sighed. "We're going around in circles. Like I told you before, I can understand your reaction, I really can. It's pretty common."

"You're right, we are going around in circles. So let's stop right now. Just arrange it, okay? Just let me know when I can see him."

"What exactly do you expect to get out of it?"

"Only the truth."

"Well, Diane, we—"

"Less of the *Diane*. To you, it's ma'am—or better still, *Ms. Peterson*."

"All right. I'm sorry. But we already know the truth."

"Do you really? Do you know the complete truth? I knew them both, remember, and from where I stand I'd say no, you only *think* you do."

The detective glanced down at his notes again. "With respect, we got a whole bunch of evidence and we got a confession, and—"

"You know the *what*. That's not *all* the truth. I need to know the *why*. Look, I didn't want to spring this on you, but I know it's part of my rights. I think it's called the Restorative Justice program. Isn't that correct?"

He whipped off his glasses and peered at her. "Well, of course there is that, but you have to remember that the primary aim of Restorative Justice in this state isn't so much to satisfy families of victims. It's to facilitate the rehabilitation of offenders by showing them the consequences of their actions."

"And so?"

A smirk—perhaps unconscious, Diane thought—appeared on his face. "The guy's seventy-eight. At that age, *there will be no rehabilitation*." The last five words were spoken with an air of finality.

"Detective, you don't know me, and you didn't know my father. So let me explain something. I'm forty-eight. I've lived with him since forever, apart from a few months when I lived with my mother. Sure, there were times when I wanted to leave him to his own devices—to go off and marry and have a family of my own. But I didn't. He was just going to be a lonely old man without me, and I enjoyed the precious time I had with him. I loved my father."

"Like I said, it's understandable for you to feel bad about what happened to him. It's normal."

"I don't give a damn about normal, and that's not the point I'm making here. And if you think I'm normal, you couldn't be more wrong.

Oh, I enjoyed the time I had with him, but I didn't exactly grow up into an average, well-adjusted adult. My father took care of everything he could so that I didn't have to trouble myself with the mundane things in life. But there was a price, and that price is that I've spent most of my adult life like a . . . almost like a mouse, not arguing my case and standing up for myself."

He nodded, clearly trying to be solemn in the face of her anger. He'd probably been trained for it.

Diane continued. "But I just can't be the person I was anymore—the person my father wanted me to be. And that's because you've got his corpse lying on a slab. Now, I want to know why it's on that slab and not in his easy chair listening to the damned music he loved so much. I want to know exactly what happened that night and why—or as much as I can find out from that man you have in the cell. And if I have to go over your head and take legal action to get my rights, I can promise you I will. I won't give up, Detective Durwood."

"All right." The detective nodded slowly. "Okay. I was only trying to prevent you from upsetting yourself further, but if that's the way you feel . . ."

"It most certainly is."

"In that case, legal action won't be necessary. As you say, it's your right, and I think you'd win if we contested the case. I honestly can't see what you stand to gain from a situation like this, but if that's what you want, we'll arrange it."

Diane exhaled a calming breath. "Wasn't so hard, was it?"

He grimaced, raising an eyebrow suggestively.

"What?" she said. "Is there something else?"

"Actually . . . Well, he seemed delirious, sort of gabbing away about how you two have some sort of bond."

"Bond?"

"Something in common. Do you know anything about that?"

Diane was taken aback for a moment. "Uh, nothing. We have nothing at all in common, except that he knew my father. He stayed over at the house plenty of times, almost like he was my uncle. But I can promise you, other than that we have absolutely nothing in common."

"Is he . . . going senile?"

"God, no. He's sharp, believe me."

"I have to admit, that's what our guys say too. Anyhow . . . we'll be in touch, although it might take a couple days."

"Not a problem. I can wait."

They exchanged polite smiles and got to their feet.

"And I'm sorry," Diane said. "I didn't mean to be forceful."

"Oh, of course not."

"No, really. I didn't. I'm sure you'd be just the same if it happened to you. I just need to meet and talk with the man who left a big bullet hole in my father's head."

Chapter 4

Warsaw, Poland, 1937

The months flew by, but a part of Asher still longed for the wide-open spaces of the farm, the toil that seemed to give such satisfaction, and the lazy afternoons fishing with Mykhail. Yes, he told his parents that he was looking forward to leaving school and perhaps getting a job working with his papa, but although Warsaw was a home of sorts, it didn't feel like *home*, and he still wasn't sure whether the friends he'd made at school were anything more than acquaintances.

One Saturday afternoon, late in the summer of 1937, when a hazy sun was doing its utmost to brighten up the dust-lined streets, Papa told everyone to put their coats on.

Asher looked at him closely. Papa had a broad smile and his shoulders were high and proud as he handed the coats out.

"It's been a good week," he said. "Today we're having a treat."

Asher was the only one not to get out of his seat.

"Come on," Papa said to him. "We're going to Baran's."

"Baran's?" Keren said, her face almost alight with joy. "Really?"

"I don't want to go," Asher said.

"You know what Baran's is, don't you?" Papa replied.

"No, but I don't want to go."

"You don't know what it is, but you don't want to go? That doesn't make sense."

"Leave the boy alone, Hirsch," Mama said.

While Papa sucked air through his teeth and shook his head, Mama handed Asher his coat.

"Asher, please," she said. "Café Baran is one of the best cake shops in all Warsaw. They have delicious food there—food we haven't even heard of."

"What sort of food?"

"Well, like . . ."

"She doesn't know," Rina chipped in. "She hasn't heard of it."

A few subdued laughs filled the room, and Rina took Asher's hand, pulling him up and out of his chair.

"Come on," she said. "I've heard things about this place, and you're not going to stop *me* going."

"It's a treat," Papa said to him. "They have cakes and desserts to make your mouth sing with joy—so I hear. And I won't be taking you there often, so make the most of it."

Mama pulled Asher close and kissed him full on the temple, leaving a wet mark. He pushed her away, both of them giggling.

"Ah, my baby's growing up. He doesn't want his mama's attentions."

Then Keren closed in. "Or his sister's either." She, too, went to kiss him, exaggerating her pout.

He was now fending off both of them, as well as his own laughter, which was coming loose and loud. He could also see Rina, waiting at the door, her coat already on, tutting at the scene, although she afforded herself a barely hidden smile.

"More kisses unless you agree to come," Keren said.

"Okay, okay," Asher said. He grabbed the coat his papa was holding out. "I guess I *am* hungry."

"Good," Papa said. "Now, let's stop playing around and get going. It's popular and the tables fill up quickly on a Saturday."

Asher could hear the sound even as they turned the corner of the street, and it was as if he could hear nothing else as the Kogans approached Café Baran. Never mind the café and its cakes; *that music* was caressing his ears, soothing his soul. He almost stumbled as they all sidled past the people sitting outside the café and soaking up the sunshine. Then he did stumble, because he realized the music was coming from *inside* the café.

"We're here," Papa said. He lifted his hands up to draw attention to the red-and-white-striped awning above them. "This is it. Café Baran."

Asher looked again at the people sitting outside the café. They were silent, some reading books or newspapers, one or two writing letters, and others simply closing their eyes and turning their faces up to the sun. All were listening and would occasionally sip from cups or use forks to pop morsels of cake into their mouths. But there was no talk and it seemed everyone knew why. The café and its environs were bathed in a calming wave of violin music. It was jaunty and tuneful, provoking feet to tap and heads to dip in time along with the meter, but at the same time calming.

"Come on, Asher," Papa said. "Let's see if we can find a free table."

Inside the café, one or two conversations carried on regardless, although many people simply gazed toward the corner, where a lone girl, her neck contorted to press her chin against her violin as though she cared deeply for it, smiled sweetly as she drew the bow back and forth, back and forth.

Asher gazed too. In Dyovsta there had been no music. This was a language he found hard to understand. There was no meaning, it was of no material use to anyone, but it was mesmerizing. So he, too, gazed, unable to take his attention away from the girl's face and the way she stroked the strings.

"Asher!" Papa said, as if not for the first time. He was pointing to a table, where the rest of the family were settling down. "You go sit down. I'll order."

Asher still couldn't speak, but nodded his agreement and eased himself slowly into a chair so he could continue watching the violinist. He hardly noticed when Papa sat next to him a few minutes later.

Soon, a large pot of coffee and five small cups were brought to the table, followed by a three-tiered tray of cakes. They were so carefully arranged—and precariously balanced—that for a few moments Asher was distracted before turning away again.

"Face the front," Mama said to him.

That was easy for her to say. She, Rina, and Keren had chosen the best seats—those facing the violinist—and if he was to face the table he wouldn't be able to see the girl at all. So he sat with his belly against the table and his neck twisted to one side.

"Don't these look delicious, Asher?" Mama said, forcing him to face her.

"We didn't have anything like this in Dyovsta," Papa said.

The mention of Asher's birthplace finally broke the spell, and he started perusing the cakes with more interest.

"Look," Keren said, her finger pointing and moving along the selection as she spoke. "Poppy cake, iced donuts, plum cheesecake, gingerbread, tree cake. And is that coffee cream cake? Is that chocolate wafer cake?"

The dark coffee was poured, the cakes were selected, and the Kogans settled back to eat and to listen. The cakes disappeared five at a time, and soon Keren was asking Asher what he wanted to do now he'd left school, Mama was asking him whether he would keep in touch with the friends he'd made there, and conversation moved on to how work was going for Keren and Rina. Throughout all of that, Asher struggled to pay attention over the beauty of the music.

"Can we come here again?" Asher said to Papa as they were leaving.

Papa puffed his chest out. "Oh . . . ah . . . we can't afford it too often; it's only a treat now and then." He checked himself, narrowing his eyes. "I thought you didn't want to come here?"

"Well . . . I . . ." Asher struggled for a moment, recovering to say, "It's better than I thought. Nice cakes."

Papa glanced over to the girl still effortlessly playing the violin in the corner, then raised one eyebrow at Asher. "Mmm, yes," he said with a crooked smile.

◆　◆　◆

The Kogans made a point of going to Café Baran on special occasions. That was good of Mama and Papa. Asher didn't stare at the violinist girl quite as much as he had the first time, but still enjoyed the music. For a boy stuck in a homesick groove, every visit was encouragement—a reminder that there were some good things about Warsaw, some things he would miss if he ever left.

In time, he started work helping Papa at the bakery, and, like Rina and Keren, had to give his pay to Papa. But no sooner had he started work than the working hours for all the family started to reduce, and with them the pay. Asher never understood why, and kept asking Papa when they would go again to Café Baran. Papa said they could no longer afford it, so he asked Mama, who told him to ask his papa.

Instead, Asher resorted to lone walks to the café. He worked out that if he stood across the street, just past Friedman the greengrocer, directly opposite the café, he could make out the slim but shapely figure of the violinist, and also just about hear her music.

The greengrocer would occasionally appear and tell him to move along, which made him run home in embarrassment. He would usually have composed himself by the time he arrived, although if he tried hard enough he could still sense the joy of the music, and picture the girl and her smile.

Dyovsta, Ukraine, 1939

Three years had now passed since Asher left the farm, and, as Mykhail's papa had predicted, harvests had grown year on year.

"And it's all down to you and your new tractor machine," his papa would say.

But Mykhail's day-to-day life on the farm hadn't changed much, for the cycle of seasons was a constant, requiring much the same attention every year. The vocation wasn't exactly dynamic, but there was a never-ending amount of physical work involved. He would help his papa with plowing, sowing, and harvesting, as well as fencing areas off and dealing with pests. It was hard work, but it was also boring.

They rented out the larger farmhouse for money, but did all the work themselves; Papa said it was better to save money rather than pay people to do work the Petrenkos could do themselves. Papa also said that if Mykhail did the work, then he would learn how to run the farm, which was much more useful than anything he could ever learn at "that schooling place."

By now, schoolwork and farm duties were leaving little time for fishing trips, and besides, it just wasn't the same on your own. Mykhail would still often think of the day, three years before, when his papa had told him the Kogans were leaving and the Petrenkos were the new owners of the farm. Those three years had been ones where friendships were fluid and loyalties anything but fixed.

During that time, he'd finished attending the government school his papa derided so much, but had kept two best friends from his schooldays. Taras was a studious but humorous sort, whereas bullish Borys reminded Mykhail more of his papa.

One day, while he and Papa were out on the tractor at the far end of the farmland, they stopped to eat the midday meal Mama had packed for them. Mykhail casually mentioned the idea of traveling.

"Traveling?" Papa said between mouthfuls. "Why would you want to travel? Everything you need is on this farm. Well, here or in the village."

Mykhail didn't reply to that.

His papa tried again: "So . . . where exactly are you thinking of traveling to?"

"I'm not sure. Probably west."

"You mean Germany? Austria?"

Mykhail shrugged. "And Poland."

Papa chewed for a few moments, then said, "You mean Warsaw. You want to see your old friend, Asher, don't you?"

"I'm just interested to learn what's become of him. What's wrong with that?"

"Oh, nothing. But, *Warsaw?* I mean . . . surely you've heard?"

"Heard what?"

"The city has become a cesspit. Too many *undesirables* in one place."

"That's hardly Asher's fault. He was my best friend. And I'd like to go to other countries too, honestly I would."

Papa tutted. "Those schoolbooks have given you some strange ideas, Mykhail. What's wrong with staying here?"

The boy shrugged shoulders that had grown melon-shaped with hard work. "I'm not saying it's wrong, just perhaps . . ."

"Perhaps what?"

"Perhaps it's not what I want. Perhaps I have ambition."

His papa laughed. "Ambition? What's *ambition?*"

"Papa, I'm not sure I want to spend my life here on this farm, sowing, plowing, and harvesting—just doing the same thing year in, year out."

"So, who would do these things, if not you?"

"If not me?" Mykhail said tentatively, leaning his body away from his papa. "Well, if I had any brothers or sisters . . ."

"Well, you don't. We . . . ah . . . we just have to accept that."

"I remember asking you a few years ago why I have no brothers or sisters. You just said it was something I shouldn't worry about."

"Yes."

"But I'm a man now, aren't I?"

Papa looked him up and down. "Perhaps a little more growing to do, some filling out, but a fine figure of a young man nonetheless."

"So tell me now, Papa. Why am I an only child?"

The breath from his papa's long sigh swirled in the strong rays of the midday sun. Even after that, it was a while before he answered. "It doesn't matter anymore. It's not worth talking about."

Mykhail disagreed, and opened his mouth to say so, eventually choosing to take a large bite of stuffed pancake instead.

In August, Mykhail's plans to travel were thrown into disarray.

He was vaguely aware of events to the west, where Germany had been "assisting" other countries with their social problems, but everyone he spoke to said it was stuff and nonsense that wouldn't affect Ukraine.

One day, they'd all just sat down at the dinner table when Papa spoke.

"Interesting news today," he said.

"Interesting good or interesting bad?" Mama said.

Papa pondered for a while and muttered, "I'm not sure anyone can answer that question yet. But you know how we've all been worried about Germany lately?"

Mykhail and Mama nodded.

"Well, it seems our Russian masters have made peace with them."

"But isn't that a good thing?" Mykhail said.

"I'm not sure. They call it a non-aggression pact."

"What's wrong with that? Doesn't it stop Germany invading us?"

"Who knows?" Papa replied.

"What do you mean?"

Papa wagged a finger at him. "I've said it many times: never trust the Russians. Only a few months ago Stalin was talking to the British and the French about guaranteeing Poland's independence should Germany feel like walking into the country. Now he turns the other way. Ha!"

"Dmytro," Mama said. "Please. No politics at the dinner table."

"Sorry," Papa said.

Mykhail thought about his travel plans, and how this news made it less likely—or even impossible—that he would travel. He was about to say as much when Mama spoke.

"Who knows the mind of a politician?" she said. "All we can do is wait and see." She pointed to the steaming bowls of borsch and dumplings. "Wait and see, and eat."

And so they ate.

◆ ◆ ◆

Warsaw, Poland, 1939

Asher had now put his farm days firmly behind him and changed—matured, he liked to think. That was probably why he knew something was seriously wrong. Like any family, there had been petty squabbles before, but this was different; he could sense it from the way his parents and sisters spoke. One-word answers to questions. No humor. No cheer. The only joy he got these days was from his secret visits to Café Baran, where the violinist had by now become more a woman than a girl. He'd also noticed the café wasn't as busy as it used to be. But the music was just as beautiful.

And there were more changes.

Warsaw was itself changing. More accurately, many of the *people* of Warsaw were changing.

It had been slow and gradual, but many of those who at first had welcomed Asher and his family to the city now crossed the street rather than talk to them. Asher spoke to these people—usually nothing more than a "Good morning" or "Hello"—but the reply was often a perfunctory smile or simply nothing at all. So Asher knew something was wrong, but didn't want to trouble his parents; at sixteen he was no longer a little boy, so he needed to take care of any problems himself.

But then, one day in August, his papa came home seemingly in a daze, staggering into the apartment.

All the children noticed, but they looked to their mama to voice their concerns.

"What is it, Hirsch?" She stepped over to him as he eased himself into a chair. "Is something wrong? Tell me."

He stared ahead. "My old friend, Mr. Petrenko, was right all along."

"Right?" She screwed her eyes up in confusion. "Right about what?"

"He always used to say we should never trust the Russians."

They all gathered around him as he continued.

"The bakery had a visit today from the police. They told the manager to . . . make plans."

"Plans?"

"Put his affairs in order for events to come." He glanced at all their faces before he spoke again. "The Soviet Union and Germany are now allies."

Mama frowned. "And so?"

"Well, the Germans have done a lot of wandering lately. The hope was that the shadow of Russia would put them off wandering into Poland. Now the two countries are more likely to help each other." He looked at his children again, and Asher saw creases on his papa's face that hadn't been there before.

Then Rina spoke up. "But didn't you hear the news, Papa? It was on the radio. Britain and France have guaranteed Poland's independence."

He snorted a laugh. "I know. That's the worrying part."

"I don't understand," Mama said.

"Herr Hitler has designs on Poland. At least, that's what the great and the good of the country think. Why would Britain and France take such action if that threat was unrealistic? No, it means it's more likely."

Mama thought for a moment before speaking again. "So, what are the great and the good of the country doing about this threat?"

He shrugged. "Preparing the army to defend us, I guess."

"Well, that's good, isn't it?"

"Mmm . . . I'm not so confident. Everyone knows we have cavalry and they have tanks. It will be horses' hooves powered by muscle versus metal tracks powered by ruthlessness."

That seemed to silence everyone.

Chapter 5

Warsaw, Poland, 1939

News of the pact between Germany and the Soviet Union cast a gray cloud over the Kogan household, leaving little appetite for conversation. By the first day of September, however, the mood was starting to improve.

"Perhaps it won't happen," Mama said as they all sat down to breakfast. "You know what these things are like, the big men with their big egos rattling their big sabers at each other."

"You keep saying that," Papa replied. "And you shouldn't."

"Why not?"

"Because it's tempting fate."

"But surely if anything was going to happen it would have—"

"Let's just eat."

"I'm sorry. Yes. Let's eat."

They ate.

"Why not tell us all how you're doing at work?" Papa asked his daughters.

Before they could answer, there was a knock at the door.

Papa tutted and got up. "At this early hour?" He opened the door, stepped outside, and shut it behind him.

"Let's just carry on as normal," Mama said. "How are we all?"

But nobody replied, all the better to hear the voices outside.

"Come on," Mama said. "It's rude to listen to other people's conversations."

"Is Asher going to start work soon?" Rina asked.

Mama nodded. "Your papa's trying to get him a job at the bakery. But there's uncertainty. We don't know—"

She stopped talking as the door opened, and they all watched Papa come back to the table, shuffling slowly, head bowed, like a man ten years his senior. He sat down, his pale face clear for all to see—until he buried it in the palms of his hands.

"What is it?" Mama asked him.

He spoke in a sluggish, despondent tone. "That was someone I work with. There are rumors."

"Rumors?"

"More than rumors. A few hours ago, German forces came over the border."

Mama laid a hand on her husband's shoulder. She silently tried to usher the children away, but they stayed where they were.

"I'm not moving," Rina said. "I want to know what's happening."

"And I'm almost twenty," Keren said. "I should know too."

Asher kept quiet, hoping nobody would argue.

Papa looked at them all in turn. "I'm sorry," he said, as though dragging the words out. "There isn't much to know."

"Surely our forces are fighting them off?" Mama said.

He shook his head. "There are a lot of German soldiers—far too many for the Polish army to cope with. They have tanks and much better ammunition too. I don't know any more than that."

"What are we going to do?" Rina asked.

Papa shrugged and shook his head.

"We can wait and see," Mama said. "It might not be all that bad. You know these politicians. Always full of surprises. Perhaps they could come to some agreement."

Papa exhaled between tightly clasped teeth. "Now that really would be a surprise."

"So, what shall we do?" Asher said.

His papa thought for a few seconds. "For now, we carry on as normal. Mama cooks, cleans, and looks after us all, and we go to work as long as we have jobs." He held his head up. "Other than that, we eat, we talk, and we listen to the radio if we have time. But most of all, we pray."

Breakfast continued, but coughs, grunts, and the clinking of cutlery on crockery easily outgunned the sound of conversation. Still no words were spoken as Papa, Keren, and Rina went to their rooms to get ready for work. When they left, there were kisses and embraces, but still very few words beyond pleasantries.

Mama cleared the table and washed up in silence, while Asher fetched one of his books to read. Then she sat down next to him with a cup of water. But she said nothing, just stared out of the window. This wasn't the mama Asher knew.

"How far away is the border?" he said.

There was no answer.

"Mama?"

She shook her thoughts from her head. "I'm sorry, my son. Did you say something?"

"How far away is the border? And how long will it take for the Germans to reach Warsaw?"

She gave him a wistful, almost pitying look before replying. "Oh, we should have a few days of peace at the very least." Her eyes seemed to be sagging a little. Like Papa, she looked older than she had done just the day before. "I'm so sorry," she said.

"What for?" Asher said with a puzzled frown. "It's not your fault."

"Mmm . . ." She grimaced as she tilted her head from side to side.

"Don't feel bad, Mama." Asher placed his arm around her shoulders.

That brought a rare smile to her lips. "Oh, I know there's always hope." She reached across for her cup. "Let's not be too pessimistic, there might—"

She stopped talking and stared at Asher, her face bloodless. As the distant drone got louder she looked up at the ceiling. Asher wanted to look up too, but couldn't drag his eyes away from his mama's face.

Then there was a whistle. Then another.

For Asher, it all seemed to happen slowly, and then again all in one panicked moment, as the noise washed over him and left a residue of acute awareness.

Mama gasped and dropped the cup. It shattered, but that didn't matter. They both felt the floor shake, the whole apartment block jolting as if thumped by the fist of the devil. Asher heard Mama scream and felt her holding on to him, squeezing him tightly in wild desperation.

The door opened, the handle cracking carelessly against the wall behind. Asher heard more screaming. Keren and Rina ran in, followed by Papa.

"They told everyone to go back home," Papa said. "Told us we should prepare for—"

The building shook again. For a second, all five of them stared open-mouthed out of the window, to where pockets of dust flew into the air from building after building. The few people who remained on the streets scattered like frightened mice, and the scene reminded Asher of when Mama used to bake and she dropped raisins into flour, each one exploding in a white puff. What he was witnessing hardly seemed real. No, it couldn't be real. How could strong, solid buildings be blown apart so easily?

He looked up at the skies, at the flying tractors he'd heard about but never seen, at the machines that sowed destruction rather than seeds.

Then he heard shouting, and knew that this was very real.

"Under the table!" Papa shouted. "Everyone get under the table!"

They all dropped to the floor and crawled under.

"So, it's started," Mama gasped.

Papa nodded, his head and arms trembling.

Mama wept, and Papa held her, kissing the top of her head. Asher saw his papa's frantic eyes and noticed his hands, grabbing at thin air to pull his family closer to him. Within seconds, all five bodies were entwined.

Asher shut his eyes, squeezing them tightly, praying for that noise from hell to stop, just praying for it all to go away. The concentration made him dizzy.

He heard someone shouting above the whistles and the crashes.

"Asher! Asher!"

It was his papa.

"It's okay, boy. We'll keep you safe. I promise."

Only then did Asher realize he was jabbering, nonsense falling from his mouth with every explosion that rocked the nearby buildings.

He was sixteen, almost a man in body, but he had to bury his head in his mama's bosom to keep himself sane.

The bombing continued for no more than half an hour, after which the droning noises faded to nothing. There were a few minutes of fretful peace, and then Papa and Asher got up and approached the window. An eerie silence lay outside. There were no people rushing by, no children playing, no people chatting on street corners—there were no people at all. All was calm, and yet it was as though Satan himself had paid a visit.

"Come back," Mama said from under the table. "It might not be over."

"She's right," Papa said, and the family gathered under the table again.

It took a while—a speechless half hour for the Kogans, but then they heard people outside. It was over. Asher got up again and went back to the window. Slowly and fearfully, the people who had scattered like frightened mice were now coming out of their hiding places.

Asher felt an urge to go out, to see the damage with his own eyes. But he kept it to himself; it would only upset his mama. They checked the apartment for damage. They were lucky. Two cracked plates. That was all.

The next day, Papa went to a meeting organized by the local authorities. There was talk of "blitzkrieg," and of setting up warning sirens and shelters as quickly as possible.

In the meantime, there was clear guidance. Go about your daily business as normal, sleep as normal, but on hearing the siren stay indoors and find shelter, preferably under a table or bed.

Papa came home and relayed that message to his family, and they laid spare blankets and pillows under the table to save time in case of a raid.

And the raids did come, causing mayhem whenever the bombs were falling, and leaving a thinly disguised foreboding when they weren't.

As with most families, the space underneath the Kogans' dining table became something of a meeting point, a place where there was, if not safety, then the *sense* of safety. Even after days of bombing, their apartment was still intact. But there was precious little talk. The raids became so frequent that the family more often than not went to bed under the table, but even when the raids didn't come, Asher stayed awake in the silent darkness, unable to relax. And he was sure that applied to the rest of his family too. During the daylight hours, the only thing that stopped them succumbing to their tiredness and falling asleep was fear.

Amid the mayhem, Asher had a secret urge. Even a week after the initial bombing, it was still there, nagging him. He'd tried to dismiss it, to overcome it, but now it had overcome him. After a particularly heavy raid, over a breakfast eaten in a respectful silence, he spoke.

"I need to go to the café," he said.

"Why?" Papa asked.

"I want to see if it's been damaged."

"No, Asher," Mama said. "It's too dangerous. Only go where you need to."

"I'll be careful, Mama. I won't be long."

"Please, Asher."

Breakfast was finished in a fraught silence, then Asher stood up from the table, only to pause as he noticed the imploring expression on his mama's face.

"I'll go with him," Papa said, grabbing their coats. He kissed Mama and said, "It'll be fine. I promise." Rina approached him and drew breath. "No," he said, cutting her off. "Not yet. Only me and Asher. We'll tell you what we see when we get back."

They left, and were hit by the gritty air, a thick dust hanging around that made them cough at first.

"Hold your handkerchief over your mouth," Papa said, pulling Asher by the shoulder.

The buildings they passed had sustained such varying degrees of damage it all seemed so unfair. Some had suffered nothing but a heavy layer of brick dust; many were dotted with deep holes. Some had only windows broken, whereas others mere yards away were little more than rubble.

There were bodies too. And parts of bodies. Asher stared.

Papa dragged him away and turned his head to stop him looking. "I know it's horrible," he said. "But we must show a little respect to the dead. Let the authorities deal with the victims."

They walked on, and soon were standing outside Friedman the greengrocer, opposite Café Baran. At least, they were standing outside what had once been Friedman the greengrocer.

The Barans had been luckier than many. Every window of their café was blown out, the ground outside a shimmering mass of crystalline fragments that crunched like sugar candy under the feet of passers-by. Even the window frames were dislodged and hanging off. The brickwork directly above the two large downstairs windows was gaping, and it was cracked further on—right up to the gaping holes where other windows used to be.

"That looks like Mr. Baran," Papa said, pointing across the street. "Come on."

He took a stride forward, and Asher wasn't far behind. The man turned to meet them.

"I'm Mr. Kogan and this is Asher, my son. We wanted to offer you our condolences."

"Thank you." Mr. Baran spent a few seconds surveying the damage, then nodded across the street to the greengrocer. "It could have been worse."

They looked with him, then Asher's papa said, "Was anybody hurt?"

"The Friedmans?" He shook his head sadly.

Papa took a gulp. "Are they all . . . ?"

"All five of them. Mr. Friedman survived a few hours, long enough to know what happened to the rest of his family. I cried for him."

"That's terrible." Papa eyed up the holes in the brickwork. "And where are you staying?"

"With my wife's sister. That is, my wife and I, and my oldest, Izabella. My other three . . . we got them out last year, they're staying with my brother and his wife in the Netherlands. What about you?"

Papa put an arm around Asher, even though by now they were about the same height. "Lucky. Very lucky. My wife, this one, and my two daughters are all safe."

"Good. I'm happy for you. Your property?"

"We lost two plates, would you believe."

Mr. Baran smiled flatly and rubbed his chin, pinching something between stubble and a beard as he spoke. "I don't think we even have that left in the café."

"It must be terrible. I'm sorry."

"It's not so bad. Most of our personal possessions upstairs were safe. Izabella was worried that her beloved violin would be damaged. It was near the window, but in its case."

"Good, good. Look, I'm sorry to disturb you, we'll . . . we'll let you get on."

"Thank you. And long may you be lucky."

"That's very kind of you under the circumstances." Asher and his papa started walking away.

Asher hadn't spoken to Mr. Baran, letting his papa take care of all the manly conversation while he'd repeated the name *Izabella* in his mind over and over again. Now he spoke. "Couldn't we help in some way?" he said.

Papa stared at him pensively for a few seconds. Then he turned back, calling out Mr. Baran's name. "What are you going to do?" he asked the café's owner.

"Do?" Mr. Baran replied.

"Do." Papa waved a hand at the ruined property. "With this."

"Well . . . it's my living. I'm going to wait and see what happens in the next few weeks, whether our forces can fend off further attacks. There's no point repairing it only for this to happen again." He pointed at the wreckage across the street. "But when the time is right, I fully intend to repair, refurbish, and reopen. It's just a question of finding people who can help."

Papa nodded. He put his arm around Asher again and pulled him into his side. "Warsaw won't be Warsaw without your cakes. You've just signed up two more strong and willing volunteers." Asher could feel his papa standing tall and proud, and noticed his grin, wider than it had been for a long time. He felt compelled to join in on both counts.

Mr. Baran's frown settled low. He swallowed and firmly shook hands with both Asher and his papa. Asher noticed him wipe a few tears from his eyes. "Thank you. Thank you so much. With your help, Café Baran will be resurrected from the ashes."

"I certainly hope so."

"And for the select few, there will be free cakes on the reopening."

Papa was impressed. "They're very good cakes. It's a deal."

Mr. Baran thanked him again. "I'll be in touch once we know the bombing has stopped."

After giving him their address they left, and Asher started repeating the name in his head again: *Izabella, Izabella, Izabella.* Her face was beautiful, her violin playing was beautiful. And now he knew that even her name was beautiful.

Chapter 6

It was the middle of September, and Warsaw was being shown no mercy, still enduring sporadic bombing raids. Those, together with stories of dogfights between the two countries' air forces, had become an accepted part of daily life. The family had returned to sleeping in their bedrooms, but sleep was often disturbed by the bombings, and once or twice Asher had lain awake thinking of Dyovsta and Mykhail. He knew that the here and now—German advances to the outskirts of Warsaw—was more important, but he couldn't help wishing he'd never left Dyovsta. And then there were the images and sounds of Izabella that would all too often seep into his dreamlike thoughts of a better life, confusing him even more.

On one of those sleepless nights, Asher felt thirsty, got out of bed, and tiptoed into the main room, heading for the sink. He stopped when he saw a shape hunched over the dining table.

"Mama?"

"Don't put the light on, Asher."

He didn't need to. A little moonlight beaming through the window caught her as she turned. Asher saw a blanket wrapped around her and a glistening under her eyes.

"I got it wrong, didn't I?" she said.

Asher said nothing, just sat down next to her, their shoulders touching. Then he felt the warmth of the blanket envelop him too. A hand rubbed his back between the shoulder blades.

"Freida kept telling me how good life was here—the people, the food, the freedoms. Now she apologizes to me, she says it had already started to change—the new regime in thirty-six . . . the new broom to sweep the city clean, so they said. She didn't tell me all of that at the time because she wanted me to come here and assumed it would only be temporary."

"I like living here," Asher said. "It feels good to be part of the flock." He drew breath before adding, "Well, it did until September came along."

She sniffed and wiped under her eyes with the corner of the blanket. Asher put his arm around her and rocked her from side to side.

"I'm sixteen now, Mama."

"Taller than me."

"And much stronger. I can take care of you. And I can fight if I need to."

"Please don't say that, Asher."

They stayed silent for a few minutes, then Mama reached out for a cup of hot milk on the table in front of them. "Here," she said. "I'm guessing you came in for a drink."

As he sipped the milk, he heard her say, "I'm sorry."

She kept repeating the words.

Dyovsta, Ukraine, 1939

News of the events in Poland took a few days to reach the Ukrainian prairies, and finished off any lingering hopes Mykhail had of traveling there.

He was in Dyovsta village center, listening to the radio—yet another of those newfangled machines his papa didn't approve of—and ran all the way home as soon as the news bulletin finished.

He found his parents sitting outside, resting in the last of the year's afternoon sun.

"They've done it," he said to them, gasping to catch his breath between words.

They said nothing, just showed him puzzled expressions.

"The Germans and Soviets have marched into Poland."

"Oh, *that*." His papa stood up. "It hardly comes as a surprise." He slapped the dry dirt from his pants. "Are you going to help me complete this harvest? I've been waiting for you to come back from—"

"Didn't you hear me? They've both invaded Poland. The Germans are bombing Warsaw."

"Yes. We heard you." Papa's look was piercing, almost threatening.

"But . . ."

"Aha." Papa nodded. "I know what this is about. Our friends, the Kogans. They're probably still in Warsaw, God bless them. But it's not the only place being invaded. These things happen. And we can't do anything about it, can we?"

Mykhail's mind raced, thinking of arguments to the contrary. His papa continued before he could put them into words.

"But we *can* do something to help ourselves. We must finish this harvest. We're nearly there, but it could be a harsh winter, so we need to collect every last grain we can find. I've made a start, and you can help this afternoon. Yes?"

All Mykhail could do was nod.

His papa spoke little more about the invasion of Poland, and Mykhail thought that perhaps his papa was right. Out here, only the weather seemed to matter. Perhaps it was irrelevant after all, and it wasn't as if they could do anything about the situation. And the crops did need harvesting. Once that was done they could relax.

A few days later, the three of them walked into the village center. There was talk throughout the marketplace and the streets. Mykhail just listened. There were heated voices, some fearing the Germans, some thinking it good that they and the Soviet Union were on the same side, and some thinking the Germans could hardly be worse than the Russians.

Someone mentioned the threats by Britain and France to intervene and defend Poland. There was laughter at the idea.

"Empty threats," one of them said.

"They wouldn't dare," another said.

"They don't have the resources," a third said. "It's all a bluff."

"It's better that we stay out of the argument," Papa said. "We're Ukrainian, not Russian or Polish. We've recovered from our own problems—that famine Mr. Stalin engineered for us. We don't want more trouble."

"That's a little harsh," Mama said. "It must be terrible for those poor people."

But Papa shook his head. "I tell you, after that mass starvation, the number-one priority of every true Ukrainian is to keep grain production high. That's much more important to us than some invasion hundreds of miles away. And who cares what other countries do about it?"

Mykhail nodded as if to agree, although that didn't feel right.

Mama bought some cloth and they all went home.

Warsaw, Poland, 1939

In Warsaw, in the middle of September, the rate and ferocity of bombings started to increase dramatically, shaking the parts of the city they didn't pulverize. Sleepless nights and hunger pangs became part of life. But for Asher there were no more tears; every crash made him feel more like an adult. The resistance to the German invasion was brave, the Polish Warsaw Army dug in deep, and from the relative safety of the apartment Asher would watch them rushing around the streets, thinking there were so many of them that they couldn't possibly lose. But the aerial bombardments were relentless. News spread that schools, medical facilities, and waterworks had all been bombed, along with the aircraft factory and the army barracks.

One day, late in September, the bombing stopped. The Kogans asked neighbors what was happening. Rumors started, and soon official notes were distributed.

Within days, the Polish soldiers who had been stationed on the street corners disappeared from the city, to be replaced with German ones.

The rumors were correct. Warsaw had fallen.

The bombing raids stopped; the tension remained. There was peace of a sort, but no less fear. People watched every move of the German troops and slept with one eye open. The message from the officials who had taken over the city was one of business as usual, and that the city would now be made to run more efficiently.

It was strange for Asher's papa and sisters to continue to go to work—for everything to be normal. There was little conversation, although once Asher heard a neighbor talk about waiting for a hammer to fall.

Everybody accepted there was not much else they could do but wait and see.

Asher thought there was one thing that they could do. It was something he'd never quite forgotten since the bombing started, even though Papa hadn't mentioned it at all since that day they'd visited the mess that used to be Café Baran.

"Perhaps Mr. Baran will want to start rebuilding the café now," he said casually one morning while the family were eating breakfast.

"Is it worth it?" Mama said, frowning.

"Of course," Asher replied. "And Papa and I are going to help."

"You're . . . *what*?" Mama's gaze hopped between Asher and Papa, settling on the latter.

Papa kept his eyes down on his oatmeal, which only signified to everyone around the table that he was aware of his wife's accusatory stare. He eventually looked over at her and smiled.

She didn't smile back.

"Didn't I mention that, Golda? You should have seen the place. The walls are still standing, but everything else is ruined and it's very dangerous, so we promised to help with the repairs in our spare time."

"I want to help too," Rina said.

The others surveyed her slender figure.

"I can do something, I'm sure," she continued. "I'm stronger than I look, and we have to show the Germans they haven't completely destroyed us."

Mama, suddenly and confusingly outnumbered, opened her mouth to speak but said nothing.

"Mr. Baran is going to pay us in cakes," Papa added.

Mama shrugged her shoulders and mumbled, "As you wish."

Throughout the winter that followed, Asher, Rina, and their papa worked on the reconstruction and refurbishment of the café two evenings a week and either Saturday or Sunday. There were one or two delays for items to be delivered, which Asher thought his papa welcomed as he looked weary once or twice. For Rina, what she lacked in strength she made up for in determination, always being full of energy and never seeming to tire. And Asher positively enjoyed the work; his papa once commented that his body was at that age when muscles relished hard labor, and as 1939 turned into 1940 his muscles seemed to have swelled due to the work. The only downside was that he never saw Izabella in all that time. Mr. Baran had talked of her, so Asher knew she was in Warsaw, and he was aware of an inner determination to wait for as long as it took to see her.

One dull day in spring, Mr. Baran gathered the handful of workers together and thanked them, declaring that the café was now looking cleaner and more stylish than it had on its opening fifteen years before. He handed out bottles of beer and lemonade, and announced that he had decided on the date of the grand reopening, which would be a dual celebration because it would also be his daughter Izabella's sixteenth birthday. All workers and their families were invited, and were told not to bring any money.

And so, on the first Saturday in April, the Kogans put on their best clothes and had all the cakes they could eat, washed down with beer for Asher and his papa, and lemonade or coffee for his mama and sisters. Most importantly for Asher, he got to see Izabella once more, and to listen to the music that he'd missed so much, which he felt had a kind of hypnotic hold on him.

Toward the end of the celebrations, Izabella came to each table, personally thanking everyone for their help in rebuilding the café. Seeing her close up for the first time, Asher could do no more than listen to her voice, which was every bit as mesmerizing as her violin playing, and admire . . . well, admire everything else about her. Warm brown eyes sat above a classically strong nose, below which lay petite but full strawberry lips, and coal-black hair draped down either side of the whole ensemble, her pure white skin a canvas to the picture. She was as delicious as any of the cakes the Kogans had just eaten, and everything about her seemed to light up whenever she talked, in turn brightening everything around her as if some magic candlelight were present. Asher could do no more than watch and admire all these things; uttering any words to her was completely out of the question. Not that his shyness bothered him. The important thing was that Café Baran was back in business and Izabella was there.

Finally, Warsaw felt like a proper home to Asher, with people and experiences and opportunities he would miss if the Kogans were ever to return to Dyovsta.

By the summer of 1940, the German authorities had exceeded all expectations where the residents of Warsaw were concerned. Yes, there were restrictions on travel and prayer, and the Kogans had to put on their Star of David armbands whenever they left the house, but the authorities had largely kept to their word when it came to letting "business as usual" prevail, and the hammer that Asher's neighbor had talked of hadn't fallen. It seemed too good to be true.

Asher turned seventeen, and his strong, youthful body was now managing to do almost as much work as his papa at the bakery, lugging around sacks of flour and anything else that needed moving. At home, there was more conversation among the Kogan family than ever, as well as smiles—and even laughter.

One evening in October, while they were playing cards at the table, there was a knock on the door.

Papa answered, and Asher saw a council official standing there. Papa went outside and closed the door behind him. They all heard raised voices. This time, Mama didn't say anything about it being rude to listen. Not that it would have mattered. Nobody spoke or moved, instead just listening to the argument, trying in vain to work out what it was about.

Papa came back in. Slammed the door. Went straight to the bedroom. Slammed that door too.

"Stay here," Mama said, and followed Papa into the bedroom.

Strained voices came from the other room, and soon their parents returned.

"I have something to tell you all," Papa said, the gravest of expressions darkening his face.

There was a stolen glance between Mama and Papa, then he said, "We . . . we have to move."

They all looked at Papa, their mouths open.

"Where to?" Rina said.

"Another part of the city. They're segregating Warsaw."

"Segregating?" she replied.

"Creating a Jewish district. We've all heard about the walls they've been building."

"But why do we have to go?" Asher said.

Papa rubbed the back of his neck nervously. "I don't have answers," he said. "That's the way it is."

It was a strange response; Asher had expected more. Exactly what, he didn't know. But nobody queried it, and within days the Kogans had placed all their belongings onto a cart and pulled it to the center of the city.

They passed guards and ruined buildings, which Asher's eyes dwelt on, and red-stained concrete, which he tried not to notice. Soon, they lined up at a gap in a large wall. When Asher had first heard about the new walls, he'd assumed perhaps they were being constructed to replace those the bombs had destroyed. But he had ample opportunity to examine this one during the long wait in line, and this was not part of any building: it was a wall and nothing more—a long one, snaking as far as he could see and eventually around a corner. It was about twice his height, with rolls of barbed wire curling along the top. It reminded him of the walls he'd heard about at school—the ones enclosing ancient cities. Those, of course, had been designed to keep people out. Asher could only guess the purpose of these walls, but he dismissed his fears, hoping he'd got it horribly wrong.

Their papers were checked, and once inside the walled area they were given directions to their new living quarters.

When they arrived, Asher felt slightly relieved. It didn't seem too bad. Okay, so it was a single room this time, but it was a large one. After they'd all looked around, which didn't take long, Papa gathered them at the table that dominated one end.

It took him some time to start speaking, making two false starts before the first words came out.

"There's something else I have to tell you," he said.

"What can be worse than this?" Mama said.

"I'm sorry," he said, "but . . . Asher and I can no longer work at the bakery." He looked at his two daughters. "You two can't work at the factory either."

"Why not?" Rina asked. "Says who?"

Again, he was slow in speaking. "Because that would mean leaving this area—the Jewish sector." Now he looked up at each of them in turn. "We aren't allowed through the wall to the rest of the city."

"What if we need to buy something?" Mama said.

Papa shrugged. "We use what we have within the walled district. Perhaps there'll be work for one of us here, who knows?"

"We'll survive," Keren said. "When we walked here we all saw shops and businesses, didn't we? They all need workers, surely?"

"We'll see," Papa said. "We will see."

Despite the upheaval, the worried faces of his family, and the uncertainty of life in the walled sector, something else had been bothering Asher. After a few days in their new home, Asher waited until he was alone with his papa, walking the streets seeking out work, before asking the question.

"Papa?" he said. "What about the Barans? Will they have to wear these armbands and move here too?"

"They're Jews. I guess so."

"But what about the café?"

"Asher, I have enough problems worrying about our family."

"But do you think they'll open a café here?"

"Enough, Asher."

"I'm sorry, Papa."

Asher didn't ask about the Barans again, and wasn't sure he wanted to know the answer, his mind churning over the possibilities. On the one hand, he wanted the Barans to run the café as before; that would be much better for them than having to start another café from scratch inside this rather rundown walled sector. On the other hand, if that were true, he wouldn't be seeing Izabella again until the Germans left and the city returned to normal, which pained him even more.

As the months went by without hearing anything of the Barans, he assumed that they had been spared by the German authorities. Yes, that was it. They had been seduced by the delicious cakes and captivated by Izabella's beautiful music, and had given the Barans some sort of special dispensation to continue running the famous Café Baran.

The thought was bittersweet for Asher, but he slept a little better knowing that they'd been spared. He convinced himself that when the walls came down and the city got back to normal, he would see her and be able to listen to her sweet violin music once more.

Chapter 7

The door to the police station flew open and Diane Peterson strode out with a feeling of quiet triumph that somehow didn't seem appropriate.

Detective Durwood was going to do the paperwork and arrange a time for her to meet the man who had—as she'd put it—left a big bullet hole in her father's head. They were blunt words, she reflected as she headed for Brad's car, but no more and no less than what was needed to sum up the scene she'd come home to that night.

That night.

A thought rushed through her mind in the length of time it took for a ripple of thunder to threaten more unpleasantness from high above her. The thought made her stop walking.

Okay, so she'd won the battle to meet Father's killer. But what exactly was she going to say to him? She'd been so preoccupied winning the battle that she hadn't given much thought to what she wanted to do with the victory.

There was only one question in her mind. She wanted to know why the hell he'd done it. It was only the one question, and there seemed no point engineering 101 different ways of asking it, so she headed for the car again.

"How'd it go?" Brad said as she sat in the passenger seat.

"They're going to let me speak to him."

"Good." He leaned over to kiss her, but drew back at her stiffness.

"Doesn't mean *he'll* speak to *me*, of course."

"No, but it's a first step. Did you need to talk about the Restorative Justice program and your rights?"

"I did. Can we leave please?"

"Sure." He started the engine and set off.

"And thanks for ferrying me around these past few days."

"Don't thank me. We both know you're not ready to drive again yet."

"No. I'm only ready for one thing."

"One thing?"

"Finding out why."

"Oh, yeah. Of course. I'm sorry."

They drove on in silence. Diane was, indeed, not ready for driving, and didn't she know it. As they headed to Brad's place, her mind was drawn back to that night. She tried to roll her mind onward, so that whatever she did think would fast-forward like those old-fashioned cassette tapes her father used to play. There—even when she was trying not to think of him, she found a roundabout way to think of him.

That night.

"I feel a little nauseous," she said.

"Open a window?" Brad said. It was intoned as a casual suggestion, not in any way an order. He'd learned the hard way.

Wordlessly, she pressed the button and the glass lowered. The air wasn't exactly a fresh sea breeze, but it was cool and moist. Then more flash frames of what had happened that night forced themselves into her head. As the car accelerated, the surge of air on her face only served to tip the balance, and she was there, arriving home that evening the previous week.

◆　◆　◆

It had been a very average but nonetheless enjoyable night out. Absolutely nothing special at all. Her and Brad and two old friends out for bowling followed by tacos and talk. The cab had pulled up outside 38 Hartmann Way, the home she still shared with her father. Brad leaned over and they kissed.

"Do you want me to come in?" he asked.

"You have to get up early tomorrow, don't you?"

"Well . . ."

She laughed warmly. It was the warmth of a long relationship, one fulfilled in all aspects apart from one—they didn't live together even after all this time. She'd worked with Brad for five years, then been good friends for four, and then been lovers for another six. A lengthy courtship by any standards—longer than many marriages, she often joked to herself.

"Actually, I do," he said. "It's an early meeting I just can't get out of. Would you mind?"

"Ah, that's okay." She kissed him again, this time fuller and holding on for longer—a proper *goodbye until tomorrow* kiss. "I'll see you for lunch tomorrow."

"Sure. And thanks." He nodded to the front door. "I'll wait here till you're safely inside, though."

But his words weren't necessary. He always waited. That was Brad—one big, soft security blanket.

A few seconds later, she waved to him, watched the cab get to the end of the street, and went inside. She was immediately aware that something wasn't quite right. After her calls out to her father weren't returned, the fear multiplied. The lights upstairs were out, but the kitchen light was on, and she could feel cool air on the back of her neck. And once she'd shut the door she could still hear the hum of the traffic from the freeway a hundred yards or so away. That was also not right—not right one bit. Above all, her nostrils twitched at the hideous, metallic edge to that cool air.

A few paces later, she was at the kitchen doorway and her face was on fire.

Her father, sitting at the table but slumped on it, blood everywhere.

The back door swinging nonchalantly in the breeze, as if a careless child had left it in a game of chase.

Her father, who'd carried her up to bed every night for a week when she'd sprained her ankle, his body now slumped over the kitchen table, a shiny pool of blood all around his head.

The door handle, smeared in blood, and above it one panel of glass broken through, more blood dripping from its edges.

Her father, the man who once drove her at breakneck speed to school to make it for the bus for the school ski trip, his form now slumped over the table, blood everywhere on one side of the room.

Blood everywhere.

A gun on the ground in the backyard, just beyond the doorway as if trying to escape, but caught in the light thrown from the kitchen. And next to that a spilled pot of paint, obviously knocked over by someone escaping in a rush.

Her father. Her father. Her father. The man who used to take her to the local park and push her on the swings until she screamed in joyous terror.

Now there was only terror.

This was no longer her father. This was a corpse with a large black hole in the side of its head. Beyond that hole, a spray and splatter of blood had found its way onto every surface and object.

That night had only been five days ago, but Diane still had no recollection of what had happened after she'd discovered the body. She was told that a neighbor had found her in the street, unable to talk, only able to point, and that the neighbor had gone in to check and subsequently called the police.

Brad drove on. Diane shut the window. Switched the radio on. Listened for a few seconds. Turned the radio off. Said nothing. Brad drove on. Brad said nothing. That was good.

Chapter 8

Dyovsta, Ukraine, 1941

It was now almost two years since the Soviet-German invasion of Poland, and for the Petrenkos, that time had gone by with little fuss.

For those interested, there had been many news bulletins about the events there and in the rest of Europe, but for most, the existence of the non-aggression pact with Germany was all they needed to know about.

And while Mykhail occasionally thought about how the Kogans were managing in Warsaw, he convinced himself he had more pressing issues to deal with. After all, that was his past life; he would probably never see Asher again. At seventeen he'd gotten into the habit of meeting up with friends in the village center to talk about girls and, increasingly, politics. Likewise, his papa had gotten into the habit of groaning every time he went there.

"You think you can change the system," he would say, "but you're too young to even *understand* the system." Or he might say, "It's easy to talk a fight." Or even, "Youngsters, anything to avoid hard work." There was, however, always a crooked grin and a twinkle in his eye when he said those things, so Mykhail knew there was a grudging respect beneath his words.

By the start of June that year, the invasion of Poland was very old news, and the minds of the youngsters had turned to fighting for Ukraine.

One lazy afternoon, Mykhail, Borys, and Taras were sitting around the village clock tower, talking politics.

Taras was shaking his head. "This Russian collaboration with the Germans is awful for us," he said. "It means we have to fight two armies for our independence."

Mykhail raised a finger. "Don't be so sure. It keeps the Russians occupied. More troops busy keeping the Poles in check means fewer troops available to fight us."

"Us?" Taras said.

"I mean the *nationalists*."

"So you're joining the nationalists?"

Mykhail held his head high. "Why not? I'm a proud Ukrainian. Wouldn't you fight for your country?"

"You, Mykhail?" Borys said. "You're going to fight against the Red Army?"

Mykhail shrugged. "I haven't decided yet. You know there are a few organizations pledging to fight for Ukraine and for Ukraine only. And they have people with ammunition and the training to use it."

"I've heard. But, you know, most of the people who would fight are in prison. Look at my Uncle Viktor. He's behind bars just for trying to organize talks on the history of Ukraine."

Mykhail spat on the ground. "What does that tell you about the Russians?"

"That they're in charge?" Taras said, laughing.

Mykhail grabbed his shirt. "Don't laugh. It's not just his Uncle Viktor. Many people have been taken away or even . . ."

"What?"

"Killed. Executed for daring to speak out against Russia."

Taras apologized, and Mykhail let go of his shirt.

"Mykhail's right," Borys said. "The Russians classify proud Ukrainians as enemies of the people. We can't accept that."

"Enemies of the *Russian* people, perhaps," Mykhail said. "But one day Ukraine will be a free nation—a proud and independent nation."

Taras smirked. "So you would take up arms? Even kill?"

"If it comes to that, yes. I'm certainly a strong, brave Ukrainian. Aren't you?"

Taras shrunk slightly at the question.

Mykhail turned to Borys. "And you?"

Borys nodded vigorously. "Of course. We should fight for Ukraine together. I'll join the underground fighters if you will too."

Mykhail looked Borys in the eye for a moment, then Borys spat on his hand and offered it out. Mykhail spat on his own hand and they shook.

"See," Mykhail said to Taras. "We fight for our country."

Taras nodded to the clock tower and laughed. "Not yet, though. First you have fields to plow."

Mykhail smiled. "Oh, very funny. At least I have ambition and courage. And at least my intentions are good."

The three friends agreed to meet again the next day, and Mykhail left.

When Mykhail got home and shut the door behind him, the noise disturbed his papa, who was sitting at the table, leaning forward as though he'd nodded off.

"Your papa's been waiting for you," Mama said.

"And he's been waiting for some time," Papa added, stretching as he roused himself. "We have fields to plow and seeds to sow. Where have you been?"

"Oh, just talking with my friends in the village."

His papa groaned.

"We were talking about the nationalists," Mykhail said.

"What about them?" Papa asked.

Before Mykhail could reply, his mama forced a chunk of bread smeared with cream into his hand and said, "Eat." She turned to her husband. "He's told you where he's been, Dmytro. In the village. Now stop moaning at him."

Papa tutted. "He's been sorting out all the country's problems, no doubt."

"Isn't it good he takes an interest in politics?"

"Pah! I wish he'd take more interest in the farm. The tractor keeps misfiring. He needs to take a look at it."

"Only because you can't fix it."

"But he's wasting his time talking when he could be working." He prodded a muddy finger at his son. "Not even eighteen and he thinks he knows it all. Yet he knows less than my little toe does."

"He knows how to fix your tractor," Mama muttered.

Papa opened his mouth wide and looked aghast for a second. Mykhail laughed, almost choking on the bread.

Papa tried to suppress a cackle of laughter and failed. "You have a point there, Iryna. Give me a horse any day. Horses I can understand. You feed them hay, they pull. That's all there is to know. They don't go wrong."

Mama stepped over to Mykhail and placed an arm around his waist. "You take after your papa—passionate about what you believe in, a proud Ukrainian. You'll settle in time, I'm sure. You'll learn which things are really important."

"I certainly hope so," Papa said. "And to be fair to you, Mykhail, I happen to agree with your politics. It's just that we don't need you talking in the village center; we need you on the farm, fixing and driving the tractor."

"Okay, okay," Mykhail said. He kissed his mama's head and headed for the door. "I'll go make my magic fingers dance over the engine."

"Good boy," his mama said as he left.

◆ ◆ ◆

It was another few weeks before Mykhail could take a break from work out in the field to celebrate his eighteenth birthday, and one evening he met up with Taras and Borys in the village center again.

Mykhail gave a firm handshake to Borys, then held a hand out to Taras, who showed a little reluctance to do the same. But they did shake hands, and Mykhail kept an eye on him as they all sat cross-legged on the dry earth.

"What's wrong?" Mykhail asked him.

"He's worried," Borys said, laughing. "He worries about anything. And he was just telling me of his latest worry."

"I'm serious," Taras said. "It's not good, all this talk of who'll fight on whose side. And with the German military building up at the border, who wouldn't be worried?"

"Ignore the Germans," Mykhail said. "It's just for exercises, everybody knows that."

"Of course," Borys said. "That's what I've been telling him. The Germans are our allies. The pact says so."

Mykhail nodded. "If anything, they could help us."

"They couldn't be worse than the Russians," Borys said.

Taras grimaced and struggled to speak for a moment. "It's just . . . I don't like talk of war, that's all. What I want is to be left alone to find a wife, run my family's farm, and enjoy life."

"And you feel you can do that with the Russians breathing down your neck?" Mykhail asked him.

Taras shook his head. "I . . . I don't know. All I know is that I don't like the way things are going. And . . ." He sighed. "Look, we're supposed to be celebrating your birthday. Could we forget wars and fighting and talk about something else?"

Mykhail and Borys looked at each other and shrugged. "Like what?"

"Like the quality vodka at my Aunt Natali's place."

The others immediately stood up and pulled him to his feet.

"That's good enough for me," Mykhail said. "Lead on."

Taras broke into a smile and they all started walking.

The farmhouse was much like any other the three young men had seen, a solid affair with whitewashed walls and a thatched roof that looked waterproof just by the skin of its teeth.

"Is this it?" Mykhail said.

"Doesn't look much, does it?" Taras said. "Nobody would guess there's a small hidden room that's been turned into a distillery."

"I'm impressed," Borys said.

Mykhail slapped the backs of the other two. "And I'm excited. I haven't tasted good vodka since . . . yesterday." He spluttered a laugh.

Taras knocked on the door, while his two friends casually rolled around on their haunches, glancing left and right.

The door was opened by a woman in tears.

Taras's face dropped. "Aunt Natali? What's wrong? What is it?"

"You haven't heard?" She looked at all three in turn. "None of you have heard?"

"Heard what?" Borys said.

"The news," she said. "It's too bad. Oh, it's terrible."

"Tell us!" Mykhail shouted.

Taras gave him an admonishing stare.

"I'm sorry," Mykhail said. "Please, tell us the news."

"The . . . the Germans have invaded."

Mykhail leaned his ear toward her. "What did you say?"

"The Germans invaded Ukraine early this morning."

Taras held a hand to his forehead, mouth agape. The other two cursed under their breath.

"I guess news travels slowly," the woman said. "But it's true. They've taken towns and villages all along the border, in both Russia and Ukraine. They're moving quickly by all accounts, sweeping away all resistance."

"Now I *definitely* need a drink," Mykhail said.

The woman went back inside and returned within seconds. She thrust a couple of bottles into Mykhail's arms.

"Here," she said. "I feel sorry for you. Enjoy it. It might be your last taste of freedom." She shut the door.

Mykhail gave his friends a confused look. "What did she mean by that?" he said.

"What do you think she meant?" Borys replied. "We'll be expected to join the army. Perhaps our families will have to move if the Germans overrun this place."

Taras nudged his cap and scratched his head. "We should go home and prepare for war. I need to tell my parents. We have to be ready to leave Dyovsta at short notice."

Mykhail looked to Borys, who shrugged and said, "I think we should have a drink. What else can we do?"

"I'm with Borys," Mykhail said. "Who knows when we might get a sniff of vodka again, let alone get drunk." He turned to Taras. "Look, if your parents don't know, telling them will only upset them, and if they do know, there's no point reminding them."

"Come on," Borys said to Taras. "One last drunken night, how about it?"

Taras bowed his head for a few seconds, then looked up and nodded. "And my aunt could be right. It could be the last chance I get for a while."

"Good," Mykhail said. "And while we're getting drunk, we can talk about who we're going to fight with."

They sloped off to a tin shed fifty or so yards away that had been baking in the sun, and sat down together against the still-warm metal.

They drank, watched the sun fall to the horizon, and drank some more. But despite the vodka, there was little talk. Eventually the cold came, and Taras said his goodbyes and left.

"Are you definitely joining the nationalists?" Mykhail asked Borys after a few silent minutes.

Borys took another slug of vodka and handed the bottle over. "Of course. I'll fight Hitler and Stalin together."

"In that case, I'll join you."

"You know, the old woman has it wrong. I've been talking with some of the nationalists."

"Your Uncle Viktor's friends?"

Borys nodded. "They've been saying for some time that the Germans could be good for us. As you said, if they get the Russians out of the way it could help the Ukrainian cause."

Mykhail nodded slowly, but said nothing.

They talked a little more, raising a toast to Ukrainian independence, but soon after that Borys also left. Mykhail stayed to finish the last few drops of vodka, and to think.

As the sun's final rays were vanishing, he shivered. It was so peaceful here, and yet at his country's brittle edges, German guns and tanks were wreaking havoc. Mykhail was only eighteen, but he knew the good times were coming to an end.

And Papa was right. Strong beliefs were easy to talk about. But now events were conspiring to test his mettle, so how much were those beliefs worth? At eighteen he could no longer hide behind the privileges of childhood. Soon he wouldn't be able to talk about fighting and step away; he might have to *do* it.

A couple of weeks ago he'd felt like a boy. Now he got to his feet unsteadily, and walked home a confused and apprehensive young man.

Chapter 9

Dyovsta, Ukraine, 1941

The next morning Mykhail was shaken awake by his papa, and found himself babbling meaningless phrases.

"Are you all right?" his papa said.

Mykhail rubbed his eyes, looked around, and sighed with relief. "I was just having a . . . a dream." Vague imaginings of fighting alongside Borys and other Ukrainian nationalists lingered in his consciousness.

"It sounded more like a nightmare," Papa said. "Probably all that vodka you drank last night."

Mykhail shook the thoughts from his head. "Why have you woken me up so early?"

"You have a visitor. And I think you know why."

"What do you mean?"

"A man at the door. Asking for you."

Mykhail looked up at Papa. *Why was he struggling with a brave smile? And why did he appear glassy-eyed?*

Then Mykhail remembered the news from the day before, and his headache became a little worse. "Tell him I'm on my way."

By the time Mykhail got to the door, buttoning his shirt as he shuffled along, the man was huffing impatiently. But he quickly gathered himself together and his face became almost as expressionless as the whitewashed walls.

Mykhail didn't speak, just listened. It only took a minute, the man reeling off the words as if he didn't really mean them. But Mykhail knew the meaning very well. And only at the end, when the man handed him the slip of paper and asked whether he understood, did Mykhail respond, nodding silently.

The man left, and Mykhail turned to his parents. Papa had his arm around Mama, who was dabbing her eyes with a cloth.

"Mmm," Papa said. "The Red Army."

Mykhail stared at the slip of paper. "I have to report tomorrow. They're collecting me at the village clock tower."

Papa nodded. "They're picking off the easy targets first. For now, they need me for food production, but I'm sure my time will come soon enough."

"But . . . it's the Red Army. The Russians. I can't fight with *them*. I just can't."

"You shouldn't be fighting at all," Mama said. "You're too young."

Papa held her closer but kept his gaze on Mykhail. "I know how you feel. In an ideal world you would be fighting for Ukraine against both the Russians and the Germans. But this is the real world—most of the nationalist leaders are locked up."

"But I don't know what to do. I mean, are the Germans good for us or not? I . . . I just don't know."

"Me neither, I have to admit. While you were out getting drunk last night, I was talking with some of the other farmers. The stories I heard from the west are of the Germans being welcomed. And why not? They can hardly be worse than the Russians. But for you, in your situation? I just don't know."

"Aargh!" Mykhail screwed the paper into a ball and threw it against the wall. "I hate this situation. I mean, who are we? Are we Ukrainians? If we are, then why do I have to fight for the Russians?"

Papa pulled his arm from around Mama. She sniffed and nodded, telling him she was okay. Then he approached Mykhail, and the two men stood square in front of each other.

"Son, I know how you feel." He placed one of his meaty hands on Mykhail's shoulder and patted it. "I know because I feel the same. I'm a proud Ukrainian, and that's exactly what I've brought you up to be. But it's time to be a man and not a boy. Sometimes you must compromise. The practical overcomes the ideal."

"You're saying I should join the Red Army?"

Papa thought for a moment. "I'm saying you should ask yourself what choices you realistically have."

"I can run."

"And be captured and shot?"

"I could join the nationalists."

"And live rough in the countryside, or in a stinking prison in the middle of a war?"

"At least I'd have my principles."

"Can you live on principles? Can you eat them? Will they shelter you from the wind and rain?"

Mykhail gulped. "I'm confused."

"At least in the Red Army you'll get trained and you'll have a rifle. You can be sure of having food and shelter."

"But . . . I'm Ukrainian, not Russian. I want to fight for Ukraine."

"Remember this, Mykhail." Now Papa held a hand against the side of his son's face. "Self-preservation is never an unworthy cause. Sometimes it's all that matters. Your mama and I want to see you again. In time we want to see you marry and have children."

"But that isn't what I want."

His papa showed him a crooked smile. "Sometimes what you want isn't the best thing for you. And who knows, the fight for Ukraine could carry on after you've helped the Red Army fight off the Germans."

"I guess it could."

"You only have a day to decide. But whatever you decide, your mama and I will always be here for you."

Mykhail nodded. Then he felt his papa's full embrace for the first time since he was a boy. It felt strong, and Mykhail sensed a little of that strength pass through into him.

◆ ◆ ◆

After breakfast, Mykhail's papa picked up his cap and headed for the door. He stood there, readjusting the cap, until Mykhail finished eating and followed.

"Wait," his mama said. "I'll come with you."

"But you only look after the chickens and goats," Mykhail said.

She gave a resigned smile. "I'll have to do more when you're gone. I might as well learn now." She put on her shoes, slung a shawl over her shoulders, and the three of them headed for the fields.

Mykhail did his best to show his mama how the tractor worked, and they spent the morning harvesting barley from the nearest field and plowing the farthest.

It was early afternoon by the time they finished, and they walked back to the farmhouse to eat. Afterward, while his parents took a nap, Mykhail slipped out and headed for the village center.

There, something was clearly different. Few people spoke or even smiled as they passed this way and that.

The conscription men had obviously been busy.

Only subdued nods of hello escaped the purge of greetings, and after a few of these, Mykhail reached the clock tower.

He waited there for a while, but there was no Taras or Borys. Taras's farm was the closest, so Mykhail headed in that direction, down a narrow track and over a small stream, eventually reaching the edge of a bright amber field where a few people were gathering wheat into bales. He squinted to see but couldn't quite make out the figures. So he stuck two fingers into his mouth and blew a piercing whistle. The workers all stopped and turned. One of them started trudging toward him.

Mykhail met Taras halfway, and immediately noticed a grimace on his face, a seriousness that didn't sit well.

"You too?" Mykhail said. "The Red Army?"

"All the younger men in the village."

"So, what are you going to do? Are you going to join?"

Taras shrugged his shoulders. Then he looked down at his dirty boots and gave a few reluctant nods. He motioned to a nearby felled log and they both sat on it.

"What else can I do?" Taras said. "I'm no revolutionary. All I want to do is sow and harvest. Perhaps if I join I can stay out of trouble. Perhaps the war will be swift and I'll return." He pulled a rag out of his pocket and wiped the sweat from his brow. "You?"

"Oh, I've been thinking about it all day."

"And?"

Mykhail shrugged. "I'm still not sure."

"You haven't come across Borys, then?"

"Borys? He's been conscripted too?"

Taras nodded. "He came here earlier. He said he went to see you, to talk to you, but there was nobody home."

"We were all in the far field."

"He said he ripped up his conscript papers in front of the official."

"My God! Really?"

"You know the way he feels about the Russians. He was still angry when I spoke with him. He said he would rather die than fight with the Red Army. That's what he told the official too."

"So he's going to join the nationalists?"

"He said it's his destiny to fight for his country—Ukraine. That's what he went to see you about. And he gave me a message if I were to see you first. He said you need to meet him an hour before sunset at the clock tower if you want to join the nationalists with him."

"Did he ask you too?"

"Borys knows how I feel. He accepted it. We shook hands." Taras frowned. "You know how long Borys and I have been good friends. And soon we could be shooting at each other, trying to kill one another. And that's without dealing with the Germans. It's crazy. But war is always crazy."

They both stood up, and Mykhail held a hand out. "I can only do the same," he said. "Whatever happens, we're friends. And after the war we'll still be friends."

They shook hands, and Mykhail noticed fear twitching the flesh around his friend's eye. "We'll both live to drink together again," he said. "I'm sure of it."

They both tried to laugh, then said goodbye, and Mykhail returned home.

◆ ◆ ◆

Later that day, just as Mykhail opened the farmhouse door and was about to leave, his papa appeared behind him.

"What are you going to do?" he said.

Mykhail said nothing, just glanced over at the sun, low in the sky.

"You haven't decided, have you?"

He shook his head. He'd told his parents what Taras and Borys were doing. All they'd said was that he had to make up his own mind, to try not to be influenced by his friends. "I'll decide on the way," he said. "I promise."

"You either fight alongside Taras or you fight alongside Borys. Either way you'll end up fighting the other one. That's some decision."

"I know. But whatever happens, they're both friends and compatriots. And I should say goodbye to Borys."

"Of course you should. So go."

Mykhail's mama appeared and hugged him. "Don't be too long. I want a final evening with my one and only son."

"Of course, Mama. I'll be back at sunset."

◆ ◆ ◆

The journey was less than a mile but seemed much longer. As he turned the corner he spotted Borys waiting for him at the clock tower.

He also passed half a dozen soldiers or armed guards—he wasn't sure which. They seemed to be going from person to person and door to door, asking questions.

It didn't take them long, Mykhail thought. *Power has gone to their heads.*

He walked on toward Borys, and the first thing the two men did—before a word was spoken—was shake hands.

"I hear you had a visitor too," Borys said.

Mykhail nodded. "And I hear that you . . . declined the invitation?"

Borys laughed. "You should have seen the man's face. I tell you, he was so angry. God, he was trembling so much I thought his stupid Stalin mustache was going to explode." He straightened his face. "But enough of this. Have you decided what you're going to do—whose side you're on?"

Mykhail's jaw dropped, and stayed there. He could see Borys's nostrils twitching in anticipation, the rest of his face frozen.

Before Mykhail could speak, he heard shouts coming from behind him. He went to turn but was flung to the side before he got the chance.

Three men appeared in front of him—three of the men he'd seen before, asking questions. He could now see they were soldiers, and all three were pointing their rifles at Borys.

"Hands on your head!" one shouted.

Borys waited for the man to shout it a second time, then did as he was told, but slowly and with a dark scowl.

Mykhail stepped forward, but the butt of a rifle in the stomach winded him. Gasping to recover, he pulled back, and the man turned his attention to Borys again.

"You are Borys Popovych of Dyovsta?"

Again, Borys didn't hurry to react. "And . . . what of it?"

"You are hereby charged with defacing official government documents."

Borys narrowed his eyes at them. "My conscription papers? If that's what you mean, they aren't official papers. This is Ukraine, not Russia."

One of the soldiers nodded to the other two, who pounced on Borys, one pulling him by the arm, one pointing a rifle at his back.

Mykhail felt his stomach turning in on itself as he watched them drag Borys away and throw him into the back of a truck. He went to the truck, running at first, then slowing to a tentative walk and holding his hands up as a rifle was pointed in his direction.

"Where are you going?" he shouted. "Where are you taking him?"

The soldier ignored him, but lowered the rifle and headed for the front of the truck.

"Please!" Mykhail quickened his pace, keeping his hands high. "Where are you taking him?"

The soldier opened the cab door and rested his hand on it as he addressed Mykhail. "He's going where all the anti-Soviet insurgents go. Prison."

"For ripping up papers? He hasn't done any harm. It's all talk."

"Oh, he's been talking all right—to the other agitators. He's an enemy of the people."

"But . . ."

The soldier pointed at the truck. "Do you want to come too? We have room."

"Just tell me which prison you're taking him to."

"He's going to Kiev."

Mykhail held his head in his hands as he watched the truck drive off.

Mykhail got home just as the golden ring of sun was about to plunge below the horizon.

His parents turned and stared at him as he stood by the door.

"I've decided," he said. "I'm joining the Red Army."

Mama let out a sharp gasp and held a hand over her face.

"Please don't cry," Mykhail said to her. "It's for the best."

"I know," she murmured, and wiped away a few tears.

"And what about Borys and Taras?" Papa said.

Mykhail was flustered for a second, then said, "You were right about self-preservation."

Papa nodded thoughtfully. "It's a practical decision."

"I'm still scared," Mama said. "Promise me you'll stay out of trouble."

"I can't promise that, Mama." He saw her face start to collapse, then added, "But I'll try."

"So, come sit down," Papa said. "It's your final night here. We can—"

"His final night *until he returns on leave,*" Mama said.

"That's what I meant, of course. We'll get out the vodka and the playing cards."

Mykhail suffered a restless night, with thoughts of Borys—and his own future—churning in his mind. He gave up trying to sleep and got up. Before sunrise, while his parents were still sleeping, he went outside and took a last look at the fields and the livestock.

The memories whirled around in his head of the sunny days spent working on the land, as well as the rainy ones when his boots became encased in mud. There were also the games of hide-and-seek with the children of neighboring farms, and the races through the long meadow grasses. Even those torturous days laboring in the sun now seemed magical.

He gave the horse a last brush, and couldn't resist giving the tractor a farewell pat on the seat. He smiled to himself as he did this, then jumped up onto it. A final sit for old time's sake.

For a few seconds he was a young child again, with a lust for learning about this new metal beast—an enthusiasm he shared with his old friend Asher.

No, his *best* friend Asher.

Asher was long gone, but not forgotten. The games, the fights, the fishing trips, and, yes, even the day when they'd been robbed and had tried to cover for each other.

"Good morning."

Mykhail turned to see his papa standing in the doorway of the tractor barn.

"Volunteering for a quick shift before you go?"

Mykhail nodded. "Put me down for one later in the year—I'll be back by then."

"I'm sure you will."

"I was just thinking of old times." Mykhail caressed the steering wheel, just as he'd done when it had been brand new. "And of Asher."

Papa dropped his smile and turned away for a moment. When he turned back, Mykhail noticed his face was a little flushed and he was blinking.

"Papa? Are you okay?"

His papa nodded, but with no great conviction.

"Are you upset because I'm joining the army, or upset because I'm joining the Russians?"

Papa let out a laugh, and a crooked smile appeared on his face.

"I know how much you hate them," Mykhail said.

"Mykhail, sit down for a moment."

They sat side by side on a rough wooden bench. Papa patted his son's knee. "Perhaps I should explain something before you go. It's something you should know."

Mykhail said nothing, and stilled himself to listen.

"You asked a few times why you were an only child. You see, after your mama had you, we waited a couple of years before trying to give you a little brother or sister, but by then we were living in the shadow of the Russians, and times were hard. We waited as long as we could and tried again, but along came the Holodomor. Thanks to the Russians we were starving, just like everyone else in Ukraine, and she . . . she miscarried."

Mykhail saw redness around his papa's eyes, then he blinked and a teardrop fell to the dust.

"We tried again the next year, but still the great famine continued, so we had the same results. And after that, she . . . didn't have the heart to try again. For many years I hated the Russians—for that and for many other things, but mainly for that."

"And now?"

"Age dulls your hatred. You see things differently. And, I guess, there's a level of acceptance."

"So I'm an only child because of the Russians?"

Papa stood up, and motioned for his son to do the same.

But Mykhail stayed seated. "I'm confused," he muttered, shaking his bowed head. "You tell me that about the Russians, and now I'm fighting on their side?"

"Nothing has changed," Papa said. "The arguments are the same. What choice do you have?"

"*What choice?*"

"You have the choice of self-preservation or self-destruction. I know what I and your mama both want."

Mykhail took a long breath to settle a heart that was running away. "But I feel like I'm betraying you."

"Nonsense. Perhaps I shouldn't have told you. Now, come on. A final breakfast. Your mama's waiting. She has sweet egg bread and meat sausage."

It took a while, and Papa waited without speaking, but eventually Mykhail stood up and forced himself to smile. "A final breakfast," he said. "Let's go."

◆ ◆ ◆

After breakfast, Mykhail fetched his sack of clothes and dropped it by the door. He turned to Mama and was immediately engulfed in her arms.

She swallowed away her sorrow and told him to look after himself.

"Don't worry," he said. "I'll be back before the end of the year."

Mama nodded, but kept her mouth tightly shut.

"I mean it," he said. "I'll see you in a few months, definitely."

"Definitely," she repeated, her face creasing up.

Then Papa opened the door and ushered him out. He followed, then shut the door, leaving Mama inside. Mykhail stopped, puzzled.

"Your mama says she can't watch you walk away," Papa said.

They shook hands, and embraced.

"There's something else," Papa said as he stepped away. "Something else I need to tell you. A confession of sorts, I guess."

"Go on," Mykhail said, eyeing him suspiciously.

Papa rubbing his silvered stubble as he bowed his head. "It's . . . it's about your old friend Asher—your *best* friend Asher."

"What about him?"

"I did it for the best, Mykhail. I was thinking of you."

Mykhail shrugged, too puzzled to speak.

"After he left for Warsaw, he . . . he sent you some letters."

"Letters?"

"I burned them."

Mykhail paused to take in the words. "You burned them? You *burned my letters?*"

"I know it was wrong. And I'm sorry."

"But . . . why?"

"I thought it best you didn't read them. I wanted you to forget him, Mykhail. I didn't want you to have false hope."

The men stood face to face for a few moments.

"It's something I regret," Papa said. "But it's something you should know."

Mykhail looked him in the eye; he saw sadness and a little shame.

"And now you have more important things to worry about."

Mykhail aimlessly flicked dry dirt with the toe of his boot, then looked in the direction of the village center. He nodded, then again, more firmly. "You're right. It's not important now."

They shook hands, and Papa gave him a slap on the shoulder. Mykhail turned and started walking.

Chapter 10

Warsaw, Poland, 1941

Conditions in the Jewish sector of Warsaw had started badly and deteriorated.

Almost a year had passed since the Kogans were forcibly moved there. By now, food was scarce and sanitation poor, allowing disease to rip through the district like an icy gale. Even the strong needed luck; the weak stood no chance.

Since the end of paid employment, Asher and his papa had settled into a routine of sorts. Thoughts of theaters and playing sports were long forgotten; they took any work that paid in food or anything that could be exchanged for food—digging trenches, loading carts and trucks, moving anything to anywhere. Nothing was beneath them—including the job few people were prepared to do: burying the increasing number of dead. But even that work was now petering out, so they begged. Sometimes the whole family begged, but half the time they were doing nothing but begging from people who had nothing to give.

Nevertheless, it was the only way to survive. They would start out by picking an area of the sector and standing on opposite sides of an intersection, where they could watch out for one another, their caps in their hands, asking passers-by for loose change. If the day was going well they would stay there; if not they would separate, each making their own choice of where to go.

On a drizzly day in summer the begging was going very badly; Asher had one coin in his cap, his papa nothing. So they separated, Papa going south, Asher going northeast toward the river, hoping that a little of the breeze brought down the river might enliven him—perhaps, even, that conditions might be better there.

They weren't.

As he trudged along street after street, the picture was the same. Yes, there were shops, but most had little for sale—a stale loaf here, a handful of sprouting potatoes there, old clothes of dubious history, bottles of milk yellowing with age. There were also just as many beggars in this area of the sector, and although many people rushed back and forth, very few had change to toss into the proffered caps. So Asher was spending more time gazing blankly into rain-streaked shop windows than he was begging; it hardly seemed worth the effort.

He heard it only a few blocks away from the easternmost wall. He walked toward it, hardly believing it, but still hopeful even as the shouts from a beggar on a street corner masked the sound. He continued on, and there it was again. He moved even closer, quickening his pace, and yes, it was definitely a violin, and it didn't sound like just *any* violin. This was no sorry, sad tune being played as a lament, but jolly, almost comical music. Comical, at least, in the mind of anyone used to dark Ukrainian humor.

Asher turned corner after corner, once doubling back on himself, unsure exactly where the music was coming from.

And then he found her, standing under a canopy next to the wall. She was even slimmer than she'd been in the Café Baran days. Her hair was matted and grayed by dust and dirt, her dress smudged and smeared with grime. But this *was* Izabella, her half-smile so incongruous in such filthy surroundings, yet still so strong and resilient in its joyfulness. And this was her music, no less beautiful than it had been before, almost rebellious in its message to the occupying forces. It was as if she were pronouncing to the Germans that she, at least, would not be beaten.

At first Asher could do nothing but stand back and watch, but after a few minutes he approached her. She looked up and her smile blossomed to fullness.

Was she smiling at him? He glanced around furtively, unsure of her and aware his face was reddening. He wanted to run, but also wanted to stay there forever. He froze for a few seconds, then reached into his pocket, plucking out the one coin he'd earned that day. He stepped forward and dropped it onto the small square of cloth at her feet.

"Thank you," she said.

Asher only nodded, unable to put his thoughts into words.

The music stopped. She removed the violin from under her chin and reached her arms out and back a few times to ease cramps.

"Don't I know you?" she said.

Asher's throat dried in an instant, as if a gust of wind had thrown a handful of sand into the workings. He tried to gulp, but his muscles wouldn't obey.

He turned and fled, only slowing to walking pace when he was a few streets away. By the time he got home he was cursing himself for being so weak. Izabella had talked to him and him alone. The vision of beauty had spoken—not to a group of people, with him somewhere among them, but to *him*. He'd had the opportunity to talk and had run away.

"Are you all right, Asher?" his papa asked when he sat down at the table.

"Fine. Why?"

"Oh, you seem a little agitated. Nothing happened to you out there today, did it?"

Asher looked downward and shook his head, too embarrassed to tell the truth.

"And do you have the coin?"

"What coin?" was all he could say in reply, his stomach turning with the fear of being found out.

"When we separated, you had a coin. Where is it?"

"I . . . I don't know what you mean, Papa."

"But it was there in your cap. I saw it."

"Well . . . I think I lost it. The rain got heavier and I had to put my cap back on. I must have dropped it or flung it away. I'm sorry, Papa."

His papa took ten seconds or so to react. Asher expected some serious scolding; instead, his papa looked him in the eye and said, "No matter. Money isn't much use anyway; there's nothing to buy."

Asher sensed his body relaxing at the words; his papa was starting to become indifferent, which was disappointing, but lucky in this instance. Somehow that made Asher stronger, as if he were now gearing up to become the man of the house. And the strength made him vow to see Izabella again the next day. And to speak to her this time.

The following morning, Asher was out on the streets again with new determination. The begging was secondary; all his effort was aimed at ensuring he got to the far eastern edge of the walled sector at some stage. Three times he suggested to his papa that they should split up; on the third occasion there was agreement, and Asher was off with little more than a goodbye.

Today was a little brighter, the warmth more in keeping with the summer morning it was, and somehow the music traveled more easily, audible from well before where Asher had first heard it the previous day. He hurried along and found her again, occupying the same spot as before.

This time Izabella stopped playing as soon as she saw him. "Hello again," she said, taking the chance to rest her arms.

Asher gulped, his mind as featureless as the concrete wall beyond Izabella. Her smile, full and sensuous, was like a snake charmer's music, numbing his mind and body.

"Last night I remembered where I'd seen you before," she said. "You came into the café, didn't you? You helped Papa repair it after the bombing."

Asher nodded, then approached her, still not knowing what to say, but at the same time burdened by a head full of questions that seemed too impolite to ask.

"I need to carry on playing," she said, bringing the violin up to rest on her shoulder and drawing bow across strings.

And again, Asher realized the moment God had created for him to speak had come and gone; he couldn't possibly disturb her while she was playing.

He listened for thirty seconds or so, secretly cursing himself but also every bit as mesmerized as he'd been the first time he saw her.

Then the violin squawked and the bow fell down, one end bouncing on the dirt below, coming to rest at Asher's feet. Izabella doubled up, coughing sharply.

Asher picked up the bow and placed an arm around her shoulders. "Are you all right?" he said. "I'm sorry. Was it me? Did I put you off?"

She shook her head, still coughing, a deep, bark-like sound coming from her as she convulsed again.

"Let me take this," he said, grabbing the neck of the violin.

She resisted, holding on tightly even as she fought to breathe.

Asher held firm too. "Really," he said. "You can trust me. I've been in love with you ever since I first saw you at the café years ago, and your music too. I know exactly how much this violin means to you and I could listen to you playing it all day."

She coughed again, this time more lightly, then froze, looking up at him in a way that stirred something mysterious yet potent in him.

She let go of the violin. "What did you say?" she asked.

"I . . . I said I remember your music from the café. It's beautiful. I assumed you were still there."

"Why would you think that?"

"Because . . . the café . . . the cakes . . . I thought perhaps the Germans might . . ."

Asher realized his thoughts converted to spoken words were ridiculous.

"You think I'm less of a Jew than you? Is that it?"

This was a different side to her. Her friendly smile and warm eyes faded away, leaving a fierceness Asher found puzzling but no less alluring.

"I'm sorry," he said. "I didn't know what to think. I was being stupid. I apologize."

She relented, the anger on her face subsiding as quickly as it had appeared.

"But it was only wishful thinking. What's become of the café if you and your parents are in the walled sector?"

Izabella stilled herself for a few seconds. Asher could see her breathing in and out deeply and slowly, trying to calm herself or control something within. And then her face stiffened, a hand covered her eyes, and Asher saw wetness on her cheeks. A few seconds later, she'd grabbed the square piece of cloth, her violin and bow, and was scurrying away, wiping tears as she went. Before Asher could think what to say or do, she was out of sight.

Asher didn't do much talking that evening. Mama asked him over the family meal what was wrong. He hesitated, and Papa told her he was fine, that begging on the streets was hard work, that she shouldn't worry.

The next day, however, just after the two of them had left the house, Papa stopped at the edge of a small park and motioned for Asher to sit on one of the benches.

"What is it, Asher? What's wrong? You can tell me." He left a pause for Asher to speak, but it went unfilled. "I know something happened yesterday. You didn't say a word all evening."

Asher shook his head and said he didn't know what his papa was talking about.

Papa's weary eyes didn't move from his face. "I can't help you if you won't tell me."

"There's nothing wrong. It's just . . ." Asher let out a long sigh. "You can't do anything to help, Papa."

"So there *is* something wrong."

"I . . . I saw Izabella yesterday."

"Oh."

A period of silence followed, both men staring straight ahead, watching the people trudging left and right along the street.

"So you know about the Barans?" Papa said dolefully.

Asher's head jerked around. "What?" he snapped, immediately feeling a little fear and sadness. He'd never spoken to his papa with such aggression.

Papa narrowed his eyes to slits. "What did she say to you?"

"Nothing about her family. Why? What do you know?"

"Mmm . . ." He sighed, then looked at Asher as though assessing him. "I didn't want to tell you, and I haven't told your mama or the girls. Earlier in the year I overheard a couple of neighbors talking about what happened. I knew one of them from the bakery, so I asked them. It's not good news, Asher."

"Please. Tell me."

Papa nodded. "The Barans were told to leave, just like us. But Mrs. Baran said they'd not long ago repaired and reopened the café, that she'd put part of her life into the place, that her husband had toiled for months to put right the damage German bombs had inflicted. She insisted she was going nowhere."

"And?"

"There were arguments for a short time. Mr. Baran pleaded with her to give in, but she wouldn't, perhaps thinking the guards would spare her. But one guard tried to drag her away, and she . . . she assaulted him."

"Oh, dear God. Did they . . . ?"

Papa nodded. "It was merciless, but quick and painless, apparently."

"So, does Izabella live alone with her papa?"

"Oh, they both came to the walled sector. But at the start of the year Mr. Baran caught a bad chest infection. I think his heart was already weakened by the stress of seeing his wife shot. He and Izabella slept together for warmth. She awoke one morning to find him dead, his arms still locked around her."

Asher stared at him in shock.

"You understand why I kept it from you, don't you, Asher? It's . . . not very good for morale to know these things."

Asher nodded. "Yes. I understand. But what about poor Izabella? Where does she live?"

"I don't know. Possibly alone, possibly with another family."

"Could she live with us?"

Asher saw pity in his papa's eyes. "We're already five living in one room. We . . . we can't manage that. I'm sorry."

Later that evening, as the family gathered around the table to eat, Mama was quiet and reserved, going about the business of preparing the meal as usual but without the usual conversation.

Everyone started eating—everyone except Mama.

"Stop," she said suddenly, her face pained. She glanced around the table, settling on Papa. "You need to tell me what's happening," she said. "I know you and Asher are up to something."

He shrugged. "Up to something? Up to what? I told you, it's just been—"

"Hirsch!" she shouted. "Tell me!"

Asher exchanged a glance with his papa. He made his mind up to stay quiet, to let his papa decide how much to tell them.

"Very well," Papa said eventually, then he told them everything about the Barans that he'd told Asher earlier in the day.

The news was met with the same shock Asher had experienced. He scanned the faces of his family. If he didn't know before why his papa had kept the news to himself, he did now. Mama, Keren, and Rina couldn't eat. It was up to Papa to persuade them to eat even if they didn't feel like it, to remind them that they could do nothing to help. So, reluctantly, and in silence, they ate.

"Well done," Papa said when they'd finished. "I know it's not easy to carry on, especially when there's nothing we can do to help. But we have to think of the family unit. We have to put the five of us above all other considerations."

"Do we?" Rina said. "Do we really have to put ourselves above anyone else?"

"We do," Papa said before anyone else could speak. "Asher even asked whether she could come and live with us." He glanced at Asher, who remained expressionless. "I had to say no. There's hardly enough space for the five of us. We're forever tripping over one another."

"We could invite her for a meal," Rina said.

Papa shook his head. "We don't have enough food to go around."

"I wouldn't mind sharing," Asher said.

"We can't," Papa insisted. "We have to think of ourselves—of *our* family."

"No, we don't," Rina said. "And I'll go further. I pledge to give up a part of my next meal for Izabella. I'll give up my whole meal for her if nobody else will. We can't think only of ourselves. We simply *can't*."

Mama brought the handle of her knife down sharply on the wooden table, making the others jolt in unison. "Stop this," she said. "There will be no bickering at the dinner table. Asher, please invite Izabella here to break bread with us when you can. Rina, it won't be necessary for you to give up your meal, we'll cope somehow. Hirsch, do you have anything to say?"

Papa kept his mouth shut and shook his head. He didn't notice Asher struggling to contain his joy.

Chapter 11

Diane took a seat at the bare table in the bare room.

"Are you okay?" she said softly.

He shrugged his skinny shoulders. "It's jail. There are worse places."

"But I mean . . . are you keeping well? Is everybody treating you okay—your food and so on?"

"It's adequate."

"Good." She nodded, conscious that this wasn't how she wanted it to be at all. She'd as good as rehearsed what she was going to say—what she was going to *demand* of him. But now his familiar old face was here in front of her, it was different. "And are you taking care of yourself?" she said.

He didn't answer. Just blinked those watery eyes of his a little and looked down.

"I'm really finding this hard," Diane said, unveiling the smile she'd promised herself she would hide.

"I know." Now he looked straight ahead and at her. He didn't return the smile. "Diane," he said. "Please don't feel under any obligation to be polite to me."

Diane's smile turned to a scowl. Then she screwed her eyes up, trying to keep the tears at bay. A few forced their way through the roadblock and she quickly wiped them with the back of her hand.

"Okay," she said, now more firmly. "So tell me, what the hell happened between you and my father?"

He glanced at the guard standing upright in front of the door like a big *A* and lowered his voice. "Diane, I never meant to cause you any distress. You do understand that, don't you?"

Her eyes took a while to rove over his face, all the way from his shiny head to the white beard. She hesitated, a force of habit, but this was different. The nature of their relationship, as a divorce lawyer might say, had changed significantly. She tried her best to keep her voice unsentimental and hard-edged. "Seeing as you ask," she said, "no, I don't understand. I don't understand one single bit."

"I'm sure. I'm guessing you want an explanation."

"You and my father are best buddies for years, then you kill him. So yes, please, I think I deserve an explanation."

His mouth opened and shut a few times, but eventually the words came. "I'm not sure where to start, but the most important thing you should know is that none of this is your fault."

Diane cursed under her breath and ran her hand through her hair roughly.

"Are you okay, Diane?"

"No, of course I'm not okay. You killed my father. You killed the man who—" She broke off and gulped, trying to control the tears. She wiped her face again and took a deep breath. "The point is, if we're not doing politeness, please don't patronize me."

He nodded slowly, the tip of his white beard brushing against his orange jumpsuit. "I'll try not to."

"I need to know why you did this. I mean, what the hell happened between you two? You and Father had been best friends for years, *brothers in all but blood* was always the joke." She focused on his eyes, unsure whether age or sorrow was making them watery, but she told herself to ignore his reactions. "You were best buddies, and do you know, I can't remember a cross word between the two of you. Ever."

"That's true," he said, sniffling. "There never was one. Not until last week."

"I just . . . I don't understand. I *want* to, but I don't. I guess that's why I'm here. I need you to tell me. I need to understand it for my own benefit. What the hell was it all about? What was so bad that it made you do that to your best friend?"

"You deserve an explanation, Diane. But I'm not sure how much to tell you."

"Jesus Christ," she hissed. "*Everything* is the answer. I want to know *everything*."

"If I told you that, I think you might understand, but it would involve telling you things you'd rather not know."

"Hey, let me be the judge of that."

"And I'm not sure your father would want you to know what we fell out over."

"I don't care. I still want you to tell me everything."

"Everything . . . ? It's a long story. Your father never told you about when we were kids growing up in Ukraine, did he?"

"No, he didn't."

"Have you ever wondered why?"

"I guess I'm wondering right now. Father's gone, and I want to hear everything you have to say about him."

"Well . . ." He glanced once again at the guard. "I'll explain it all to you the best I can. But it has to be you alone, and you must swear never to tell the authorities what I tell you. I'll deny everything if you do."

Diane screwed her eyes up again, this time in confusion. "What the hell does that mean? What does it matter to you what the authorities know? You're going to prison, and you're going to . . . to . . ."

"You can say it. I'm going to die in prison."

"Okay. You're going to die in prison. There. Happy? Because I certainly am. You killed the man I loved. And you're going to die in prison for it."

"It's nice that you can say that about your father. We both know he wasn't perfect."

"*Excuse me?*" Diane said.

"I'm sorry. I shouldn't have said that. All I meant was that . . . Oh, I don't know."

"And while I think of it, what's all this crap about some sort of bond between you and me?"

"Oh, you know about that."

"What the hell did you mean by it?"

"Well . . ." He thought for a moment. "It's hard to put into words. Something in common in our pasts, I guess."

"I have no idea what you're talking about."

"Perhaps I'm being presumptuous."

"Perhaps you are, with a little arrogance on the side."

"Well, I'm sorry you feel that way."

"Okay, let's cut the bullshit. Just tell me why you killed my father."

He glanced at the guard standing next to the door.

Diane did the same, then said to the guard, "Could you leave us alone please?"

The guard kept his head straight and looked down along his nose. "You must know I can't do that, ma'am."

"Why not?"

"Why can't I leave you alone in a room with a man who's confessed to murdering your father? Are you serious?"

"He's seventy-eight. He has cuffs on. And we're old fr—" She huffed. "We *used to be* old friends. Perhaps we aren't anymore, but I still don't think we're likely to harm each other."

"I'm sorry. I can't just take your word for it."

She turned away from the guard. "Well?"

He shook his head. "I can tell only you, Diane. Nobody else. I'm sorry, but there are certain things . . . . things I promised your father I wouldn't tell the authorities."

"You *promised* him? Do you have any idea how empty that promise sounds now? You murdered him, and now you're . . . somehow *honoring* him?"

He narrowed his eyes, looked at the guard and then at Diane. He opened his mouth as if to speak, then shook his head and lowered it. "I'm sorry, I just can't."

"Why not? This guy's a guard, not a cop."

"I'm sorry, Diane. This has to be just between you and me."

She stared at him for a full ten seconds. "Right," she said. "You'd better get your excuses good and ready, because I'm gonna sort something out here even if it gives me a nervous breakdown." She stood up sharply, her legs knocking the chair away.

Chapter 12

Kiev, Ukraine, 1941

Mykhail's papa had told him he had more things to worry about than letters from Asher. The words were becoming painfully true. The German blitzkrieg machine advanced with such speed that troops had to be rushed out to defend western Ukraine before they were fully trained. And it was to no avail.

Mykhail and Taras found themselves fighting in the same regiment, and together they witnessed their country being overrun with frightening ease. They dug into one line of defense, lived through days of blood and bullets, then were ordered to destroy anything that might be of use to the Germans—often razing whole villages to the ground—before retreating to the next line, where the cycle repeated itself. It was like a recurring nightmare, the smell of cordite and rotting flesh alternating with that of burning buildings.

By September, after months of unrelenting death and defeat, the Red Army had been pushed back to within a few days' march of Kiev, the capital city of Ukraine.

There were many losses at that position. Taras and Mykhail had to help drag half a dozen corpses out of the small trench they were occupying. But by now they were accustomed to such tasks.

During a lull in the fighting, Mykhail lit a cigarette, took a long drag on it, and closed his eyes for a few moments. He felt a rush of ecstasy that, for that brief time, took him away from the bloody reality.

He crouched down next to Taras, who was sitting on the floor in the mud. He almost passed the cigarette to his friend, but took another dose of relief himself instead. He slowly exhaled before offering it over.

But Taras didn't respond.

"Here." Mykhail gave his friend's face a tap with the back of his hand and placed the end of the cigarette against his lips. "Taras," he said. "Take some of this. You'll feel better."

Still there was no movement. Mykhail grabbed his friend's chin, pulling him to look. "Taras. Snap out of it. You have to."

But Mykhail saw glazed eyes that looked through him.

"I can't," Taras said. "I've had enough."

Mykhail grabbed his shoulder and gave it a shake. "Oh, come on. You've said that before."

And then they both flinched as a rifle grenade exploded yards away from them. Gunfire and more grenades followed.

Mykhail poked his head out of the trench and fired his rifle indiscriminately, the cigarette still drooping from the corner of his mouth. He took a break to reload and looked down. Taras was still sitting there, staring into space.

"Taras! Stand up and—"

An explosion interrupted him. A few minutes of bombardment followed, and when Mykhail looked down again, Taras still hadn't moved.

A bullet glanced off Mykhail's helmet, making him stumble and drop down to his knees. He could hear Taras mumbling to himself. Mykhail pulled him close, forehead to forehead. "What is it?"

"I want to sow and harvest," Taras said to him. "I'm not a fighter."

Another rifle grenade exploded nearby. The blast forced Mykhail onto Taras's body.

"Don't say that, Taras! You'll be shot for cowardice." He grabbed him by the lapels. "Come on! Perhaps we can hold Kiev. But you have to fight!"

Then they heard a voice screeching out commands above the gunfire. It was the voice of their corporal and he was telling them to retreat.

Mykhail tightened his grip on Taras and tried to pull him to his feet. The two men fell into the mud.

"Leave me here," Taras said breathlessly. "I can't carry on."

Mykhail tried pulling him to his feet again, but realized he was almost as weak and tired as Taras—low rations and precious little sleep had seen to that.

He tried once more, but was disturbed by that same assertive voice from behind him.

"Is he shot?" the corporal asked.

"Just weak and tired," Mykhail replied, giving Taras's arm another pull.

"Go!" the corporal said to Mykhail. "You go, and I'll deal with this."

"But . . ."

"It's an order! Retreat!" He got his pistol out and waved it toward the city behind them.

Mykhail got to his feet, grabbed his rifle, and started scrambling up and out of the trench. Keeping on all fours, he crawled along a few yards. Then he glanced back to see the corporal pointing his pistol at Taras's temple. Taras had his eyes closed. Despite the gunfire and shouting, his face looked to be at peace. Moments later, one shot rang out above the rest, and Mykhail felt nauseous.

The corporal crawled toward him and Mykhail lifted his rifle, for a second thinking the unthinkable. But the corporal shouted out, "Let's move!" and Mykhail came to his senses, lowering the rifle.

"You didn't have to do that," he said.

The corporal glanced back to Taras's body. "He as good as killed himself. We couldn't leave him for the Germans to capture and interrogate. We both know they would do far worse to him."

The blast from another grenade made them both duck.

"We could have carried him," Mykhail shouted, the noise of the grenade still ringing in his ears.

"We can't carry people. Now move on, Petrenko. We need to move farther into the city and make defenses."

The corporal crawled on. Mykhail yelped as he caught a bullet in his upper arm, then looked up to see the corporal turning back.

"Petrenko!" he shouted. "Do you need help?"

Mykhail shook his head and followed as best he could. As he scurried along, he kept repeating the words of his papa. *Self-preservation. All that matters. Self-preservation. All that matters.*

By the next day, the bullet had been removed from Mykhail's arm and the wound had been dressed. The only anesthetic had been vodka and a rag to bite down on, but at least he'd slept well afterward.

Now it was back to reality. And for some, even talk was dangerous. "That's it," they would say. "If Kiev falls I'll surrender."

The sergeants and corporals threatened instant executions for any soldiers who did, and punishments for those who even spoke openly of it. So soldiers were more guarded in their words, although not completely silent.

Mykhail's arm was deemed fit for him to fight, but over the next few days there was no fighting. Instead they retreated even further; they were running away like wounded dogs.

Eventually, as they reached the outskirts of the city, an ugly gray building dominated the view. It was surrounded by two layers of fencing, each topped with barbed wire.

"Anybody know what that is?" Mykhail heard one of the soldiers ask.

"We're in Kiev," someone else said. "I visited here many years ago. That's the prison, where they keep all the insurgents, the dissidents, and the agitators."

Mykhail turned to the man. "Are you serious?"

He nodded. "And the poets and nationalists—the dreamers."

They marched past and settled about a hundred yards from it, at a deserted crossroads, where they started piling up abandoned carts and the debris from bombing raids into makeshift barricades.

Mykhail kept glancing over to the prison, wondering about Borys.

After the barricades were complete, Mykhail approached his corporal.

"Do you know about the prison?" he said.

"In what way?"

"Well, what happened to the inmates."

The man looked puzzled. "They're still in there."

Mykhail looked around at the deserted streets and buildings.

"So we just leave them there?"

The man nodded casually before lighting a cigarette.

"I know someone who's in there," Mykhail said.

"And?"

"Could I look for him?"

A small cloud of smoke blew from the man's mouth. He took another breath before shaking his head. He drew his forefinger slowly across his throat.

"I don't understand," Mykhail said.

He pointed. "Just watch."

By the time the corporal had finished his cigarette, the prison door locks had been blown off and a few hundred soldiers had run inside.

"What's happening?" Mykhail said. "Are they going to bring them out?"

The man laughed. "All of those enemies of the people? The insurgents, agitators, Ukrainian nationalists? What do you think?"

Then the gunfire started, and Mykhail started to tremble.

"But . . . I don't understand. They can't just kill them."

"This is war, young Petrenko. People die. We can't leave them in there, and we can hardly let them out."

"Why not?"

"Are you mad? These prisoners are enemies of the people. If we leave them there the Germans will liberate them. Do you want to fight the Germans *and* those prisoners?"

Neither man spoke for a few minutes, and by the time Mykhail forced himself to turn and walk away, the flamethrowers had moved in and the whole building was ablaze.

His corporal followed him and patted his back.

"I'm sorry about your friend," he said. "But these are orders from the top. We're here to obey. And don't forget, friends or not, these people are all troublemakers. They deserve to die."

Mykhail stopped and threw the man's hand off him. "What did you say?"

"Look. The Red Army has no time for these people, and you are a serving member of the Red Army, so neither should you. Did you know that many of the towns and villages in Ukraine have actually been *welcoming* the German forces? They see them as liberators. Can you believe that?"

Mykhail pushed the man aside and walked away.

Mykhail had seen the flames from the prison lick the clouds above, and was now watching the smoke swirl high above the charred remains.

And as the wreckage smoldered, so did his anger. Taras was gone; now Borys too. Both killed by Mykhail's own side.

He was sitting on the ground, his back against a low wall, when another soldier approached and stood next to him.

"Petrenko," the man said, "you'll do yourself no good."

Mykhail just looked up and scowled.

"I heard you arguing about the prison with the corporal."

"And?"

"We all feel the same. Always on the back foot. Outnumbered, outgunned, and outmaneuvered. Then they do this." He nodded to the burned-out shell. "It disgusts me too."

"You knew people in there?"

"It doesn't matter whether I did or not. The corporal is right. We are an army, and they are orders."

"Well, I feel no allegiance to this army," Mykhail said, the venom clear in his voice.

"Shh!" The man glanced around. "You want to see what they do to cowards?"

Mykhail stood up quickly and faced the man, eye to eye. "I'm no coward."

The man was taller than Mykhail, but pulled his head back and took a step away. "I'm sorry," he said. "I'm only telling you how it is."

Mykhail opened his mouth to reply, but the man's expression switched instantly to one of shock, his eyes bulging, his head trembling. It took another second for the rattle of aircraft fire on concrete to register with Mykhail, and then the man slumped to the ground, blood seeping from his mouth.

Soldiers ran left and right, each searching for cover. Shouts were heard above the noise, which now included the screaming engines of the aircraft themselves.

Mykhail ran in a jagged path. The prison didn't matter now; all that mattered was survival. He fell beneath the back end of a tank, praying that the thing wasn't going to move.

The aerial bombardment continued long enough for Mykhail's legs to go numb, and when the aircraft gave up and left, their armory spent, the ground was spattered red.

He crawled out from under the back of the tank, focusing on the prison again, trying to shake all thoughts of Borys and Taras from his head. Whatever had happened to them wasn't important now. He'd survived yet another onslaught. *That* was important.

He lit a cigarette and once again took himself away from reality, closing his eyes and pointing his face toward the sun. Soon they would be retreating yet again, he thought, but there was no rush—not until the aircraft returned.

The tank fired up, the noise startling Mykhail. But the engine gave up as soon as it was started. It was cranked over once more, and grunted for a few seconds before stalling again.

A nearby corporal cursed. "What have you done to it?" he shouted up to the soldier's head poking out of the driver's hatch.

"I don't understand," the man replied. "But we can try again." He did, and still it spluttered and gave up.

"Perhaps it needs refueling. Check the fuel level."

"Fuel level is good."

As they argued, Mykhail wandered over.

"You," the corporal said. "Put that cigarette out. We're about to refuel the tank."

Mykhail took another drag. "It uses diesel, not gasoline." He noticed the glare of the corporal, apologized, and put the cigarette out. "And it won't be a fuel problem, because it's turning over." He walked around the tank. "My guess is it's either the air intake or the exhaust."

"You're an engineer?"

He shook his head. "I know engines. I've worked on many."

"Well, do you think you can help?" The corporal flicked a thumb at the tank. "We need every tank we can save."

Mykhail approached the engine, just behind the turret, and took a few seconds to examine the air-intake grille. "Looks okay," he said. Then he walked around to the exhaust.

"Ah," he said, pointing at the underside of the pipe. "It's damaged."

The corporal walked over and stood next to him.

"You see? The opening is okay, but farther back something's crushed the exhaust pipe, pinched it. Probably a chunk of concrete thrown up onto it."

"So?"

Mykhail glanced around until he spotted a metal fence post—a sorry casualty of the aircraft's bombs. He dragged it over. The corporal helped, and together they poked the post into the back end of the exhaust.

"Careful," Mykhail said. "Just use it as a lever to open the pipe out, to get rid of that pinch point."

A few minutes later, they'd just done that, and the exhaust pipe—although mangled—was now open.

"Try that," Mykhail shouted up to the driver.

The tank fired up and revved, and a few seconds later it started moving.

"I'm impressed," the corporal said. "You want to work more with tanks?"

Mykhail gave the man a sideways, wary glance, then nodded.

"You know it's not a safe option, don't you?"

"What *is* safe around here?"

The corporal nodded. "Good. Consider yourself part of the tank maintenance team."

Mykhail spent most of the next few weeks looking after the tanks and other army vehicles. It wasn't peaceful, and when he wasn't being a mechanic, he was retreating, but it kept him away from the worst of the action. Tanks and engines were mechanical beasts. They showed no fear or anger, had no allies or enemies. They would not turn on you unexpectedly.

A little of that robotic attitude rubbed off on Mykhail. He was still sore over the killings of his friends, and the work helped him keep himself to himself and quell feelings of anger that, if given vent, would surely see him get punished.

He didn't talk to other soldiers, but he did listen. The words were always spoken after a glance over each shoulder to make sure no corporals were within earshot.

"I never wanted to join this damn army in the first place."

"Months of bloody retreat after bloody retreat. I've had enough."

"I was conscripted against my will anyway."

"Do the generals know what the hell they're doing?"

"It's humiliation week after week, losing battle after battle."

And there was talk of what his fellow Red Army troops had done to captured German soldiers—things so horrible they made Mykhail feel more ill than he already was.

By now there was also talk of rebellion every day, but it came to nothing.

Ultimately the Wehrmacht and the rest of the enemy did the job for them. By the end of September 1941, the Nazi blitzkrieg machine had encircled the last remnants of the Red Army in the city. There was nowhere left for them to retreat to, and they were finally ground into submission.

The soldiers were gathered into groups and told that they were surrendering to the combined forces of German, Hungarian, and Romanian troops.

Those in command said, "You should be proud of yourself," and, "One day the courageous Red Army will live again," and, "You will continue to fight the good Soviet fight for your people."

The rank-and-file soldiers muttered, "Thank God," and, "Anything but more fighting," and, "Damn the Russians."

Whether embarrassing capitulation or blessed relief, the plain fact was that the Germans had taken Kiev, and with it something in the region of half a million Red Army soldiers.

◆　◆　◆

A strange, almost ethereal, sense of relief fell upon Mykhail. There were no bombs exploding left, right, front, and back. No aircraft fire strafed the ground in front of his eyes, no friends fell on him, grasping, their fresh wounds spraying blood onto him. The fighting had stopped.

The civilians of Kiev started to come out of their houses, like bemused pit ponies being brought to the surface. There was an air of normality—a peace of sorts. For the first time in months, Mykhail could relax. Yes, there would be a price for that. But so be it.

He was not alone in this release. Nobody seemed to be considering the practicalities of housing and feeding so many prisoners of war. Instead, there was only relief, and little of any other emotion.

The German troops approached warily. Arms were surrendered at gunpoint. Now Mykhail felt naked. There were raised German voices. A translator shouted out the orders in both Russian and Ukrainian, and they were all ordered to march.

Mykhail was lucky; he still had boots. Some of his comrades had to march across the rubble-strewn streets in blood-soaked rags or bare feet that were soon cut to shreds.

About a half-mile on, some of his fellow soldiers started talking and pointing up at the trees lining the streets. Some branches seemed to be bent vertically to point at the street below. Mykhail was confused.

Then he realized. They weren't branches, but blackened objects hanging from the branches. And as the marching prisoners and escorts got closer, the reality became clear.

These blackened objects were the remains of soldiers—German soldiers—suspended from branches by their tied hands, hanging lifelessly, occasionally swinging and spinning in the breeze.

The entourage slowed to a halt. The Germans looked up, at first astonished, then gritting their teeth in anger.

Mykhail squinted to look more closely. The lower halves of the soldiers hung up in the trees were charred and shrunken.

"What happened?" Mykhail whispered to a soldier next to him.

"You don't know about Stalin's socks?" the man said.

Mykhail looked at him quizzically, then back up at the trees.

"Captured German soldiers. They tie their hands together over the branches, douse their feet in gasoline and . . ."

Mykhail's stomach turned as he looked up. His weakened heart struggled to pump harder. He dragged his eyes away from the wizened forms hanging from the trees and looked down, a dribble of cold fear escaping from his mouth.

Then there was shouting. The Red Army prisoners turned to see the normally unflappable German soldiers arguing with each other as they pointed up into the trees. Scuffles broke out, some of them even raised their rifles to one another.

Then their weapons turned, and instinct took control of Mykhail. By the time he was conscious of what was happening he'd already hit the ground. Submachine guns had been let loose, powering vengeance into the Red Army. A body fell onto Mykhail's legs, cracking his knees onto the concrete below. Another fell on his right arm and shoulder. He turned his head and met a face at close quarters. It belonged to a lifeless corpse, eyes bursting from its sockets in shock, blood pouring out of a neck wound.

And the shooting continued.

A shout rang out. "For Stalin's socks!"

Mykhail closed his eyes and started crying. The gunfire continued. For a few seconds he considered getting to his feet—even charging at the German troops. At least that would end it. But even if he wanted to do that he couldn't—he was pinned to the ground.

And then there were shouts in German, desperate and unrelenting. Voices were fighting bullets. Even Mykhail understood that they were ordering their troops to hold fire—and within thirty seconds the shouting had beaten off the gunfire.

Jackboots approached Mykhail.

"Those who are able, stand up."

Mykhail didn't move.

Louder: "Stand up if you can. It's safe."

Mykhail struggled at first, pulling his legs from under one corpse, pushing away the other. The German soldier grabbed his arm and helped him to his feet, but Mykhail stepped back—back toward the bigger mass of Red Army prisoners who had escaped the initial flurry of gunfire.

The Germans still argued, pointing and shouting. The prisoners steeled themselves to fall to the ground again. But no. Even the angriest of the German soldiers eventually breathed deeply, nodded agreement, and relaxed their weapons.

A few of them approached the prisoners.

"Wounded, come away," they shouted.

Men holding their blood-soaked arms or limping from bullets to the leg went where they were directed, moving themselves to a grassy area to one side. "On the ground," they were then told. "Face down."

There were more whispers from the Germans. Some lined up in front of the main body of uninjured prisoners and pointed their weapons at them, holding them steady. Others approached the wounded.

In a short burst of gunfire all the wounded soldiers were shot dead, and below them the blades of grass were soon poking through pools of blood.

"We can't carry any injured," the German soldiers said, then picked their way through the mass of bodies lying on the ground, putting a bullet in the head of any that showed signs of life.

For a moment Mykhail envied those comrades. Perhaps he should have stayed on the ground.

A few days later, the men were behind barbed wire.

This was a POW camp, but it was hardly a prison, merely an encirclement of fencing and armed guards. No buildings. No shelter. No sanitation. Food came only every other day, water only when it fell from the skies.

The sea of bodies at least provided a little warmth, much needed in the October chill. When the prisoners turned into corpses, their clothes were plundered. Occasionally those too weak to defend themselves were victims of the same crime.

Mykhail was lucky. A man next to him had a thick field coat but no boots. In the cold and wet, his feet got diseased, rotted, and soon afterward took him with them.

Mykhail took the man's coat and covered his whole body up in the increasingly cold nights that followed. A youth of eighteen, his body seemed more resilient than most. Whenever food appeared at the gates he was one of the first to react. He was like the sturdiest of the litter: better suited to surviving, hence stronger, and hence more likely to stay stronger. Self-preservation was everything.

Yes, he was weak, permanently chilled to the bone, infected with scabies and God knows what else, but in a sea of rotting flesh he was strong—as strong as a farm horse.

Chapter 13

Warsaw, Poland, 1941

The night after Asher's mama gave him permission to invite Izabella for a meal, he'd hardly slept for excitement, but still managed to find her within a half hour of leaving home the next morning. She was a couple of streets away from where she'd been before, and when they met this time, the timid numbness of his mind parted to make way for a confidence that surprised even himself.

At first he stood back for a few minutes, just watching her play that same tune. This time there was no vacant grin: his face held the smile of a young man simply enjoying the moment.

When she stopped for a break he approached her, clapping his hands in appreciation. She blushed, but also frowned in mock disapproval of his actions.

"Hello again," she said.

Asher held out a hand. "Do you want me to hold anything?"

She offered him the violin and bow, which he took, showing great care.

"It's very early," he said. "When did you start playing?"

"Dawn—as soon as people appeared on the street. And I'll go home at dusk."

"I'm sorry I upset you yesterday," Asher said. "I just wanted to know more about you."

She gave him a coy, sideways glance. "What do you want to know?"

"Well, where do you live now?"

"With my aunt in the north of the sector."

Asher nodded. "The one you stayed with while they were repairing the café?"

"How do you know about that?"

"I worked on the repair, remember? I heard your papa talk of you." He noticed her smile drop. "I'm sorry, I'm sorry. Forget I mentioned your—"

"It's all right. You helped him. I should be thanking you."

"Oh, I made sure your papa thanked me; I think I ate my weight in cakes that day."

They both laughed, although a glance at each other's figures, their waistlines shrinking by the month, lent a bittersweet edge to their laughter which neither wanted to mention.

"Are you happy living with your aunt?"

Izabella grimaced. "Mmm . . . they're nice, but her and her husband and four sons, all in one room? Let's just say I don't mind being outside all day. Besides, if I don't beg, I don't eat."

"Doesn't your aunt get the rations?"

"Not for me."

"Really? You must suffer from hunger a lot."

She nodded.

"In that case, how would you like to come to my home for a meal?"

"When?"

"Whenever you want to. How about today?" Asher peered into her eyes, trying to read what she thought of him, whether the lure was the food or spending time with him. It was probably the food, but that was understandable. "If it was up to me, you would come to our apartment to eat every day."

"You have an apartment?"

"I'm sorry. A slip of the tongue. We used to have an apartment before we came to the Jewish sector. Now we have one room, and it's very cramped with five of us sharing, forever getting under each other's feet." He checked himself. "Of course, not as cramped as seven would be."

She shrugged. "It's a roof over my head. I'm used to it by now."

"So, you'll come for a meal?" Asher said.

"Definitely." She reached for her violin and bow. "What time?"

"Six o'clock tonight. Shall I come here for you?"

"Of course," she said, drawing bow across strings as though warming them up.

Asher was conscious of his face flushing, and shifted from foot to foot, trying to quell his nervousness. "That's good. I'll come to fetch you." He took a pace back.

"One other thing," she said.

"What?"

"Your name?" she said. "You haven't told me your name."

Asher cursed himself. Now he could feel his skin almost burning with embarrassment. "I'm sorry, I should have said. I'm Asher Kogan."

"I'll see you here just before six, Asher. Now I have to work."

She started playing, and Asher watched for a few minutes, closing his eyes once or twice to allow the music to permeate better, then turned and ran. He had his own begging to do.

Later that day, Asher turned up early, finding Izabella studiously caressing the strings of her violin as usual. She flashed him a coy grin but continued playing, and Asher lost all sense of time while he listened, unable to take his eyes off her—so much so that he was a little startled when she stopped and took three paces to stand face to face with him. She said hello, and he paused before returning the greeting, as though snapping himself out of a trance.

The reaction clearly puzzled Izabella. "I'm sorry, Asher. I thought you were taking me to your home for a meal today. Am I being presumptuous? Tell me if I—"

"No, no. You're right, of course. It's all been arranged. Follow me please."

Izabella put her violin in its case, and Asher insisted on carrying it for her. They walked side by side, Asher talking about the room his family lived in, Izabella nodding agreeably. Whenever their arms brushed together he paused, his heartbeat quickening. Once or twice their hands touched, Asher feeling her warm flesh for only a second. As they approached the apartment block he felt the urge to gently place his hand over hers, which he resisted, although the mere thought made him lose the thread of what he was saying.

They arrived just as the bowls were being laid out on the table, and there was enough time for brief introductions to be made before the soup was served.

"It's a lovely room you have here," Izabella said as they all started eating.

"Oh, it's not much," Asher replied. "We used to have an apartment with two bedrooms."

"We *used* to have a farmhouse," Rina added from the sidelines.

"Asher told me," Izabella said, smiling sweetly. "But this is still a nice place. You have light, a table, it's clean. It's so much better than . . ." Her sentence trailed off to a sigh.

"Better than what?" Asher asked.

Rina hissed his name from across the table.

"What?" he hissed back.

"Don't be rude to our guest."

Asher wanted to tell his sister that Izabella wasn't *their* guest, she was *his*. But he noticed Izabella and Rina exchange a glance. Rina gave her head the slightest of shakes to show despair at her brother, making Izabella smile.

"You're right, Asher," Izabella said. "This is better than where I live."

"So, where do you live?" Keren asked.

"The other side of the sector," she replied.

"Whereabouts?" Papa asked. "I might know it."

"I don't think so." Izabella took a spoonful of soup and picked up a chunk of bread. "You have better food than me too. This soup is delicious, Mrs. Kogan. You have potato, carrots, and even a little onion in here. And the bread—oh, I can't remember the last time I held fresh bread in my hands. Where did you get this from?"

"That's a good question," Papa said. He turned to his wife. "Golda, where did you get this from?"

"The oven," she replied.

"No, I mean—"

"Izabella," Rina interrupted sharply, "tell us about your family. They live in the Netherlands, don't they?"

Izabella told them what she knew, which wasn't much because she hadn't heard from them for such a long time, but she said she missed them terribly and hoped that one day, when the country was free again, they could all live together once more and make up for lost time.

The mention of the country being free again kicked off a heated discussion between Papa, Rina, and Keren, leaving Mama to gather up the empty bowls while Asher and Izabella did little more than listen, occasionally glancing at each other.

Not long after that, Izabella stood up and reached for her violin case.

"Are you going so soon?" Mama said.

"I'm afraid so," she said. "But I can't thank you enough for your food and hospitality. I haven't felt so welcome in a long time."

"You deserve it," Rina said before anyone else could speak. "Nobody deserves to starve and nobody should have to beg."

"Nevertheless," Izabella insisted, "I'm very grateful. You're a kind family."

"Asher," Rina said, "aren't you going to walk Izabella home?"

"There's no need," Izabella said.

"I'd like to," Asher said. "Please."

Izabella paused, as though carefully weighing the offer up, before accepting.

"Only halfway, though," she said to Asher as they left the apartment block a few minutes later.

"Don't you want to show me where you live?"

She stopped walking and turned to him. "It's a horrible place," she said, holding his hand and squeezing it. "So please, turn back when I ask you to."

Asher nodded, his mind busy wondering whether she really was holding his hand or he was imagining it. A quiet "Yes" was all he could manage.

"Your sister Rina is a very confident woman, isn't she?" Izabella said as they started walking again.

Asher paused before replying. "Sometimes having her as a sister is difficult," he said. "Not that I don't like her. It's just that often I prefer the company of Keren. She's easier to get along with."

"I can see that, but I like both of them. I like all your family."

Asher almost said he'd like to meet Izabella's family one day, but thought better of it, and soon Izabella stopped at a street corner. She told Asher once again how much she'd enjoyed the meal and meeting his family, then reached up on tiptoes to give him a kiss on the cheek.

He stood, open-mouthed, and touched a fingertip to the spot where those petite strawberry lips had been, feeling the ghost of her warm kiss. This time there was no wondering; she definitely had kissed him.

"Now go," she said.

"Are you sure you'll get home safely?"

"I walk these streets all day, Asher. Just go, and I'll see you soon. I promise." She smiled the happiest smile Asher had seen on her since the days of Café Baran, then she ushered him away with one hand. "Go!" she hissed, starting to giggle.

Asher took a step back, then another, then turned and started running, not stopping until he got back home. The first thing he did there was ask Mama whether he could invite Izabella to eat again. She raised an eyebrow but agreed.

◆ ◆ ◆

Asher saw Izabella during the next week, but didn't dare make any physical contact, preferring to simply look and listen. Whenever she had a break from playing the violin they would sit and talk. They discussed the old days in free Warsaw—the glory days of Café Baran. Asher told Izabella more about his life before Warsaw, of days on the farm in Dyovsta with his old friend Mykhail, of mornings toiling in the sun and afternoons fishing in the nearby river. In return, she told him of her childhood days in Warsaw, when her two brothers and sister lived with them, before the specter of German invasion became an imminent threat and they'd fled to the Netherlands.

During that same week, while Mama and Papa were out of the house, Rina and Keren cornered Asher and asked him whether Izabella was just a friend. He tried to play his desires down but it was no good. Somehow, they knew; probably because they were women.

"You need to take the initiative," Keren said. "You like Izabella, so show her that by kissing her."

"I'm not sure," he replied.

"What do you mean?" Keren said.

"You don't know how to do it, do you?" Rina said.

His lack of a reply was all the answer they needed. They laughed. Asher blushed.

"It's easy," Keren said. "First of all, hold one hand. Then, if she likes that, hold both hands."

"And if she likes that," Rina continued, "pull her toward you—gently, though—so that your face meets hers."

"Then lean in," Keren said gleefully, "and touch your lips against hers."

Asher felt his face reddening. "But . . . how will I know whether she wants me to do that?"

Rina giggled. "You'll know," she said. "You'll know."

◆ ◆ ◆

The next meal Izabella shared with the Kogans was a more relaxed occasion, mostly taken up by reminiscing on better times.

Again, Asher accompanied Izabella halfway home. At the corner he held her hand, and she seemed comfortable with that, her hand squeezing his, which he took as a sign of encouragement.

He remembered the coaching Rina and Keren had given him a few days before, repeating their words inside his head. He made Izabella put down her violin case, held both her hands, and now turned to her, that beautiful face filling his view. His eyes roved over the long coal-black hair, her skin—perhaps too dirty to be pure white but still pure to Asher—those eyes, now warmer than ever but just a little sad, and that lovely strawberry pout. He wanted to do exactly as his sisters had suggested, which was to plant a confident but gentle kiss on her lips, but at the final moment his nerve failed him. His kiss was indeed confident and gentle, but landed on her cheek. Still, it was progress. And still, it felt wonderful.

There was a response, but not the one Asher expected. He felt her hands wriggle free from his, then felt one snake under his arm and around his back and the other firmly grasp the back of his head, pulling at his hair just a little.

And then he experienced the most exquisite feeling of his life so far: her warm lips on his, pressing just hard enough that he felt the outline of her teeth, not letting him breathe for some time.

He let out a short gasp as her lips let go, her fingers still tugging at his hair. Then her face—flushed and serious—was once more in front of his. She bit down on her lower lip, her nostrils flaring, then told him he had to go, he just had to leave *now*. He nodded, taking a few extra moments to move legs which now felt weak and heavy, but he was soon running home, this time with his heart feeling strong and a giant grin on his face. He had to stop before going inside, just to take a few minutes to calm himself down. He didn't want his sisters to start asking awkward questions.

The meals with Izabella became a regular affair, and Asher would see her most other days, when they would talk of times gone by and increasingly their hopes for the future. It was after the fourth meal, when Asher was walking Izabella home, after she'd kissed him with so much passion that he felt dizzy, that she told him she loved him. He started to reply, but couldn't get the words out at first, so he gulped, took a long breath to ensure his voice would sound manly, and told her he loved her too, that he always had, ever since he'd seen her at Café Baran.

For Asher, those were weeks of extremes. The horrors, the worries, the arguments—these didn't go away. But they were also the happiest of his life. He saw Izabella every day. There were days when she would shed tears for her family, tell Asher she was scared, and he would put an arm around her to comfort her and tell her he would take care of her. And they both said they would always love each other. Asher believed that.

For Asher, the second half of 1941 was a carnival hidden within a tempest. Despite the worsening conditions inside the Jewish sector of Warsaw, the joy of time spent with Izabella took him to a better place and made the hardships easier to cope with.

But soon, as the oncoming winter shortened the day, Izabella became less keen on that intimacy, often pulling away when Asher kissed her. Asher accepted this reluctance. Perhaps it was what he'd overheard one of his papa's friends call "feminine reserve." So yes, he accepted the reluctance, assuming her reaction to his attentions would improve, given time and patience.

As the end of the year approached, however, Asher was becoming increasingly frustrated. Izabella was indeed his carnival in a wretched world. Starvation and disease permeated his every waking moment— except for the precious time he spent in Izabella's company, when Izabella smiled, when Izabella talked, when Izabella played the violin. Just to be with her was a relief from the real world around him. So he didn't ask about her reluctance. But he did tell her he loved her and wanted to be with her as much as possible. Again, her replies echoed his, but, like an echo, they appeared to fade with time.

Eventually the stolen kisses were rejected outright, Izabella pushing him away.

"What is it?" Asher said one chilly day early in 1942. "Don't you like me?"

A pained expression gave him one answer, but it was an answer at odds with her actions.

"Don't say that, Asher," she replied. "Please, it's . . . it's not that. You're a kind, strong man. I enjoy your company. You and your family are fine people. But when we talk about loving one another . . ." A slow shake of her head finished the sentence.

"What?" Asher said, secretly understanding but not wanting to understand.

"I remember what you said when you first spoke to me. You talked of love even way back then. I'll always remember that."

"I said it because it was true. And it's just as true now. I'm in love with you, Izabella. There, I've said it again. This time I'm not spouting the words like . . . like some star-crossed fool; I'm telling you that because I know you well and I mean it from my head as well as my heart. I'm in love with you."

"And what if I say the same, if I tell you I'm in love with you and I promise you my undying love for evermore? What then?"

"I don't understand what you mean."

"Oh, Asher. Look around you. People are starving, many even dying. We're both in a prison with no release date. So we have love. But what do we do with it?"

Asher thought for a few seconds, but was still puzzled. *"Do with it?"*

"Yes. Do we get married? Do we start a family? Asher, I can't tell you how grateful I am for your company and friendship, for your family's hospitality. You've brightened up days that would have been my darkest, but this is not a place for love."

"But . . . but I love you."

"And in a better place I would love you too. Honestly, I would. And perhaps when all this is over and we have our freedom, I will. But not now, not with so much suffering all around us. I'm so sorry, Asher, but we'd be torturing ourselves if we let our emotions take control."

Asher stayed quiet for a few moments, his head bowed. Then he looked up and said, "Can I still meet with you?"

She nodded and frowned, looking almost hurt. "I'd like nothing more. You know how I feel about you. That hasn't changed."

"And the meals?"

"I'm so grateful to your family. I know how hard it is to share food that's been hard fought for. But I think it's better that I don't come anymore. It feels wrong after I've said these things to you."

"Oh." Asher smiled glumly.

"Asher, I'm not rejecting you. Please don't think like that. As I said, perhaps we can become closer in a better time, a better place. You won't forget me, will you? Please promise me that much."

The words brightened Asher up and he felt the corners of his mouth twitching upward instinctively. "Of course I won't forget you, Izabella. As you say, another time. I give you my word I won't forget you, and when that other time comes I'll tell you I love you again."

"So you're not bitter? I'd hate it if you were bitter."

"No, no." Now he smiled. It was a smile edged with sadness, but still a full smile. It was also a lie. He *was* bitter, although not at Izabella. "I'll be happy just to listen to you playing the violin on the streets. All I want is for these horrible walls to come down and for Warsaw to return to normal."

"And they will one day, Asher. But for now, just listen whenever you're near. If you hear the violin, I'll be here."

Asher left Izabella, telling her he had to go and meet his papa. When he was out of her sight he stopped to wipe away a few tears. He stood for a few moments listening to the violin. He knew he'd lied to her, although one thing he'd told her had been perfectly true. Watching her play, or watching words tumble from her ripe strawberry lips, or gazing into her warm, brown eyes—any of that would be like torturing himself. No, he couldn't do that. It would only tempt him to strike up conversation with her, which would only tempt him to hold her and kiss her once more. And any of that—even, perhaps, his presence—would make her feel awkward, and he didn't want that either.

But he wouldn't forget her, and one day when this sorry mess had gone away, he would track her down again. Then they would share love.

He pulled himself together and returned home.

There, he found his papa talking to a neighbor. When the neighbor left, Asher explained to his papa what had happened, that Izabella no longer wanted to be an inconvenience to the Kogans. He also said he didn't want anybody else in the family to ask him about it.

His wishes were respected—although his family couldn't hold back the pitying looks—and soon life in the Kogan household returned to as normal as it could ever be in an occupied city.

Asher's self-imposed abstinence lasted less than a week. Despite all the thoughts that seeing Izabella again would only make him suffer, conditions were deteriorating by the month, and just like anybody else with a spark of hope, something told Asher it was a spark to be nurtured, to be coaxed into a glow and then into a warm fire.

One sleepless night, he got up in the early hours, silently drank a cup of milk, and crept out. By the time he reached the other side of the sector, dawn had broken, and on every street corner he stilled himself, tuning his ears to any noise that sounded like music. He searched street after street, and yes, there was music—from a banjo player, from a flutist hardly worthy of the word—but not from any violinist. No Izabella. By noon Asher had walked every street and crossed every crossing in the Jewish sector. He returned home to an unwelcome interrogation.

"Your papa's been out looking for you all morning," Mama said. "Where in God's name have you been?"

"I couldn't sleep."

"And you've stayed out of the house for . . . what is it, five hours or more?"

"Please, Mama, I can't talk now. I need to rest."

"I should think so." She stepped over to him, held his head in both hands, and examined his face. "You *are* tired, aren't you?"

He wrestled his head away. "I am, and I don't want to talk. I'm here and I'm safe."

"And you're a little bad-tempered too," she muttered.

"I'm sorry, Mama. I just need to rest."

She nodded. "Okay. It's good. I should be grateful you aren't harmed in any way. I worry when I hear what's happened to people recently."

Asher felt a rush of fear. "What do you mean?"

"I thought you didn't want to talk?"

He grabbed her arm. "Tell me, Mama. Tell me."

She eyed his hand and he let go.

"I'm sorry," he said more quietly. "But tell me what you mean. Please. Then I'll rest."

"Your papa says there are rumors of people disappearing."

"Disappearing?"

"Here one day, not here the next. Nobody knows what happens to them. Or if they do know, they're not telling."

Asher's mind spun with the possibilities.

"But anyway. You need rest. I have to go out with the ration card and see what magic I can conjure up with it, so I'll leave you alone in the house. But please stay and rest, won't you?"

"Yes, Mama. I'll be here when you get back, I promise."

Asher stayed in the house, but didn't sleep.

When his papa returned an hour or so later, Asher asked him about the rumors.

"What rumors?" he said, hanging up his coat.

"The rumors of the people disappearing."

Papa shrugged. "That's it. That's as much as I know. Did your mama tell you we were worried senseless about you this morning?"

"I'm sorry. I just needed to go somewhere."

Papa thought for a moment, rasping his fingernails against his stubble. Then he put the coat he'd just taken off back on and grabbed Asher's. "Let's go for a walk," he said, handing Asher his coat. "And talk, man to man."

"You need to tell me if you go anywhere," Papa said a few minutes later, as they walked along the street.

"Does it matter where I go?"

Papa held a hand against Asher's chest, stopping them both still. "This is no time for games, Asher. I need to know where you are if you go out alone, especially so early in the morning like that. I don't want you to be one of those people who disappear."

Asher nodded and apologized. They started walking again.

"So where did you go this morning?" Papa said.

"If you must know, I was looking for Izabella, and I couldn't find her anywhere. I hunted the whole sector."

"What about where she lives?"

"I don't know where she lives. She didn't want me to know."

"I thought you walked her home?"

"Only halfway. I think she's embarrassed about where she lives."

"Oh, I see. Well, she could just be sick."

"She would still play the violin on the streets even if she was sick. She needs the money for food."

"Could she have found a job?"

"*A job?*" Asher squinted at his papa.

"Mmm . . . No. I can see that's a stupid thing to say. Look, I'll do you a deal, play along with your game. I'll help you look for her and I won't tell your mama or sisters, as long as you promise me not to go out alone without telling anyone where you're going."

It was a deal Asher accepted but was to regret.

He and his papa spent hours the next day looking for Izabella. And hours the next day too.

On the walk home that day, Asher couldn't bring himself to speak to Papa. It was left to Papa to sit him down on a bench near their block and tell him that perhaps they weren't going to find Izabella.

"No!" Asher shouted. "We'll find her. She must be somewhere in this sector. She *must!*"

His papa nodded in support. "The thing is, Asher, I can see this girl still means a lot to you, but there comes a point where—"

"I won't stop looking for her. *I won't.*"

Papa sighed. "You're in love with her, aren't you?"

It was the first time Asher had heard someone else put his feelings into words. He was confused, unable to answer.

"That's to say," his papa continued, "do you still think about her every waking minute? Do you get breathless at the sight of her and also breathless at the thought of never seeing her again?"

"I don't think she wants to see me," Asher said after a long silence. "But I still don't think I can live until I know she's safe. That's all I want."

Papa stood. "In that case, we'll carry on searching tomorrow. Now come, we need to eat."

So they searched the next day, and the next, Asher's mind becoming more ragged and desperate with every wasted hour. Then Papa told him that they needed to spend some time begging—that surely Asher could see that. Asher didn't reply, but the next week they spent four days looking, and the next, only two. At the end of that week, Papa sat Asher down and told him that they simply couldn't afford to spend any more time looking for Izabella when they could be begging instead.

Reluctantly, Asher was forced to agree. Papa also told him that if God meant for them to be together, they would meet again one day, and in the meantime survival was more important. He said a date with destiny would be useless if Asher wasn't around to take advantage of it.

So eventually Asher put thoughts of Izabella and her mystical violin music to the back of his mind, and concentrated on the task of survival.

Chapter 14

Warsaw, Poland, 1942

On the streets of the Jewish sector of Warsaw, some people looked fitter and healthier than others, and Asher had worked out that these were the new people.

It was hard to believe, but more people came into the ghetto every day, all crammed into the same square mile of Warsaw. When asked where they'd come from, the answer was always some other Polish town or city. The country was being trawled for Jews, and the catch dumped inside the walls of this city prison.

Early in the year, however, there was a seed of optimism for the Kogans.

They'd all heard the rumors of work—although they dared not even bring the subject up for discussion. But one day, while Asher's mama was cooking, his papa returned home with the closest thing to a smile Asher had seen for a long time.

"There's work," he said, taking his cap off and twirling it on his finger. "Hard work, but any work is good work."

"Is it dangerous?" Mama said. "I need to know."

"Not really," he said. "Let's sit down and eat." He sniffed the air. "What are you cooking today, Golda?"

"Some kasha, and a few pieces of challah."

"Any gravy?"

Mama shook her head.

"Never mind," he said.

They all sat down to eat, and Papa spoke with hope for the first time in many months.

"I've signed Asher and myself up for it. It's good, honest, physical work. And no . . ." He lowered his voice. ". . . no bodies."

It gave Asher a warm feeling inside. He was going to help his papa provide for the family. He was going to be a true man at last.

"Asher too?" Mama said, frowning. "Hirsch, you know he's not old enough for heavy physical work."

"Pah!" Papa said with a laugh. "The boy can cope. He's almost as strong as me." He patted Asher on the shoulder. "Eager muscles. Young bones. He'll be fine."

"Don't you think you should ask him first?" Rina said.

"Rina," Mama said. "Don't speak to your papa like that."

Asher noticed that Rina's stare persisted.

"I don't mind," he told his sister. "We need all the food we can get, don't we?"

"But you don't know what the work is," she replied.

Asher shrugged. "I don't care. It's work, so it's food."

"So tell us," Mama said to Papa. "Where's this work?"

"The brick factory. They need to increase production."

Rina laughed. "They build huge walls all around this place, then wonder why there's a brick shortage?"

Papa continued. "They've just been granted a big order by the authorities. They're allowing more coal to come in to fire the furnace, and also more food for the workers."

"The furnace?" Mama said, slapping a hand down on the table. "I don't like the sound of that."

"Calm down, calm down. Asher and I won't be anywhere near the furnace. We'll be helping to load the bricks onto the trucks."

"Are you sure that's all it is? You can't trust anyone these days. How can you be sure?"

"*Sure?*" he said. "What can anyone be sure about in these times? It's a job. Even a chance of a job is good news."

"We'll see."

Papa tutted at her.

"Have they told you what the bricks are for?" Rina asked.

"I don't really care," Papa replied. "But apparently there's an important construction project to the east that needs a lot of bricks. It's an urgent project so the work is all day, every day."

"But that will kill you," Mama said. "Both of you."

Papa waved the thought away with the back of his hand. "Ah, so what's happening now? Look at us, we're all losing weight. Without food we'll all be dead in six months anyway."

Asher ate the kasha, but his mouth tasted something more. He imagined fruit, perhaps even meat.

"Come on," Papa said. "We should be grateful for a drop of good news in an ocean of bad."

At first, Papa's optimism proved well founded. He and Asher worked like dogs at the brick factory and were exhausted at the end of every day. But there was food on the table. Compared to many around them, they ate like kings.

Nevertheless, by the spring of 1942 they were all still underweight, and Papa had developed a bad cough which was proving hard to shift. But, as he kept telling his family, they were all still alive when so many had perished. Weight could be put back on, and coughs could get better.

One day, Papa and Asher returned from work and washed while Mama prepared a meal. It was awkward with only one sink, but they managed.

Keren was reading a book.

"Hey, come on," Mama said to her. "Help me. You can lay the table."

Keren closed the book and put it down. Then she stopped. A glance out of the front window down to the street below had become a stare. There was also a grimace of disgust.

"Keren?" Mama said. "What is it?"

But Keren simply pointed to the street.

Mama came over and looked.

Asher came over too while he dried his hands, then Rina joined them.

"No, no," Mama said. "Don't look."

But it was too late. They saw the body lying on the street outside. The woman's legs were twisted, her head resting at an unnatural angle, her coat soaking up a nearby puddle.

"Is she dead?" Rina said.

They all knew the answer. But all Mama could say was, "Come away from the window, all of you. Asher, sit. Rina, Keren, help me prepare the meal."

But they didn't move, and soon Papa had finished drying his face. "What are you all staring at?" he said, ambling over. "What's happened?"

His face dropped a little as he saw the sorry scene. He spoke softly. "Let's all move away from the window," he said, ushering everyone to the table. "I know it's horrible, but what can we do? People are dying everywhere, inside houses and on every street. Asher and I must have passed a dozen dead bodies on the way home."

"Sixteen today," Asher said.

Mama turned to Papa. "Can't you move her?"

"Who? Me?"

"Well, you and the authorities. Can't you carry her away somewhere and bury her?"

"Carry her where? Bury her where?"

"Carry her off the street."

"But to where?"

"Anywhere. She's human. She deserves a proper burial."

"But there's no space. No land."

"Yes, but—"

"And besides, we have the living to think of. The last grain delivery was three days ago, and they say half of that was weevils and beetles. Money or no money, soon there will be no food to buy."

"I don't care about that now. She's a human being and if you don't—"

"Mama!"

They turned to Keren, who had crept back and was peering through the window.

"Don't interrupt your mama," Papa said.

"But look."

They all looked. A man and a woman were kneeling next to the dead body, searching through the woman's pockets. Then they talked to each other and tried to lift the body up.

"Well," Mama said. "Thank God there are some decent people left in this neighborhood."

Asher noticed Papa exchange a knowing glance with Rina. They said nothing, but gave Mama a pitying look.

"What?" Mama said. "What is it?"

At first Asher didn't understand either. But the five of them carried on looking outside. The two people kneeling beside the dead woman lifted her up to remove her coat, and then manhandled her to take off the rest of her clothes. They left the naked corpse splayed out, then got to their feet and scurried away.

Mama carried on staring out of the window. Even when Papa pulled the curtains shut she still stared.

A few minutes later, Papa started to scoop boiled potatoes onto the dishes.

"I can't," Mama said. "I'm not hungry."

"And I feel sick," Keren said.

"Listen," Papa said. "Both of you. Sit. Sit and eat."

"I agree," Rina said. "You don't have to enjoy it, but you have to eat."

Keren shook her head. "I really can't."

"Sit down!" Papa gestured to a seat at the table. "It's not a question of whether you want to eat." He pointed toward the window. "It's whether you want to end up like that."

Mama shook her head and covered her face with her hand.

Papa continued. "Have you forgotten the starvation ten years ago in Ukraine? Just consider all those who died back then. If you aren't eating for yourself, think of *them*."

Mama sighed and guided Keren to the table.

"Just eat what you can," Papa said. "It's a duty, not a pleasure."

Work at the brick factory continued, although the rewards were increasingly worthless.

Yes, Asher and Papa carried on loading bricks onto trucks, and yes, they brought home money. But, as Papa had said, they could only buy what people were prepared to sell, and now that wasn't much. The bakeries, vegetable shops, and butchers that had once been well stocked now had little or nothing to sell. And what they did have was often barely edible.

Even more bodies lay in the gutters. More people were diseased. Papa still had his cough, and now Mama had developed it too.

While Asher and Papa worked for worthless money, Mama and the girls went out begging for food. But they only ever seemed to meet more beggars.

"Why do you still work?" Mama would ask Papa. "Nobody has anything to sell you."

At first he would reply that he was buying food. Not much, but some. And some was more than none. He would also complain about the influx of people, about how still more people were arriving and were somehow being squeezed into that small area of Warsaw. "One dead body is carried out, two living ones arrive," he would say. "Net result: one more mouth to feed."

One evening, while Papa was resting on the bed, there was a knock at the door. Asher answered it, and a man asked for Papa. His papa groaned but he went out to the man, shutting the door behind him.

Asher listened. The two men argued for a few minutes, then Papa came back in, slamming the door behind him. He sighed and hesitated before speaking.

"Everyone, stop what you're doing and sit down." He waited until he had their attention before trying to continue. "They say . . . that is, the authorities say . . ."

"What?" Mama said. "What is it?"

"Well, they talk of a shortage of housing."

She glanced around the room, at the sink at one end, the table in the middle, the bed and mattresses on the floor at the other. "And that's supposed to be news?"

Papa looked down toward his feet. "We'll be sharing this room with a young Polish couple."

Mama laughed, but Asher could see it was an empty, desperate laugh.

"We can't do that," she said. "Tell them no. We won't accept it."

Papa held a hand up. "No. Look. It's happening."

"You mean, eating, sleeping, and washing with *strangers*? I don't think so."

"*Please!*" Papa roared.

Mama's face trembled. She shook her head in dismay.

"I'm sorry," he said. "I'm sorry for shouting, Golda. But . . . this is not a choice."

She nodded slowly. Papa put an arm around her and beckoned their three children toward him.

"We don't have a choice," he continued. "And neither do our new guests. We must welcome them."

"Well, yes," Mama said, huffing. "I guess you're right. We can't complain to them or blame them."

"And we won't," Rina replied. "We all know whose fault this is."

Oskar and Sala Slominski arrived late one evening. They were clearly weak and very frightened. They apologized for the inconvenience, speaking in short, nervous breaths, nodding hellos to everyone, and glancing furtively around the room.

Asher thought they were probably not much older than him, perhaps early twenties. Sala was a petite woman, Oskar was tall and thin, towering over the Kogans, almost threatening to fall over like an unstable building. The fact that he had a red birthmark on his face, covering one cheek and the side of his neck, made him look even more fragile, and at first Asher found it hard not to look at the mark.

"Sit down," Papa said to them. "Relax. And you don't need to apologize."

They still seemed uncertain, clinging on to their suitcases.

"I'll get you some sweet milk," Mama said. "I'm afraid it won't be hot; heating is in short supply."

The Slominskis thanked her, settled their suitcases in a corner of the room as if they contained fragile ornaments, and sat at the table with the Kogans.

It turned out they only spoke Polish, but the Kogans had learned the language to varying degrees, so they found common ground to converse well enough.

"How far have you come?" Papa asked them.

"I'm not sure," Oskar said, still a little disoriented.

Sala continued. "We've come from a small town in the north, not too far from Danzig. We were only told early this morning. We had to pack everything into two suitcases each."

"At gunpoint, I suppose," Mama said from the kitchen end of the room.

Sala nodded, her face pained.

Oskar held her hand. "It was more like the middle of the night when they came for us. Sala was very frightened." He paused for a moment. "Me too. I don't like guns."

"We weren't told anything about where we were going," Sala said. "We'd all heard the stories of camps where the living conditions are unbearable." She looked up at Oskar and squeezed his hand. "But I feel better now. This is a nice apartment. You're good people."

Papa raised his eyebrows at his children. "You've caught us on a good day."

Mama brought over the two cups of milk. "I'm sorry, we have little food. We can only offer you a small piece of challah each."

Oskar looked to Sala, and she gave her head a little shake.

"Thank you," Oskar said. "But right now we need rest more than food." He looked behind him. "Will we have a separate room?"

Mama and Papa exchanged glances. "What you see," Papa said. "The one room. This is it."

It took a few moments for the arrangement to sink in, then Oskar and Sala looked down at their cups of milk. Oskar took a sip and let out a gasp. "Delicious," he said. "Thank you."

"So what do you do for a living?" Keren said after a long pause.

"Oh, yes," Oskar said, now a little animated. "Sala is a seamstress and I'm a chemical engineer with the local—" He stopped himself and his enthusiasm quickly drained away. "I mean, I *was* a chemical engineer."

"That's all right," Rina said. "Papa once owned and ran his own farm. Now he's only a laborer, reduced to breaking his back by loading bricks onto trucks."

"Rina," Papa growled. "I can talk for myself, and it's a good job, an important position at the brick factory, helping . . ." His words trailed off to a guttural grunt. "Oh, she's right. I don't like it, but she's right. I'm a laborer."

"But the war will end," Sala said, forcing a smile. "Because all wars end, and when it does, life will return to normal."

"Of course," Papa said. He gave an assured nod, and talk turned to the street layout of the Jewish district and the meager food provision, after which they all lay down and slept, the Slominskis using cushions from the two easy chairs.

Living in such close proximity to strangers was always going to be awkward, but after the first few days the worst of that feeling fell away. Mama borrowed a needle and thread from next door, and she and Sala created a makeshift curtain, which they put on a piece of string tied across one corner of the room, where Sala and Oskar slept and kept their personal belongings.

Keren designated that area "Slominski house," and she also organized a schedule for "family hour," whereby for one hour every day either the Kogans or the Slominskis would leave the house to give the others some space, and to allow some privacy for washing at the sink.

Over the weeks that followed, the five Kogans and two Slominskis gradually got used to sharing the room without bumping into one another too much as they walked around the table or approached the sink. They also tried their best to restrict complaining to "family hour." At least, the Kogans did; Asher had no idea what the Slominskis got up to during their family hour—although they always seemed a little flushed and flustered when the Kogans returned home.

One day, while Asher and Papa were at the brick factory, Papa was called over by a guard. Asher carried on working, lifting the bricks onto a truck, but stopped when he saw, out of the corner of his eye, Papa gesticulating wildly. There were angry words. The guard's rifle barrel was raised for a moment. Papa returned and started loading bricks again, but didn't speak or look at Asher.

On the way home Papa still didn't speak—not until they were outside the apartment building, where he stopped and turned to Asher.

"I have some bad news," he said. "And I feel I should tell you first."

Asher felt his throat trembling. "Is it about Izabella?"

A deep frown appeared on Papa's forehead. "No. No news of her, I'm afraid. The news is that there's no more work at the brick factory."

A hundred words of fear and apprehension played on Asher's tongue, but he could say nothing, could do nothing except follow his papa inside.

Papa gathered the family around and told them that work at the brick factory was to cease. The one big order for bricks had been completed, so there was no more work for him and Asher.

There were arguments about what they would do, but all questions went unanswered.

"What do you want me to do?" Papa said to them all. "I don't have solutions."

After that, Asher and Papa stayed together during the long, miserable days, trudging through the walled area of the city, searching for food or work of any sort. "Let me do the talking," Asher's papa would always say to him.

Asher went along with that, but telling everyone they met that they would do absolutely anything in exchange for food for the family didn't seem such a hard thing to say.

It didn't take long, however, for Asher to realize that actually it must have been a very hard thing for Papa to say.

Soon after the brick factory closed, in the summer of 1942, there seemed to be a little hope. Many Jews were being taken out of the walled city within a city. The official story was that people were being taken somewhere else in Poland with more space and better housing—a heaven of sorts.

Asher heard the rumors of what was really happening, and assumed the others did, but the family didn't talk openly of such things. Asher assumed this was out of optimism.

And Mama said it was good news for those who remained in Warsaw, with more space and perhaps more food.

Within months her hopes were dashed. Because so many people had been taken away on trains to that "heaven," the authorities reduced the walled area of Warsaw further. They were back where they started, shrinking bodies in a shrinking prison. And whereas until then it had felt like being imprisoned in a walled city, now it really did start to feel like a prison.

The only work seemed to be running errands for the soldiers that patrolled the area, or carting dead bodies around. Those duties provided some food to supplement the most basic of rations, but the cords holding up their pants and skirts were tightened some more. Strangely, Sala looked slightly fuller in the belly, even though her face looked leaner. Asher's mama and papa had long since lost the appetite for polite conversation, but now their faces seemed expressionless and their talk often descended quickly into petty squabbles.

The only spark of hope for Asher was how well Rina was coping. One way or another, she was bringing in as much food as the rest of the family combined. Whenever she did this she said nothing, just hurriedly put it away in the cupboard. But Asher noticed.

And so did Papa.

One dark evening late in the year, they all sat down to a meal of potato soup and dumplings. A lot of dumplings.

"Why are there so many dumplings?" Papa said to Mama.

"Are you complaining?" she replied.

"No, but . . ."

Asher noticed that Rina was staring straight ahead, and Keren was giving her a suspicious look.

"I just wondered why," Papa continued.

"Because I had lots of flour," Mama said.

Papa thought for a moment, then nodded to himself. He lifted his spoon and held it above the nebulous steaming liquid, lowering it slowly. As soon as it touched the soup he dropped it and let out a frustrated grunt. He stared at Rina, then at Oskar and Sala, as though daring each one of them to speak.

"I can't take this anymore," he said to nobody in particular. "It's Rina, isn't it?"

There was silence.

"She got the flour, didn't she?" he added when it became clear his question was not going to be answered. He turned to his wife. "Golda, where did you get the extra flour?"

"I found it."

"Found it?"

"In the cupboard."

"But . . ." He turned to Rina. "Look at me, Rina."

But she could do no more than glance at him.

"*Rina?*" Papa said again.

Now her look was direct. "You prefer to starve, is that it?"

"No, but . . ."

The two were like a pair of stags locking horns.

"Papa, don't ask, because I won't tell you."

His voice softened, almost cracking. "But I worry for you. Is that so wrong?" He turned to Mama. "Do you know what she's doing to get this food?"

"Nobody knows," Rina said. "And it has to stay that way. But please just believe me, Papa, it's not what you think."

"I'm not sure what I think," he mumbled. He shrugged and turned to Oskar. "Oskar, if it was your daughter, what would you think?"

Oskar blinked a few times and looked toward Sala for encouragement. She nodded at him. "We're just grateful for any extra food we can get," he said. "We need it . . . I mean, *Sala* needs it more than ever."

Papa glanced at Sala. "Really? Why?"

Oskar put an arm around his wife. "She's . . . expecting a baby."

Everyone stopped eating and stared at Sala.

"Oh," Papa said. His jaw lowered as if to say more, but he froze for a couple of seconds as his stare met with that of Oskar, and he lifted his spoon to his mouth.

A long silence followed, nobody else even daring to eat for fear of making a sound.

Then Papa sighed. "And, uh . . ." He glanced at Sala, then Oskar. ". . . have you considered where the extra food is going to come from?"

"Hirsch!" his wife said. "Don't be so rude."

"But it's true. I just wondered whether they thought about—"

"Mr. Kogan," Oskar interrupted, "I appreciate your concern, but what else can we do?"

His wife leaned forward. "And the war might be over by the time my child is born."

Papa gave a harrumph. "You really think so? I think you're deluded."

"Stop this," Rina said, slamming her hand on the table, which made her papa visibly back away. "Stop it now. Don't you all see you're letting them win if you argue? Let's try our best to live normal lives. All of you, think what you would really want to do in an ideal world. If you can do it, do it. Don't give in."

"That's all well and good," Papa replied. "They're worthy words, but we're only just getting enough food as it is."

"It will be okay," Rina replied.

"But how?"

"We'll manage. Don't worry, and don't ask. Just eat."

"What's this? My own daughter ordering me about?"

"Telling you not to worry isn't an order, Papa."

Papa shook his head, bemused, but started eating, and they all followed. There was no more conversation until well after the spoons and empty bowls had been taken away, but Asher thought about Rina that night. Like everyone else, he didn't know exactly what she was doing to get the extra food, but he knew she was brave.

That they survived the year was mainly due to her efforts, whatever they were.

Chapter 15

Diane pretty much threw herself into the passenger seat and slammed the car door shut. "Let's go."

Brad had driven them three blocks before she said another word. "Damn bureaucrats," she muttered.

He waited for an explanation that didn't come before taking a guess with, "So, it's a no-go, then?"

Another two blocks went by, including a thirty-second wait at the lights.

"Now he's saying he'll talk, but only to me."

"Is that a problem?"

"He means alone, with no legal guys or even guards listening in."

"Oh."

Another two blocks went by.

"So, did you ask the manager or whoever?"

"Deputy and a couple other guys. They said it was out of the question for us to meet with no guard present."

"They figured you'd . . . what . . . take revenge on the old guy?"

"Clearly I'm untrustworthy. I even told the sons of bitches they could search me for weapons, cuff my hands to the table legs, whatever the hell they wanted except cover my ears."

"So that's the end of it?"

Brad glanced to the side to see Diane shaking her head.

"That's the end of it *for today*. I argued, like, forever, and said it was my father who'd been killed and I had to have some closure here."

"I don't get it. So what's happening?"

"They're going to consider setting up some video surveillance system to keep lookout, to make sure I don't do anything dumb. If that meets their regulations, they'll do it tomorrow."

"Sounds positive."

"Except for one more sleepless night wondering what the hell happened between him and my father. And even then, that's only if I'm lucky. It's so goddamn annoying."

They pulled up into Brad's drive.

"Relax a little," he said. "We'll cook, watch TV, I could call Emma and David, see if they want to go for a drink—anything to take your mind off things."

But Diane was already shaking her head. "I want to be alone," she said.

They got out of the car.

"Alone?" Brad asked.

She rolled her eyes just a touch. "Alone *with you*."

Brad put an arm around her shoulders and kissed her. "Listen. After what you've been through, you get to have what you want."

"Ah, yeah, talking of which . . . ah . . . could you drive me back there tomorrow?"

"Hey, you don't need to ask."

The next morning, Diane and Brad lay in bed together listening to the morning news on the radio alarm clock. She lay on her side, curled up into a ball as if she were cold, and he lay behind her, his face nuzzling her hair, his hand caressing her arm, his naked chest pressing against her naked back.

"Have you thought about what you'll be doing?" he said, kissing the crown of her head.

"About what?"

"I mean, like, you're not going back to your father's place, are you?"

Diane felt herself shudder at the thought. "I can't even visit there, let alone live there."

"So where are you going to live?"

"As soon as I'm done with finding out why that son of a bitch killed my father, I'm going to visit Mother in Baltimore."

"To stay permanently?"

"I have nowhere else to go."

An ad jingle so grating that Diane cursed it came on the radio. Brad reached across her, turned it off, then lay on his back.

"Hey, where do you think you're going?" Diane said.

"Sorry."

Diane felt his chest warming her back again. "No, I'm sorry," she said.

"For what?"

"Saying I have nowhere else to go."

"That's okay."

She thought she could detect an edge of sourness in his words. She turned her head to look at his face, to see if he had that half-smile of acceptance he always had when he couldn't be bothered to argue. And yes, it was there.

"Is it really okay?" she said.

He kissed her and they settled back into position. She closed her eyes as he spoke again.

"I'm guessing staying with your mother is only going to be a temporary thing."

"I'm a mess after what's happened. I'm not so sure what is and isn't temporary."

"I've told you, you're welcome to move in."

"You have."

"So . . . in time you might be able to tell me where I stand?"

"At the moment, you stand between me keeping sane and me with my brain turned to jello."

He let out a half-stifled laugh. "I should get one of those 'Here to Help' badges."

"Don't ever think I don't appreciate what you're doing, Brad."

"I know. But I'm just thinking that if you feel like that . . ."

"What?"

"Well, you always told me you never got on so well with your mother, so I can't see that staying with her for any length of time is going to help you."

"It's more complicated than that."

"How so?"

Diane was silent.

"Come on. You can tell me. Really."

"No, no. I wasn't not answering, I was just trying to work it out myself. You see, when we first met, I told you I never really got on with my mother. It's closer to the truth to say I was never really allowed to get on with her. After the split, I tried to keep the peace between Mother and Father like any good kid would, but that was a lost cause. They asked me what I wanted to do, and I said I wanted to live with Mother, so I did, and Father called me regularly and occasionally visited. Then I went to live with him, and he always told people that I changed my mind and decided I wanted to live with him."

"I remember him saying that. You didn't disagree, as I recall."

"It was the official line, I guess. And I liked to fool myself. It made me feel better that way."

"And the truth?"

"When he called me at Mother's place he would ask how I was and how school was. Later on, there was stuff that made me feel terrible. He'd say how he hadn't seen anyone outside work for two weeks, that he was fine with his own company. He'd really lay it on thick—just for my benefit. Sometimes, when he visited and had to leave, he got upset and was almost in tears. I don't know whether they were tears of sadness, anger, or deceit. All I know is that it worked."

"That's when you went back?"

"Yes. And after that I guess I found it hard to escape."

"What did your mother have to say about that?"

"I think she was still just a little in love with him, or at least didn't want him to be lonely and unhappy. You've met her. She's the gregarious type, always was. But he was the opposite; he didn't much care for other people."

"That's a harsh thing to say about your father."

Diane shrugged. "It's the truth—or my version of it. You weren't there when I brought boyfriends home and he would almost interrogate them and then tell me what was wrong with them. I challenged him about it when I turned twenty. He would tell me he was only being a proud father and trying to protect me. I would say I didn't believe him, and then he'd get all tearful, telling me his only sin was he could never accept that any man was good enough for me. I swallowed that, and I was almost thirty when I realized it was kind of an act of his. He just found it hard to contemplate me moving out."

"I don't get it, Diane. I know you're not quite as confident as you come across. But if that dawned on you when you were thirty, why didn't you make the break then, get your own place not too far away, ease yourself away from him?"

"I guess after all that time together I got as weak as him. And he was my father. I know he was possessive of me, but that doesn't mean he didn't love me."

"Doesn't it?"

They both relaxed in silence. Diane sensed Brad's head lift up. She knew what he was doing: checking the time on the alarm clock.

"No, it doesn't," Diane said. "For instance, there was the time I mentioned to him that I wanted to socialize more—to meet more people. He said it was a coincidence, because he was thinking exactly the same thing. So we held a few house parties, invited a few people from his workplace, a few from mine, some neighbors. Somehow I knew his heart wasn't in it, but he persevered. After they'd gone he would bitch about them, and during the third one he started being rude to people. Not aggressive or anything, just bad-tempered. I asked him what the big deal was, especially when he'd said he wanted the parties just as much as I did. He had a face like thunder, and I knew then that he'd never really wanted the parties. It had all been a way to please me, to make me happy living there. So even though his motives were selfish, he *tried* to make me happy."

"You don't think he was holding you back for his own purposes?"

"Mmm . . . I guess we all act in our own interests more than we care to admit. We all have a weaker self."

"You don't think he had some sort of hold on you?"

"Of course not. Well, look, I just didn't want him to be lonely. Is that so wrong?"

Brad opened his mouth to reply but seemed to downgrade it to a nod.

"We had our ups and downs but we got on fine together. I miss him. I *really* miss him. We had the same tastes in food and TV—at least, so he led me to believe. And that made it even harder for me to move out."

"Is that it? Was that the reason for all those years? You just didn't want him to be lonely?"

"I don't want to talk about it. Not now."

"Okay, but talking of moving out, have you seen the time? We need breakfast, then we have to call in to find out if your video shoot is on."

Diane turned to him. They embraced. She thanked him.

Chapter 16

Mykhail knew from the passing of the seasons that he'd now been in the POW camp for about a year. A sea of men stretched over the horizon. Starvation and disease were everywhere, beatings and shootings commonplace. Just as food, shelter, and clothing were rare.

For Mykhail, eating was only out of animalistic habit. When the food arrived at the gates he would fight his way to the front, knocking over people who he knew he should have thought of as comrades or compatriots—or fellow human beings, at the very least. But he fought them for what little food was provided.

There was plenty of time to think, and so many of his papa's words kept spinning in his head—talk of being a proud Ukrainian, talk of self-preservation, doing what was necessary to survive. After all, those ideals had gotten him so far while Borys and Taras and millions of others had perished.

But even with those memories of his papa's words rattling around in his head, Mykhail's spirit, if not his conscious self, was starting to give up. How much longer could he survive? Another year? Another five years? And what after that—a country controlled by Nazis rather than Soviets? He'd seen many prisoners attack guards for the finality of being shot, choosing to be put down like sick and useless farmyard animals.

Then there was the goading by the guards. They'd obviously learned a few Ukrainian and Russian words: *useless, filthy, disgusting, subhuman, unworthy, ungodly*—the list went on and on. The only merciful thing was that most of what they said was in German.

Today was different. This one happened to speak good Russian. "Time for your supper, Russian peasants," he said as he cast scraps of food onto the ground.

It took a while to register with Mykhail's stunted mind. But he listened more intently.

"Looks like we've discovered a new variety of pig. The Russian Weakling Pig."

Mykhail grabbed a piece of moldy bread from the ground and started gnawing on it. But he kept his eye on the guard.

"Why are you Russians so filthy?" the guard shouted out, flashing a smile. "Is it in your blood or do you have to learn it from your Russian pig fathers?"

Mykhail couldn't help but answer back. "I'm not Russian," he said as he grabbed another chunk of bread from the dirt.

The guard laughed. "What did you say, Mister filthy Russian vermin?"

"I'm not Russian," Mykhail said more firmly. "And my name is Mykhail Petrenko."

The guard's smile dropped. He reached out and grabbed Mykhail's jacket, pulling him forward. Mykhail was so weak that the action made him dizzy for a second. He fell to his knees.

The guard twisted the lapels of his jacket up in his fist. "You speak to me like that again, *Mr. Petrenko*, and I'll kill you, you dirty piece of Russian shit!"

Mykhail thought for a second about self-preservation. He thought it stank. Or perhaps he no longer cared; there wasn't much of him left to preserve. "I'm Ukrainian," he said. "And if you call me Russian again, I'll *make* you kill me."

At this, every trace of humor dropped from the guard's face. He walked back, dragging Mykhail along by his knees. That wasn't hard; the guard was a couple of inches shorter than Mykhail but he was fit and well fed. As he pulled Mykhail back he cracked his rifle against the back of Mykhail's hand, making him drop the moldy bread into the mud.

They stopped at the fence, where the guard spoke in Ukrainian as if a switch had been flicked. "You're Russian," he said. "You're Russian and you're a pig. You're a filthy, disease-ridden pig." He lifted his rifle up to Mykhail's throat. "So go on, Russian pig. Make me kill you."

Mykhail said nothing, just froze and looked the man in the eye.

After a while the guard withdrew his rifle, smirked, and started walking off.

"Ukrainian!" Mykhail shouted out after him. There was no reason, no logic, no element of self-preservation. It was suicidal. Perhaps that was the idea.

Within seconds the guard was standing above him again. This time he didn't raise his rifle, so Mykhail repeated the word, sensing the end— the end of his suffering. His heart didn't race; it had no energy for that.

The guard burst into mocking laughter. "You're a brave man," he said. He pointed to Mykhail's face. "Is that where you got that scar, from fighting?"

"I'm not brave," Mykhail replied. "Look around you. What do I have to lose?"

The guard cast his eye over the mass of bodies—alive, dead, and a hundred stages in between. "I'm Ukrainian too," he said. "Tell me, where are you from?"

"Dyovsta," Mykhail replied.

"I've heard of that." The guard thumbed his chest. "I'm from a tiny village near Tarnopol in Galicia."

Mykhail had heard about Ukrainian men joining the SS—that there was actually a Ukrainian SS regiment—but never quite believed it. Here was proof.

"You must really hate the Russians," the guard said.

"I remember what they did to my people," Mykhail replied. "In the early thirties."

"Me too. Stalin's starvation. Yet you fought alongside them?"

Mykhail shrugged, and winced at the pain in his emaciated shoulders. What could he say? He could mention that the Russians effectively prevented his mama having more children. But so much had come to pass since he'd struggled with his principles on the issue.

Then the guard said, "You hate the Germans too?"

Mykhail cast a lazy arm at the prisoners behind him. "The Germans who keep me in this living hell? Germans who treat us worse than animals?"

"But what if you were allowed out of the camp?"

Mykhail, puzzled, hesitated. "To where?" he said. "For what purpose?"

"Labor is needed in Germany and elsewhere. People we can trust. Just tell me you're not Jewish."

"I'm not."

"You know, if you're lying I will find out, and I really will kill you."

"Do what you need to. I'm not Jewish."

"In that case I could recommend you, and you could get out of this place."

"What would you want in return?"

The guard grunted a laugh. "Don't fool yourself; you have nothing I might want in a million years."

Mykhail, for weeks thinking he couldn't feel any more wretched, now felt one inch tall. But the guard didn't need to ask twice, and Mykhail didn't need to take another look at the POW camp.

◆ ◆ ◆

Mykhail was dragged out of the camp the very next day—not told anything, just ordered into a truck at gunpoint. He was taken to somewhere they called the Trawniki camp. It was a strange place, a kind of training facility in Poland for people who should have been enemies of the Germans but had been "persuaded" to work for them.

Mykhail was confused, although he did find out why the guard at Kiev had saved him: he was on a commission of sorts for providing reliable labor for the German war effort.

Mykhail spent the first few weeks at the camp getting his health back—that and getting used to sleeping in a bed again after so long sleeping in muddy fields. He had no idea what they needed him for, but in time they assessed every aspect of his skills, involving tests and interviews.

It was soon after these that he was summoned from his barracks and marched to a worryingly official-looking building, into a room dominated by three men seated behind a large desk.

The men talked in German among themselves, then Mykhail heard his name and they all perused sheets of paper before one of them looked across at him and spoke in passable Ukrainian.

"They say you're good with engines, Petrenko?"

"I've repaired tractors and—"

"Speak up!" another one of the men said.

Mykhail cleared his throat and decided to speak with a measure of confidence, hoping it wouldn't be taken as a sign of insolence or arrogance.

"I was brought up on a farm, and when the farm first acquired a tractor I learned the basics of how it operated and how it needed to be maintained. I became well known throughout the surrounding villages for being able to diagnose and fix most mechanical problems. From there I learned about civilian vehicles—both gasoline and diesel—and during the last few weeks of fighting in and around Kiev I was responsible for tank maintenance."

The three men looked slightly shocked, and Mykhail could feel his heart racing, wondering if he'd said too much, but eventually they started muttering among themselves, after which Mykhail was marched back to the barracks none the wiser.

The next day he was taken to a workshop, the inside of which was almost entirely filled by a large tank. In front of the three men he'd seen the previous day, he was asked what he knew about the vehicle.

Still unsure what the hell this was all about, Mykhail decided he had little to lose and a lot to gain, so spoke again with confidence.

"It's a German model," he said, "whereas I'm more familiar with Soviet tanks." He sauntered around the vehicle, peering at the air intake, checking the brackets around the exhaust, opening the engine cover and tapping his fingers on a few of the components inside. "But the principles are much the same," he continued, and proceeded to explain—from the fuel and air intake to the compression cycle and to the emission of exhaust gases—precisely how the engine operated, to the approving nods of the onlookers.

They were clearly impressed, but still didn't tell Mykhail what they had in mind. And he didn't dare ask.

Soon afterward he was shipped out of the training camp, with no idea where he was going or why.

When he arrived, it seemed a pleasant place—a small settlement of huts and buildings in the middle of the countryside. It even had its own dedicated railroad station, with the name "Treblinka" on the platform. A set of carriages pulled up, holding more people than seemed possible. The people looked quite ill and were shoved this way and that by guards with rather nasty-looking dogs. Mykhail was told not to look at them—which was difficult considering the number of people—and was shown to his quarters. The building was like an army barracks, not much more than a shed, but it was a palace compared to the hell of the POW camp.

He was told he would be collected for work within the hour, and decided to spend that time resting in his bunk, which was still a paradise of sorts and to be savored.

As well as rumors about Ukrainian SS divisions, there had always been rumors about secret camps hidden all over Germany and the countries under its command, where conditions were desperately poor for prisoners—mostly Jews.

Mykhail wondered whether this was one such camp. He was unsure for two reasons. For one thing, there weren't many guards or other staff. For another, there simply wasn't the room—perhaps only twenty or thirty buildings, mostly small. And Mykhail didn't feel like a prisoner, although he told himself never to show complete trust in anyone.

After a while he heard voices outside and sat up. The doors opened and a handful of men came in. They were speaking Ukrainian. Mykhail immediately felt better: this far from home, these men were as good as brothers. He got up and introduced himself. They talked openly of the routine of roll call, mealtimes, and suchlike. They weren't exactly happy, but they looked to be in relatively good health.

Then Mykhail said, "So, what's the purpose of this camp?"

They all stopped what they were doing for a second and glanced at one another. One gave Mykhail a very worried look.

"I mean, what have you just been doing?"

Still they didn't speak.

"You'll be told what part you play in good time," one of them said.

Mykhail was puzzled. These men were all able-bodied, and although slim didn't look dangerously ill. So whatever they were doing, it wasn't harming them.

Thinking he might have somehow offended them, Mykhail got back into his bunk and kept quiet.

A few minutes later, someone else entered—a uniformed guard—and told Mykhail to follow him. He spoke Ukrainian too. He didn't utter another word until they reached a narrow path, camouflaged on both sides. He told Mykhail it was referred to as the *Himmelstrasse*. Mykhail clumsily repeated the word, and then the guard told him in Ukrainian what it meant: "Road to Heaven." A polite smile played on Mykhail's lips. Was this man joking? It sounded a strange name for a path.

That was when Mykhail heard the noise—a distant throbbing—which got louder as they walked on. At the end of the Himmelstrasse they came to another section of the camp, hidden from the rest, and Mykhail was led to a large brick building. At the nearest door—which was shut—a few people rested outside. Two were German guards, the rest appeared to be civilians.

The civilians were naked. Mykhail could feel his body starting to tremble as his imagination ran wild.

The throbbing noise was coming from inside this building. Now Mykhail recognized the noise: it was a big engine, whether diesel or gasoline he was too numb to consider. He was taken to the far end of the building, where the guard opened a door and told Mykhail to go in.

It was some sort of pump room, quite warm and dark, with an oily smell. But the room was dominated by the sound and sight of something Mykhail knew well—an engine from one of the tanks he was used to working on.

"You're the mechanic," the guard said. "Your job is to keep the engine running."

"All day?" Mykhail asked.

"Most of the day, most of the night, every day, every week. You stop the engine when you are told to, you start the engine when you are told to. It must not break down under any circumstances. Your life depends upon it."

Mykhail glanced at two medium-bore pipes, which he determined from the orientation of the engine to be the intake and the exhaust. They both went through the wall into another room of the same building.

"What is it for?" he said.

"If fuel gets low you have to tell me or another guard. If you need to stop it for maintenance you must tell me or another guard. If there are exhaust leaks you must stop them and tell me or another guard. You must keep the level of carbon monoxide produced as high as you can. Do you understand all of that?"

Many questions were rattling around in Mykhail's mind. But he didn't want to know the answers. He nodded, and the guard left.

It wasn't long before Mykhail found out why he was there.

At first he didn't know the full details, but he heard the screams and shouts coming from the other side of the wall, and wished the engine was even louder so it would drown out those sounds of a place worse than hell. Even deafen him, perhaps.

And then, worse, there was a blur of the darkest emotions when he did find out, a sense that he wanted to be elsewhere, that this couldn't be happening. There was a commotion, rifles being used. Mykhail was called outside. He was told that others were supposed to carry out the task, but they had refused and been shot. So Mykhail had to step in, removing the still-warm bodies from the chamber, dragging them away and dropping them into nearby pits dug deep in the earth.

In the POW camp there had been constant physical suffering.

Mykhail wondered whether this was any better.

Chapter 17

Warsaw, Poland, 1943

Nobody spoke again of the food Rina was bringing into the Kogan household. It appeared in the kitchen, Mama cooked it, and they all ate it. It was mainly due to that food that the Kogans and the Slominskis survived into early 1943 in reasonable health. Papa often forced the idea home, saying this food was *reasonable* or the room was *reasonably* warm. It was only during the increasingly frequent arguments that Papa's veil of optimism slipped, when he said in anger that even *being alive* wasn't reasonable under the circumstances. Words were only words, but Asher knew Papa's health was not good, the cough having now taken up permanent residence in his chest.

One day, during a silent breakfast, there was another knock at the door. Everyone looked to Mama, who turned to Papa. He didn't move for a few seconds. It was as though they all had now come to recognize an "official knock." Mama offered to answer it, but Papa said no, and slowly got to his feet and ambled over.

He opened the door. There was a man. There were also soldiers. A few words were exchanged, then Papa turned back and called for Oskar to join him, closing the door behind them. The others waited, not speaking.

When they returned inside, Papa did no more than bow his head, as if to hide his expression, while Oskar stared at the faces of the others, their mouths agape.

"What's happened?" Mama said. "What is it?"

"We have to leave," Oskar said. "They say it's our turn."

Mama gave her husband a look of horror. "Is this true, Hirsch?"

He nodded solemnly. "It . . . could be a good thing."

"What do you mean?" Rina said. "Where do you think they want to take us?"

"Somewhere better than this," he said flatly.

"I agree," Mama said. "Let's try to hope. You never know, it could be a place with more room, perhaps space to grow our own vegetables again and even keep a few chickens."

"What are you talking about?" Rina said. "Haven't you heard—"

"Rina!" Papa said. "Don't talk to your mama like that."

"But—"

Rina shrieked as his fist hit the table.

"Stop it!" He took a breath, coughed a little, and struggled to lower his voice. "The guards are rounding up the whole street. We have no choice. Thousands have been moved out in the last few days, and hundreds who argued have been shot dead. Do you want that?"

Rina said nothing.

"And look around you. Think of what we've been eating for the past year. We manage better than many, but it's still mostly scraps hardly fit for animals. We all keep losing weight. Could it be any worse than this?"

"When do they want us to leave?" Keren said.

He sighed. "Now. We have to go *now*."

"This minute?" Mama said. "Without warning?"

Papa nodded. "We each have to pack as much as we can into a single suitcase. The guards will accompany us to the meeting point next to the railroad station."

Nobody spoke for a few moments.

Then Rina said quietly, "I'm not going."

"Oh, come on," Mama said. "There might be jobs. Think of us living a better life. You heard your papa; it can't be any worse than this broken shell of a home."

Rina shook her head. "But surely we all know the rumors. Papa? Oskar? Keren?" She looked at each of them in turn. "You must know all those people have gone to their deaths? And you, Asher." She stared at him, her eyes wide and questioning. "You're happy to simply give yourself up to these people?"

Asher opened his mouth to speak. Yes, he knew the rumors, but also knew not to talk of them for fear of upsetting people.

"I say we should stay and fight," Rina said. "Asher?"

"I . . . I don't know," he replied. "What do we fight with?"

"Leave that to me," she replied. "I have contacts."

"You know people who can supply guns?" Papa asked.

Her face blushed. "I . . . I know people who need bullets."

Papa gave her a sideways look, then shook the thought from his head.

"I say we stay," she said. "Who's with me?"

Asher thought for a moment, torn between loyalty to his parents and the courage of his sister. "I am," he said quietly. He glanced at the other shocked faces, then added, "I want to fight too."

"Well done," Rina said. "And what about you, Oskar? Do you want to fight or leave the city?" She glanced at Sala, her belly now full and round. "I'm sorry, I forgot."

"Of course," Oskar said. "There's no way we could live in hiding places. Besides, I'm a pacifist. I will not point a gun at anybody on principle." He looked at Sala, who held his hand and nodded agreement.

"I agree with them," Mama said. "I don't want to kill people. And I certainly don't want to stay here."

"Me neither," Keren said.

Mama turned to her other children. "Rina, Asher, come with us. Please."

Asher looked at Rina and felt her stare willing him on.

"No," Rina said. "I don't trust them."

"We don't know what awaits us at the other end of the train journey," Mama continued. "But we know what's here. It's dangerous—very dangerous. This is the center of a war zone and we'll be shot if we stay here. Maybe I'm optimistic, thinking of growing vegetables and keeping chickens, but it's like your papa said, wherever they're taking us, could it really be any worse than here?"

"Oh, yes," Rina replied. "It certainly could. So I still say we should stay and fight."

"Well, I don't," Mama said.

"Oh, look," Papa said. "All this bickering is getting us nowhere. We only have ten minutes." He took his cap off and gave his head a hurried scratch. "Those who want to stay, stay. Those who want to leave, leave. But I go where my wife goes. And I won't be sorry to say good riddance to this rat's nest."

"No, Hirsch," his wife said flatly. "We can't split the family up."

"Then what do you want me to do?" he replied. "We're all adults. It's the only way to decide." He turned to Rina and Asher. "You definitely want to stay here?"

First Rina nodded, then Asher.

"Very well." Papa sighed and rubbed his chin. "If that's the way you feel, we need to find somewhere in here for you to hide." He peered around the room, then looked at Asher and Rina. "You realize what you're doing is very dangerous, don't you?"

"We know," Rina said.

"And you'll probably be killed if they find you."

"No! No! No!" Mama shouted. She burst into tears, and the others looked on in silence. "I'm not leaving . . ." She sniffed and gulped a short breath. "I'm not leaving my children to the dogs."

Rina went to speak, but Papa held a hand up to silence her. He turned to Mama.

"Golda, please. I know it's hard, but . . . our children aren't children anymore."

"*Well, they are to me!*"

He heaved a sigh. "Then I don't know what else to do."

"Please, Mama," Rina said, stepping over to her. "We haven't much time. Asher and I want to take our chances here."

"But if they find you they'll—"

"We'll make sure they don't."

They embraced. Mama beckoned Asher over and embraced him too.

"Are you two absolutely sure?" Papa said.

Asher and Rina nodded.

"Okay. But we have to be quick." He walked to the far side of the room and opened the wardrobe doors. "We'll put you in here and cover you with clothes."

"Good," Rina said.

"The best I can think of," he said with a shrug. "Grab your food and water; you might have to stay there for a few hours, until you hear nothing and nobody outside." He turned away from them. "Everybody else, it's time to pack."

Asher watched as his mama, her face shiny with tears, hurriedly put a few clothes into a suitcase. Keren did the same.

There were hugs and a few more tears, then Papa pointed to the wardrobe. "Get in now, before I change my mind and drag you along with us."

Rina and Asher started emptying clothes from the bottom of the wardrobe. They each fetched a cup of water and put bread in their pockets.

"I'll lock the door on my way out," Papa said. "So if you hear it being broken down, you'll know to keep still and quiet."

"Papa," Rina said, "do you really believe you're going to a better place?"

The furrow on his brow held back his emotions. "I feel as if I'm being forced to make a choice between being shot or being hanged. But we've both made our decisions. Come on, let's get you hidden."

They got in, one each side, facing each other with their cups of water under their knees. Their papa gave each of them a lingering kiss on the forehead, then threw the clothes back onto them, rearranging them once or twice.

Asher had no way of knowing in the darkness, but he thought he heard his papa crying. Then he heard a fractured voice whisper, "Rina, be joyful. Asher, be blessed." He heard the creak of the wardrobe door being closed, followed by the muffled sounds of people leaving the house.

Soon, all Asher could hear were distant shouts and his own nervous breathing.

"I'm sorry, Asher," he heard Rina whisper. "I didn't mean to pressure you. It's just . . ." The sentence trailed off as her voice trembled.

"I know," Asher said. "You think they're being taken away to be shot."

She sniffed a few times. "And I think they know it too, but . . . there's a chance they'll survive."

"And us?"

"A chance also. A greater one or a smaller one. Who knows?"

"We both know," Asher said. "We'll see them again."

Beneath the huddle of clothes, Asher felt a hand grab his ankle and give it a gentle squeeze. "Thank you," she said. "Thank you for staying with me."

"I wasn't sure," he whispered. "I'm scared."

"Me too."

"But from now on I'll take care of you," he said. "We'll take care of each other. Don't worry."

"Of course."

"And Rina?"

"What?"

"Did you . . . did you smuggle in bullets? Is that why we had extra food?"

"It doesn't matter now."

"You should have told Mama and Papa."

"I will, Asher. I'll tell them when this is all over."

"Do you think that will ever happen?"

"Of course it will. You have to be strong. Try not to worry."

"But I do. I still worry about . . ."

"Izabella?"

"Of course. I don't know what happened to her. I miss her. I can't get her out of my mind."

Asher felt his sister's hand on his ankle again, now squeezing tightly.

"Listen to me, Asher. I promise you'll see her again one day. She's alive. I feel it in my bones. And I know God meant for the two of you to be together."

"Thank you," he whispered.

"But for now, we should be quiet in case guards come in to search the place."

They both stopped talking.

It might have been the clothes muffling Asher's ears, but he could hear nothing—not one thing except his own breathing and the faint echo of his own resting heartbeat. And in his safe cocoon he'd lost track of time. Had he been drifting in and out of sleep? It was hard to tell.

"Rina?" he whispered.

He heard nothing. He moved his foot forward and tapped hers.

There was a muffled squeal, then Rina said, "I'm sorry. I was asleep."

"Me too. It's so dark and quiet. And my legs are getting stiff."

"We can't move," Rina said. "We should wait a few more hours."

"How do we know what hours are?"

And that was a fair question: hours or minutes could have already passed.

"Let's just stay here as long as we can bear it."

"Okay," Asher said, and drifted back into that state that was neither awake nor asleep, more an acute awareness that important events were happening outside and sooner or later he would be at their mercy. He was never completely sure if his eyes were open or shut. His balance, too, seemed to have no frame of reference, and more than once he had the sensation of falling down a hole, only to wake with a start.

Then.

A crack. One single crack, like a piece of wood being broken.

The door, perhaps?

His senses went into overdrive. *Should he ask Rina if she'd heard it too?* No, too dangerous. Be silent. And breathe quietly, all the better to hear.

A hand on his ankle again. Squeezing. This time so tightly it hurt.

So, Rina had heard it too.

But what to do?

Nothing.

Be quiet. Be still. One false move and the wardrobe could become a coffin.

Another cracking sound. This time Asher was definitely awake, and he heard it loud and clear. The sound didn't come from the door, but from the other side of the room. It was like wood splintering.

A third crack, and now there was movement—like a hinge in need of a drop of oil.

Asher heard a thumping sound and felt it too, as if someone had just landed on the floorboards.

Were those footsteps?

It was hard to know.

Now he felt Rina's grip tighten on his leg, her desperate nails almost breaking through his skin, making him clench his teeth rather than yelp in pain.

Another creak, this time lighter.

The wardrobe door?

The next thing Asher became aware of was the bundle of clothes being dragged off him, followed by the smell of soot and sweat from the hand clasped over his mouth.

"Shh!" he heard.

The hand came away from his mouth, although slowly, as though not quite trusting. But Asher was too confused to speak.

Then there was a face. It happened in a flash—the flash of a match being lit.

On the other side of the match was the blackened and furtive face of a man.

Asher squinted to see past the wavering yellow light, unsure for a moment whether he recognized him.

The man used his free hand to pull the clothes off Rina and then cover her mouth too. When he pulled it away he held his index finger up to his mouth. "Don't scream," he whispered. "You must be Rina, yes?"

Rina, too shocked to speak, didn't reply, didn't move.

The man now looked at Asher. "And you are Asher? You're the two Kogans, yes?"

"Yes, we are," Asher said.

Then the tiny light between them flickered and died, and soon another match lit up their faces.

Yes. Asher knew this man.

"I'm Josef," he said. "I worked with you and your papa at the brick factory."

Asher went to speak, but Josef held up a silencing finger. "We can talk later," he said. "For now, just follow me."

They crawled out of the wardrobe, gently and quietly unfolding their limbs, taking a few moments to stretch their backs.

Now Asher could see a little moonlight casting a bluish hue onto the window. The wooden frame was crooked, hanging by one hinge, clearly wrenched off.

"Don't speak, and try not to make any noise," Josef said. He lifted the window frame to one side, and in the half-light Asher saw two wooden stumps leaning against the outside wall.

He felt a nudge from Rina, asking him to go first.

A moment later, he was leaning out of the window, peering down to the street below. He could just make out another man standing at the foot of the ladder.

"Quickly," Josef said. "The guards will patrol this area soon."

Asher scrambled out of the window and as good as flew down the ladder. Before his feet touched the ground, the man standing there gave two raps on the ladder with his knuckles.

Before Asher knew it, Rina was with him. They stood next to each other, both scanning the street.

Another two raps on the wood and Josef's feet appeared at the top. He was halfway down when they all heard a commotion at the end of the street, and looked to see vague figures in the distance, shouting and weaving left and right.

Josef's feet thumped down onto the ground, and Asher felt his muscles tighten as he watched him pull out a pistol and shoot in the direction of the figures.

"Follow me!" the other man shouted, and they all ran, Josef occasionally turning back to fire more shots.

The next few minutes were frantic. Asher and Rina were led down one street here, up another there, through the front door of one house, out the back door, up a back alley, and out onto another street. At each turn there were shots—in both directions, Asher thought. At one stage Josef and the other man swapped places, with Josef leading them through the front door of a house and immediately through another door.

Now there wasn't even moonlight to help them, and Josef lit another match.

Asher looked around. They were in a kitchen—a very ordinary-looking one. Before he had time to ask questions, Josef opened the oven door and in his whispered rasp said, "In!"

Asher looked at the oven, a fairly large but otherwise unremarkable affair. He looked at Rina, and then at Josef.

"It's all right," Josef said. "Just get in. Go through."

Shots from outside made Rina react first, dropping to the ground and forcing her head into the oven. She stopped and turned, looking up at Josef.

"Just crawl through," he said.

Asher watched, barely believing his eyes, as first her torso, then her legs disappeared from view.

The match went out. The gunfire was getting closer. Asher turned and saw the moon shadow of the other man, standing in the doorway, shooting further down the alleyway.

Then Asher felt his arm being grabbed and he was forced down, his head entering the blackness of the oven. He felt his head thump against the back panel, which gave way. He continued crawling through, soon falling a few inches onto soft earth.

As soon as he got to his knees he felt his hand being grabbed and pulled to one side.

By the light of a single candle he saw Rina. He turned to look at where he'd just come from and saw a hatch. It flipped open once more and Josef fell to the ground. He'd hardly rolled out of the way when the other man appeared, and Josef gave a quick tug on a piece of string. There was a noise that Asher recognized as the catch to the oven door.

Then Josef placed a piece of wood across the hatch, preventing it from being opened again.

"Not a sound," he whispered, then spat on his finger and thumb and reached for the candle flame. Asher heard a faint fizzle as the light went out.

In the full darkness, with his sense of hearing heightened, Asher heard muffled noises through the wall. He understood no words, but knew what was happening: the guards were shouting and running back and forth, then shouting some more, then asking questions of one another. Eventually, after more angry discussions, there were groans of frustrated acceptance, and the noises faded away.

For a minute or so there was silence in the darkness, and Asher might as well have been alone. His senses turned to the damp mustiness of the place. A match ignited, providing his eyes with some reference, and then its fire was transferred to a candle.

Josef lit another two candles. "It's okay now," he said. "We can speak."

"So speak," Rina said. "Tell us what's happening."

"He told you," Asher said. "He worked at the brick factory."

"I was also a part-time resistance fighter." Josef shrugged. "Since the factory closed I have more time for those activities."

"But how did you know where we were?" Rina said.

"Your papa got a message to me while he was waiting at the meeting point."

"And what are you going to do with us?"

"Now you're in the resistance too," Josef said. "That is, if you want to be."

Rina looked at Asher, who nodded. "Yes," she said. "Yes, we do."

Josef smiled. "Good. Welcome to our bunker—your home now."

They all got to their feet, and Asher looked around.

It was a strange room, so narrow he could touch both walls, but so long that the far end wasn't quite visible.

"There are no doors or windows," Josef said. "The hatch is the only way in or out."

Asher looked up to see a few ventilation grilles, then behind him, where a shelf displayed packets of food. Two beds—in reality no more than small mattresses on the floor—were arranged end on end halfway along, against the wall.

Rina eyed up the two beds. "The four of us are going to live here together?" she asked.

Josef shook his head. "One more. We can sleep in shifts on the beds."

"Oh."

"You know, most resistance fighters are living in the sewer system, or even in shallow underground pits. This is a hotel by comparison."

"Of course," Rina said. "I'm sorry."

Josef pointed to the opposite end, where a rusty bucket lay on the floor, and something else was jutting out of the wall above it. "And we have a water valve over there."

Rina's face still held a worried frown, but she nodded. "It's good," she said. "Perfect. So we fight from here?"

"One of the many locations across the Jewish district." He wagged a finger at her. "And listen, we need all the hands we can get. I want you to know you'll be safe here—well, as safe as any Jew can be in this city. The toilet facility is right at the end, beyond the bucket. You, uh, cover it with earth."

Asher and Rina peered beyond the makeshift beds, into the darkness at the end of the room.

"If you need privacy just ask. But . . ." He let out a little laugh. ". . . I can't vouch for the spiders." He looked at the other man, who smiled back at him.

"Never mind spiders," Rina said firmly. "Do you have guns for me and Asher?"

"Do you know how to use one?"

She glanced at Asher. "We can learn."

"Good," Josef said. "That's good. And I'm sorry, we need a bit of humor here to while the hours away."

"Humor is good," Rina said.

"You like humor?" Josef pointed to the other man. "This is my friend, and your new brother-in-arms, Adolf."

Rina cracked a rare smile.

"And yes, before you ask, he speaks very good German."

"How do you talk to each other?" Asher asked.

Josef leaned across and patted the man on the back. "Adolf speaks good German and a little Polish. I'm Polish but speak a little Russian, as well as Yiddish. And you?"

"We both speak Polish and a little Russian, as well as Yiddish and Ukrainian."

Josef laughed out loud, then chided himself for making such a noise. "Sounds like we have all languages covered. We can be translators if we fail as soldiers."

"So, you're Jewish?" Rina said. "Do you have family?"

His laughter quickly dissolved. "Well, I did."

"You *did*?"

"Now, I'm not so sure. A wife. Three children. A mother-in-law. We survived until three weeks ago. We hid whenever they came to take us away. Then they came one last time with loudspeakers. They said the deportations had ended, that any remaining Jews would be fed and moved to better housing. My wife . . . she . . ." Josef took a few deep breaths. "She said she and her mama had had enough of hiding. We argued. I told her it was a trick. She disagreed, and I was torn, I didn't know whether to go with them or not. Perhaps I was a coward for staying hidden."

"No," Rina said. "You're no coward. Any fool can see that."

"Thank you."

"Have you heard from them?" she said.

He gave his head a disconsolate shake. "They were deported, I'm left to assume."

"Oh. I'm . . . I'm sorry."

"Do you know where to?" Asher said.

Josef stared at each of them in turn. "You must have heard?"

"We've all heard rumors."

"Of course," Josef said. "I don't know the details for certain. Some say they become slaves, some say they are all shot. I only know they are never seen or heard from again."

"So it's possible they're still alive?"

"Let me put it this way." He took a deep breath. "If a dozen people leave the city and you never hear from them again, so what? If a thousand people do the same—just disappear—it's suspicious. But *hundreds of thousands*? Something is very, very wrong."

Rina's face creased up.

"I'm sorry," Josef said. "Your parents. Your sister. I'm being insensitive, but I'm trying to be realistic."

"That's all right," Rina said, wiping away a tear.

"Right." Josef put on an artificial smile. "We have to keep our spirits up so that—"

A sound made him stop. Asher recognized it: the oven door was opening. Then there was a distinctive rap on the hatch.

Josef held a finger up to his lips and took a step back. He lifted the piece of wood holding the hatch shut and pulled out his pistol, pointing it at the hatch.

A body fell through—a young man, not much older than Asher. He pulled on the string to close the oven door.

Josef held out a hand to help the man up and they exchanged a few words. Asher only half understood, but this was clearly the final member of the group Josef had mentioned.

"This is Anatoli," Josef said. "He's a Russian soldier. He's not Jewish, and for that matter, neither is Adolf. But they both believe in the cause. They fight for humanity rather than their countries." He glanced at them both. "And because they are Gentiles, it's easier for them to smuggle guns and food to the resistance."

"So where are *our* guns?" Rina said.

Josef looked embarrassed, a crooked smile slightly spoiling his revolutionary demeanor. "We only have three. But you won't be left out. I promise."

Chapter 18

Warsaw, Poland, 1943

Asher lost track of the days and weeks passing in the dark cocoon they were all hiding out in, but Josef was true to his word about including him and his sister in missions to disrupt the Nazi cleansing of Warsaw, although for the first few missions Asher and Rina were little more than observers.

Then came their first practice. Josef stressed, as he always did, that Rina and Asher could stay in the hiding place if they wanted to, but were also welcome to come along. Each time, it was an easy decision: the hiding place was like a prison cell.

Asher and Rina kept low while the other men shot an isolated group of four SS guards at a sentry point. On the way back, the group detoured through an abandoned hall of some sort, and Rina and Asher took turns to shoot at targets scraped into the bare plaster walls. "Learn quickly," Josef said. "We can't waste bullets."

The next mission was more involved—and more frightening, as far as Asher was concerned. They'd climbed onto the roof of a housing block and were all leaning over the edge, looking down at a regiment of guards—SS, Wehrmacht, or police, it was hard to tell from above.

Josef offered the gun to Asher. He hesitated to take it.

"I'll try," Rina said.

And she did, keeping both hands on the gun and gently squeezing the trigger as she'd practiced. Directly below them, a splash of blood appeared on the top of a cap, and a man collapsed to the ground. Before his body hit the earth there were more shots, killing six or seven guards, Asher guessed. In the course of the arguments and panic below, some guards looked up, spotting the source of the gunfire.

"Follow me!" Josef shouted.

A jump across onto another roof, onto a third by balancing on a length of piping, down a flight of stairs, through a hole in the wall, down more stairs, and out into a backstreet. Into and out of another house, around a corner, then into the house where their dummy oven lay waiting for the heroes to return.

"You did well," Josef said to Rina between hard breaths, as they rested on the floor of their hiding place a few minutes later. He glanced at Asher. "You can shoot on the next mission."

Again, Josef was true to his word.

Asher was told it would be a simple mission. Ground level. Along the way, Anatoli disappeared for a few minutes, rejoining them with a large box under his arm. The team made their way through ruined buildings—too many for Asher to keep count of—before settling inside one, crouching below three large holes in the wall, which afforded good views of a small square outside.

"Our intelligence tells us they often meet up here," Josef whispered to Asher. "It's just a question of waiting."

Walls full of holes and no roof to speak of allowed a bracing wind to cut through, and as Asher hunkered down he had time to work out where they were—or what this place had once been. Blackened objects, row upon row of them, occupying equally black shelving cabinets of some sort. A few fragments of printed paper, shapeless and edged in brown, fluttered down next to Asher. This had been a library, a place of peace and learning, now of no use except as a barricade, a piece of guerrilla-war machinery.

The noise of a vehicle approaching snapped Asher out of his thoughts.

Josef handed him a gun, but held Asher's hand down. "Wait," he whispered. "There will be more."

He was right. Within minutes more vehicles had arrived, guards were chatting, helmets were removed, and cigarettes were being exchanged. One or two guards opened small flasks and swigged from them.

"Okay," Josef hissed, and nudged Asher toward one of the holes in the wall. He turned to Adolf and Anatoli, who nodded, then he whispered a countdown.

Asher pointed the pistol at the nearest soldier, stilled his breathing, and squeezed the trigger. Before the man's body fell to the ground there was more gunfire from Josef and Adolf, and then an explosion made Asher jump. He looked left to see Anatoli lobbing hand grenades over the top of the wall.

Asher looked through the hole in the wall again. The soldier he'd shot was sprawled, lifeless, on the ground where he'd fallen. Asher should have been pleased with himself; he should have been proud. It was an excellent shot for a first kill. One less Nazi. But he felt sick, and for a few seconds was unable to breathe. He'd always thought ending any life was unacceptable. And he still did. But there was no time to consider his feelings: the return fire had started.

"Let's go," Josef said, not panicking, not shouting, merely speaking as if suggesting it was time to leave the library for the matinee performance of a show.

They started running.

Again, Asher couldn't keep track of the number of ruined buildings they entered and exited, nor the number of streets and alleys they crossed. At one point they came under fire again, and Josef shouted for them all to go back. They turned, and Anatoli took the lead. Asher didn't know how, but Anatoli somehow led them all back to the hiding place, and they got through the oven before the guards even reached the same street.

Whether Asher liked it or not, and even though it sounded ridiculous, this dark, fetid place was now his and Rina's home.

In the darkness, they stayed silent as the sound of the guards came and went.

Josef put an arm around Asher and squeezed him. "You're getting used to it," he said. "Aren't you?"

Asher nodded, although it wasn't true.

The next mission was a similar operation, an ambush of soldiers taking a break. The ruin they were in was even more unsettling than the library. It had once been a synagogue—one Asher had been inside when it was in full possession of its glory and solemnity. Today, it was merely another part of a battlefield.

Asher shot and killed two guards—they looked like local police. Again, the feeling was one of nausea, not glory, and he felt unable to shoot more. Josef grabbed the gun back and continued. This time there were no hand grenades, and they quickly ran out of bullets.

And this time the retreat to the hiding hole didn't go so well; bullets flew around their ears as they weaved and ducked. At one point Anatoli—in his customary position bringing up the rear—yelped in pain. Asher looked back. The man had taken a bullet in the shoulder. He shouted at Asher, telling him to carry on, and quickly.

They reached their street and dipped into the house, to the sound of guards running after them. After a frantic clamber through the oven, Josef pulled the door shut only a few seconds before they heard the clatter of boots on the kitchen floor.

As before, Asher heard the guards talking, arguing, walking out then back into the house, all melded with the sound of the five resistance fighters gasping for breath but trying to keep those gasps quiet.

When the guards could no longer be heard, Josef lit a candle, which showed off his crooked smile of crooked teeth. By now Asher had a lot of respect for this man. After all, he'd been living in these horrible conditions for much longer than Asher and Rina, and seemed happy to kill guards, whereas Asher felt uncomfortable ending someone's life. The same could be said of Adolf and Anatoli too.

And Anatoli was now paying the price for that bravery.

"Anatoli took a bullet," Asher said to Josef.

But Josef was more interested in Adolf, and was staring, wild-eyed, across at him. Asher, Anatoli, and Rina looked too. Adolf had a concerned, almost pained expression on his face—as if he were the one who had been shot.

Josef asked him a question in German. He didn't reply. Josef asked again, more firmly. Now Adolf replied. Asher couldn't understand, but there was no doubting the fear in the man's voice.

Josef and Adolf exchanged a few more words, then a deep frown sat itself on Josef's forehead.

"What is it?" Rina said. "Tell us what Adolf said."

Josef pursed his lips for a moment, then drew breath and spoke in a measured tone.

"He heard a little of what the guards outside were saying. He said they kept mentioning the kitchen wall, how it doesn't look right from the outside."

Even the warm, flickering candlelight could not imbue the faces Asher saw with any confidence. They all bowed their heads, rubbed their chins, scratched their heads. Anything but speak the unspeakable.

"We have to be honest here," Josef said after a few minutes. "Perhaps we should move. There are other hiding places—ones Adolf, Anatoli, and I know about."

"You think we'll be safer there?" Rina asked.

Josef looked at the other men. He faced Adolf and opened his mouth to speak, but suddenly turned to Anatoli. "I'm sorry, Anatoli, I forgot. You have a bullet wound?"

Anatoli screwed his face up slightly and pushed one side of his jacket over his shoulder, revealing a bloody shirt. "I think it's just a nick," he said.

The amount of blood implied otherwise, Asher thought. Yes, this was a brave man, but one in need of medical attention.

Josef and Adolf talked some more in German, then Josef addressed the others.

"From what he heard, Adolf thinks they will come back here later, perhaps take some measurements. He suggests we pack up what food we have and leave here as soon as possible, and I have to agree. If they find us, they'll kill us."

The others nodded.

"I could do with some iodine and bandages," Anatoli said. "What about the hideout in the basement of the medical center?"

Josef nodded, then asked Adolf, Rina, and Asher. All agreed.

"Good," Josef said. "We'll wait ten minutes for things outside to settle, then go there. In the meantime, we celebrate quietly. We all did well today." He looked over to Asher, and even by the flickering light of the candle, Asher's unease at killing must have showed. "It's hard, I know," Josef said. "You know you're snuffing the life out of someone— someone with a wife, a mama and papa, perhaps children."

"I think it's more that he's lovesick," Rina said.

Asher told her to shut up. There was a little laughter. Asher joined in.

"Ahh," Rina said. "He's pining for his violinist girlfriend."

"No, I'm not," Asher said. "Well, perhaps a little."

"It's nothing to be ashamed of," Josef said. "I miss my wife every minute of every day." He let out a frustrated sigh and gazed into the darkness. Then he forced a smile onto his face and said, "This violinist girl of yours, she's not the black-haired one who used to play on the east side of the sector every day, is she?"

"How many black-haired girl violinists do you know within the sector?" Asher replied.

"Asher, don't be rude," Rina said. "Please excuse my brother."

"No, no," Josef said. "It's a fair point. She's a good musician, and very pretty too."

"You mean, *she was*," Asher said with more than a hint of bitterness. "*Was?*"

"She . . . she disappeared a few months ago."

"You mean, she disappeared from the Jewish sector." Josef cast a questioning glance over to Anatoli. "Isn't that what you told me?"

Anatoli nodded. "I heard that the nuns smuggled her out."

Asher crawled over and grabbed him by the arm. "What did you say?"

"I don't know for certain. I just heard."

Rina scolded Asher once more from the other side of the room.

"I'm sorry," he said to Anatoli. "But please, tell me what you know."

"I don't think they told me her name." He paused, recalling. "But I think she used to play in some café run by her parents before they put the wall up."

"Café Baran?"

"Yes." Anatoli nodded, uncertain at first. "Yes, that was it. Café Baran."

"So, what nuns are you talking about?"

"There are Catholic nuns in Warsaw," Josef explained. "The authorities trust them and they're, shall we say, sympathetic to our cause. They've smuggled hundreds—perhaps thousands—of children out of the Jewish sector, and quite a few adults too, usually because they're sick and in need of medical attention."

"And where is she now?" Asher asked them both.

Josef and Anatoli both shrugged. "We have no idea," Josef said. "I take it this girl means a lot to you?"

Asher hesitated. Rina spoke for him.

"He was in love with her. Well, as much as anyone can be in love in this place."

"I'm sorry we don't know any more," Josef said. "But we have contacts. We can ask."

"Don't be sorry," Asher said. "You've given me hope."

"We all need a little of that," Josef said. "But now we should go. Let's collect up what food we have and head for the medical center."

They all stood up, and Josef moved toward the shelf of food.

Before he reached it, they all heard a deep, threatening rumble from outside. They stopped completely still, each holding an uncertain, worried stare.

"What in God's name is that?" Josef hissed.

Then the whole room shook, and a wall crashed in as if a sudden earthquake had hit. Asher tried to crouch down but felt his frame being bowled over by the force of a dozen bricks, and saw the whole room engulfed in a billowing cloud of dust. He got to his feet and took a few seconds to check himself. There were some nasty cuts and bruises on his arms and legs, but nothing more serious.

He looked up at a vision that was almost celestial. Where there had once been the clear yellow light of the candle, there was now bright white light. And yet, he could hardly see his hand in front of his face. Then the tickle in his lungs was too much, and he convulsed into a coughing fit, leaning over, hands on knees.

His ears were still full of the sounds of others coughing and a dull ringing, but beyond those he couldn't ignore the shouts.

They were angry shouts.

In German.

Asher, blinking and trying to clear his eyes with dusty fingers, realized the bright light was sunshine streaming through the haze of brick dust. A few seconds later, the fog cleared enough for him to make out the four figures of his fellow resistance members, all gasping for fresh air and wiping their faces.

He went over to Rina. They briefly held hands, and Asher wiped a chunk of mortar out of her hair.

The haze cleared more, to reveal a pile of bricks in front of them. Beyond the rubble, an armored vehicle of sorts reversed away, its brakes squealing as it stopped, then sped off down the street.

Also, a few yards in the distance, Asher could just about make out those uniforms he had come to despise and fear. They stood in line, ignoring the dust whirling about them. Oblivious. Victorious, even.

One of them approached the resistance members, picking his steps between the rubble, and started shouting, his rifle aimed at them.

There was no mistaking "*Hände hoch!*" All Jews had heard those words before. The same could be said for "*Kommen Sie her!*"

In seconds there were more guards and more guns, and no way out other than over the rubble and through the large hole in the wall.

Now the shouting conveyed more anger. "*Hände hoch!*"

They all obeyed, struggling to keep their tired arms aloft.

Anatoli was the first to start clambering over the bricks, occasionally dropping his hands for balance, each time being reminded not to by a bullet flying a foot or so from his head. The others followed, each stumbling and falling but somehow keeping their arms away from their bodies.

A few minutes later, all five stood in a row outside, hands aloft. All were frosted in brick dust, flecked blood-red in parts. Each one had a guard standing a few feet away, a rifle pointing at their head. Now, in the daylight, Asher noticed a wound above Rina's eye, and a dust-caked streak of blood down one side of her face.

For a minute or so, nobody spoke—not even the guards. And in the silence, Asher's mind momentarily drifted off to a better place. There had been too much terror, too much killing. If they wanted his body, they could have it.

The sun was full, and he took a second to bask in its warmth. What else was there left to enjoy? He was distracted by a noise and glanced down the street, where the small armored vehicle had been driven—to hunt out more Jews in hiding places, no doubt, like forcing rabbits out of a warren. He also saw a man holding a portable flamethrower, apparently setting anything and everything he could find on fire. Any parts of the city that hadn't been bombed were clearly now being destroyed by more manual methods, courtesy of the flamethrower and the armored vehicle.

The leader of the guards, a bespectacled SS officer in a meticulously pressed field-gray uniform, barked an order to the guard on his right, who marched over to Anatoli, standing awkwardly at the end of the row. He was having difficulty holding one of his arms up—where he'd taken the bullet in his shoulder. The guard screamed at him, and Anatoli's face contorted as he tried to obey.

The guard patted the sides of Anatoli's jacket, eventually coming across the pistol. He held the pistol in the palm of his hand for a second, as though examining it or trying to guess its weight. Then he put the muzzle of the pistol against Anatoli's temple and pulled the trigger.

Josef immediately took a pace forward and shouted at the guard, but the guard pointed the pistol straight at him and he stopped, gasping for a moment.

"*Hände hoch*," the guard said, and Josef returned to his place in line, staring at Anatoli's corpse and the splatter of fresh blood on the bricks behind him.

The guard looked at the pistol again, nodded approvingly to himself, and said, "*Mmm, das ist gut.*"

Then he moved on to Adolf, searching him too.

And again, he found a pistol. But Adolf bolted, moving quickly for a tall man, sprinting down the street, jerking left and right. The guard laughed for a second, then lifted both pistols and sent four bullets into Adolf's back.

He sighed, then looked at the pistols again. He nodded, impressed, and turned to Josef.

Josef's hand immediately fell to his pocket, but the guard pulled his arm away. He stood in front of Josef, their faces inches apart, and put his hand into the pocket Josef had reached for.

Again, a pistol was pulled out.

Then the officer, standing behind the guard, said something to him. It was intoned as a question, and Asher heard the word *Josef* being mentioned.

The guard stepped in front of Josef and said, "*Du bist Josef Kurowski?*"

Josef gulped, then took a few breaths, but didn't speak.

"*Josef Kurowski?*" the guard said, their heads now inches apart. "*Ja oder nein?*"

Josef spat in his face.

The man sneered, took a step back, pulled a handkerchief out of his pocket and cleaned his face, taking his time to wipe every last drop of spit from every last crease and wrinkle.

While this was happening, Asher decided he would do the same as Josef. Yes, he would spit in the man's face, perhaps punch him, even knock him over. They were all going to be shot anyway, so what did he have to lose?

The guard folded the handkerchief, again clearly taking more time than necessary, and turned back to face his officer. A few words were exchanged.

The guard shouted down the street, toward the armored vehicle and the man holding the flamethrower. He made a beckoning motion with his hand, and the man with the flamethrower started walking toward them.

Josef started speaking, then babbling, and finally pleading. As the guard talked to the man who had just arrived, Josef fell to his knees and put his hands together. Asher didn't understand the words, but he knew the man he had come to respect and admire was now begging.

The guard took a step back and barked *"Ja!"* to the man, who pointed his contraption at the still kneeling, still praying Josef. He pulled the trigger and Josef became a whirling, screaming fireball, his arms flailing, his body thrashing around on the ground. But the man didn't stop, adding more fire just to make sure.

Time was meaningless in Asher's state of mind, but it probably took something in the region of a minute for the flamethrower to do what a bullet would have accomplished in half a second. Josef's slumped figure was motionless, but still the flames caressed it. Asher felt the coldness of a dribble coming from the corner of his mouth. He took a few gasps to stop himself from being sick, then turned to see that Rina was lying motionless on the ground, eyes closed. For a second his eyes searched her coat for blood-soaked holes, then he came to his senses. Whereas he had almost been sick at the punishment, she had fainted.

He lowered his arms and bent down to reach for her, but a guard screaming in his face changed his mind. The smack of a rifle butt on his cheekbone sent him down to the ground. He was told to get up, and obeyed without question. All thoughts of punching or spitting at the guard were placed back in their box, locked there for as long as the flamethrower was around. Even then, the guard only stopped screeching once he'd given Asher another thump, this time in the middle of the chest.

Another guard stood over Rina, opened his water bottle, and splashed her face. She groaned. He bent down and gave her a slap across the face, then another. She stirred, bringing her hands up to protect herself. The man shouted at her, and within a minute she'd struggled to her feet, albeit staggering and stumbling.

The guard who had searched the other three men now did the same to Asher, and Asher felt unable to do anything other than hold his breath, brace himself, and pray.

The guard found no gun. He stepped back and looked Asher's dust-caked figure up and down. "You have no weapon?" he said in confident Polish.

Asher could do no more than cough. They stared at each other for a few seconds, then Asher gasped as the guard's pistol was raised, the muzzle pressed low against his forehead. For a moment he looked the man in the eye, saw the rash of stubble on his chin, the greasy sweat on his cheeks. Then he closed his eyes.

"They wouldn't let us have weapons," he heard Rina shout.

Words were exchanged between the guards, but still Asher felt the cold, hard steel against his forehead, pressing against his skull. Now he opened his eyes, and beyond the blurred image of the gun at his head, he saw another guard searching Rina.

"They didn't trust us," she said. "Told us we were only children."

The guard found no weapon on her.

And still Asher had the gun against his head.

There were more heated discussions between the guards. "*Nur Kinder,*" one of them kept repeating. Asher heard the guard in front of him sigh, and felt hot breath momentarily warm his face. Then the man took the gun away.

Now Asher was being shoved forward, staggering and gasping like he'd just run a mile. Soon, he and Rina were walking down the street, helped by the muzzle of a gun occasionally prodding them in the back.

A few minutes later, Asher and Rina were deposited at the meeting point next to the railroad station. They sat down on the earth next to each other. Asher put his arm around his sister and looked left and right. The square was contained on all four sides by either brick or solid fencing, and was patrolled by those armed guards the authorities seemed to have an endless supply of, whether SS, Gestapo, or Stormtroopers.

Asher had often walked past the square over the past couple of years, and each time it had been thronged with people waiting to be taken away.

Today it was less than half full.

They had chopped off all the meat and were now scraping away the gristle.

But where exactly were they being taken? Asher looked around, his eyes falling on a man a few yards away, gnawing away at a potato. *Would he have any more idea what was happening?*

The man noticed Asher staring at him and stopped gnawing. He put his hand into his pocket and pulled out two more small potatoes, then reached over and handed them to Asher.

Asher thanked the man, but there was no reply: he stared straight ahead again and continued gnawing away.

Then a dot of darkness appeared on Asher's knee. Then another. He looked up and got a splash in the mouth. It tasted good. Soon the raindrops were bouncing off their heads, and Asher grabbed Rina's arm, pointing toward a wall at one side of the square. They both stood and hurried over, settling down there with their backs leaning against the wall. Asher took his coat off and held it over both their heads. He handed Rina one of the potatoes, and they both started chewing.

For a second, Asher considered using the rain to clean the mud off his meal, but even a little mud would fill his belly a tiny bit more than the wood-like flesh of the raw potato alone, so he left it on. And the little seed sprouts added variety, as well as providing something to hook his teeth onto.

The rain continued after they'd finished eating, the drops dancing on Asher's already soaked back. He used his wet sleeve to wipe the blood from the side of Rina's face, and they huddled together; it was starting to get cold.

"At least we might find out what happened to Mama, Papa, and Keren," Rina said.

Asher said nothing. He wasn't sure he wanted to know.

Chapter 19

Diane sat down and tried not to smile, tried not to show any signs of friendship. It was a hard habit to break, but the "friend of the family" stuff would have to go. And if it struggled, she would have to put it down.

"You got what you wanted," she said. "Just the two of us. So tell me what happened."

He nodded and then waited, drawing a long, wheezy breath before speaking.

"You said you wanted to know everything—everything about me, everything about your father, and the reason for his unfortunate death."

"The reason why you murdered him, yes. But please, take your time. I really would like to know everything."

"Very well. There's a lot to say—more than you might think. But I want you to hear it."

"Good."

"He told you we were born within a few days of each other in Ukraine, didn't he?"

"Yes, and you kind of lost touch with each other some years later. So what happened after that?"

"I'm going to tell you everything, Diane. That includes the childhood we shared, how we came to be brothers in all but blood, how we lost contact, what happened to us both in those years, and how we made contact again, which you probably already know. But I warned you there was a lot to say, and you need to hear everything to really understand the reasons behind what happened between us last week."

"I'm not sure any of that will help me understand," Diane said. "I get that you were close as kids and I get that life was tough for you back then. But it was tough for my father too."

"Oh, I agree. And it didn't get any better for a long time. We both had hard decisions to make—decisions that followed us around for the rest of our lives. But I want you to know what sort of man your father was."

Diane peered at him, as though trying to bore holes in his face with her eyes. "Hey, he was my father. I know all about that."

"But do you? I mean, how well did you really know your father?"

"What are you getting at?"

"Do you think he was a good man?"

She nodded immediately, then stopped, uncertain.

Yes, her father had carried her up to bed every night for a week when she'd sprained her ankle. Yes, he'd once driven her at breakneck speed to school for that ski trip and he used to take her to the swings at the local park. But there was also the way he behaved at those house parties and how he'd sabotaged her love life. In her teens she'd referred to him as General Grump whenever he got bad-tempered and grouchy. By her twenties she'd realized that the word *grouchy* didn't quite cut it in this instance, and the General Grump joke had started to wear thin. In hindsight, it should have been clear to her that he was in the habit of spiraling into a pit of self-obsession or insecurity or paranoia, or a mixture of all those things. In reality, she didn't want to think that way, and he probably wouldn't have wanted her to think that way either.

Images of his sullen face drifted into her mind. When she had no boyfriend and he had her all to himself, he was almost a model father. Companionship, help around the home, a friendly ear and encouragement when she needed it, someone to hear her laughter when she watched TV—he ticked all those boxes. But whenever she brought a boyfriend home or went on a date, he would turn into General Grump for days afterward. He would grunt instead of speak, never get her a coffee when he was getting one for himself, and make remarks about anything she cooked—usually not even finishing it. She knew this was all down to his fear that she would leave him, a fear he'd made clear to her that day she would never forget, many years ago. In more recent times he seemed to accept Brad more readily—partly because he'd known him since he and Diane were just friends, and partly because after all these years it seemed a given that Diane would never move out of Hartmann Way.

So yes. She knew her father. She knew the good, the bad, and the abominable. She also knew that what was private should stay private.

"Do I think my father was a good man?" she said. "Well . . . actually, yes. If I have to choose between yes and no, then yes; I think my father was a good man. He wasn't perfect, but he was perfect to me when I was growing up."

"And when your parents split up, why did you decide to live with your father rather than your mother?"

Her face froze for a few seconds. "You know, that's a really horrible question to ask."

"I'm sorry. Yes, it is. But once or twice, when your father was drunk or melancholy—usually both—he'd let slip one or two things he used to do. I know he was very needy where you were concerned, very . . . well, it's hard for me to say any more because I have mixed feelings about him."

"And did you have mixed feelings about him when you shot him?"

His composure immediately dropped, a look of shock flashing across his face, his small eyes opening fully for once. He recovered quickly. "I think you've just matched me in the horrible questions category," he said.

"I'm sorry, but you seem a different person to how you've been all these years."

"I'm really not, Diane. But I guess it's reasonable for you to think that way."

"And please stop patronizing me. I'm sorry for the horrible question, but I'm trying to figure out what the hell my father did to you to make you hate him so much."

"That's what I'm going to explain to you."

"So, you *did* hate him?"

"Mmm . . . that's a tough question. We really were like brothers, so I guess it's okay to say I hated him because I loved him too. I still do, come to think of it. And I miss him. You might find that hard to believe, but I really do."

"You know, I remember how well the two of you got on, so somehow I do believe you. But I need you to tell me what happened."

"Very well." He took a sip of water.

Then he started telling Diane about how the Petrenkos and the Kogans shared a farm, how both families welcomed sons into the world in 1923, how the young Asher and Mykhail played together and fought together, and how they shared food and an interest in tractors and fishing trips.

And he carried on further, describing how they were parted when Asher left for Warsaw, and how each boy coped without his best friend—his brother in all but blood. Asher suffered in Warsaw and ended up fighting with the resistance, whereas Mykhail joined the Red Army and was captured, becoming a puppet for his Nazi masters.

And there they were interrupted by a guard and told they had five minutes left.

"We haven't finished," Diane said. "Could we carry on again tomorrow?"

The guard shrugged. "That's entirely up to the old guy."

"Of course," the old guy said.

They stood up, Diane grabbing her purse.

"Where are you staying?" he said.

"With Brad at the moment, till I sort out Father's house. Then I might stay with Mother."

"You're not moving in with Brad?"

She paused, then shook her head. "I've missed out on a lot with Mother."

"You've missed out on a lot with Brad, I'd say."

Diane screwed her face up. "*Excuse me?*"

"I just think you deserve a little happiness, that's all."

"The man who killed my father tells me I need a little happiness. You're a real piece of work sometimes, you know that?"

"Yes. It sounds bad, I understand, but I do care about you. I can well imagine the games your father used to play to keep you from leaving him."

"Look, I've had enough. My head's spinning. I'll see you tomorrow."

They both left the room. Diane went into the parking lot and called Brad to pick her up.

Chapter 20

Warsaw, Poland, 1943

Asher and Rina were now on the train—headed for where, they weren't at all sure.

It looked and felt like a freight carriage, and was packed so tightly with people that their shivering bodies were starting to warm up and their clothes were merely damp rather than soaked through. Most of the other people were wrecks of bodies, their rag-clothes baggy, their faces craggy. Asher had tried talking to one or two, to ask if anyone knew where they were going, but had found no appetite for conversation.

Only Rina would talk. "Do you think we'll find out what happened to Mama, Papa, and Keren?" she said.

Asher's mind was dry of words. It wasn't making any sense. *Rina* wasn't making any sense. She must have known the most likely fate to have befallen them. Surely she knew.

"I hope they found that heaven Mama was talking about," she said. "A nice, sunny place in the country with enough room to grow vegetables and keep chickens."

Asher was about to tell her she was talking nonsense, deluding herself, but then he saw a hardness in her eyes.

Now he understood.

"I like the sound of that," he said, nodding. "I'm sure they're in their own heaven."

He blinked to rid his eyes of the wetness.

They didn't speak for the rest of the journey.

Nobody spoke.

Asher looked around at the faces, empty of flesh but full of fear. To one side, a man lay completely motionless on the floor, his head in the lap of a woman who had passed the first part of the journey gently stroking his brow. Then, with just as much care, she closed his eyes for him.

Most of the others were curled up like babies, their eyes half closed, their bodies hardly moving. Occasionally somebody would adjust their position and urinate where they sat.

But nobody spoke.

Asher knew it was hard to have hope. He ignored the smell of disease and the groans of despair, instead choosing to close his eyes and dream of his own heaven, somewhere much like Dyovsta, with clean air and seas of golden wheat shimmering in the bright sunlight. He felt warmer than he had for some time, and was soon rocked to sleep by the rhythmic rattling of wheels on track.

Asher woke up only when the train jolted to a halt. He rubbed his sleepy face, and turned to see Rina doing the same.

Their fellow passengers started mumbling and pointing to the cracks around the doors, where daylight streamed in and highlighted planes of dust gently dancing up and away, as if trying to escape. There were loud noises from outside: strident shouts, boots marching, dogs barking.

There was also a very distinctive smell.

Asher sniffed a little more.

The carriage doors opened with a squeal, and a wave of that same smell engulfed the carriage. Asher's next breath made him feel sick.

Rina looked at him and screwed her face up. Nobody could have ignored the stench.

But horrible smells they could deal with; the armed guards shouting at them were the more immediate issue.

The disheveled bodies around Asher started dragging themselves to their feet and stepping out of the carriages. A few stayed on the floor and looked like they would never move under their own steam again. The guns and snarling dogs were hardly necessary; ramps to help the weak and injured onto the platform might have made more sense.

But what *did* make sense here?

Asher and Rina stood together on the platform, holding on to each other like comfort blankets, scanning their surroundings.

There were no streets or shops or housing blocks to speak of, only a few buildings half hidden by trees and bushes. And the whole area was surrounded by barbed-wire fencing, although it looked like an attempt had been made to disguise it with foliage. Were they trying to hide something here? To make something look pretty when it was anything but?

Asher looked behind him and read a large sign. It said "Treblinka." He thought for a few moments, but no, he'd never heard of the place before. Was it some place constructed especially for Jews? A new village in the country? There must have been something here for the place to have its own railroad station.

Rina looked around in all directions, then nudged him. "Do you think this is where Mama, Papa, and Keren came to?" she asked hesitantly.

Asher didn't dare tell her what he thought. The rest of their family plus hundreds of thousands more Jews brought here from Warsaw? If so, then where had they all been accommodated? There were nowhere near enough buildings. But surely the authorities wouldn't go to the trouble of taking that amount of people many miles across the country only to shoot them?

"Perhaps this is only a junction point," Rina said. "Perhaps there will be another train to take us away to . . ."

Her voice trailed off to a faint whimper. It was clear to Asher that even she didn't believe what she was saying.

She forced down a gulp, her face contorting. "Oh, Asher," she said, now stuttering the words out. "I'm scared. What's . . . what's happening?"

Asher looked around again. Ahead of them was what looked like a ticket office. On the walls were large pieces of paper full of writing—like timetables. And above them were clocks, as if arrivals and departures were to be expected.

"It's . . . a railroad station," he said to Rina. "A proper one. At least . . . as far as I can tell. Perhaps you're right; perhaps we're just changing trains here."

Shouts and shoves from guards forced the crowd along the platform.

"Stay with me," Rina said, now crying freely. "Stay with me, Asher, please. I'm scared."

"Don't worry." He put an arm around her and held her close. "They'll never separate us. You know I'll die before I let that happen."

As they were carried along by the flow of bodies, Asher glanced across at the buildings. Some were wooden cabins, and some looked familiar. But how? He'd definitely never been here before. Also the voices. The voices were . . . Yes, he was hearing voices in fluent Ukrainian. It was surreal. *Was he dreaming this?*

He looked around. The voices he recognized were coming from some of the guards. Yes, some of the guards were talking in Ukrainian. He shoved his way through the crowds to them, pulling Rina along with him.

"Are you Ukrainian?" he said.

They didn't reply, just eyed him suspiciously, but they clearly understood.

"We're Ukrainian too," he said. "Both from Dyovsta."

"Get back in line!" one of them shouted.

No, this definitely wasn't a dream.

The crowd was forced into single file, around a corner and down a ramp, ending up at a desk underneath a canopy. Asher held Rina's hand until they reached the desk.

"Names and occupations?" the man said in Polish.

"Why do you need to know that?" Asher asked.

"Because this is a labor camp and we need to find the most suitable work duties for you."

Asher and Rina told the man their names, and said they would be prepared to do anything. He scribbled this down in a book.

Then he looked up. "All your valuables on the table."

"I'd . . . rather not," Rina said.

"It's not an option," the man said. "All money, jewelry, valuables of any sort. Put them all here. You'll have a shower to get rid of the lice, and then you'll get them back."

"Are you Ukrainian?" Asher asked.

The man snorted a laugh. "Yes. Would you prefer me to ask you in Ukrainian?"

"But we're both Ukrainian too," Asher said. "We're compatriots. Can't you let us keep them?"

"It's only for safekeeping. Please, don't be awkward or it could get unpleasant for you. Now, empty your pockets." He laughed again. "Would a fellow Ukrainian lie to you?"

Asher could see the reluctance on Rina's face, but she removed the two rings from her fingers, took a bracelet from her pocket, and placed them on the table. Asher pulled a few mangled zloty bills from his pocket and put them next to the jewelry.

"Are you absolutely sure that's it?" the man said. "No gold, spectacles, dentures, or false limbs?"

They shook their heads.

"Very well, women go this way toward—"

A German official interrupted, talking to the Ukrainian guard. At close quarters, Asher could make out the death's head insignia on his cap. This was an SS man.

The Ukrainian guard nodded to the German, then pointed at Asher. "You go that way," he said, pointing in the opposite direction, to a much smaller line of four or five men, all in relatively good health by the look of them.

Asher could feel Rina gripping onto his arm.

"My sister," Asher said to the guard. "We stay together."

"No, you don't," he replied loudly. "You go this way, she goes that way. You can meet up together after the delousing shower."

"But—"

Then Asher hit the ground. He felt something trickling down in front of his ear. He wiped it and saw blood.

"Do as you're told!" the guard shouted, pulling his arm. "Get over there!"

Asher scrabbled to his feet and obeyed, glancing back to see Rina in the crowd, staring at him, her face creased up in distress. Seconds later, she was merely another figure in a tide of women and girls slowly drifting away. This was his big sister, the woman who had assured him as a little boy that she wouldn't allow him to be lonely, who had kept the family fed by risking her life, who had bravely fought in the resistance. Now she looked like a little girl who knew she was drowning.

Asher told himself he would see Rina soon, perhaps later that day or the next. If this was a labor camp, they were bound to see each other again.

In all the panic and drama, he'd become accustomed to the strange smell that enveloped the place, and for the moment it hardly mattered.

The buildings, however, were still bothering him; they still seemed familiar.

A few minutes later, a guard started barking orders out in Polish and beckoning the men toward him. As Asher followed he got a good look at the others. They were all young men, stronger and fitter than the average Jew from Warsaw.

They were shown through a security gate into an enclosure surrounded with barbed wire, and from there into a long cabin. A large burner stood in the middle, with a row of bunk beds along each side. The men were told to occupy the beds along the left-hand side, and that someone would return later with food and water. The guard left and locked the door.

Asher asked the other men what was happening, what this place was. He was answered with shrugs and a "How would I know?"

The men all chose bunks, and Asher settled back on his, trying to rest, trying to put his apprehension to the back of his mind. He had to be positive. This was a prison of sorts, but at least he would see Rina again. She was probably in a similar cabin, and whatever was going on at this place, there would be time to see her one day soon.

It was many hours before the cabin door opened again, and it wasn't for food to be provided, but for more men to enter the barracks. Asher sat up and watched them trudge in and collapse onto the beds on the opposite side. There were about twenty of them—all young, but very different to those on Asher's side of the cabin. These men were sinewy and sunken-chested—rake thin, even—and filthy. Their eyes not only seemed to have retreated into their sockets, but were also devoid of any emotion. There was no talk between them, and no obvious acknowledgment of Asher and the new arrivals.

The man on the bunk below Asher stood up and faced them. "So, what goes on at this place?" he said. "Is it some sort of labor camp?"

"You could call it that," one of them replied.

"But what have you been doing?" the man persisted.

"You'll find out soon enough," another one replied. "But you should rest while you have the chance."

Asher sat back for a moment. He thought of Rina, and how her headstrong, confident manner had been chipped away to a bare fear of everything. He decided he had to ask for her sake, if not for his own.

He jumped off his bed and strode over to the others.

"No," he said. "Why don't you tell us what you've been doing?"

Nobody replied. A few glances were exchanged, one or two shook their heads, the others simply curled up on their beds. Now Asher was close to them he could see how their bones jutted out of fleshless skin, how the outline of their teeth showed through their cheeks.

He pointed to one. "You," he said. "Why do you look so ill?"

Again, there were a few knowing looks.

"Just rest," the man said. "Rest and eat as much as you can."

"But what are we here for?"

"If you really want to know," another said, "we are the *Totenjuden*."

"What does that mean?"

"It means we do as we're told."

Asher hesitated, but thanked the man and returned to his bed.

One or two of the newer men gave him curious looks.

"What?" he said to them.

"You don't speak German, do you?" one said.

Asher shook his head.

"The word *toten* means anything to do with killing or death."

Asher lay back on his bed and wondered what was going on.

Later that evening, there was food. It was only a watery potato soup and a chunk of stale bread, but Asher was getting accustomed to sleeping on a rumbling stomach. He was cold too, but at least he was sleeping on a bed; that was something to be grateful for. He spent a few minutes convincing himself that the rest of his family were safe, that Rina was sleeping not too far from him, the others farther away but also safe. It was a comforting thought, and eventually he drifted into a deep slumber.

He was woken up by a raucous metallic banging. While pulling himself out of sleep, he had to think where he was. But that nauseating smell seemed stronger than ever. And he was still cold. So yes, he was still in this camp, whatever it was.

The guard, waiting just inside the door, stopped banging on his metal tray for a moment to shout out instructions. He told them to get up immediately and follow him. They were led out of the cabin, along a path enclosed with barbed wire, and past a few buildings—more of those that Asher found worryingly familiar.

He told himself they didn't matter just now. They entered a forest of huge pine trees and were led to a small clearing, where they were told to wait while the guard took two of them away.

While they waited, Asher peered beyond the edge of the forest. Between the trunks and foliage, he could make out a large clearing, like a field, but with smoke rising from something—some structure raised a few feet off the ground with objects lying on it.

It looked nothing like any field of crops he'd ever seen.

For a second he thought they looked like bodies of some sort. But he'd heard no gunshots, so they couldn't have been people—and certainly not on that scale; the structure was quite long—perhaps a hundred feet or so. What were those things on it? Animals? No; that didn't make sense either.

As he was straining to see, one of the guards moved toward him and shouted, pointing in the other direction.

Asher looked away, toward the tall trees, and between them the sun just poking over the horizon. It reminded him of his childhood, tending to the fields on the farm in Dyovsta, of the glorious sunrises and sunsets he'd witnessed during the harvest season, when they'd worked every daylight hour. He thought of Mykhail—of their games, their fishing trips, of their shared enthusiasm for tractors. He cursed his mama for taking the family away from Dyovsta, and immediately felt sick with guilt at that thought. It wasn't her fault, and even Warsaw, busy and congested as it was, had never had this heavy stench hanging over it like a shroud of malevolent fog.

The two workers returned carrying lots of axes, dropping them in a pile on the floor for the other men to pick up.

The guard led the men farther into the forest, to another clearing where trees had recently been felled. There, the smell of pine and cut wood was a blessed relief. A few minutes later, they were all chopping the felled trees into more manageable chunks.

Asher didn't know why they were doing this. For a moment, it crossed his mind that they were simply producing firewood for the cabins, but this was a huge amount of wood for a dozen or so cabins.

At first it didn't seem so bad; at least he was generating some heat. However, after half an hour he was soaked in sweat and exhausted. A bucket of water was brought by the guard and placed nearby, and each man had his turn drinking from it.

An hour later, Asher was beyond exhaustion, and still they were being told to chop more. A few times he felt faint, almost keeling over.

And still, after a couple of hours, with the sun way above the horizon, they were told to continue. The more wood Asher chopped, the more logs there were to arrange into piles. By now his muscles were numb, and he felt no pain. Even the discomfort in his throat, sticky-dry again from dehydration, was ignored.

Finally, after what Asher thought was probably three hours, they were ordered back to their barracks. Now he understood—indeed all of them did, judging by their faces—what the other Totenjuden had meant when they'd told the new men to simply rest and eat as much as possible. Nobody spoke; they all merely collapsed on their beds and rested.

They had ten minutes. After that, a different guard came in and gave them some more orders. It was an effort for Asher to move his stiffened muscles, but again he followed the others out of the cabin.

Outside, he could hear a distant hiss, and looked across to see steam pulsing out above another train. He stopped for a moment to listen, and heard the clatter of shoes on concrete—hundreds of them—and the faint hubbub of voices. A shout and a crack of a stick on his shoulder made him move on.

They were led to a nearby building, where a few more guards were casually leaning against the walls, talking and smoking cigarettes, and they were told to wait inside.

It was another large cabin, with lots of sacks piled up along one side. Asher opened one of them, and then another. It took a moment to register, and he quickly checked a third sack. They were full of hair—yes, *hair.* How strange. And it looked like human hair. But if it was from people, there must have been thousands of them.

The guard fetched scissors from a closet and handed them out.

Even stranger.

The clatter of shoes and the blur of voices got closer, and the guard called Asher and his fellow Totenjuden to attention.

"Your job is to cut off the hair of all the women and girls who pass through here."

Asher had to think that through. Had he really said that? More importantly, had the rest of his family been here? He glanced back at the sacks again. Were Rina's locks—freshly cut the day before—somewhere in that mass of hair?

The guard continued: "Take care to cut the hair off as close to the scalp as possible. No waste."

"What do you think they do with the hair we remove?" Asher whispered to the man next to him.

The man shrugged. "I can't say I care. I'm just hoping my hands still work after all that digging."

Asher clenched his aching hands and was about to agree, but before he got a word out the room started filling up. Women and girls entered, the men and boys waiting outside. Clearly, these people represented the next batch of Jews, like livestock being delivered to a farm.

Perhaps now Asher would find out what had happened to the rest of his family.

Another guard started talking to the new arrivals. "All of you, be quiet and listen. You are going to have a shower to rid you of any lice, but first, while the boys and men wait outside, the women and girls must have their hair removed just in case the lice have laid eggs. It's nothing more than that."

Before Asher had time to consider what was going on, a girl had been placed in front of him. She started crying. Asher placed an arm around her and squeezed her shoulder gently. He told her it would be all right, that he would be gentle and not hurt her, and that getting rid of the lice would be for the best. His own hastily arranged words echoed in his head as he then whispered into her ear, asking her to keep still.

He started cutting.

Chapter 21

Treblinka, Poland, 1943

Cutting hair didn't seem such hard work compared with chopping wood, but after a few hours Asher's back ached so much it brought tears to his eyes, and his fingers had an arthritic quality to them, the joints stiff and swollen.

But together the men had worked their way through the entire crowd, and by the end the scene before them looked like a nightmare. This was a room full of hundreds of women and girls with hair so closely cropped they were as good as bald. Asher had never seen a bald woman before, and judging by the looks of fear and disgust on their faces, the women were also unaccustomed to the feeling.

The Totenjuden were then ordered back to their barracks. More orders were given as Asher walked toward the exit, this time to the girls and women.

"Clothes off!" was the command. "Now!"

Some of the older women questioned this.

"Do as you're told," the guard replied, giving her an assured look. "Your clothes will be disinfected and returned to you after your delousing shower."

One woman was brave enough to continue arguing. A guard stepped up to her.

But by then Asher was outside the building, and his mind was adjusting to a new scene of distaste. Indeed, every Totenjude stopped for a second, startled to be confronted by the boys and men, all naked, all shivering and huddled together, their clothes in a pile against the wall.

Asher glanced back to see the shaven-headed women and girls undressing too, many cowering from yet more embarrassment.

As Asher was marched away, his thoughts turned again to the rest of his family. Was this what had happened to them? And to Rina only the day before? All of them would have been uncomfortable, to say the least, undressing in front of strangers. An image of his mama, cold and naked, nothing more than rough stubble covering her head, flashed into his mind. He stopped walking at the thought, only starting again when the men behind shoved him in the back and forced him onward.

In the cabin, Asher collapsed onto his bed. Physical relaxation was easy; the thought that he was in the bowels of some hell on earth prevented his mind relaxing. Nevertheless, he closed his eyes and tried to make the pulsing sensation in his fingers go away. It didn't take long for the exhaustion to conquer his unpleasant thoughts, and he slept.

He was woken by a distant throbbing sound—deep and regular, like nothing he had ever heard before. Well, actually, no. It was like the engine of a truck or a tractor, only louder and deeper in tone. But Asher had been woken from a dream—a dream of being on the tractor in Dyovsta once again, driving up and down the fields with his papa and his best friend, Mykhail. Perhaps that was why the noise reminded him of an engine.

As he was rousing himself, a group of guards entered, yelling orders. Asher's back ached, and he took a little longer than the others to get up. They were marched back to the same building as the day before, and told to gather up all the clothing and shoes and take them to another one.

There, Asher took a few seconds to look around. The edges of the room were piled to head height with clothes. There were pants, jackets, shirts, and dresses—clothes of all sizes. Underwear and footwear too. It was effectively a warehouse or a huge clothing store, with some clothes neatly stacked and some in messy heaps, yet to be sorted. If the clothing they'd moved today belonged to hundreds, there must have been the clothes of many thousands in here already.

A few more trips back and forth were undertaken to move all the clothing, and Asher didn't want to believe what he was thinking.

Perhaps it was better to just do as he was told, and not to think.

But Asher couldn't shake off that unpleasant feeling—the one he didn't want to give in to. Were these people really going to get their clothes back? Surely if they'd all been shot, he would have heard gunshots. But there was nothing—nothing except that maddening throbbing sound.

He felt weak, and had to sit down on one of the smaller piles of clothing.

His darkest thoughts had caught up with his conscious mind and a revelation was occurring, an admission of what he should really have known all along. The thousands of people who had been through the camp—*no, hundreds of thousands*—were nowhere to be seen or heard.

Now Asher knew. Not the details, not exactly how, but he knew.

As he leaned to his right his hand fell upon something soft. He picked it up.

It was a baby bonnet, knitted from blue wool, with yellow flowers sewn into the edges. He looked down and saw a matching blanket, not much bigger than a handkerchief. It had a Star of David sewn into it.

A guard was shouting, but Asher ignored him and threw the baby bonnet back down as though it were possessed. He suddenly felt very ill and eased himself forward, resting on his knees.

Within a few seconds, a pair of shiny black boots appeared in front of him. He didn't look up.

"I told you to leave," the guard said. "Now."

Asher's legs wouldn't move. He continued to stare at the ground. The guard spoke again, this time in Ukrainian. At this, Asher looked up.

Ray Kingfisher

"So now you understand?" the man said.

"You're Ukrainian? So am I. From—"

"Shut up. I don't care. You get up or you get killed. Three seconds."

"You would kill a fellow—?"

"Three!"

The muzzle of a rifle appeared, an inch from Asher's forehead.

"Two!"

By its smell, it had been used recently. Asher stood.

Asher saw it coming, but could do nothing to avoid it. A thump to the head and his world turned upside down. For a second he felt still and settled, his head resting on the ground. Then the blows started on his back. He screamed and curled up into a ball, but the blows continued. One caught his shoulder blade and he felt his skin split. He glanced up, only to meet the butt of the rifle swinging toward him, hitting him full in the face. It was like a hit of ammonia, waking him up all over again, an electric shock to his brain.

"Do as you're told next time!"

Asher coughed and spat out blood.

"You have one second to stand!"

Somehow Asher stood. It probably took more than a second. Perhaps the guard was feeling generous.

There was no respite, not even a moment to wipe the blood from his face or check the wound on the side of his head. He had to follow the others out of the building.

Now that rhythmic throbbing noise was louder—so loud he could feel the thumping vibration making its way through his feet and up into his head.

And just when he thought he could take no more, the noise stopped.

He strained to listen—to be sure he could no longer hear it. But there was no time for that. They were taken along another path, enclosed in yet more of that barbed wire. Along the way he heard one of the guards say something in German. The other guards laughed.

"What did he say?" Asher heard one Totenjude whisper to another.

"They call this the Himmelstrasse," was the reply.

"What does that mean?"

"It's German for 'the way to heaven.' It's a joke."

Asher stumbled at the thought, but recovered.

At the end of the path they came to a large building—half buried, so it seemed. It had a familiar look to it, just like some of the other buildings. It had three sets of large doors, outside which other Totenjuden were waiting. There was an unpleasant atmosphere—one of silent acceptance. Asher thought of all those people who had stripped naked. He started feeling queasy again.

The men were led to one of the sets of doors, outside of which were piles of excrement. Asher glanced across and saw the same mess outside each door. Normally the stench would have been unbearable, but it could hardly have made this place smell worse.

A guard gave one of the Totenjuden a broom, and he swept the mess away from the door. Asher turned to another and showed him a puzzled frown.

"It's the women," the man muttered. "They process the men first, and leave the women and children waiting outside, so they know what's going to happen to them."

"Process?" Asher said. "What do you mean by 'process'?"

Before the man could answer, the doors were opened and clouds of sooty smoke flew out. What Asher saw answered his question.

He blacked out for a second, and staggered as he tried to remain on his feet. It took a few moments for him to regain his composure, to force himself to believe what was in front of his eyes—what was spilling out of the room—and to accept it, for the sake of his life.

Some of his fellow workers—slaves, to be correct—turned and retched. Others looked away for a few seconds, composing themselves, then started work.

The room was a sea of dead, naked bodies—so many they were spilling out of the doorway. Some of the corpses had their hands over their mouths; others were frozen as they might have been when they had gasped their final, deadly breaths. Some had even tried to climb above the others to reach fresher air. All had faces stricken with pain and desperation.

And Asher recognized the oily, sooty smell that hung around the room. He knew it well from his days working with tractors back in Ukraine.

He knew what had killed these people: the exhaust fumes from an engine.

A guard stood next to him, rifle in hand. The guard said something and pointed into the room of corpses. Asher nodded to him and held a hand up; he couldn't speak. The guard must have sensed Asher's shock. After all, it couldn't have been uncommon. He turned away and told someone else what to do.

Slowly, and grimacing with disgust, Asher joined in with the rest. They were each given a leather strap and shown how to attach the belt around the ankles of a body and drag it out of the building.

At one point, Asher turned to walk away, unable to even look at what he was doing.

A guard forced him back. "Do it," he said, quietly but firmly. "You'll get used to the sight, I guarantee it."

Asher didn't want to get used to it, but his mind was too much of a cauldron of disgust and fear to do anything but obey. He gulped, and slowly reached down for the legs of one woman, her eyes still open.

"Stop a moment," a man said. He bent down to the woman's head. A pair of pliers hung on a hook from his little finger, and he used both hands to open the woman's mouth and peer inside. "You can take this one," he said. "No gold here."

Asher tried to compose himself. But it was useless. Had his mama and papa had their mouths searched in this same fashion earlier? His sisters too? Had their lifeless, naked forms been dragged along, bound by leather straps, like carcasses in an abattoir? The woman at Asher's feet was someone's wife, someone's mama.

He tried to dismiss the thought, but it wouldn't let go of his mind. And he couldn't carry on.

A few words from a guard made no difference.

The barrel of a rifle brought him to his senses.

Yes, it was likely that this woman had once been proud of her looks, been keen to bring her children up well, and had worked hard to keep her house clean.

Those times had passed. He told himself over and over again that this was now merely a corpse. The woman was gone.

He tied one end of the leather strap around the body's ankles and tugged, leaning back. After dragging it a couple of yards he stopped, leaned down to shut its eyes, and then continued dragging it backward, digging his heels into the earth. The corpse had very little weight to it, but Asher had very little strength.

He dragged the body around the side of the building, just following the rest of them. And there were many, because there were other doors to the same building, each with their own set of Totenjuden, each with their own sets of families and forgotten lives.

All that consideration of lives snuffed out was dismissed in an instant when Asher rounded the corner, because what he saw there made him fall to his knees.

There were two structures of some sort, one to his left and one to his right. They were long runs of metal bars, like wide railroad tracks, except there were about a dozen bars rather than two, a hundred or so feet long and held up off the earth by metal supports. Each set of bars had burning wood underneath and a mass of bodies on top.

Yes. Bodies. Human cadavers being roasted like cheap meat.

The smell—the same smell the men had experienced before but magnified a hundredfold—made a few of them collapse and retch. But at that moment, disgust and shame were vying for Asher's feelings.

Bodies. Thousands upon thousands of them.

For a second, Asher's thoughts were disturbed by cracking sounds. The sound of bones cooking or merely chunks of wood splitting in the heat? *Did it matter?*

He'd been so foolish, denying his instincts, relying on convenient excuses. Of course he'd heard no gunshots; perhaps the Nazi authorities considered that a waste of bullets.

The bodies must have been stacked five or ten deep on the pyres to his right; it was hard to tell among the tangled knots of limbs and torsos, all in various stages of incineration.

And how long had this been going on? Perhaps hundreds of thousands of them had been through this "process."

The other pyre, to his left, wasn't stacked so high, and held a mixture of assorted limbs, carbonized flesh, and ash.

One of the guards beckoned the Totenjuden toward the emptier pyre. But they didn't move. One of them let go of his belt and started running—running and screaming at the top of his voice. Two guards chased. Two shots rang out.

The orders to approach the pyre were repeated.

The men looked at each other, then to the ground.

What else could Asher do?

The men dragged their corpses toward the pyre, Asher included.

After a few paces the guard then told them to halt, to stay exactly where they were. And the rumble of an engine gave precious relief, drowning out the noise of the cracking bones and bursting skin.

A huge vehicle appeared beyond the pyres. It was something Asher had never seen before: an earth-moving device like a tractor but much bigger. And it wasn't moving earth; its cargo was bodies—more bodies, which it proceeded to drop onto the pyre in front of them.

"Okay," the guard said once the earth-mover had left. "Onto here with the rest."

The men didn't move. The guard looked at them, then back at the pyre. Then he sat down and held his belly. He turned and beckoned over two more guards who were stationed by the security fence. As they approached, he vomited on the ground between his boots. Words were exchanged, and he walked off uneasily.

"What did they say?" one of the Totenjuden asked.

"He's had enough," another said. "Even some of the guards can't take it."

They carried on, all playing their parts, collecting more bodies and dragging them to the pyres, or collecting the odd body—or body part—that had fallen off it.

Asher now knew why they'd been chopping such large quantities of wood.

After all the dead bodies had been slung onto the burning racks, they were ordered back to the cabin. There were few words, none of them from Asher's lips; his head was spinning with images of hell on earth, and his fellow workers were clearly feeling the same. They were offered potato soup with raw rice, but few had the inclination to eat.

Asher curled up on his bunk and closed his eyes, but struggled to sleep, his mind a mess of images of limbs and lifeless faces—hundreds of bodies disposed of like offal.

Now he knew what had happened to Rina, and probably the rest of his family too. Yes, he had begun to accept the unacceptable.

His mind turned to the good old days of his papa strolling around the farm back in Dyovsta, joking about the tractor—saying how it was such a new-fangled thing and would never replace horses. He thought of his papa in Warsaw, weary from loading bricks, his face noticeably aged from the never-ending physical work.

That was when Asher sat up in the bunk, startled.

"Bricks," he whispered. He wiped the cold sweat of fear from his face and repeated the word.

Now he knew why the buildings in this wretched place looked familiar. It wasn't so much the buildings, more the bricks they were constructed from. Asher's own hands had held these bricks, fresh from the kiln, still warm. Still warm, like the bodies he'd just dragged to their unholy cremation. Yes. The bricks had been made in Warsaw and loaded onto the trucks by him and his papa.

Was there no cruelty too far?

This place—this place that God had clearly turned a blind eye to—was the "important construction project to the east" that had urgently needed all those bricks.

Asher tried to sleep, part of him hoping never to wake up.

But Asher did wake up, disturbed by a persistent creaking noise, and in the half-light he saw something moving back and forth in time with the sound. No, it was swinging left and right. It was swinging on the end of a leather belt hung from a high wooden beam. Clearly it wasn't only German soldiers who'd had enough.

The body went on the pyre with the rest.

On that second day, Asher was still shocked at what he was doing—shocked, ashamed, guilty, his mind twitching with self-loathing.

By the third day his mind was numb; it was starting to be just a job.

On the fourth day there was a change. His team of Totenjuden cut hair and removed clothing just as they had on previous days, but as they were carrying clothing back to the warehouse they heard shots. They all stopped for a second, but then continued as if they'd heard nothing.

After the clothes had been taken to the warehouse, they started on the bodies again, dragging them out of the gassing building and throwing them onto the pyres. Today, some fluid was splashed over the bodies, and they caught fire more quickly and burned more aggressively. But after the last few bodies were flung on, the guard told the Totenjuden to follow him.

They went through another barbed-wire corridor and behind some hedging, where they found some bodies lying on the earth.

Yet more dead bodies. As if Asher hadn't seen enough. But these were different: they were fully clothed and had bullet holes in their skulls.

That would explain the shots Asher had heard earlier.

After the guard spoke, the twenty Totenjuden started taking one corpse each. Asher was one of the first, and duly manhandled his allotted corpse toward the smoldering pyre.

"Who are they?" he asked one of his fellow Totenjuden.

The man let out a lazy laugh. "Haven't you heard? They're *us*."

Asher frowned. "I don't understand."

"These men are us in three or four weeks' time."

It took a moment for Asher to get the message. Then he shook his head slowly. "Dear God, no," he said.

"How long do you think we'll last, being worked like dogs? These are the Totenjuden from three or four weeks ago. Time will move on. In a few weeks *we* will be the corpses with bullet holes in our heads, and another, fresher set of robots will be here, burying us. A month after that, they will be dead too."

And as much as Asher wanted to argue—to say that what he was hearing couldn't be true—he then saw something that silenced him.

At first he wasn't sure. But he scanned the scene of blood, flesh, and soil before him once more. Yes, there was something there. The man's corpse was tall and stick thin. It had a red birthmark covering one cheek and the side of its neck.

Its name used to be Oskar. Oskar the pacifist, the protective husband and father-to-be, the man who had been so grateful to the Kogans.

The more Asher stared, the weaker his body became. He was relieved when the body was thrown onto the heap, where he could no longer see it.

The next few days were ones of relentless drudgery—hour after hour of body-breaking physical work combined with sights and sounds that lodged like sharp splinters in Asher's mind.

But he had to ignore his feelings. That was the program. Use the body as a tool, don't think beyond the physical. Never think. Never try to remember. Just do. Get with the program or die.

The throb of that big bad engine, the smell of charred flesh.

Do.

Ignore.

Repeat.

Just like the rest.

Chapter 22

Treblinka, Poland, 1943

In his first few days at Treblinka, Asher had kept in the back of his mind the hope that somehow, possibly, some of his family were still alive.

That thought had long since perished, along with his humanity. Now he spent his time dealing with meat—ignoring the faces contorted in pain and the limbs twisted at unnatural angles, dragging them to the pyre, throwing them on the heap, splashing gasoline on the mass of flesh, watching the skin pop and the flesh cook. All of this was merely his job, and these bodies were never people with their own loves, interests, opinions, and beliefs. Self-preservation was all that mattered, and any thoughts that threatened that were banished.

Self-sacrifice was for others, and it happened regularly. Waking up to a body swinging from the rafters no longer startled Asher. A fellow prisoner in a deranged fit charging at a guard and being gunned down was no longer worth watching.

Do.

Ignore.

Repeat.

By the summer of 1943 a few shards of hope appeared for those men who had managed to blank out the horror and keep their bodies— if not their minds—alive.

In his first few hours at the camp Asher had been frightened to move or speak unless ordered to. Like the rest, he'd been petrified of the consequences of doing otherwise.

But now the camp was starting to wind down. Fewer trains arrived, and those that did were half full and often contained more Roma gypsies than Jews. The Totenjuden were given more freedom to move around the camp and to talk.

The talk was of another camp about a mile away—not an extermination camp like here, but a forced labor settlement for Jews. The workers from there occasionally visited and exchanged information in secret. The news was encouraging: not only had the German war machine lost the crucial battle for Stalingrad, but there had also been major German losses in North Africa.

That meant the Nazi powers and their collaborators were not invincible after all. They were human and could be beaten. This idea—which had seemed unlikely for so long—galvanized the prisoners. But for a long time it was merely rumor with no substance, until late one night in July, when Asher was shaken awake and by the light of a candle saw the face of Stefan, a fellow Totenjude.

"Shh!" he whispered. "Get out of your bunk. Go to the far end."

In the dimness, Asher saw a few men carrying their wrecked bodies over there, and Stefan moving on to wake up the others. When they had all gathered, Stefan started speaking in hushed tones.

"This meeting is also happening in other cabins. There is an escape plan. And we know the risks. Do we all know what happens when an escape fails?"

"Not really," one man said.

"Perhaps you aren't aware," Stefan said. "There have been escape attempts before—two men going through the fence, a few tunneling under it. For every prisoner who tried to escape, ten were executed in reprisal. And that is why this is different. We are planning a total revolt against the camp authorities. I would ask anyone who doesn't want to be a party to this to go back to bed now."

He waited. Nobody moved.

"Good. I expected nothing less, but it's good. I've had meetings with the committee members. As you are aware, there has been a strong and steady supply of Jews coming here from Polish towns and cities, with a few Roma from elsewhere in Europe. And we all know why we are here: our job is to, shall we say, *process* them. But there are now very few Jews left in Poland. We have to ask ourselves what will happen to us, the Totenjuden, when that supply has run completely dry."

"We'll be shot," someone said.

"Of that," Stefan replied, "we can be absolutely certain. But it would also be reasonable to assume that the authorities have guessed we have worked this out and will act accordingly. And because of that, the escape must happen soon."

"I agree," another Totenjude said. "If we wait much longer there won't be enough of us left to revolt."

"Exactly," Stefan said. "To that end, a date has been set."

"Which is?"

They held their breath, but Stefan shook his head slowly. "I can't tell you," he said.

"*What?*"

Asher heard groans and saw faces of confusion in the dim light.

"Shh!" Stefan hissed. "Please listen. This is crucial. Remember that we'll get only one chance at this. If it fails, then realistically we'll all be shot. This has been planned at a higher level, and that's why I don't even know the date myself. Everyone will be told on the day or the night before. I would ask you to remember that secrecy is our main weapon. The more people know the date, the greater the chance that the authorities will find out. And I repeat, if we fail, each and every one of us dies."

Stefan swung his head left and right to meet the faces of all the men. When his glare settled on Asher, the iron resolve in the man's eyes was clear.

"I'm completely with you," someone said.

"Me too," another said. "You're right, Stefan; it's for the best."

Seconds later, every man had agreed.

"A question," one said. "You say secrecy is our main weapon. But surely we need more powerful weapons?"

"We do," Stefan said. "And I promise you shall have some. Not necessarily a gun each, but something. Please remember that this revolt is being planned with precision, and that our plan is to destroy the camp and get every prisoner out of this wretched hellhole. *Every last man.* Any more questions?"

"What do we do in the meantime?" someone asked.

"I'll tell you what you do. You go back to bed. You were never awake. I never spoke to you. You know nothing of any plan. You do what the guards tell you to do. Everything is normal."

The men all nodded and returned to their bunks.

For days there had been a calm atmosphere—unnervingly calm, with even the guards appearing more relaxed. Deliveries of new prisoners had all but stopped, and the Totenjuden had been gathered together and told there would follow an exercise to dismantle the site.

They've finally done it, Asher thought. *They've bled Europe dry of Jews, bar the odd few specks such as the Totenjuden. And what will happen when those specks have served their purpose?*

It was no idle thought. Asher knew—they all did—that their lives were more at risk now than ever before. Was the dismantling plan merely a ruse? Would they all simply be led to a ditch and disposed of?

And then there was the revolt plan—the plan nobody talked of, but also one that was in everyone's thoughts all day, if Asher's own mind was anything to go by. They all waited and expected. Asher knew that the longer he stayed at the camp, the more likely he was to be killed. If he escaped, either he would be captured and killed, or he would evade capture and need to find his way to a safe country.

Between the site-dismantling plan and the revolt plan, it was clear that his life was on a knife edge.

In deference to Stefan's request there were no furtive speculations as to when the plan might be put into action, no whispered guesses in quiet corners. Few words at all were spoken in the cabin. The days were hot, the mood calm, the undercurrent tense. The end of July came, and still there was no word from Stefan.

And then, late one night, Asher was woken up again for another meeting.

"It's set for tomorrow," Stefan told the gathered men. "I know you've been ready for a long time, and I'm sorry, but now it looks good. As far as we can tell, the authorities don't suspect a thing. It's set for late in the afternoon, so we have the maximum time of darkness on our side when we escape."

"What about guns?" a man said.

"All planned. In the afternoon we'll distribute money, guns, and grenades to various people. You'll be told individually where yours are— perhaps in a bucket, in a sack, or under a pile of potatoes. You'll be allocated areas to go to, where you'll pick the guards off in ones and twos, however you can, but as quietly as you can. When you hear the explosion, that's the signal to storm the gates. Is everybody clear on this?"

They all nodded.

"So sleep well," Stefan said. "Sleep well in the knowledge that, one way or another, this will be your final night in this cabin."

All the men shook hands with one another, wished each other good luck, and said they would miss each other's company, but nothing else.

Asher slept well.

Asher tried his best to treat the next day like any other. When he started chopping wood soon after dawn, it seemed that the morning would last a lifetime. He kept looking beyond the fence, dreaming, imagining himself sprinting through the forest, effortlessly evading the gunfire from the watchtowers.

At one point he noticed a guard looking in his direction. The guard walked over, stood a few yards from Asher, and peered through the forest to where Asher had been looking.

Asher promised himself he would not look again. What would happen would happen. He would deal with it at the time.

And the morning flew by.

Bread and cheese were brought out for the midday meal, and they were told to stop chopping. There was other work to do, and Asher found himself sweeping storage cabins clean.

It was only early afternoon, but there were no clocks, and he could do no more than wait, his senses heightened to hang on to every voice and every set of footsteps.

A guard sauntered along in front of him. He glanced at the area Asher had swept and nodded approvingly. Then Asher gulped. Behind the guard, in the far doorway, he saw Stefan. Stefan was agitated, eyes darting left and right. When the guard sauntered away, Stefan ran in.

"It's now," he said. "Follow me."

Asher followed without speaking, and a short dash later they entered their cabin, where four other men came out of hiding from behind the farthest bed. "What's happening?" one of them said. "You said late afternoon."

Stefan shook his head. "There's been a change. The guards found money on one of the men. They're talking to him."

"Talking?"

"You can guess. But it ruins everything if they find out at this late stage. So we go now. The others have been told too, and also told where their weapons are. I'll get yours now."

He climbed onto the top bunk, reached up to a beam, and pulled himself up. After the last few weeks the feat seemed superhuman to Asher, but as he watched, he could feel adrenaline imbuing his own body with more strength. From the top of the beam Stefan dropped two knives and four guns onto the bed. Then he came down.

"You two, the kitchen block. You two, the clothing warehouse. Asher, you're with me. Remember what you've been told. Only kill guards out of sight of other guards. And quietly too. If you can use a knife instead of a gun, much better. Then drag them out of sight. When you hear the first grenade explosion, head for the main gate and kill any guards you see."

He handed out the weapons, hiding one of the guns in the back of his pants under his belt, giving another to Asher. "Take care. The guns are loaded. Let's go."

A few minutes later, Asher and Stefan had reached one of the buildings used to store sacks of hair and glasses. They hid around a corner, Stefan peeking out occasionally.

"We'll wait here until the guards come in," he said. "But have your gun ready."

Asher plucked out his gun and weighed it in his hand. "Where have the arms come from?"

Stefan cracked a rare smile. "From the camp's own stores, so I'm told. Someone said children were used to get them, but who cares? Let's be quiet and be ready."

Asher said no more, just tried to judge the number of spare bullets in his pocket.

"Right," Stefan said a few minutes later. "Follow me. Put your hands behind your back. Relax. Be normal."

They stepped out and called over to a pair of guards, who strolled over. They were both fresh-faced, Asher thought, perhaps only seventeen or eighteen.

"What are you doing out of barracks?" one of them said.

Stefan pointed a thumb at Asher. "My friend here wants a pair of these spectacles. Is that okay?"

The guards both laughed.

"But he can't see without them," Stefan protested. "Perhaps some nice silver-framed ones, yes?"

Now one guard stopped laughing and gave Asher and Stefan a sideways glance. Soon the other also realized something wasn't quite right and pulled his face straight.

Both guards reached for their rifles, but as they did so each instantly had a pistol pressed firmly against his chest, just below the rib cage. As the ends of the pistols pushed deep into flesh, the triggers were pulled, the close range deadening the sound as efficiently as it deadened the guards.

"Quick!" Stefan hissed. They dragged the bodies to the back of the room, behind some sacks. "Now we just do the same again," he added. "Until we hear the grenade."

They stood in position again, but only had to wait a couple of minutes before they heard the dull boom of a grenade. "That's it," Stefan said. "Good luck, my friend."

"Perhaps one day we'll celebrate this," Asher said, and gave Stefan a slap on the back.

"I hope so," he replied. "But first we need to get out of this cesspit."

As they left the building, the sound of another grenade exploding jolted them, but they managed to break into a run, both firing as they ran between the cover of buildings.

They made their way toward the camp gates, Asher's mind sharp with fear and determination. Another explosion—a bigger one—knocked both men off their feet. One side of Asher's face felt painfully hot and he could smell his singed hair. It was the camp fuel tank, once used to hold gasoline for the pyres, but now hidden in a rage of yellow fire and dark smoke. It made Asher grin—not smile, but grin. If he died now, a part of him would die happy.

Asher scrabbled around for his gun, lost in the fall, but Stefan pulled him away and onto his feet.

"No time!" Stefan shouted. "To the gates!"

Asher noticed other buildings were on fire too, and the air was alive with bullets. They ran on, dodging fireballs and gunshots until they reached the gates.

"Someone's already gone over!" Asher shouted, pointing up at the top of the fence, where a section of heavy cloth had been slung over the top, covering the barbed wire.

Both men started climbing. Asher reached the top first and swung both legs over. He heard a shout of pain from Stefan and looked down. There was a mass of blood and flesh where Stefan's elbow should have been. Asher could see a sharp section of bone poking out of his jacket.

Asher looked up to the nearest watchtower, where a machine gun was flashing with gunfire. For a second, helpless across the top of the gate, he forgot about Stefan and prayed the guard up there would spare him.

"Help me!" Stefan shouted, bringing Asher back to his senses.

Asher reached down and grabbed Stefan's other arm. He tried to pull, but could only hold Stefan steady. He looked farther ahead and saw a guard running up toward the gate. He grunted as he strained to pull Stefan up, then heard a bullet whistle past his ear.

That was when he let go of Stefan and threw himself back. Both men hit the ground at the same time, Asher outside the gate, Stefan inside. Blood spewed from Stefan's mouth, but still he looked at Asher and held a grasping hand out.

Save yourself, Asher told himself, *save yourself,* and he raced away into the woods, darting left and right as the gunfire continued behind him.

◆ ◆ ◆

Fires blazed at every corner of the camp. Only the brick buildings were untouched. The prisoners had done their best to wreck the sturdy gas chamber block, but burning the wooden doors and dislodging a few bricks with grenades was hardly recompense for the deathly offenses against human decency inflicted there.

The door that they knew held the secret—the source of the killing fumes—was bombarded and battered, but personal freedom was more important, and soon they either escaped or were shot by guards.

Inside the engine house, one Mykhail Petrenko cowered in a dark corner behind the oily mass of the engine, in no doubt as to what was happening outside and what would happen to him should they break through. He'd been dragging the last of the victims out of the chambers when the fighting had started. He'd heard shots, then grenades, then seen guards shot by prisoners, and had run back into the safety of the engine room before the fires and major explosions started. He'd shoved everything movable—tables, tools, fuel containers—against the door to barricade himself in. He'd heard guards ordering him to open up, then heard gunfire, then heard the mob trying to break the door down.

Like a cornered animal, Mykhail sat in his own personal darkness, knees to chest, rocking his lonely figure, trembling and wide-eyed, and mumbling nonsense to himself.

By now the mob had left, and he could only hear the crackle and roar of an inferno, but in his head Mykhail still heard the voices demanding vengeance, telling him to open the doors, screaming that they would break them down and kill anyone inside.

He was to hear those voices for a long time.

Chapter 23

Diane slumped into her seat, and slumped a little more before reaching for her seat belt. "Thanks," she said.

"How'd it go this time?" Brad replied.

"Let's just get out of this place," she said, pointing to the exit.

They'd traveled a mile before either of them spoke again.

"Is everything good?" Brad asked.

He spoke as sympathetically as he always did when she was giving him the silent treatment. And she knew she was giving him the silent treatment right now, but felt powerless to do anything about it. As always, he accepted it, and it seemed to work, without either of them getting upset. He would just wait; she would eventually give in.

They stopped at a set of lights. She gave in.

"I'm going to live with Mother in Baltimore for a while," she said. "I mean, in a few days, when I'm done listening to that murderer back there and done dealing with Father's house."

"Okay."

She glanced right. "What does 'okay' mean?"

"It . . . it means it's fine with me." The lights changed and he set off again. "It's just . . . I thought you might want to stop longer at my place, perhaps even make it permanent."

"I need a bed in Pittsburgh while I sort out Father's stuff, and I'm really grateful it's yours, but eventually I'll go stay with Mother."

"And her new husband."

"So she's remarried. So what?"

"Nothing. But you know I'd like you to move in permanently— when you want to, that is. And there's your job here to consider."

"Screw my job."

"All right. As long as you know the offer's there. Just promise me you'll consider it."

"I *am* considering it—right now. And I've just told you, I'm . . ." She let out a long, frustrated breath. "Brad, I'm sorry. I'm not trying to give you a hard time. I'm grateful for all you've done, really, but I think I owe it to Mother." They drove another few hundred yards before she continued. "I don't expect you to understand, but we missed out on a lot of time together because of Father. And as for moving in with you permanently, thank you again. Perhaps one day. I don't know. I'm a mess at the moment. You may have noticed."

"Whatever works for you. It's not a now-or-never offer. I could visit you and your mom in Baltimore at weekends—that is, if you'd like that."

She laid her hand on his arm. "Hey, that'd be lovely. And I'm sorry I'm such a pain in the ass right now."

"Hey, will you cut that out? You've had a hard time. Just do what you feel you have to. If you really want to move in with your mom, then move in with her. It's not gonna kill me." He grimaced. "Sorry. Unfortunate choice of words."

Once Diane had given that some thought, it brought a smile to her lips, which brought a smile to his lips.

"I guess you'd like to know what just happened back there?" she said.

They stopped at another set of lights, and he looked to the right. "You don't need to tell me the details, just whether it was worth it."

"Worth it?"

"Did he tell you what you wanted to know?"

"Hmm . . ." She pursed her lips tightly.

"I'm guessing he didn't, right?" Still he got no answer, so he said, "On the other hand, if you'd rather not tell me anything at all . . ."

"No, no," she said. "It's not that. I'm thinking. He did talk. He talked a lot. But it was all about him and Father growing up together in Ukraine and what happened to them during the war years. I never realized Father had such a hard time of it. It's so easy to forget that your parents had a life before you were born. I guess that's a pretty universal thing."

"I get that," Brad said. "Does that mean he didn't tell you why he killed your father?"

"Not yet."

"Uh, so you're going back?"

Diane nodded. "I need to find out, and he sounds like he needs to tell me. But it's good. It was quite friendly, considering what he did. And we talked about what Father was like."

"What he was like? In what way?"

"Whether I really knew him."

"And?"

"And I'm beginning to think . . . well, perhaps I didn't. At least not as well as I thought I did. And I have to admit he knows a hell of a lot about my father's life, considering there was such a long time when they didn't see each other—over sixty years."

"You always told me your father never really liked to talk about the old times. You said you assumed it was all too painful for him and he wanted to put it behind him."

"That's what I thought. I asked him once what happened to him during the war and why he came to America. He said the whole thing was horrible and I didn't want to know. I told him I did, that he should try talking about it. He got angry with me, like he was about to have some sort of fit or breakdown, so I backed off, told him to forget it, and I never broached the subject again."

Brad shot her a glance. "You never told me that before."

"Sorry." Even after all this time, she wasn't sure why she was still unable to tell Brad the whole truth about her father.

Another few minutes of silence passed. During that time, the things Diane *hadn't* said about her father ran through her mind. There was the trick he would pull whenever she hinted—as she had once or twice a few years before—that she was thinking of moving in with Brad. There was the tiredness that seemed at odds with his ability to walk miles every day. There were the continued reassurances—announced in a weak, throaty voice— that he'd be okay on his own because he liked his own company and no longer felt wanted by the world anyway. Most importantly, there were also the nights—anything up to three of them a week throughout his life— when he would talk in his sleep, spouting out seemingly random words of Ukrainian in a deep and threatening tone. Diane had faint memories from when she was a little girl of asking him why he talked in his sleep, and how he'd told her never to talk about his "episodes" to anyone—even him. When her parents split up she'd even thought that it might have been a factor. It was only soon afterward, when she stayed with her mother, that she found out the truth, which was much worse. Perhaps, she'd mused many years later, she stayed with him to prevent him having some sort of breakdown—to stop those truths coming out. Moreover, perhaps he knew the threat of that might just make a good reason for her to stay. So, had it been her concern to keep the peace at all costs, or his emotional blackmail? She could take her pick: both were partly true.

Back at Brad's place, he cooked, and they talked all evening. They talked about the place where they'd worked together and about coworkers past and present. They talked about the vacations they'd shared. They talked as they walked around Brad's flower garden—the one Diane had planned and planted largely on her own.

They didn't talk about Diane's parents, or Baltimore, or the murder case, or what she was going to do and say at the county jail the next day. That was good.

Chapter 24

It might have been an hour since Asher escaped from Treblinka or it might have been three, but he stopped, exhausted, and fell to the forest floor. He'd heard gunfire, horses, and vehicles on various occasions, but had evaded all of them, running when he had the energy, walking when he didn't.

Now he was utterly spent, and the sun was going down. In the near darkness he climbed a tree and tied his jacket to a branch for safety, thanking God this wasn't one of those bitterly cold nights. He fell asleep immediately, and was woken before dawn by a rain shower. It was welcome, and he collected and drank the water as best he could. Before daylight broke he got down and started moving again.

This time, weak and stiff, he could do no more than stumble between the trees, but he eventually reached a river. He looked long and hard at the rushing torrent, listened to its hypnotic thunder, and concluded it would probably kill him, and hence would be a last resort. He turned back under cover of the forest and started walking alongside the river.

Soon he spotted a building between the veil of tree trunks and slowed to a stealthy prowl. It was a farmhouse on the edge of the forest, with a small field beyond. His eyes were drawn to the cattle in the field, to the chickens to the right of the farmhouse, but mostly to the small orchard next to the wooden barn on the left, which backed onto the edge of the forest.

Within minutes Asher had entered the orchard's edge via the forest and was picking plums, pears, and small apples, cramming what he could into his mouth, storing more in his pockets and in the crook of one arm. He heard a door open and ran into the barn. On one side was a ladder leading up to a hayloft. He climbed up and headed for the darkest place, where he sat in silence. He heard nothing, so ate, gorging himself on sweet fruit. Then, as bloated as a medieval king, he fell asleep.

Asher's slumber was peppered with dreams of fire and nightmares of the dying, but they paled to nothing as he stirred, disturbed by something heavy crawling on his outstretched legs. As he started to wake up he sensed pressure on his chest and heard close breathing.

He gasped, and the nightmares were forgotten as he woke to the rancid breath of a dog. He grabbed the thing by its wiry hair and was about to push it away when his eyes met with something just beyond—the muzzle of a shotgun.

It took him a moment to look at the other end, where he saw an elderly woman in dirty gray clothes and a headscarf. She was staring right into his eyes, her finger poised on the trigger. She whistled, and the dog hopped off Asher's chest and trotted away to sit by her feet.

"Polish?" she said.

"Ukrainian," Asher replied in a croaking voice.

She asked whether he was a Jew. The black holes of the rifle barrels forced the answer back down his throat. *Should he lie to save himself?*

As he considered his reply, the woman's eyes bobbed down to the side of his leg—to the dark red streak on his pants.

"Treblinka?" she said.

Asher gave a single nod and held his breath. The muzzle of the rifle stayed where it was, and Asher closed his eyes and prayed. He prayed for whatever was going to happen to happen quickly.

He couldn't hold his breath long, and let out a wheeze and some tears as he opened his eyes.

The muzzle was still there, and her eyes were still on him.

Then her eyes moved to the side, to where he'd thrown the plum stones.

"I'm sorry," he said in his most polite Polish. "I was so hungry."

Her nostrils twitched, and the tip of her tongue peeped out between her cracked lips and lodged in the corner of her mouth. Slowly and steadily she backed away. "Stay where you are," she said, and climbed down to the barn floor.

Asher crept over, conscious he was disobeying but unable to resist. He poked his head far enough over to see her standing in the doorway below him.

She called out toward the house, and soon a man joined her. She talked to him while he wiped his hands on a rag, and at one point she cast a hand back in Asher's direction. There were heated voices, hand gestures, after which the man strode past her and approached the ladder.

Asher quickly threw himself back to where he'd been told to stay, and the man's head appeared seconds later. He climbed up and walked over to Asher.

"You're Jewish?" he said. "Escaped from the camp?"

Asher nodded, not taking his eyes off the man. "I'm Ukrainian. I was in Warsaw, then Treblinka. I escaped from there. I don't mean you any harm. I'm just desperate."

Then the woman appeared again at the top of the ladder.

The man glanced back to her and said to Asher, "We're the Malinowskis."

"Asher Kogan."

"On your own?"

Asher nodded.

"You can stay with us," he said. "But not in here."

"Thank you," Asher said, heaving a sigh. "I'll repay your kindness."

Now the woman was standing next to the man. He put his arm around her. "Forgive my wife," he said. "The farmhouse belonged to our son and his wife. They took in a family of Jews two years ago, sheltered them. The Nazis found out and shot them all. They said we should think ourselves lucky they let us have the farm."

Then the man's eyes grew heavy; he blinked to hold back his tears. Asher looked at the woman. "I'm sorry," he said. "Really."

She nodded and said, "Me too, but thank you."

"Anyway," the man said, "we're old now. It hardly matters. We'll protect you, and if it kills us . . . so be it." He shrugged. "Not that we won't fight."

Back at the camp, Mykhail had listened from his cocoon to the fires burning themselves out and the shouts turning to talk. He knew he'd probably slept but couldn't be sure, his mind having hopped from reality to nightmare and all stages in between. But he would starve if he stayed in the engine room.

The first things he saw on removing the barricades and opening the door were rifles pointed at him. As one guard searched him for weapons, he cast his eyes over the scenes of the prisoner uprising. Dead bodies—a mix of guards, prisoners, and fellow Trawnikis—were strewn about. Blood tainted the earth everywhere. Most of the buildings still smoldered, smoke lazily drifting above. It was so quiet compared to what he'd heard during the revolt.

"Did you know anything about the prisoners' plans?" the guard asked him.

Mykhail shook his head.

The guard briefly spoke with his superior, then turned back to Mykhail. "You have to clear up," he said.

Mykhail nodded. Whether he understood or agreed or was just relieved not to be shot, he wasn't quite sure.

Over the next few days he worked all the daylight hours. People who had been shot in the uprising were divided into two: bodies of guards were shipped out for a proper burial; those of the prisoners simply added to the mass of bodies. With no prisoners, it was left to the Trawnikis and guards to do the dirty work. Prisoners who had been shot, prisoners who had been recently gassed, and exhumed bodies all had to be dragged away and loaded onto the enormous pyres. The men scattered the resulting ashes far and wide, digging them into the sand and earth. They weren't told why they were doing this, but they all knew because they'd heard the rumors: the Soviet troops were advancing, and the Germans wanted to cover up what had been happening. They were even told to dismantle and destroy what remained of the camp buildings, effectively erasing all traces that it ever existed—bodies, buildings, records, everything.

Eventually the place was restored to nothing more than a forest clearing. The only clues as to what had happened there were to be found a few inches below the surface.

A few miles away, on the farm, Asher took a few weeks to do nothing more than rest and eat. It turned out that there was a large gash along the outside of one leg, the pain of which had been covered by adrenaline and exhaustion. But Mrs. Malinowski dressed the wound daily and it recovered, along with his body weight.

Mr. Malinowski constructed a compact hiding hole behind the log pile in the storeroom just off the kitchen. Asher went there whenever there was a knock at the door, ready to squeeze into it if he heard the code word that signified the presence of Nazi guards. Additionally, Mrs. Malinowski would spring into action, ensuring there were no giveaway signs such as a third plate or cup on the table, and rolling up Asher's makeshift bed and storing it away. Their efficiency sometimes made Asher slightly fearful—but so grateful.

They asked for nothing in return, and after one particular visit, once the Nazis had gone, Asher asked Mrs. Malinowski why she was helping him, risking her life when there were much easier options. "It's what our son would have wanted," was the reply.

For those first few weeks Asher spoke very little, and was rigid with the fear of those inhuman knocks at the front door. But the Malinowskis made him feel that there was good in the world after all. He stayed there for a year, safe and cared for, his mind and body gradually healing.

During that time, they all listened to the foreign news on the radio and heard reliable rumors from neighboring farms. Every month there was news of more German and Axis losses to the west; every week there was news of more Soviet advances in the east. There were also unpleasant rumors of what the Germans were doing to towns and villages they were retreating from.

One day, in the summer of 1944, when the Treblinka uprising was merely a memory and the search for escapees had long since been abandoned, Mr. Malinowski ran into the house, quickly followed by a younger man and woman, both soaked through and with muddy hands and feet.

Mr. Malinowski called out to his wife and Asher. Mrs. Malinowski fetched towels for the pair, then all five sat in the kitchen, where Mr. Malinowski told them there was danger.

"The rumors are true," he said. "Asher, this is our niece and her husband. They ran a farm just across the river."

"*Ran?*" Mrs. Malinowski said, confused.

"It's just a burning wreck now," her young niece said through tears. "They set fire to everything, killed our cattle and pigs. We only escaped by swimming across the river. We're lucky to be alive."

"You must be so scared," Mrs. Malinowski said.

Her niece's husband nodded. "But not too scared to fight."

"I'm glad to hear it," Mr. Malinowski said. "The same is not going to happen here; they'll have to kill us first." He looked at them all in turn. "We're not running. Agreed?"

Asher nodded with the rest of them.

Mr. Malinowski fetched a key from the back of a kitchen drawer and took it down into the cellar, where he unlocked a small cabinet. Asher couldn't count the exact number of shotguns and rifles inside it.

"I knew this day would come," he said. "Upstairs we have a window on each side, two at the front. We take one each, and shoot at anything that looks like a German, yes?"

The wait was long and boring—two days and nights. Then, just after dusk, two German soldiers approached the door and knocked on it, lifting their rifles up. There was no answer, so one steadied himself to kick the door in. Before he could manage that, both men were shot dead from above.

More soldiers quickly arrived, shooting and smashing the windows. While the wooden barn was set alight and the livestock shot dead, the battle for the farmhouse carried on. Soldiers attacked the building from every angle, but were also shot at from the upstairs windows.

Eventually, with a few dozen soldiers lying dead around the house, there was nothing more to be shot. Asher and the Malinowskis waited, looked, and listened, but only heard voices and vehicles slowly receding into the background.

"They've given up!" Mrs. Malinowski eventually shouted out.

"They've moved on to the next farm," Mr. Malinowski replied. "God help the owners."

The five prayed for them, and kept guard for another day and night, but the only sounds they heard were birds twittering during the day, and owls hooting and wolves howling at night.

But there was no time to relax. There was no knowing whether the guards had given up or would try again. By day and by night there were always two people on guard, and the guns were kept loaded and to hand.

Early one morning, while Asher was on guard and struggling to stay awake, he heard Mr. Malinowski, who was sharing guard duties with him, shout from the other side of the house.

"Asher! Asher! Someone's here!"

Asher shook the slumber from his head and rushed across.

"See," Mr. Malinowski said, pointing toward the forest. "Movement. Definitely some people."

And yes, Asher could make out a few figures moving around in the dark forest.

Approaching.

He and Mr. Malinowski lifted their rifles and set their sights on the edge of the forest.

Three figures stepped out from the trees and into the dawn's half-light.

"Look," Mr. Malinowski said: "Rifles. Definitely soldiers."

Then there were six, then ten, and soon there were too many to count.

Mr. Malinowski gulped. "My God, so many of them. Do we start shooting?"

His words registered with Asher, but Asher was struggling to think, let alone reply. It seemed too good to be true. He waited to see a little more clearly, and yes, he was right. "Look!" he said, pointing at the nearest soldiers. "Can't you see?"

"See what?"

"The uniforms."

Mr. Malinowski squeezed his eyes to gray slits and peered at them. Then he gasped and tears filled his eyes.

"They're *Soviet* troops," Asher said.

All Mr. Malinowski could do was smile.

◆ ◆ ◆

By this time, with all obvious traces of the Treblinka extermination camp destroyed, Mykhail had found himself transferred back to the Trawniki camp to train other men. But that camp was eventually abandoned too, again because of the approaching Soviet troops.

From there, Mykhail became a gun. Nothing more. Not even a gun for hire, but a gun to be commanded. With the rest of the diminishing band of Trawnikis, he was transported to one place, told to shoot people, then transported elsewhere and told to do the same.

He tried not to consider who the victims were. He shut down his conscience. The excuse he gave himself was hope—hope that the Germans might control Russia one day and give Ukraine independence. Behind the excuse, he was a robot. In his head it wasn't him who was perpetrating the killings: it was the gun he'd been given. When he was shooting, he took his mind to a better place. Some of the other Trawnikis seemed to enjoy what they were doing. Not Mykhail. Nor did he hate it. He just did it. He aimed and pulled the trigger like he was back on the farm in Dyovsta destroying pests. He considered himself a non-human.

Self-preservation was everything.

Chapter 25

After welcoming the advancing Soviet troops, Asher and the Malinowskis rejoiced at the land being Polish once more. Asher stayed on the farm for a few more days, but was soon conscripted into the Red Army.

But by the summer of 1944 the war in Poland, like the German fighting machine, was on its last legs. Yes, there were battles to fight, but Asher managed to avoid those duties. A few months later, the Soviets took Warsaw, and soon after that, the rest of Poland.

Asher heard that the war was over, but didn't dare believe it. It had been five and a half years since he'd witnessed those bombs dropping on Warsaw. The war had cost him his family and had effectively left him homeless—without a country as much as without a home.

Was he ready to believe this was the end?

He read the newspapers, listened to the radio, and got his papers to leave the army. So yes, the war really was over, Asher's obligations to the Red Army were fulfilled, and before he knew it, he found himself being deposited in Kiev.

Kiev was, after all, the capital city of Asher's country of birth, and as good a home as any, but only on a temporary basis. Returning to Dyovsta was an option, and there was a lure, he had to admit—a burn of nostalgia. But would Mykhail and his parents still be there after nine turbulent years? If so, would they welcome Asher? Would they even recognize him? And how would he settle there with no job and no property?

No. He had so many happy memories of Dyovsta and of Mykhail, perhaps it would be better to keep it that way. And he had another home—one of even happier memories, as well as bitter ones. There was a time he'd been content in Warsaw. Before the wall went up. And there was a compelling urge to find out what had become of Izabella. If he found her, they would talk and he would find out whether she still wanted to marry him. Now the war was over there was no barrier to them being together. He would have to be brave—he could no longer live on his dreams of her; he would find out whether those dreams were realistic.

So Asher found work repairing tractors in Kiev, and by summer 1946 had saved enough money to board a train bound for Warsaw.

But sitting on the train, he was having second thoughts. Perhaps he was wasting his time. Had he and Izabella really been in love? Perhaps it was only the closest thing to love they could find. Had she really been honest with him about wanting to be with him when the war was over? By now she could be a completely different person. She might not even be alive.

Every permutation of every possibility whirled around in his mind, one moment urging him to stay on the train and find out, the next moment telling him to get off—to leave his sweet memories of Izabella to be savored in future years like fine wine.

The jolt of the train made his decision for him, and for the briefest moment the jolt took him back to that other train ride—the one departing Warsaw.

An old man struck up conversation, and within a few minutes they were chatting about what they did for a living, whether tractors really were better than horses, moving on to how hard the next winter would be and what might happen to the price of vodka. And Asher's reservations were forgotten. He was on his way to Warsaw.

◆ ◆ ◆

The journey took a day and night—a sleepless one for Asher—but on a still Saturday morning he stepped off the train and set foot on Warsaw ground. He gasped, partly at the fresh, cooler air, and partly at his memories of this place. His first few steps were staggers.

"Careful!" the old man said, his grin showing Asher yet again all eight of his brown pegs. "I'm not strong enough to hold you up. Are you okay?"

"I'm sorry. Yes, I'm fine, thank you."

"You don't look fine." The man glanced around at the scene Asher was scanning. "I guessed from what you said last night that you've been here before—in less pleasant times and more dangerous circumstances."

Asher nodded. "I'm a little frightened, if I'm honest."

"Listen to me," the man said. "Walk quickly. Get where you want to go. Don't dwell, don't pause for thought, don't stop to admire. That will only make you think back. You're still a young man and you need to think of your future. Concentrate on where you're going, not where you've come from."

"Thank you. I'll try to do that. It was . . . nice knowing you."

"Good luck."

Asher set off, only glancing at the square, which had been the meeting point not too long ago, shaking from his mind the memories of him and Rina chewing on raw potatoes in the rain. He headed for Café Baran—or where it used to be. But forgetting his horrible time in this place was easier said than done. The reminders were all around. Even the wall was mostly still standing, holes smashed in it at intervals to allow the free access that so many had died trying to achieve a few years ago.

As he carried on, he allowed himself to think where he and Izabella might live together. What if she wanted to stay in Warsaw? Could he bear to stay in this place, with so many images haunting him? What if they argued about it?

After twenty minutes, he turned the corner, and felt weak at the sight of it. It was different now, with a new awning, different tables and chairs arranged outside, different menu signs. But it was still called Café Baran.

He slowly wandered up to the door, his head feeling light and dizzy, and stepped inside. His first sight was of the corner where Izabella used to play the music that had enchanted him so much. In her place was just another table and chairs.

He breathed a little more easily and looked around. The interior had hardly changed. Well, *of course* it had hardly changed; it had been refurbished only six years ago by his own hands, among others.

"Table for one, sir?"

Asher turned around, slightly startled, and cleared his throat. "Is the owner of this café here?"

The young man shrugged as he wiped his hands on his apron. Asher's lack of reaction must have told him this answer wasn't enough. "You could ask the manager." He pointed to another man, slightly older, carrying plates behind the counter.

This was better. The man looked vaguely familiar.

"Hello," Asher said to him. "I'm looking for Izabella."

"Izabella who?"

"Izabella Baran. She used to play the violin here." Asher glanced to the corner. "Just over there."

The man set down the plates he was carrying and stared into space for a moment. He started nodding very slowly and a sad smile spread across his face. "Ah, yes. Izabella."

"You remember her?"

"Of course, now you mention it. Very happy days, when I was just fifteen and Mr. and Mrs. Baran owned the place."

"Do you know where I can find her?"

The man shook his head. "New owners. She has nothing to do with the place now." He turned to the side. "Magda!" he shouted to the other end of the counter. A middle-aged woman looked up. He beckoned her over. "You must remember Izabella, the violinist?"

"Of course I do, so beautiful."

"Do you know where she lives?" Asher said.

She shook her head. "I'm sorry."

"Oh."

"But I occasionally see her buying food for her family at the Banacha. Do you know where that is?"

"The market? Yes. I . . . I used to live in Warsaw."

"Try there. Saturday or Sunday mornings."

Three hours later, Asher had given up looking, although not for good. He took a break, eating at a café—but not Café Baran because he found the prospect of returning there disturbing, taking him back to the time it was a mere ruin. And he thought. And what he thought was that something was niggling at him, something Magda or the man at the café had said.

No, it didn't matter. He dismissed the thought.

He returned to mingle with the crowds at the market, searching, but still he found no Izabella. He'd already considered that the council offices might know her address. But they would be unlikely to give any details to a strange man, and besides they were closed until Monday.

He settled into a cheap hostel, slept soundly, and waited for the market to open. But he felt unable—too impatient—to wait in the hostel, so walked halfway toward the apartment he'd moved into in 1936, before deciding against the idea. He bought a pastry from a street seller, sat on a bench to eat, then returned to the market, checking clocks along the way.

He was early, so the market was quiet, half the traders still setting up their stalls, talking with each other, arranging their fruit, vegetables, bread, and meat.

And there she was.

There was no mistaking her beauty. That long coal-black hair contrasted against pure white skin, the warm brown eyes, the petite strawberry lips, the strong nose. Asher wanted to look away and look back, to be sure he wasn't dreaming, but his eyes were under the control of some other force.

He walked toward her, his eyes locked and unblinking. This was Izabella. She was alive, and he had found her. He could finally kiss her as he had done many years ago. She was alive, and he would talk and she would talk, and they would rekindle their love and they would look back on sadder times and perhaps—just perhaps—look forward to better times together.

And then Izabella looked down, at the baby carriage her hand was holding on to. She reached in and picked the infant out, clasping it to her chest. She kissed the baby's head, rocking the precious bundle slowly from side to side.

Then a man appeared behind Izabella, placing an arm around her shoulders. His other hand stroked the baby's forehead, pushing aside a lock of hair. He leaned over and kissed the baby.

Asher stopped walking.

Of course. Now he remembered. The woman in the café. Magda. She'd said she'd seen Izabella out shopping for her family. *Her family.*

Asher felt weak, and turned his back on Izabella so she wouldn't see his face if he were to fall. He stumbled, took a few deep breaths, and started running haphazardly, knocking stalls askew along the way.

Twenty minutes later, he was on the platform, waiting for the train back to Kiev, thoughts of Izabella still whirling in his mind. He could have spoken to her, he could have asked how she was and how she'd escaped the walled sector, but without a doubt he would have then told her he was still in love with her, and how would she have replied to that? What *could* she have said with her husband standing next to her. No, it was better to keep his memories, and not to break the spell.

On the way back Asher cursed himself and his stupidity. He could have talked to her, at least exchanged polite conversation. He *should* have talked to her. But no; he was on his way back to Kiev.

He would have to be content with mere memories of Izabella.

Chapter 26

Pittsburgh and Detroit, 1997

The Troy Hill neighborhood of Pittsburgh, on the north side of the Allegheny River, boasted houses of varying designs and colors, all packed together like they trusted one another with their lives. Accompanied by a well-judged smattering of trees, it could almost have been a pretty village in some hidden corner of Europe.

A car pulled up into the driveway of 38 Hartmann Way, a modest but smartly kept house, and the car door opened.

Michael Peterson swung his legs to the side. He was sprightly for his seventy-four years of age, but still had to grunt a little as he grabbed the door pillar to pull himself out.

He walked up to the front door and pulled out his house key, but the door opened and his head jerked back with a little surprise. It wasn't a big issue as he didn't live alone; it just caught him off guard. For a second it occurred to him that he was becoming rather easy to spook in his senior years.

"Hi, Diane," he said in an accent that was almost completely apple-pie American. Almost. He took a step toward her, then stopped. "Diane? What's wrong?"

"I didn't want you just coming inside, Father, and . . . I thought it best if . . . Look, some people are here to see you." She stood aside.

He looked up and down the street, looking for what, he wasn't quite sure—just something out of the ordinary, something that might explain his daughter's worried expression.

When he stepped into the living room, two men in dark gray suits stood up. He gulped and took a step back, but all they did was smile at him.

"Michael Peterson?" one of them asked.

He nodded.

"Lieutenants Schneider and Gomez. Office of Special Investigations."

"Office of *what?*"

Both men got out their badges and showed him. "It's a unit of the Department of Justice. We need to talk to you."

He shrugged. "So talk."

"Uh, at the police station."

"What? Now?"

"Yes, sir. Whenever you're ready."

"What's it about?"

Schneider glanced at Diane. "Better if we tell you down at the station."

"It's okay," Michael replied. "She's my daughter. She's my one and only. You can speak in front of her. I have nothing to hide."

"As you wish," Schneider said with some uncertainty. "We need to formally interview you regarding allegations of war crimes."

He almost dropped his shopping bag, but turned and placed it on the couch. "Say that again."

Schneider displayed an embarrassed smile. "It really would be better for everybody if we talked to you down at the police station."

"You said 'war crimes'. You did, didn't you?"

"Yes, sir."

"But . . ." He sat in a heap, right on the bag he'd just put down. "War crimes? Me? This is madness."

"We just have some questions to ask you, that's all. We're here so we can talk about it, and so you can have your say about the allegations."

"He's never harmed anyone in his life," Diane said.

"I even put the catch back in when I go fishing," Michael said, then turned to his daughter. "Isn't that right, Diane?"

"It must be a case of mistaken identity," she said to the gray-suited men.

But the men said nothing. They just stood next to her father.

"All right," Michael said, pulling himself back onto his feet. "How long will it take?"

"I guess that depends on the outcome," Schneider said.

Meanwhile, two hundred miles away on the other side of Lake Erie, Asher Kogan was at home in Detroit, beginning his well-rehearsed morning routine. He listened to the radio while he made his breakfast of hot oatmeal with a pat of butter, followed by a handful of blueberries. Then he prepared potatoes for his potato soup lunch—just one serving—and then grabbed his reading glasses, put on his hat and coat, and left the house.

He pulled the door to and locked the padlock, which fixed the chain, which kept the door bound to the doorframe of his shack of a house. As if there were anything worth stealing.

Asher had been living much like this for the last fifteen of his seventy-four years. The five years before that he didn't like to even think about, let alone talk about. Now his life was the way he liked it: simple, unadorned, uncomplicated. Like oatmeal.

He started walking.

As usual on a Monday morning, he headed for the local library to read the weekend newspapers. It was much cheaper that way.

His route took him along the shadier edge of the local park, where the homeless hung out, their lives' possessions covered by a tarp. He scuttled past the area as briskly as his worn-out knees allowed.

Soon he was at the library.

He liked it there. It was quiet, peaceful, and warm. He'd made a few friends there, but for conversation they would visit a nearby coffee shop. He'd tried them all and knew the cheapest ones. It was always him and one other friend. Only the one at a time, because any more than that was just too many people to talk to and too much to take in.

Today it was Arnie, who just like Asher had worked for Ford at Dearborn, although they'd never met at that sprawling town of a factory that had sucked in all and any labor it could get after the war—and spent the next few decades spitting it out.

They talked about old times, when Henry Ford's blue oval was more like a national flag, then Asher went back to the library to read some more.

At midday, he left and headed for the Marist Center soup kitchen—known locally as the Catholic Club. Like most days, he did a shift there, serving the homeless and cleaning up afterward. The Catholic Club had kept him alive for those five years he never talked about, so he liked to return the favor. Then he headed home, hurrying past that part of the local park again. Back behind his padlock, he switched the radio on and started heating up his potato soup.

Later that same day, at Zone One Police Station, Pittsburgh, Schneider switched off the tape recorder and said, "You're free to go, Mr. Peterson."

"Is that it?" Michael replied.

"For now. We'll be in touch."

"But I've told you everything. You've got my goddamn life story here."

Schneider just coughed, and looked at Gomez.

"I mean, are you gonna charge me or not?"

"Uh . . . It doesn't quite work that way—not with charges of this kind. We have to discuss the interview tapes with our specialists."

"So when do I get to hear what they say?"

"I can't tell you that, sir."

"And when do I get my passport back?"

"I'm afraid I can't help you with that either."

Michael let out a long sigh. "Well, can you tell me who made these allegations?"

"Sorry. No."

"You're very helpful. Has anyone ever told you that?"

They all stood up.

"I'll just see you out, Mr. Peterson."

"Your kindness is stifling."

"And remember to come here in person and let us know if you intend to stay away from your home overnight for any reason."

"How 'bout I give you a call whenever I go to the can?"

"No, sir. Only if you—"

"Yeah, yeah. I get it. You gonna let me out now or what?"

One signature and two security doors later, he heard, "You're free to go now, sir."

"And you're free to go to hell," he muttered, but only after he'd turned and taken a few steps toward the door.

Outside it was starting to darken, so the flash made him yelp and lift his hands up as if to defend himself.

"Hey! What the hell . . ."

Another flash made him squeeze his eyes shut. His reactions weren't what they used to be.

By the time he'd gathered his senses together, the man and his camera were fifty yards away. All Michael could do was send some profanities in his direction.

The next Monday, Asher started his usual routine. Oatmeal followed by a handful of blueberries for breakfast. Prepare lunch—potato soup for one. Then out into the big bad world and a slow walk to the library, speeding up for the park section.

At the library, he headed straight for the newspapers and put his reading glasses on.

He always read through the previous day's *New York Times*—at least, he read through the national news, international news, health, food, weather, and arts. But sports, showbiz tittle-tattle, fashion, and the rest? *Ah, who cared?* He used to read the technology and science sections to keep up with progress, but didn't any longer because—

Damn! He laughed to himself, because there was no point getting angry. Someone had beaten him to it. There was no *New York Times*. He stalked up and down, peering over people's shoulders to find the guilty party.

But that person had clearly taken their guilt home—along with the goddamn *New York Times*.

Why did people steal newspapers? This was a public library. As in, *for the public*.

He sighed quietly and returned to the rack of papers. Three hours to kill. But that was always the life of the penniless.

He took a minute to peruse the various newspapers and the magazines about computers and music and . . .

The *Detroit News*. He hadn't read that in a while. That would do. But then something else caught his eye. It was the *Detroit Jewish News*. Even longer since he'd read that one. And quite a while since he'd thought of himself as Jewish.

For a second, Asher was a young boy again, his playground the expansive Ukrainian prairies, with seas of shimmering wheat dotted with whitewashed farmhouses. But that was so long ago it felt like three or four lifetimes had passed rather than merely one. Back then, in the 1930s, he didn't even speak English. He'd spoken Yiddish half the time, Russian half the time, and Ukrainian half the time.

Ha!

Well, it was funny in the 1930s.

He sat down with the *Detroit Jewish News*—the warm-up read.

Hell, he was out of touch. It had been a while. Some plans for a new synagogue. An interview with some young pop star.

He turned another page. Some politician on the receiving end of anti-Semitic slurs. Nuclear weapons in the Middle East.

Then another page. There he stopped. In a second, his mouth turned dry, his face burned, and his hairs bristled. He gulped and almost stopped breathing, then tilted the page toward the light.

The brightness perfectly complemented the expression of the man in the photograph. He looked scared, clearly flinching at the shock of the flash.

Asher stared at the photograph for five minutes. It was a long time to stare at one image, but then again, it had *been* a long time.

And the name. The name was . . .

A minute later, the newspaper was folded up inside Asher's coat and he was casually walking past the counter, smiling and nodding politely as he headed for the door.

When the fresh air hit him he almost collapsed with fear. He'd always been a good boy. He'd never stolen anything in his life. Not until now.

He passed the park, walked up to his house, unlocked the padlock around the frame of his front door, and he was inside. Sanctuary. Today the Catholic Club would have to cope without him. That felt a worse crime than stealing the newspaper.

He hurriedly put his reading glasses back on, sat down at the kitchen table, and unfolded the newspaper. He flattened it against the tabletop and looked at the photograph again. It was still the same picture, but now he was on home turf his mind was working a little better. Now he could read and think properly.

He read the article until it quoted the name—the same name that was in the caption. It said the man was Michael Peterson. Except it didn't say it was Michael Peterson, it said it was "Michael Peterson, who was interviewed Monday regarding historic war crimes,"

"Michael Peterson," Asher said to the cold potato soup. "Michael Peterson . . . Mykhail Petrenko."

He read the article all the way to the bottom three times, then stared at the photo. The face in general was vaguely familiar, but there was one huge pull for Asher, a feature he could hardly drag his attention away from. It meant there could be no mistake. Under the man's left eye there was a distinctive vertical scar, cutting the bag under that eye in half.

"Pittsburgh," he muttered. "Hmm . . ."

It took no more than a few minutes to decide.

He grabbed a paring knife, went up to the bedroom, and pulled the linen closet away from the wall. He shoved the knife between two floorboards so one section popped out.

Then the old candy tin was in his hands.

It was hardly worthy of the words *life savings*, but it was all he had. And what else was he going to spend it on—more potatoes? No, it wasn't much, but it would certainly run to a bus ticket and a night or two in Pittsburgh.

He'd seen it in the movies. If he went there, any phone booth would have a local directory. And how many people called Michael Peterson could there be in Pittsburgh?

He left the house, grabbed a plain chicken sandwich for his journey, and headed for the bus depot.

It was a long journey, and as the daylight fell away, his mind wandered to a better world—a simpler world of farms and horses and harvests and fishing in the local river. And it *was* a better world. Perhaps they had little food, but they had enough. They had so little, yet they had so much. And life was so much simpler then, before . . .

He shivered at his next thought, of a perverted world where blitzkrieg, genocide, and the industry of human extermination were the norm.

He switched the light on above him and adjusted it to point directly at his face. That would keep him awake.

By the time he got to Pittsburgh, Asher was fit for nothing except checking into a cheap hotel and going to bed.

The next morning, after a quick breakfast, Asher asked for the telephone directory. That made much more sense than hanging around phone booths. He returned to his room and looked up every *M. Peterson* in the book.

The newspaper report said this Mr. Peterson was a resident of Pittsburgh city, not the larger metro area. That whittled it down to fourteen of them. But six were female and one was down as *Martyn*.

Seven numbers to call.

He called the first, and heard that he'd reached the voicemail of Matthew and Gillian Peterson.

He tried the second. Malcolm wasn't too amused at being woken up this early.

He checked the third number, and his finger hovered over the phone.

What exactly would he say if the man confirmed his name was Michael? Hell, he'd only just considered that.

Hi there. Is your real name Mykhail by any chance?

What if he hadn't been called that for a few decades? Would he slam the phone down when he heard his real name being uttered? Would he be angry or scared, thinking it was someone asking about these war crimes? If so, then Asher might never find him again.

And Asher didn't want him scared off; he wanted to be friends. Sure, turning up on the doorstep would be more of a shock than a phone call, but he could explain better in person.

He scribbled down the five addresses and checked out.

He bought a pocket map of Pittsburgh and circled the addresses—his targets. Two were way to the south, and it made sense to try the closest ones first, so he took a cab to the Hill District.

He stood in front of the door, his collar suddenly feeling too tight, and took quite a few large breaths. His hand trembled as it knocked on the door.

Asher held his breath when the door opened, and was a little startled when a black man appeared. A very large one.

"Yeah?"

Asher felt his chest tightening, his sticky throat closing up.

The man looked beyond Asher and up and down the street.

"Say, you want somethin', buddy?"

His tone didn't suggest aggression, just no nonsense, but it hinted at a pretty damn scary aggression if the need arose.

"I'm looking for someone called Michael Peterson."

"You found him."

"Oh."

The man shrugged. "And?"

The next moment, Asher felt the man holding his shoulder.

"You okay, old fella?" he said. "You don't seem so good on your feet there."

The man was right. Asher did feel slightly dizzy. He looked more closely at the man. There was no anger in his eyes, just concern.

Asher had to do this. He had to. And the quicker, the better. He took more deep breaths. "I'll be fine," he said. "Thank you for your help. I just . . . made a mistake. I'm sorry I disturbed you."

Ten minutes later, Asher had managed to hail another cab.

"Could you take me to the Troy Hill district please?"

Chapter 27

Pittsburgh, 1997

Michael Peterson had long since finished breakfast. An early riser all his life, he was just back from his morning stroll and was about to settle down, fishing magazine in hand, in the sunroom that was tacked onto the back of the house.

He sat, but found it hard to get comfortable. He tried to read, but found himself scanning the lines without taking anything in. He tried a newspaper instead, but movie reviews or sports scores or what some politician had or hadn't said to "a source" didn't seem to matter. Everything else faded into sepia when you stood accused of something that could wreck your life and destroy everything you'd spent fifty years building up.

Okay, so he'd changed his name when he'd come to this country all those years ago. So what? It avoided all the "How do you spell that?" and "Is that Russian?" crap. It was simpler, goddammit, just SIMPLER. Easier to spell, pronounce, remember, write down. If changing your name to fit in was good enough for Kirk Douglas and Tony Curtis, then it was good enough for him. But the rule seemed to be that unless you were a star, it was assumed you were trying to hide some part of your past.

A few days after the police interview he'd had a legal briefing. He'd been told that any witness statements from that long ago would be torn apart by any half-decent attorney, and that was if it even got to court. As long as there was no physical corroborating evidence, such as photographs or official records, there was no way they would be able to lock him up or extradite him for trial elsewhere. Add the fact that the legislation quoted was relatively new and had little precedent, and there were a hundred and one legal obstacles they could put in the way.

So they said.

But could he trust legal people?

Some music might take his mind off these things. Perhaps a little André Rieu.

He groaned as he pushed himself up and out of the chair, and groaned again as the doorbell went off before he reached his tape player in the kitchen.

The press? he thought as he approached the front door. He'd had one or two of those damn parasites visit him since his picture had appeared in the papers. Then again, it could be the mailman with one of those certified mail things that had to be signed for. He'd received a few of those in the past few days: one from the court, some from his attorney.

He froze.

There's nobody home, whoever you are.

The doorbell went again. He waited, his only movement a chew on a nail. It went a third time. He took a few deep breaths and told himself not to be so damn paranoid. He'd spent decades worrying about every knock at the door and every phone call. He didn't want to go back to those dark days.

He opened the front door and saw an old man. Well, about the same age as him.

"Yes?" he said, but even as he spoke he felt weak and nauseous. The man in front of him had a familiar look about him. His memory was sprinting to catch up and failing badly.

"Mykhail," the man said. And it wasn't a question.

His throat jammed as if something had grabbed it. His eyes flitted to the man's hands, fearful that they might hold something more dangerous than a letter. But they were empty. The man's face, however, held something he wasn't quite sure about.

Asher knew as soon as the door was opened. Time makes hair thin and gray or even absent, it turns skin saggy and sallow, but it does little to the structures underneath. Or the scars. And Asher didn't take his eyes off the face of the man he hadn't seen for over sixty years.

But the man who now preferred to be called Michael didn't speak. Well, that was understandable after all this time.

"Mykhail," he repeated. "It's me, Asher." As he spoke he felt a tear fall from the corner of his eye and wiped it away before holding a hand out.

The man who was really Mykhail pulled back slightly at the gesture, but Asher thought it was probably the shock. And eventually he did hold his hand out to meet Asher's.

"It's so good to see you, my friend," Asher said, smiling.

Mykhail's eyes were blinking, his lower jaw moving aimlessly. "Asher?" he said uncertainly. "But . . . *Asher?*" It looked like he was struggling to breathe. Then he looked Asher up and down. "Is it really you?"

"I hope you don't mind me turning up like this," Asher replied.

Mykhail looked like he was in some sort of trance, until a noisy motorcycle behind Asher broke the spell. He stood aside and said, "You'd . . . better come in."

Ten minutes later, Asher and Mykhail sat themselves down in the sunroom with a cup of coffee each. Asher had recounted how he came across the photograph in the newspaper by complete fluke, and Mykhail had explained that for practical reasons he no longer went by the name Mykhail, and that being Michael Peterson just made life simpler.

Asher laughed. "You'll always be Mykhail Petrenko to me, but I guess it is a bit of a mouthful for the average American. Asher Kogan isn't so bad."

"Okay, I'll make an exception for you. You can call me Mykhail."

"I'm not sure I could do anything else."

"So . . ." Mykhail said, his face stiffening briefly. "A photo in the newspaper, you say? I remember that being taken."

"I recognized you immediately and I couldn't stop myself. Isn't it an incredible coincidence?"

Mykhail nodded thoughtfully.

"After I read the article it just needed a little detective work. You know, I knocked on the door of this huge—"

"It's all lies, you know."

"Uh, what?"

Mykhail pulled his lips back, exposing a flash of yellow teeth. "The case against me. The newspaper story. It's poppycock."

"Oh, of course."

"I have legal people working on the case—not that I really need them."

Asher placed his cup down and clasped his hands as if in prayer. "Mykhail. We haven't met for sixty years, but nobody changes that much, not inside, not the real person. You were a good kid, so you grew up to be a good man. It's probably mistaken identity."

"That's exactly what my daughter says."

"You have a family?"

Michael smiled awkwardly. "I have a daughter, Diane."

"Oh, I see."

"No, no. I'm not widowed. Jenny left me."

Asher's expression didn't quite know what to do. "I'm sorry to hear that," he said.

"That's okay. She's history. I haven't seen her in a long time. Diane stayed with her at first, then said she preferred living with me."

"And she still lives with you?"

"She thought about moving out once or twice, but I don't think she ever seriously wanted to. She's happy here. I still think she needs me, although she'd never admit it."

"It must be good having family?".

Mykhail took a sip of coffee. "Oh, I don't know what I'd do without Diane. Well, yes, I do, but you don't want to hear that. What about you, Asher? Are you married?"

Asher shook his head. "I had a circle of friends when I was younger, when I worked at Dearborn. I . . . uh . . . I had a difficult time a few years back. Now I like to keep life simple." He laughed, and looked Mykhail up and down again. "I just can't believe it. After all these years."

Mykhail smiled and looked Asher in the eye. "I know. I never thought I'd see you again this side of heaven."

"We have a lot of old times to talk about."

Mykhail nodded. "If we can remember them." He laughed. "Tell me, what are your plans for the next few days?"

"I just stopped the night in a hotel and . . ." Asher took a breath. "I was thinking we could talk about the old days. In Dyovsta."

"Mmm . . . the old days." Mykhail thought for a moment, then grinned. "Sure. Of course."

"Good."

Asher looked around the sunroom and glanced back into the living room. The wallpaper was clean and neat, there were photographs and ornaments evenly spaced on shelves and cabinets. It was such a contrast to Asher's own house. "You keep the place nice," he said.

"Well, *Diane* does. You got a place in . . . did you say Detroit?"

Asher nodded. "Nothing as nice as this. Little more than a shack, really."

"Did you drive down here?"

"Bus. Last night. No need for a car most of the time. Like I said, I try to keep life simple."

"Tell me about it. It's this new technology that gets me. I'm happy as I am."

Asher snickered. "You know, it seems after all these years you and me are still pretty much alike."

"Like brothers."

"Close brothers at that." Asher's face turned serious. "You know, I always wondered what happened to you after I left Dyovsta."

"Yeah, well, I spent a lot of time thinking how you got on in Warsaw. It . . . it *was* Warsaw, wasn't it?"

Asher nodded. "Sounds like we have a lot of catching up to do."

"Like I say, I've half forgotten about those days, but . . . how long are you down here for?"

"Until you get bored of me, I guess. I don't have commitments."

"Why don't you stay?"

"Seriously?"

"We have a spare room. Full of junk, but I think there's a bed in there somewhere."

"That's . . . that's very kind of you."

"Like you say, we got a lot of catching up to do."

"So, tell me," Asher said, "what happened to you during the war? How did you end up here?"

"Well . . ." Mykhail gave his bald head a pensive rub. "No. You go first. I'm still in shock at opening my front door to find my oldest buddy standing there. Tell me what you've been up to these past sixty or so years."

Asher shrugged. "As you wish."

And so Asher talked about his difficult early years in Warsaw, about finding Izabella at Café Baran, about the horrible days in the ghetto, and about his days fighting with the resistance, which only ended, he said, when he was captured and sent to Treblinka.

At that point he stopped and gave his old friend a puzzled sideways stare. "Mykhail?" he said. "Are you okay?"

Mykhail breathed out long and hard, then nodded slowly.

"You don't *look* okay. Do you want a glass of water?"

"No," Mykhail croaked. "I'm sorry. It's just the mention of . . . that place."

"Treblinka?"

Mykhail nodded. "I've never been there, you understand, but I've heard of the horrors."

"Heard?" Asher shot out a short laugh. "If only you *had* been there, my friend. It was *beyond* horror. Thousands of bodies—probably hundreds of thousands. The innocents. Probably a few guilty ones too. But no human who ever lived deserved the—"

"Please. You can spare me the details. I've read up since then."

Asher nodded. "Perhaps you're right. Better not to dwell on the details."

"Why not tell me what happened to you after the war?"

"Okay." Asher drew breath and exhaled loudly. "Well, I was something of a lost soul. I went back to Warsaw, to Izabella, but . . ."

"She'd gone?"

"Mmm . . . let's just say it didn't quite work out."

"I'm sorry, Asher."

"You know, she said she wanted to marry me when the war was over."

"Really? She told you that? Wasn't that a little forward in those times?"

"Oh, *she* didn't tell me. *Rina* told me. She said Izabella confided in her one day while they were alone together."

"I can understand your disappointment."

"I'm over it—by about fifty years." He smiled sadly. "So I simply couldn't stay there. And I knew there was nothing left for me in Dyovsta; I hadn't been there since I was thirteen. So I settled in Kiev for a while—at least, I *tried* to. I went back to my old favorite, a job in a tractor factory. Oh, I had grand ambitions of starting a new life there, of kicking those demons and horrible memories out of my mind. But life was hard, and I never felt any sense of belonging; I hardly knew the city. The place was still recovering from being overrun by armies of various flavors. There had been so much destruction over too long a time. There were few opportunities and too many reminders of bad times."

"So when did you come to the land of opportunity?"

"Oh, about two years after the end of the war, as I recall. I still had very few friends in Kiev, but I'd started reading a lot. I came across a story about a huge factory over here that was starting to manufacture tractors by the thousand and needed as much labor as America could supply and then some. And I still liked the idea of spending all my days dealing with the mechanics of those beasts. Also, America was on the other side of the world, so there would be no easy way back. I liked that. It cost every ruble I'd saved to get over here."

"You're talking about Dearborn, I'm guessing?"

Asher nodded. "My career never really took off as well as I thought it might. I wanted to become a professional engineer or scientist, but I think any drive I had was left behind in Warsaw. In any case, the simple life of a production line worker was enough for me. Well, it was enough until I got laid off in the 1970s."

"What did you do then?"

"I survived. That's all that matters. And now I pay my way, have a few friends, just one or two luxuries, and I manage to do a little charity work when I have the time."

"As long as you're happy."

"Oh, that's a work in progress. When you've survived Treblinka, you should never be ungrateful, so I try not to be." He took a long breath in and out. "So that's me done," he concluded. "Now, tell me about *your* journey here."

Mykhail tried to compose himself, but didn't speak for some time, instead blinking and breathing heavily.

"Mykhail? You're trembling. What's wrong?"

"Nothing. Nothing's wrong. You know, I think I will have that glass of water after all."

"Of course, old friend. Where would I find a glass in this kitchen?"

A few minutes later, half the glass of water drunk, Mykhail started talking, slowly at first, but soon gaining momentum.

"There's no way I can match your story," he said. "Let me pitch that one out there first."

"It's not a competition."

"Of course not. Well, as you might imagine, life on the farm continued as best we could manage after your family left. It was tough, but we had big improvements on crop yield year on year. Then, of course, came the German invasion."

"They called it Blitzkrieg, didn't they?"

"My God, it was frightening, the speed they came at us."

"So, what happened when they reached Dyovsta?"

"I was drafted into the Red Army well before that. I saw a lot of action, but we were pushed back and back, eventually as far as Kiev, where we surrendered. I ended up in a POW camp. Such a horrible place, Asher. I can't bear to describe the conditions in there."

"I can understand that. I can guess how it was. Move on, if it upsets you to talk about it."

"Right, well, yes." Mykhail took another gulp of water.

Asher waited, but Mykhail looked up at the clock.

"And?" Asher said.

"You know we've been talking for over an hour?"

"That long?" Asher replied.

"You hungry? I've probably got something in the fridge."

"Well, if you don't mind."

◆ ◆ ◆

Twenty minutes later, they were both sitting at the kitchen table, finishing off the microwaved beef casserole.

"That was delicious," Asher said, scraping the last of the gravy from the plate. "Did you make it?"

"Diane."

"Ah." He placed his spoon down and took a slug of water. "Where were we?" he said.

"What?"

"You were in this POW camp in Kiev."

"Asher, did I ask you whether you ever got married?"

"You did."

"Oh." Mykhail started nodding, then stopped as if something had just occurred to him, and said, "But you didn't really say *why* you didn't marry."

"You want me to explain that?"

Mykhail gave a confused frown. "Uh . . ."

"Surely I told you about Izabella?"

"Really? She's the reason you never got married?"

Asher leaned in and lowered his voice. "Mykhail, old friend, I can trust you, can't I?"

"Sure you can."

"I can be honest?"

"As honest as you want to be. I'm . . . I'm interested. Really."

Asher's jowls seemed to drop a little. "I'm not sure I've ever told anyone this before, but . . ."

"Go on."

"Well, for many years I was kidding myself. It sounds strange after all this time, but I told myself it was somehow disrespectful, even unfair, to have a wife and family when so many others don't even have their lives." He stared into space, gritting his teeth a little. "Even growing old sometimes feels wrong when so many will be forever young."

"You said you were kidding yourself?"

Asher snapped himself out of his trance. "Yes. I was. You see, all that's true—the feelings I have about finding love, feeling bad about surviving—but in my later years I've come to know the truth . . . why I never found a woman. It's because I lost Izabella. I kept thinking I'd get over her one of these years, but while I was busy thinking that, I kinda went and got old."

"I know what you mean, old-timer."

"You know, I feel better for saying that, getting it off my chest." Asher paused, forced a smile onto his face, then said, "Anyhow, come on, tell me how you got out of this POW camp in Kiev."

Mykhail hesitated. "Well, there isn't much to say."

"I know it's a hard thing to talk about, but at least tell me what happened between the POW camp and Pittsburgh."

"Oh, it's very boring. You don't want to know."

"Don't want to know? *Are you kidding me?* Mykhail, tell me how you got out of the camp, how you got to America, why you settled in Pittsburgh."

"Well, I'm not sure I can remember, to be honest."

"It'll come to you. Just start from when you were in the camp."

Mykhail huffed a few times. "Oh . . . uh . . ." He stood up from the table. "Another coffee?"

"Playing for time?" Asher said, laughing. "Getting your story straight?"

Mykhail laughed too. "My friend, sometimes bringing buried memories back to the surface takes a little time."

"Of course. I'm only joking. Take whatever time you need. And yes, I'll have a coffee please."

Mykhail made the coffee in silence, and they returned to the sunroom.

"So?" Asher said.

Mykhail blew across his hot coffee and took a tentative slurp. "Well," he said, "there isn't much I can say. It was such a horrid place. I don't really know how I survived two winters in there. Luck, I guess. I only found out the scale of it much later. Do you know, there were about six million Red Army prisoners in all the camps combined, and about half of them perished there. That's a lot of people. Anyhow, eventually the Red Army liberated us. I was still able-bodied, so after recovery I had to fight again with them. But I kept my head down and managed to stay away from the front line and out of trouble, which wasn't too hard as the Germans were retreating by then."

"So you saw no more active service?"

"Nothing to speak of. I went back to Dyovsta, but found my parents had perished in a German concentration camp. I guess I was a broken man. I'd seen so much horror that I didn't want to stay in Ukraine—especially under Soviet rule. I wanted a better life for myself, and everybody said this country was the land of opportunity, so I aimed for New York."

"When was that?"

"Oh, I can't remember. It's too long ago, but soon after the war. I remember getting to know a few people on the ship over who taught me a few words of English and told me more about America. They told me it was common for immigrants to change their names when coming here, to make them easier to spell and pronounce. It seemed obvious I should choose *Michael Peterson*."

"And Pittsburgh?"

"Well, as they say, everybody's gotta live someplace. I spent a year in New York, training as a car mechanic and learning English. I think

I heard Pittsburgh was a steel town and figured there would be a lot of cars here. I had notions of opening my own place—nothing special or ambitious; just auto repairs and servicing—but it never happened, I just carried on being a grease monkey. But I married Jenny, who gave me a daughter and then divorced me. Then I, uh, carried on working. When I stopped doing that, I retired. And that's where you come into the story, knocking on my door and surprising the hell out of me." He let out a long sigh and lifted the coffee to his lips.

"You're right," Asher said.

Mykhail frowned as he swallowed. "About what?" he said.

"It *is* boring."

Both men stared, stony-faced, at each other for a few seconds.

Then they burst out laughing.

"I think it's a shame," Asher said as their laughter subsided.

"You surprising the hell out of me?"

"No. It's a shame when a marriage . . . I mean . . ." Asher shook his head.

"No, go on. What is it?"

"Well, if it's not too personal a question . . . what the hell happened?"

Mykhail shrugged. "I guess we just grew apart."

"I hear that a lot. What does it mean?"

"It's no big deal," Mykhail said, then waited, as though that was a complete answer. But Asher just stared, so he continued. "We started out okay. We were happy for a few years. Then in time we wanted different things, so we started to live different lives. She had her circle of friends and I had mine, and after a while there was nothing between us, so I guess we . . . we stopped caring about each other."

Asher nodded slowly. "I see."

"Good, because it's the best explanation you're gonna get. Anyhow, in the end it was quite amicable. Like I say, it's no big deal."

They drank their coffees, and the conversation turned to which sports they followed, what vacations they'd had, and what their dream cars over the years had been. Mykhail did most of the talking for all of those.

Eventually, Asher checked his watch and drew a sharp breath. "Look, my bus is due to leave in forty minutes. Are you absolutely sure I can stay here?"

"I said so, didn't I? And we've still got lots of catching up to do."

"Well, thank you again," Asher said with a hint of a gracious bow. "You're really being so hospitable."

"Ah, it's nothing. You're an old buddy."

"You know, Mykhail, I'm so glad I came across you again."

"Me too."

"And isn't it good we can talk like this, about our love lives, when we've just met up again?"

"What else would you expect?" Mykhail said. "We're brothers in all but blood."

Chapter 28

Diane had just spent her second day listening to Asher. He'd told her about the horrible events both he and her father had experienced during the wartime years, and everything she didn't know leading up to the time they'd met again in 1997.

"I know that part," Diane snapped when he started to detail the events of that year. "The newspaper photo. The charges."

"That's right. Except by then he'd changed his name to Michael Peterson."

"Right."

"I guess he didn't tell you about his days at Treblinka?"

Diane had nothing to say to that question. The news—or at least, Asher's allegation—that her father had helped run the gas chambers at Treblinka had left her numb. She was so numb that Asher's retelling of how he'd tracked down her father in 1997 washed over her like an ambient breeze, and at no time did it occur to her to interrupt him or ask questions or even argue the case for her father's innocence; he had, after all, not been charged after being investigated back then.

Equally, when she and Asher were interrupted and told that the day's session would have to end, she could only nod in silent acceptance.

"Diane," Asher said as he stood up to leave, "you have no idea how sorry I am that you had to hear all of that. I hope you understand the reasons for your father's actions."

Still Diane said nothing.

"Tomorrow I'll tell you exactly what happened between myself and your father earlier this year—how we fell out."

Asher waited, looking down at Diane's forlorn figure sitting at the table, until a guard led him away. Diane stayed there a while longer, still trying to come to terms with what she'd just heard, until another guard suggested she leave.

"Of course," she said, then silently walked out of the building.

She called Brad to pick her up and waited in the cool air of the parking lot, her mind burning with thoughts.

Now she had a good idea what they'd fallen out over, and perhaps why Asher had killed her father. It was the information she'd wanted, but a part of her wished she'd settled for a benign ignorance.

As she waited, her thoughts started to brew. It occurred to her that Asher had made a serious allegation with no evidence whatsoever. Yes, he'd told her what had happened, but was it the truth? How could she be sure he wasn't making it all up?

She was still cursing him when Brad arrived to pick her up. He leaned over to open the door, and she jumped in. He drove off. He talked on the way, but Diane only heard discrete, disconnected words; no meaning registered with her. No, she was too preoccupied with turning Asher's story over in her head, gently folding those thoughts over and over, perhaps accepting that he might be right about her father. But even if she accepted Asher's version of the truth, there was something else troubling her: regardless of his confession, Asher still didn't seem the murdering type.

◆　◆　◆

They were both back home—Brad's home—before she realized she hadn't uttered more than a few syllables to him since he'd picked her up. And, being Brad, he hadn't asked for any more than that.

But in the quiet of the living room she felt compelled to say something, to get those spiraling thoughts out of her head before they took control and twisted her mind in knots.

"Brad?"

"What?"

"I . . . uh . . . could I get a drink please?"

"Sure."

"Just a soda please."

"Of course."

They settled on the couch—he at one end, she at the other.

"I don't know how to explain this," she said. "It's too . . ." She took a nervous sip.

"Just . . . say it as it comes." He waited, but it didn't come. "Or just leave it, tell me when you feel—"

"No," she said. "I have to talk. I won't be able to rest until I do."

"Okay. So, did you find out why he killed your father?"

"Not exactly, but I've got a good idea. I'm going in again tomorrow."

"Seriously?"

"It's definitely the last time."

"If he didn't tell you why he killed your father, what *did* he say?"

Diane's eyes were stark and resolute. "He told me some things about my father I found hard to believe."

Brad waited for thirty seconds, not speaking or even daring to drink for fear of missing something. "You don't have to tell me," he said. "I get that certain things have to remain private or secret. He was *your* father, and you were the one who needed to know, not me."

"Part of me needs to tell you, but I guess it's still sinking in and I'm figuring out a way to understand it all. You really wouldn't mind if I didn't tell you?"

He put down his glass and took a few seconds to get himself comfortable, which told Diane it would be one of his longer, speech-like talks. She usually liked them; he was good with words. But just lately, nothing was good.

"Diane, you know how I feel about you. You've stayed over at my place since this whole ugly thing blew up, and I've loved every minute, despite the circumstances. It's the longest period we've been together, apart from vacations, although I've been dating you since 1995."

"Six years. I know."

"The six best years of my life. After three years I asked you to move in with me permanently. You said the time wasn't right, so I waited and asked you again a couple times. And I remember the millennium celebrations, when I took you and your father and Asher to that big party at that swanky French restaurant, when I—"

"Don't, Brad. I can promise you I remember it better than you do. You asked me to marry you and I turned you down. I remember it because it made me cry for all the wrong reasons."

"Point is, that was when I stopped asking you to move in with me. I could say it's been a real hard twenty months since then, but it hasn't; it's been just great. I've known you for fifteen years in all and I like to think I know what makes you tick. But, you know, after all that time I still don't understand the mystical hold your father had on you. Now, he's gone, and I can see it must be terrible for you, but if that means I can start asking you that question again with some purpose, why should I care if you prefer not to tell me why Asher pulled that trigger?"

"That's kind of the problem."

Brad thought for a moment. "I . . . I don't know what you mean."

"Well, just like you think you know me, I've known Asher for a few years. We had days out together—the three of us—and Asher stayed over with us a lot. On one or two occasions, when I was alone with him, he used to tell me about a few incidents from his past. He had some

284

hard times after getting laid off. He didn't go into detail, but I could make a good guess, and I got to know what makes him tick. I think I have a feel for how he reacts. And this week, when he opened up and told me his life story, I learned even more, and . . ."

"And what?"

"Well, a part of me finds it hard to believe he did pull that trigger."

"Excuse me?" Brad's face went rigid, his nostrils twitching with suppressed anger.

"I know the guy. I know it sounds illogical, but I have serious doubts."

"But you told me they have a confession?"

"They do. And the evidence. His blood on the glass door panel that was smashed to break in. His blood and Father's blood all over the grip of the pistol found in the backyard. Paint on his shoe. And they have eyewitnesses."

"Well, isn't that everything apart from a motive?"

"It's all so straightforward, but then again, it isn't. There were one or two things Asher told me that don't add up."

"Such as what?"

"Well, in his younger days he shot a few Nazis."

"Jeez. Really?"

Diane shrugged. "It was the war. I guess it was a way of life."

"Well . . . yeah, I guess so."

"But he said he hated it—that he never got used to the idea that ending any life was acceptable, even the enemy's. And he really doted on Father, thought of him as his brother. I find it hard to accept he'd kill anyone, but kill Father?" She shook her head dolefully.

"Unless he's lying to you about that. Unless he really got a kick out of killing Nazis. Most people would."

"Why would he lie to me about how he found it difficult to kill? Why would he even do that?"

"He might think saying he enjoyed killing would make him sound like a monster."

"But why would he try to make himself appear empathetic and some kind of pacifist, but at the same time take himself to a cop station and confess to murder? If he'd just got on the bus home to Detroit that night, he might easily have gotten away with it. You do realize that, don't you?"

Brad didn't reply, just thought.

"Surely you can see that something here doesn't make sense?"

"I can. And I can see this whole thing is tearing you up. You haven't slept properly for days."

Diane felt her eyes grow weary at the observation, almost self-fulfilling.

"Why not give it a break? You should try to get back to your normal routine just a little bit. Why not relax and let me cook?"

She let out a long sigh. "Sure. Thanks. Perhaps I could do with a little normal right now."

◆ ◆ ◆

Brad cooked pasta, while Diane showered off the smell of the jail. They ate listening to Easy Hits FM, then tried to watch a movie, but had to admit defeat when Diane couldn't keep her eyes open.

"Been a hard few days for you," Brad said as he turned the bedroom light out a few minutes later.

Diane didn't reply, just lay back on the bed and closed her eyes to the mess of the world outside. She felt her shoulder being stroked, and moved across, letting his arm encase her shoulders, her head resting on his chest, her hand absentmindedly caressing his belly.

Then she burst into tears, not really knowing why because she hadn't cried once over this whole damn affair. But today she'd learned more about her father's life than ever before.

Brad understood—Brad always understood—and so the bedside lamp stayed off, his mouth stayed shut, and a box of Kleenex appeared in front of her. Most importantly, his arm was still around her shoulders.

A good few minutes of wiping and sniffing later, it was Diane who spoke.

"Have you heard that quote from the Bible?" she said. "The one about the sins of the father being passed down the generations."

"It's bullshit," he said, the profanity rare for him. "And whatever your father did, whatever it was that provoked Asher to kill him—"

"If he did kill him," Diane said as Brad paused for breath.

"As you wish, *if he did*. But whatever sins or crimes your father committed, I don't care. They were his. Not yours."

"Not that simple."

"How so?"

"After talking to Asher today, I understand a lot more now about Father. And Mother. How it affected me."

"You mean, like, the breakup?"

Diane didn't reply, prompting Brad to ask if she was upset again.

"I'm good," she said. "But thanks for asking."

"I guess you're right. It can never be that simple. If you're not ready to tell me about what happened to your father in the war, can you tell me about your parents' split? Don't think you have to, but . . ."

"You know, I think I should."

Diane put the bedside lamp on and eased herself up to sit cross-legged on her side of the bed. Brad turned to face her. He went to speak, but she shushed him. "Just listen," she said.

She waited, gathering her thoughts before speaking again.

"I didn't realize what was going on at the time. I guess a lot of kids don't. And although I was sixteen, a kid is exactly what I was; I just didn't realize it. Just like our neighbors I'd heard the arguments, but when it came to a head it was such a shock, I'm surprised my hair didn't turn white. I went to stay with Mother, and she told me all about it. She said it happened gradually over about ten years, so gradually that it was hard for her to see, let alone control. Every argument they had she ended up giving in just a little more. He wanted to know exactly where she was going and when and who else would be there. He wanted to know the names and details of every man she worked with. But she had good friends, and in time she fought back. In the end she got stronger, and neither of them would give in. I remember Father packing me off to summer camp, and when I returned Mother was gone."

"But . . . wasn't that a good thing? Protecting you from the fallout?"

Diane shook her head. "I only found out later what had happened. She wanted to go out to the movies with a coworker, and he wouldn't let her. She told him to go to hell, that she was going out whether he liked it or not. And when she came back he locked her in the house for three days."

Brad stared open-mouthed at her.

"Yeah," Diane said. "I would have been a bit inconvenient in the middle of that."

Brad shaped his mouth to speak, but it took some time for any words to come. "I'm confused. I knew your father for a long time—at least, I *thought* I did. He never seemed like that."

"That all happened a long time ago. And he's good at pretending."

"But . . . I mean, no disrespect to your mother, but these things have a habit of being exaggerated. I mean, locking her in the house? Really?"

"I was there a few weeks later when the cops came and cautioned him about it."

Brad nodded. "I'm sorry. Jeez. So why the hell did you stay with him? Why didn't you stay with your mother?"

"I tried. God, I tried. After the split I went to stay with Mother but promised Father I'd come stay with him, and when I did he . . ."

"What, Diane? What is it?"

"He said he couldn't live alone, that everyone else had left him, and if I did, he'd . . ."

"What?"

"He'd . . . shoot himself."

"God. That makes it *worse*, not better. Another reason to move out."

"I was sixteen when he said that, Brad. *Sixteen*. And, hell, I loved my father. Whatever else happened he was a *good* father to me and I didn't want to lose him. I told myself he'd get over it in time, promised myself I'd move out before I was twenty. But a few more years passed by. He made it easy to stay and I enjoyed life. Then, somehow, I was almost hitting thirty and the time to act had passed me by, although I tried a couple times and suffered for it. And when all's said and done, I had a good time there. We enjoyed each other's company, watched the same TV shows, and he never stopped me having friends and going out. It just seemed an unwritten agreement that I'd never leave him."

"I'm shocked," Brad replied. "I don't mind admitting it, but I guess I come from a . . ."

"Normal family?"

"Hey. Don't say that."

"It's okay," Diane said. "Don't be so polite." She leaned over and kissed him softly on the lips. "And thank you," she said.

"For what?"

"Asking me to move in permanently. But I need a little more time."

"Of course."

"Just a little. Now let's get some sleep." She turned the light out and they settled side by side.

"I'll try," Brad said. "But sleeping after what I've just heard isn't going to be easy."

"It's all said now. I've got it all out in the open. Relax."

Brad's arm tightened up a notch around her. It was welcome support in the sleepless hours she endured that night.

She tried to banish them, but the arguments she'd had with her father—the ones she hadn't told Brad about—wouldn't stop spinning around inside her head.

"I remember what you did to Mother."

"It was a long time ago."

"She warned me what you were like."

"I'm not like that with you. I love you, Diane."

"You love me still living at home. It's not the same thing. It's like Mother all over again."

"Do I open your mail?"

"No, but—"

"Have I ever stopped you having friends?"

"You know what I'm talking about. I tried to move out, get a place of my own, have a measure of independence. It took me until I was thirty. You said I was being ripped off for rent, that it was so cramped you wouldn't let a rabbit live there."

"And I was right."

"And I gave in to you. So the next time, when money wasn't so tight, when I'd spent weeks toughening myself up to tell you I was moving out, all you could do was ask me why I hated you so much."

"Well, why do you? We have a good time, don't we? Do you honestly regret staying with me all these years?"

"I regret not trying harder."

"And have I ever stopped you seeing men?"

"No, but only so long as it never works out, only so long as I end up staying here."

"Take Brad, for instance. Have I ever put you off seeing him? Or any other man?"

"You don't get it, do you? I'm a middle-aged woman who still lives with her father. You don't need to put men off me."

"Well, I'm sorry."

"Not as sorry as I am."

By the time Brad had come on the scene, the threat Diane's father had made—that ultimate one—was long in the past. And whatever the arguments, however harsh the words between them became, Diane would never, ever mention the threat he'd made. She always promised herself that one day she would call his bluff, but she knew she could never live with the consequences if she lost that particular standoff.

Perhaps one day, now that threat had reached its natural expiration date, Diane would be able to tell Brad the complete truth about it.

Or perhaps, even better, one day the memories would slide, and she wouldn't have to.

Chapter 29

Detroit, June 2001

After meeting again in the nineties, Asher and Mykhail got on like the true long-lost brothers they thought of themselves as. No charges were ever brought against Mykhail; the authorities concluded there was insufficient evidence for that. It was something both men were relieved about but didn't like to dwell on. It simply wasn't mentioned. So they called each other every week, and once a month Asher came down to Pittsburgh, staying in the spare room, for a weekend of reminiscing and discussions about the politics of the day.

That had now gone on for four years.

And then, one morning while Asher was busying himself getting ready to go to the library, he had a coughing fit. He'd had a persistent cough for weeks, despite various treatments, but this morning it seemed to take on a life of its own and made him double up in convulsions. He recovered enough to leave the house, but only managed a few steps before falling, clutching his chest.

A neighbor, working on a car in his front yard, was over in seconds. "You okay, bud?" the man inquired.

Asher, his face red and fit to burst, his lungs feeling like they already had, and the pressure squeezing tears from his eyes, just looked up.

The man wiped his hands on a rag as he looked closer. "You got chest pains?"

Asher managed a couple of nods, which sprang the man into action, and two hours later Asher was in hospital, wires and beeping machines his only company. But he managed to get his neighbor to pass the news on to his old friend over in Pittsburgh, who couldn't get up quickly enough, complete with Diane in tow.

Asher was sitting up in bed as they entered. After the exertions of his brisk walk across the large parking lot and through the labyrinth of hospital corridors, Mykhail had to take a seat and rest for a moment before talking. Diane took the opportunity to wish Asher a speedy recovery and show him a few small gifts they'd brought along, then left her father to it.

By now, Mykhail had just about finished coughing to clear his throat. "Jeez, look at us both," he said. "We both have heads as bald as bowling balls, both have chest problems. We might as well be real brothers."

"That's right, mock the afflicted, why don't you?"

"That would be both of us. Anyhow, what's the latest?"

Asher hesitated, then said, "I might have brought you here under false pretenses."

"You're not ill?" Mykhail made a point of looking at the monitoring equipment attached to Asher's body.

"They've checked my heart and it's fine for my age."

"So, what is it? Did they tell you?"

"Oh, sure," Asher said. "But I couldn't even pronounce the words, never mind remember them. It's an infection, but it's not tuberculosis, which is a huge relief."

"Tuberculosis?" Mykhail screwed his face up. "What the hell made you think it could be tuberculosis?" Then his face straightened to a grave expression. "Oh, I'm sorry. Treblinka, right?"

Asher started laughing gently.

"What? What's funny?"

"That would be a convenient excuse. But I have no excuse at all." The furrows in his brow became deeper in an instant. "My friend, when we met up again four years ago there was something I didn't tell you."

"Oh?"

"It's something I've always felt ashamed of, but something there's no point hiding now."

Mykhail gave his head a confused shake. "I honestly have no idea what you're talking about."

"Well, now it's time to tell you. I told you Ford laid me off in the seventies, didn't I?"

"You did. That must have been tough."

"The word doesn't even come close. Anyhow, when that happened, something inside of me broke. I couldn't cope. And I . . ."

"What?" Mykhail leaned in closer.

"I had no family, and all my friends were at Dearborn. When I lost my job I, uh, I started drinking too much. At the time I didn't quite know why, but it was all I felt like doing. Before long I'd drunk my severance pay. But I carried on drinking, and soon after that I became a bum, living on the streets."

"You mean, what they call a homeless person these days?"

"That's right, a dirty hobo, hanging around the local park, sleeping under a tarp, drinking anything alcoholic I could lay my filthy hands on."

Mykhail grimaced. "I'm sorry, Asher. It's not rare, you know. Unemployment does that to people sometimes."

Asher was already shaking his head.

"What? I don't understand."

"Well, it wasn't exactly the unemployment, that's not why I feel ashamed."

"I don't get it. You're talking in riddles here, buddy."

"Shut the door," Asher said.

Mykhail hesitated, but did as his friend asked and sat back down.

"You never had any brothers or sisters, Mykhail, did you?"

"Hey, thanks for pointing that out."

"I'm sorry."

"I'm kidding. What about it?"

"I told you about Rina, right?"

"That she died in . . . in that place, together with the rest of your family. Sure, you told me."

"Was killed, Mykhail, *was killed*. There's an important difference."

"Yes. I'm sorry. Go on."

"You see, I find it easy to say that now. *She was killed*. But in 1946 I couldn't even think it. I knew what had happened to the rest of my family, but it was different for Rina. Even now my mind still drifts back to the last time I saw her, just after we got to Treblinka, when we were being herded like cattle. I can still hear her pleading with me, and I can still hear my own voice assuring her that I won't let them separate us, that I'll die before I allow that . . . The guard says we can see each other after the delousing procedure, so she goes. And I see her being taken away, just a worthless piece of driftwood being carried along by the tide. I tell myself I'll see her soon. But I don't. Not ever."

Mykhail, staying silent, fetched some Kleenex from the dispenser and handed them to Asher, who took a few moments to wipe his face dry.

"And after the war ended and the camp was cleared, I still never felt one hundred percent sure that my poor sister was dead. Of course, I was in denial. There was one small part of my mind that imagined scenarios where she'd escaped or been freed, and somehow had returned to Warsaw. I daydreamed that one day I would find her, but not yet. Even when I was in Kiev, I thought one day in the future I would somehow contact her, but not yet. Not just yet. It was all nonsense, of course, because the only people who survived that cauldron of evil were guards and a few helpers like me who escaped. I knew that but didn't want to believe it, so I told myself I was too busy building tractors and cars to look for her. I told myself that one day I would have the time to track her down. And finally, when the factory laid me off, I realized I now had that time I'd always promised myself. I could have done some research on the place, but I couldn't bring myself to do that because it would break the spell, because I knew precisely what it would tell me. So I had to find something else to do." Asher looked in Mykhail's direction, but through him. "And I did find something else to do. I drank."

"Oh God, Asher. Why didn't you tell me this before?"

"You know the one thing that pulls on my heart more than any other?"

"What?"

"The thing that still churns me up inside is that I never thought something like that would happen to Rina. She was the strongest of women. She, above the rest of my family—including me—could have done something really worthwhile with her life. Yes, I stopped crying for her when I dried out in the seventies, but the feeling is still there. It's just like a crack in a wall that's been papered over."

"That's awful. But . . . you recovered, right? You got yourself off the streets?"

"There's a soup kitchen in Detroit—the Catholic Club. They fed me for years. I'd have died without them, for sure. I met another old war survivor, one from the Vietnam days, who was doing some volunteer work. It took some time, but he got me out from under those tarps and into a house. But I know some of those homeless guys had tuberculosis. I know I'm being irrational, but it's worried me ever since." He took a heavy breath, which turned into a coughing fit.

Mykhail stayed silent for a minute while he recovered, then said, "Hey, buddy. It's no big deal. Not to me. I'm just pleased there's nothing seriously wrong with you. Tell me, what treatment are they giving you for this infection?"

"Strong antibiotics. They say I should be okay in a few months—if not weeks."

"Well, that's good."

"Mykhail, there's something else I have to tell you."

"More?" Mykhail started to laugh but cut it short. "Of course. What?"

"Well, do you remember that millennium celebration we went to?"

Mykhail shrugged. "Uh, yeah. So what?"

"And what I said then?"

"To tell you the truth I was too busy keeping an eye on Diane and that boyfriend of hers. You know he proposed to her? Can you believe that?"

"It's what people do."

"Thankfully she had the sense to turn him down."

"You should give her more freedom, Mykhail. You can't keep her forever."

"Look, never mind telling me what to do. What's your point?"

"I promised myself I would do something. But I guess I just lost my nerve, completely put the idea to the back of my mind. But this chest infection is a warning. I'm getting old. I don't have much time."

"Tell me about it." Mykhail lifted up a hand, its knuckles swollen and the fingers twisted. "These things are useless. I can hardly hold a pen, let alone write. We're both getting older."

"I didn't mean it like that. I mean, I'm running out of time to do stuff."

Mykhail eyed him quizzically. "What are you getting at?"

"I'm going back home."

"Home?"

"Dyovsta—or whatever remains of it."

"You're kidding?" Mykhail struggled to produce more than a croak for a few seconds. "All these years you complain about journeys, and now you're rushed to hospital with chest pains and—"

"I wasn't rushed here, and I'm fine."

"You're not fine. You're still very ill. Shouldn't you be concentrating on getting better rather than planning a vacation to Europe?"

Asher strained to pull himself up into a sitting position. "Mykhail. My little health scare has only served to strengthen my resolve. You know we've talked about this plenty over the years—returning to see what's left of the old farm and the village center."

"No, Asher. *You've* whined on about it once or twice, but always accepted you could never afford it, and *I've* always said it was another life that I have fond memories of—memories I don't want to spoil."

"Are you not even curious?"

"A little. But only a little. Accept it, Asher, we're seventy-eight. We're old and our lives are here. The stress of going back there would kill us, especially you, and especially after *this*." Mykhail motioned toward the medical paraphernalia surrounding Asher's bed.

"But that's just it," Asher said. "Now I have to go more than ever."

"What?"

"My mortality has been pointed out to me. My best years are far behind me, and whether it's my chest or my heart or something else, I'm going to die sometime. I might as well die while I'm doing something I want to do."

"Can you afford it?"

Asher shook his head. "I've worked that out. I need to take a few weeks to recover. After that I can get a job, just working at a checkout or something. I don't spend much. I can earn enough money in a few months to pay for a cheap flight, and accommodation shouldn't cost much over there."

"Asher, please, my friend. Stop this. It won't do you any good."

Asher stared straight at him. "I'm not doing it for me."

"But you should rest. You've contracted a serious chest infection, for Christ's sake, not had a tooth extraction. You can't *work*."

"I have to do this, Mykhail. And I'm going to."

Mykhail pursed his lips. "I'll pay," he said quietly.

"You won't, you goddamn idiot."

"*You're* calling *me* an idiot?"

"I was once a beggar, Mykhail. Never again."

"You're not begging; I'm offering—even though I don't think you can cope with the travel and the stress."

"We'll see."

"Okay, okay. Just promise me you'll think about my offer. I really don't want you to go back. But if you're thinking of getting a job to pay for it, talk to me first. I'll pay. And the hotels too. No strings, just a gesture between old friends."

"I'm not a charity case."

"Shut up, won't you? I have a few cents stored away. I can afford it. Just get yourself better first."

Asher looked down, surveying the instruments attached to his decaying body. He glanced at Mykhail out of the corner of his eye. "I'll think about it."

Mykhail smiled and held his hand out. "Brothers in all but blood, remember?"

Asher grabbed his hand and gave it a strong shake. "All but blood."

In July, after many weeks of treatment and recuperation—not to mention a lot of soul-searching—Asher took advantage of Mykhail's offer and flew to Kiev. He killed a little time researching history in the library, then took a train and taxi to Dyovsta.

He meandered through the village, its streets now clogged up with cars, its rural charm now cluttered with shops and adverts for things that hadn't even been invented in 1936. He had a coffee to prepare himself, then headed for the lane leading to his old farmhouse.

Later, back at the hotel he was staying at, he called Mykhail to tell him what he'd seen. He told him about the village center, then Mykhail asked him about the farm.

"There's nothing left," Asher replied.

"Nothing left of what?"

"Well, nothing left of anything. The farmhouses we grew up in, the outbuildings, they just aren't there. It's one enormous field—much bigger than the fields we had in the thirties."

"Really? Nothing?"

"Not one brick."

"My God."

"Even in the village center, the clock tower's about the only thing left from the old days. There are more stores, more houses, and more people." He sighed down the line. "It's . . . it's a bit of a disappointment."

"Did you find out what happened to the villagers during the war?"

"That wasn't a disappointment. Well, more sad than disappointing." His voice broke and wavered a little. "Very few of them survived."

"Really?"

"Once the German forces took over, any who were lazy or difficult were sent to concentration camps, and most of the others died of starvation or disease."

"You mean the crops failed?"

"Oh, the yields were good by all accounts, but the Germans used the food for their own people and let the Ukrainians starve."

Mykhail cursed under his breath. "That's terrible. Awful. And I don't suppose you . . . . you found out what happened to my parents?"

"Now that was interesting."

"Go on."

"This is difficult, Mykhail." The line went quiet for a few moments. "I could have sworn you told me you checked immediately after the war, and found out that they died in concentration camps."

"Oh, yes. Of course. I mean . . . but . . . I wasn't sure, it was a hell of a long time ago and I could have gotten it all wrong."

"Uh . . ."

"Asher? Are you still there?"

"I'm here. It's just that . . . you did get it wrong. Yes, they were sent to a concentration camp. And it's true that millions of Ukrainians—non-Jews—died in those places. But not your parents. They survived. Your father died in 1958, your mother three years later."

Mykhail let out a heavy gasp, but didn't speak.

"Mykhail?"

But there was nothing.

"Are you still there, Mykhail?"

A few seconds later, there was a weak "Yes."

"I'm sorry. It must be hard for you to take. It looks like they spent their later years on the same farm, quite a peaceful existence from what I can gather."

Mykhail took another few seconds to compose himself. "Oh, that's . . . that's good. And it's very good of you to check. Thank you, my friend."

"That's no problem."

Mykhail sniffed and took a few deep breaths. "So, what else is there to do there?"

"Not much. That's why I've decided to visit Treblinka."

The line went silent again.

"Mykhail? Are you still there?"

"What?"

"Are you okay?"

"You didn't tell me you were planning to visit that place."

"I've only just decided."

"But that wasn't part of the agreement."

"What?" Asher stuttered to reply. "What agreement?"

"When I offered to pay for your flight out there."

"Oh, Mykhail. Why are you being like this?"

"I'm only thinking of you, Asher. I'm worried your heart might not take the strain. Why not just stay in good old Ukraine?"

"Because there's not much left of the old Ukraine. You wouldn't even recognize it."

"Or, better still, go to Warsaw instead. Yes, that would be better. Visit Warsaw. Anywhere but Treblinka."

"I have bad memories of Warsaw, Mykhail. You know that."

"But you have even worse memories of Treblinka, surely?"

"Oh, of course, but Treblinka . . . well, that's where my family are. I know it sounds strange, but it's as if I can hear them calling. I really need to visit them."

"At least you have good memories of Warsaw as well as bad ones. You told me you enjoyed many happy days there before they put the wall up—evenings out with your family, meals at the apartment, there was even that café and the violinist girl."

"Oh, I have my memories, for sure, but—"

"Well, go there instead. Going to Treblinka will only upset you. And, of course, you could track down the violinist girl—what was her name?"

"Izabella."

"Yes, Izabella. You could see her again if you went to Warsaw."

"And remind myself of what I could have enjoyed all these years?"

"No, no. To reminisce about your joyful time together, to connect with the better times of your history. If you go to Treblinka . . . well, I hear very little is left there. You'll be on your own."

"I won't be on my own, Mykhail. The rest of my family are there, and I feel I should pay my respects to them. Surely you can see that?"

Asher waited for a reply, but all he could hear was heavy breathing. The longer neither of them spoke, the more he started to accept that Mykhail might have a point. "Well . . ." he said slowly. "I guess it might be good to see what they've done to my old haunts in Warsaw."

"And it would be better to see where your family last lived than where they . . ."

"Mmm . . . you could be right. But I'm tired now. I'm still recovering from the journey."

"Good man, Asher. Listen to me, you go to Warsaw and leave it at that."

"Oh, all right. And I promise I'll come see you as soon as I get back, okay?"

"I'll look forward to that."

"Me too," Asher said.

Chapter 30

The next morning, over a breakfast of orange juice, bagels with cream cheese, and a bowl of oatmeal he had to put in a special order for, Asher came around to the idea. Mykhail had a point: visiting the concentration camp museum would only be torturing himself. He'd spent the best years of his life doing that. No, he'd *wasted* the best years of his life doing that.

Warsaw must have undergone many changes since the war, he figured. Like everywhere else, it was probably so much brighter, happier, and more relaxed—what the marketing people called "vibrant" these days. It would be interesting to find out. And to avoid unnecessary stress, perhaps he should steer clear of where Café Baran used to be. That would be good.

By the time he was washing breakfast down with a cup of coffee, he was positively looking forward to the visit.

He was pleased to find out that the journey was considerably quicker than it had been just after the war. Most people flew that sort of distance these days, but Asher wanted to step off a train and onto the platform again. That might put those demons down. It was still, however, an overnight train, and this time Asher treated his old bones to a sleeper ticket.

When he woke the next morning, he found himself in Warsaw once more, and was pleasantly surprised at the color, the music, the number of shops and the variety of food for sale. This might as well have been a different city, so the memories didn't exactly come flooding back. But in time he spotted things—an ancient church here, an old council building there, a few statues somewhere else—that gave him a sense of place. It felt good. This was still Warsaw, but it had moved on. It made him think that perhaps he should too, and forget what might have been.

He spent the morning visiting the apartment his family had first lived in when they moved here in 1936. But it wasn't there; in its place was a hardware store. He moved on to the other place they'd lived in—that single room within the walled Jewish sector. It had been torn down and replaced by a smooth-faced office block. It made him smile. Yes, Warsaw had certainly moved on.

He wandered along to the streets where Izabella used to play the violin and beg for loose change, effectively begging for her life. At least that street was still there, even if the wall behind it had long gone. If he listened hard enough he could even hear her sweet music. And he was still mesmerized by it.

As for visiting the café—or what remained of it after all this time—he was unsure, almost fearful of his reaction. And he was very tired, even though it was early afternoon. He checked into a hotel and took a nap that lasted until it was time to freshen up for an evening meal.

The next morning, over pancakes and coffee, Asher decided it would be madness not to visit the café. He'd come all this way; it wouldn't do any harm, and might brighten him up. Warsaw had changed so much, and all of it for the better. He got the feeling the more of it he saw, the more good it would do him.

He walked more slowly this time—he'd worn himself out the previous day—but despite his tiredness it didn't take long to reach the part of town Café Baran used to be in. And the first thing he noticed was that it still displayed the name *Café Baran* above it—albeit in a modern typeface. They'd kept the old name. How sweet. It brought a proud smile to his face.

Of course, everything else had changed. The street outside was now pedestrianized. There was no awning on the sidewalk sheltering three or four tables, but a huge marquee tent covering about a dozen bistro tables and chairs. Everything was either frosted glass or brushed steel or white plastic covered in advertising slogans.

He tried to rein in his smile and went inside.

He was met with more frosted glass and brushed steel, but also noticed other things: electric coffee machines, a far greater variety of pastries and cakes, strange vegetarian options, and a hundred different types of coffee, all with exotic names.

Actually, no. No, none of this was strange. It was just like any of the coffee shops back in Detroit or Pittsburgh. It just *felt* strange—strange for Café Baran. His eyes were drawn to the corner, to where Izabella used to play the violin, but saw only another table and chairs. He took a seat, found out that the waitress spoke passable English—much better than Asher's Polish these days—and ordered a coffee. Then he spent a few minutes trying to imagine what the place had been like the first time he'd set foot in it as a boy. He remembered getting the mortar mix on his hands during the refurbishment, and his papa telling him to rinse it off quickly. He remembered Mr. and Mrs. Baran arguing—they often did. He couldn't help but smile as he remembered the grand reopening, when he almost made himself sick by eating too much cake. But, above all else, he remembered the first time he heard that enchanting violin music. Yes, Mykhail had been correct—there *had* been good times here. Before . . .

He took a sip of coffee and wiped away a single tear.

Out of the corner of his eye he saw a waitress—who was clearing up a table—stop for a second and glance at him. Then she went blurry. He hurried to pull a Kleenex from his pocket, dabbed his eyes.

"Are you okay?" the waitress said.

He smiled at her. "I'm perfect, thank you." He took a long breath, then noticed her still looking. "It's just that I was here a long time ago," he continued. "I can remember when the place was actually owned by the Barans. Mr. and Mrs. Baran baking the cakes and serving; their daughter playing the violin to give it a special something."

The waitress frowned and glanced back to the counter, where an older woman was serving.

"What?" Asher said. "What is it?"

"That woman is Katarina Baran. She is the owner."

Asher felt the flesh on his face tighten. He couldn't make sense of it, and expressed this with a grunt, causing her to repeat what she'd just said. He looked at both women in turn, narrowing his eyes to slits.

"I have work to do. I will ask her to come over to see you."

Asher said nothing.

He was still confused when the stream of customers died down to a trickle and the woman at the counter wandered over to Asher and sat down opposite him, smiling warmly.

"Katarina Baran," she said, shaking Asher's hand.

"Asher Kogan."

"I hear you know my mother and father?"

Her face looked familiar; she was about thirty, Asher estimated, with a small but full pair of lips and short-cropped black hair.

"Not exactly," Asher replied. "I'm not sure. I'm a little confused at the moment. What's your father's name?"

"Marek."

Asher repeated the name. "It doesn't ring a bell. But I *did* come here, during the war years. There was a young girl called Izabella who used to play the violin over there." He nodded to the corner of the room.

She frowned. "Izabella?" Within seconds her frown had faded and her eyes lit up. "Ah, yes. I have a great-aunt called Izabella."

Asher gasped, and had to fight to catch his breath. "How old would you say she is?"

"I'm not sure. Mmm . . . she must be well into her seventies by now. She has an apartment not too far from here."

"Dear God," Asher said. He was unable to say more for a minute or so.

"Are you okay?" she said. "Do you need a drink?"

Asher needed a vodka more than ever—a double at that. But he was still dumbstruck.

"Has she lived in Warsaw all her life?" he eventually said.

"I am twenty-nine. I don't know."

Again, Asher didn't know what to say.

"Are you an old friend of hers?"

"You could say that. Tell me, is she married?"

"She was. Her husband, he died."

"Oh, I'm sorry to hear that. And . . . children?"

"No children."

"None? Really? Are you sure?"

Katarina looked back toward the counter. "I have customers now. Would you like to meet my great-aunt?" She took a step away.

Asher's throat locked. He wanted to speak, but could only nod.

Katarina nodded too. "Good. I will give her a call when I get time and tell her you are here. Asher Kogan, did you say?"

"No," Asher said, with more force than he intended, causing a few customers to turn their heads. He lowered his voice. "Please call her, but don't tell her my name. Just tell her I'm an old friend."

Katarina gave him a curious look. "You want me to ask her to meet you, but not tell her who you are? That does not seem fair."

She was right. Asher preferred the "old friend" routine because it wouldn't give Izabella the chance to turn him down. But it was hardly fair. And if she really didn't want to see him, he shouldn't trick her.

"I'm sorry, yes. Please tell her my name. She might not even remember me."

Katarina quickly called her father to get the number, then called her while Asher stood alongside. She spoke Polish, but Asher got the general idea.

"Aunt Izabella. It's Katarina. Yes, Katarina . . . I have a friend of yours here in the café . . . yes, name of Asher Kogan . . . that's right." There was a long pause. Asher held his breath. "Oh, I see . . . uh . . . all right . . . are you sure? All right . . . have it your way."

"She doesn't want to see me?" Asher said when she hung up.

"No. She wants to see you. But she does not believe what I tell her. She is getting the tram right away." She flapped the napkin in Asher's direction. "You better be who you say you are, mister."

Asher sat down.

By the time the slender figure in the long cerise coat appeared in front of the café window and stared through at him, Asher had run through all the possibilities. Would she remember him? Would she believe it was really him? Would there be anger at someone dragging her past up? Or suspicion of his motives for coming back after so long? The paper napkins on the table had come in useful for patting the sweat from his brow.

And by the time she came through the door and approached him, his heart was thumping away at what those Detroit doctors would call "an ill-advised pace."

And then she smiled. It wasn't a big, wide smile—not with that petite mouth—but her eyes joined in to compensate. It was something that hadn't registered all those years ago: the eyes smiled as much as the mouth.

She sat down opposite him, her eyes seemingly trying to cover every pore of skin on his face. Then again, he was doing the same to her. And yes, that hair was still the darkest of blacks. Almost immediately, two fresh coffees were brought to the table.

Izabella spoke a few words in Polish. Asher tried, but the words came slowly and soon there were more frustrated grunts than words, so he reverted to English. Without pausing for breath, Izabella switched to English too. Asher's eyes widened in pleasant surprise.

"I was a language teacher for many years. It's easy to keep up my skills. English is everywhere. You live in Britain now?"

"America. Ever since the war."

She smiled warmly. "Oh, Asher. I couldn't believe it when Katarina told me. But it's you, it really is. And you've hardly changed. Well . . ." She glanced at the top of his head and smirked.

Asher smirked too, and ran a palm over his shiny head. "I must say, I didn't expect your hair to be still so dark."

She leaned in and lowered her voice to a whisper. "It needs a little help these days—but don't tell anyone."

"Whatever you do, it works."

"You know, my mind was racing on the way over here, wondering if it really could be you, and trying to think why you would come back after all these years, what you were like now, and . . . and . . . well, we seem to be getting on as if we'd never parted."

Asher's face dropped a little on hearing the words. "I wasn't sure about coming to meet you either. But it's so good to see you. We have a lot to catch up on."

"We do. So, first of all, tell me what happened to you after I left Warsaw."

Asher drew breath. "The first thing that happened was that I searched high and low for you. I had an idea what happened to you, but didn't want to believe it. How did you get out? One moment you were living with your aunt and her family, the next you'd disappeared."

She thought for a moment. "Oh, yes, now I remember. I told you that, didn't I? I made you turn back halfway when you insisted on walking me home."

"You did. I hated that."

Her hand drifted across to his and covered it, giving it the briefest of squeezes. "I'm sorry, Asher. The truth was I was living on the streets. There was no aunt."

"*On the streets?* My God, why didn't you say so?"

"Does it matter now?"

"No, no. Of course not. I'm sorry. But I guess it does explain one or two things."

"My black hair helped disguise the fact: it didn't show the dirt. But a lot of people lived on the streets in that place—sleeping in doorways at night and begging during the day. Not many with violins, I grant you."

"Ah, the violin. How can I forget your violin-playing? That was how I found you. I heard your music and recognized it from this very café. Do you still play?"

Izabella shook her head firmly. "I've never touched a violin since then. It just has painful . . ."

"Associations?"

"Yes. Does that seem a shame?"

"You and I, Izabella, we're two of the few people living who understand. Anyhow. You were telling me how you got out of the ghetto."

"Oh, yes. Well, one day I was heading to one of my usual begging spots, where I had a few friends I could trust, and I turned the final corner only to see soldiers emptying the place. Everybody there—both inside the buildings and outside in the streets—was being escorted away. I had no idea what was happening. Of course, now I do."

"Did any of your friends survive?"

Izabella's face dropped. "Sadly not."

"Oh, I'm sorry, Izabella."

"A few out of millions. I often thought over the years what might have become of them, just like my own family." She gave a sad smile before continuing. "So I was too scared to go begging again, and hid in the backstreets. I became very ill. That was when some Catholic nuns took pity on me. They dressed me up as one of them and I just walked straight through the checkpoint and out of the Jewish sector forever. I don't remember much about what happened after that, but I went to a hospital and wasn't in a fit state to rebuild my life until well after the war ended. I did think of you, Asher, I promise I did. But I had no way of knowing what happened to you and your family. I assumed . . . you know, Treblinka."

Asher nodded. "Yes, they took us all there."

She gasped and held a hand up to cover her open mouth. "*You survived Treblinka?* How?"

"For me it was pure luck, nothing more. The rest of my family . . . they weren't so lucky."

"Oh, Asher. I'm so sorry. I've never forgotten the Kogans— especially Rina, such a strong woman. But what about you? I mean, very few people got out of that place alive. Did they spare you? Did you escape?"

"I was . . . well . . . please, Izabella. Perhaps in time, but I can't talk about it yet—not in public, at least."

"Of course. I'm sorry." She leaned across and covered his hand with hers.

"And I know it's unfair," he said. "Because I want to know everything about you."

"Oh, my life's been very uneventful since I got out of the ghetto. And, if I'm honest, I like it that way. While I was recovering in hospital, I had some visitors. My brothers and sisters had come back. Then we all lived together for a few years in Warsaw after the war. We thought it would be what our parents wanted, and it made up for lost time."

"You got married, so I hear?" Asher glanced down at her hand, the fingers still slender and elegant, one of them encircled by a ring holding a single clear gem.

"This?" She held it up. "Yes, I still wear it as a reminder. I married Paul in '52, he died three years ago last March."

"I'm sorry to hear that," Asher said. Then he narrowed his eyes to slits. "Did you say 1952?"

"Yes."

"Mmm . . . and . . . children?"

"Oh, we tried for many years, but it just didn't happen. Of course, we didn't have the technology back then, so I can't be certain of the reason, but I always thought the time I was starved behind those walls— my formative years—must have damaged me somehow. Anyhow, it's all in the past. I don't dwell."

"Good," Asher said. "I mean, it's good that you don't dwell. And I'm sorry. But . . ." Asher left his mouth open, struggling to speak, sitting back in his seat, then leaning forward again.

"What?" Izabella said. "What is it?"

"Well . . ." He took a sip of milky coffee to help his dry throat. "I swore to myself that I wasn't going to tell you this, but I came back here before—1946, it must have been."

"Oh?"

"I searched for you."

"Oh, Asher. You're making me cry."

"I'm sorry. But I have to tell you. I came here, and I went to the market—the Banacha. I saw you there . . . and . . ."

"I don't understand, Asher. I don't remember it at all."

He gave his head a sharp shake. "I feel so stupid about it now. And I don't know why because it was such a long time ago. I saw you at the market. I was about to reach you, to take you in my arms and tell you how I felt about you, but . . ."

Izabella pressed a paper napkin underneath her eyes.

". . . I was almost within touching distance, but then you picked a baby up and held it. A man appeared from behind you. He put his arm around you and . . . and I assumed . . ."

"Oh, Asher." Izabella's face contorted in pain, the tears coming freely. "I remember those days well. I'm sorry, Asher. That wasn't my child, and that wasn't my husband."

Asher didn't speak for a few minutes, just took a few breaths. "So, who were they?" he said. "No, I'm sorry, that's personal, I shouldn't ask."

"No, no. Please. I think we're both a little too old for the jealous lover routine, don't you?"

Asher said nothing, just waited while she dried her eyes.

"You see, the man was one of my brothers, Marek. It was the time he and my other brother and my sister all lived together here. Marek got married in '45. Early the next year his wife gave birth to Marek Junior, but she passed away in childbirth. I helped bring up Marek Junior." She glanced around the café. "It was Marek Junior who bought this place back for the Baran family many years ago. Of course, he's not so junior now. The woman over there who called me is Katarina, his daughter."

Asher's gaze hopped between Katarina and Izabella a few times as the news took some time to sink in. "Oh God," he said, his voice trembling. "I feel such a fool."

"Don't punish yourself. You weren't to know."

"But if I'd had just a little more courage, if I hadn't been so weak, who knows what might have happened."

"But that's just it, Asher. Who knows? We both might have had a better life if we'd met then, but we might not. I guess sometimes your decisions in life are made by the sort of person you are. And you always were a shy boy. That was your charm."

"Charm? Is that what you call it?"

"Yes, I do. You used to watch me without speaking. It sounds like it should have been strange, but I didn't think so at the time and I don't now. It was so sweet."

"Strange?" Asher let out a laugh. "That sounds more like me. But forgive me. I'm just feeling sorry for myself."

"Well, don't. Just tell me, how has life turned out for you?"

"So-so."

"Is that it?"

"There isn't much to tell."

"There's that shyness again. Come on, Asher. Did you marry? Have you any children?"

Izabella paused, but Asher didn't speak.

"I'm sorry. Am I being forward, asking about marriage?"

Asher laughed at that.

"What?" Izabella said, laughing along. "What did I say?"

"Nothing. It's just that . . . well, I know you told Rina you wanted to marry me once the war was over."

Izabella frowned at him. "I told her no such thing. I thought it. Of course I *thought* it. I didn't tell anyone. But Rina told me that *you* wanted to marry *me*. She said you confided in her one day when you were alone together at home."

Asher thought for a moment. A tear escaped and ran down his cheek. "Rina," he said, a grin breaking through the sadness. "My dear Rina. She said it to both of us. Played us like fools."

"Ah, I see." Izabella nodded. "Perhaps she knew it was true?"

"And, as it turned out, she was right."

"She certainly was."

Asher picked up his cup. "It's not much, but I raise a toast to Rina."

Their cups touched. "To Rina," Izabella said. They drank and placed their cups back down.

"Listen, Asher, I know you can't talk about certain things—the war. But I want to know everything about you. I'm interested. Life in America must be exciting."

Asher caressed her hand. "It's nice for someone to be interested in me. You're right and wrong. It's not very exciting, but I should tell you."

So Asher did, and once he started talking he couldn't stop. All the details of how he ended up in Detroit, his work at Dearborn, how he met Mykhail again, how Mykhail had changed his name—all things that tumbled from his mouth faster than he could think of them. Izabella also talked, of her happy marriage, her teaching career, and her vacations. Before either of them knew it, almost two hours had passed and they were starting to tire.

"I have to go now," Izabella said, glancing at the wall clock.

The words made Asher's heart skip a beat. "But . . . can we meet again?"

"You know, Asher, it's been lovely talking, and I'd be upset if I didn't see you again."

They arranged to meet up the next day, when they spent hours talking, Izabella taking him to her favorite restaurant for dinner. There they talked even more freely: Izabella of her feelings for her husband and how she missed him, Asher of his difficult issues after he got laid off from Dearborn.

On the third day, they met at Izabella's apartment and spent the day touring the city's museums and art galleries. When they got back to the apartment, Izabella fixed a meal, they relaxed, and Asher started telling her about his experiences at Treblinka all those years ago.

It was on the fourth day that they both decided they wanted to see more of each other—that this week shouldn't be the end. Asher knew he should have felt awful about all those years of missed opportunities, but somehow he didn't. In fact, he was happier than he could ever remember being.

Also on the fourth day, with dark memories swirling around his mind, Asher realized that Mykhail had been wrong about returning to Treblinka.

He made his decision accordingly.

Chapter 31

Pittsburgh, July 2001

Asher rang the doorbell of 38 Hartmann Way. He cursed at the music coming from inside the house and the noise of the kids playing next door, and went around the side into the backyard.

"Hey, Asher," Mykhail said. "Didn't expect to see you yet." He was sitting on a stool, a paint pot perched on a brick next to him. He held a large paintbrush in his hand—the way someone might hold a hammer.

"I did ring," Asher said. "But . . ." He glanced behind him, across the tall wire fence, to where kids were shooting a basketball while apparently making as much noise as humanly possible.

"My music drowns most of that out," Mykhail said, nodding toward the kitchen. "How long have you been back?"

"Oh, I was only home a few hours. I dumped my luggage, grabbed a change of clothing, and caught the bus over." He pointed at the woodwork on the outside of the sunroom. "Keeping the wood rot out, huh?"

Mykhail nodded. "I've painted it every three years ever since moving in. It's become a kind of barometer. Each time it's just that little bit more tiring. Now I find it hard to kneel, let alone paint."

"It's looking good," Asher said.

"It better had, because it's the last time I'll be painting it. Son-of-a-bitch arthritis in my fingers. How was Europe?"

"That's what I need to talk to you about."

Mykhail eyed his brush. "I'm a little busy right now."

"You carry on." He pointed into the kitchen. "Can I get us a coffee?"

"Cold drink would be good. Got some apple juice in the fridge."

Asher went into the kitchen and got the drinks, to the accompaniment of that orchestra.

"Still on the old cassette tapes, huh?" Asher said as he brought the drinks outside a few minutes later.

"Oh, yeah. Diane keeps telling me to buy stuff on these new discs or even some new gizmo in a tiny box. I can't be bothered." He took a sip of apple juice. "So, tell me about Ukraine."

"Oh, finish your painting first."

Mykhail dipped the brush. "I can paint and listen at the same time. Tell me, did you manage to take any photographs of Dyovsta?"

"For what it's worth."

Mykhail kept his eyes on his painting line. "What does that mean?"

"I told you on the phone. The farmhouse buildings we lived in as little ones were demolished long ago. The area's nothing more than one small section of a vast wheatfield."

"And your accommodation?"

"Comfortable."

"And Warsaw?"

"I went there. And I found Izabella."

Mykhail's head jerked around. "Your Izabella? Really?"

Asher nodded silently.

A lopsided smile broke onto Mykhail's face. "So, how is she? Was she happy to see you?"

"She was. It was . . . quite magical."

"I'll bet," Mykhail said as he continued painting.

"It was almost like we'd stayed in touch all these years. We seemed to have so much in common. It was nice."

"I'm really pleased for you, Asher. You deserve some happiness."

"Thanks. We spent four wonderful days together. We swapped life stories. I told her about what happened to me during the war. And when I told her about it, I realized I just had to go."

"Go? Go where?"

"To Treblinka."

Mykhail halted his brush mid-stroke, staring at it. "Oh," he said. "Okay." He carried on, painting in silence for a few seconds.

"Why don't you ask me how I got on there?"

"Sure. How was it?"

Asher was quiet for a few seconds, his nostrils twitching. "Have you ever been there?"

Mykhail didn't look at Asher, but shook his head.

"Not even during the war?"

Now Mykhail turned to Asher. "What are you getting at?"

"It might be better if we sit in the kitchen," Asher said, his voice wavering.

Mykhail shrugged. "Okay." He placed the lid back on the tin and balanced the brush on top. Then he eased himself to his feet with a groan, and motioned for them both to go into the kitchen.

There, Mykhail pressed the stop button on his tape player to silence André Rieu's orchestra. A pained frown drew itself on Asher's face as the two men sat down opposite each other. They each took another sip of juice.

"So, what's this all about?" Mykhail said with a little shrug of his shoulders.

"Well, you remember all those years ago, when I tracked you down to this house?"

Mykhail nodded.

"The story in the newspaper?"

"Yes, but . . . I still don't understand."

"The newspaper report didn't go into great detail, did it?"

"I can't say I remember. It was years ago and it was all nonsense. And I don't see—"

"I never asked you about the allegations that were made against you. I trusted you."

Mykhail sneered slightly, an edge of forced humor showing through. "Where's this going, Asher?"

"I just want you to tell me—"

"You think I lied? Is that it? I'm lying about what I went through during the war?" Mykhail's fingers fumbled to shove up one arm of his shirt. On his upper arm was a section of skin, the only hairless section. He prodded a finger against it, and it wrinkled like the skin of a milk pudding. "Take a look. Go on, take a good look. And then call me a liar."

Asher wiped a nervous hand over his smooth head. "Shall I tell you about my visit to Treblinka?"

Mykhail shrugged. "Only if you want to."

Asher let out a long sigh, took a moment to gather himself, then spoke.

"What they've done with the place is nothing short of a miracle. It's quite beautiful, although there's something wrong about beauty in such ugly circumstances. But it's a very peaceful area, in the middle of a forest. There's a museum with exhibits, but I couldn't face that at first, so I had a walk around the grounds. It was so strange, smelled so fresh and clean—like a pine forest should always smell. And I heard no engines or screams or gunfire or crackles from burning pyres. For a few minutes I was completely alone. I closed my eyes and heard birds high above, calling one another.

"Of course, there wasn't much left of the original camp in terms of buildings or structures. The Nazis saw to that; they wanted to destroy every last shred of evidence so that they could deny it ever existed. But the Poles have done a good job of bringing back the spirit of the place. You know, they have a big area covered by stones sticking up out of the ground—thousands and thousands of them, like nothing you've ever seen. It's a sea of ragged tombstones to represent an ocean of ragged bodies."

Mykhail stared impassively, while Asher took a breath and continued.

"Anyhow, eventually I went to the museum, where they had a film show, maps of the place recreated from the memories of prisoners and staff, and a few artifacts that simply wouldn't stay buried—or perhaps rose to the surface."

"It must have been so hard for you."

"I can't convey how upsetting I found the whole experience. They also had a few photographs."

"Photographs?"

"Yes, of the buildings, some of the prisoners, the bags of hair, the clothes. And a few of the staff."

Mykhail gave a puzzled frown. "I would have expected photography to be banned."

"Oh, it was, officially. But one or two guards wanted mementos for their private collections. Anyhow, I didn't look properly; I wasn't in the right frame of mind to take anything in—too many people around me. So I left the building and took a walk."

"And . . . what did you see there?"

"What did I see? In that beautiful place I heard the sounds of my yesterdays—the noises that still stain the human race but gave me a perverse comfort in my old age. I heard the railroad trucks hissing as they drew up. I heard the shouts from the guards, ordering people to leave their belongings for collection later, and officials telling the innocent and the unaware that the first step was to have a nice shower after their arduous journey, that afterward they would be fed and shown to their living quarters. The hint of a laugh—guards actually *laughing*—as they told people to follow everyone else along the Himmelstrasse. Do you know what that means?"

Mykhail, unblinking, shook his head.

"I heard the mothers consoling their frightened children, telling them to stop crying, telling them everything would be fine, that this was a much nicer place to live in than Warsaw. But the children seemed to know more than their parents—or were more honest.

"And I heard the first murmurs of discontent as they were told to take their clothes off. Spectacles, shoes, pants, dresses—all in different piles for ease of sorting. Now murmurs turned to half-suppressed panic. They stayed calm but were clearly not—with darting eyes, quivering faces, shivering bodies. Questions were asked. But the guards had experienced this many times before and could dismiss them as if they were batting away troublesome moths. Those who kept asking were told by a gun barrel to obey. Discontent turned to naked fear as their heads were shaved. And then to rigid terror as they were marched along the Himmelstrasse.

"They were told to get inside. And that was when the unfettered panic started. Very often the stragglers got the message. They fought, but bayonets silenced their concerns.

"The doors were locked. The signal was given. The engine started. The show was over."

Mykhail stared, almost looking through Asher. Asher took a deep breath and continued.

"I stood at the top of the Himmelstrasse and spent a few minutes doing nothing but looking all around. I wanted to take in the atmosphere. I guess it was a way to connect. I was standing on the very spot where my papa, my mama, and my two sisters last lived—where their hearts gave out their final beats. I like to think there was a little of them with me that day. It was nice. It gave me a little peace.

"Then I returned to the museum building, this time a little more collected of thoughts and calm of nerve, venturing farther along the exhibits. I stopped in front of a display of photographs. Very, very few must have survived. The Nazis tried to obliterate absolutely everything, but one or two people with a conscience—or perhaps with a view to making money—held on to some rare items.

"It was then that I saw it. At first it was merely another one of those wrinkled brown photographs that can be so amusing in different circumstances. But I wasn't in the mood to be amused, of course. I found the whole display very sad. These were all real people—guards, helpers, prisoners. They once had loves and aspirations. All long gone. Most of them.

"One photograph kept pulling my eyes toward it. The young man's face was pointing at the camera. He was almost posing, yet somehow you could tell he was ashamed. I was sure I recognized him, and my mind went back to those days of hell and dread. My mind went through my fellow Totenjuden one by one, and also the guards I got to know. Then I had a realization I didn't want to have. I knew, but didn't want to know. My whole world wanted this to be a mistake on my part, but I knew it wasn't."

Asher could feel Mykhail's stare from across the kitchen table, almost willing him to stop talking. He didn't. He couldn't.

"I had to put on my reading glasses to take a better look, to examine the old photo. It was small, old, and very faint, but the scar under the left eye was definitely there. I couldn't deny it, although I wanted to. As my mind burned, I collapsed and needed help. They had to bring a wheelchair to collect me, and I was taken to a first-aid center of sorts. They were very kind, but I didn't say anything to explain my episode because I couldn't; my mind was elsewhere."

Asher leaned across the table and grabbed Mykhail's shirtsleeve, pulling and grasping. "That's why I need to know, and I'm not leaving this house until you tell me."

"Tell you what?"

"Mykhail. Please. Stop playing for time. I just need to hear it. I need to hear what the charges brought against you in '97 were."

The table jolted as Mykhail pulled his arm away from Asher's grasp. His cheeks flushed a little. "I told you," he barked. "No charges were ever brought against me."

"Okay, okay. So I mean *allegations*. What were the allegations?"

"Does it matter? It was just one man's word, which my attorney discredited immediately. They decided very quickly there was insufficient evidence to proceed with the case."

"But clearly enough evidence for you to get legal people involved."

"Asher, please. The whole thing was a complete fabrication of an unbalanced mind. It was a stupid nonsense story made up by some deluded old man."

Asher paused, taking a few calming breaths. "I need to know. Okay, so it was nonsense, I believe you. Just tell me what this deluded old man said."

"Does it matter?"

"It matters to me."

"Honestly?"

"It matters enough for me to track down the man or the journalist on the case or do whatever is necessary to get to the truth."

Mykhail lowered his voice. "You would go that far? Seriously?"

Asher nodded.

"You trust me that little?"

"*Tell me*, Mykhail! For God's sake, just *tell me!*"

Mykhail thought for a few seconds, then nodded. "Okay," he said. "Okay. If you really need to know, the allegations were that I was a member of staff at a Nazi concentration camp."

"At which camp?"

"I don't know."

"*What?*"

"Does it matter? I was never there anyway. They were no more than nasty allegations."

"But you must remember the details, if only the name of the camp?"

"I've forgotten."

"You can't have. Tell me which camp, Mykhail. *Just tell me!*"

"What does it matter?"

"Just tell me, Mykhail. *For God's sake, TELL ME!*" Asher threw his glass onto the floor, where it shattered.

"Okay, so it was Treblinka. But remember, no charges were ever brought against me. They couldn't prove the allegations were true, because they weren't. Are you happy now?" Mykhail sat back and folded his arms.

Asher nodded slowly, as though weighing up the odds. Then he lifted his head up and leaned forward. "Mykhail. I need to know. I need you to be honest with me." He gulped and beckoned Mykhail closer. "What I'm saying is . . . I need you to look me in the eye and tell me you were never at Treblinka, tell me that isn't you in the photograph— the photograph that's now displayed there."

Mykhail nodded. "Very well." He leaned closer, so his face was inches from Asher's. "All right. I have never, ever been to Treblinka." He sat back and folded his arms again. "Is that good enough for you?"

Asher's face trembled, his lower lip not knowing what to do with itself. "Oh God," he muttered.

Mykhail stayed silent.

"Oh. My. God." Asher stayed there, his eyes locked onto Mykhail's. The two men stared at each other.

"What?" Mykhail snapped eventually. "*What?*"

"LIAR!"

"How can you say that?"

Asher stood up, let the chair fall over, and took a step back. "Mykhail Petrenko, I know you like nobody else does—nobody on the planet—and I know when you're lying."

"*Bullshit* you do."

"Yes. I do."

"So now you can read my mind?"

"Don't, Mykhail, just don't. Please. It was the same when we went fishing together all those years ago and you told those men we hadn't caught anything, and it was the same when you told your papa you put up a fight against them. And a hundred other times. I can't describe it, but I know that expression on your face. I *know*, okay. So please, don't try to deny it any longer."

Mykhail sighed and covered his face with his hands. He stayed like that for a few minutes, then muttered, "Look. It wasn't—"

"DON'T LIE TO ME!" Asher shouted, so loudly he brought on a coughing fit.

Mykhail stayed silent while Asher recovered and spoke again.

"You know, for many years my soul died just a little bit more whenever people tried to replace the truth with wretched falsehood. But I've mellowed. The fire in my belly is merely a handful of glowing embers. But please, Mykhail, don't lie to me. At least, not about this. I know for sure you lied about your parents. You never did go back to Dyovsta when the war ended, did you?"

Mykhail stared at Asher for a few seconds, then looked away. "You know how much that hurts? Knowing if things had been different I could have seen them again?" He shook his head wearily. "But I couldn't go back. It just wasn't possible."

"So it *was* you in that photograph."

Their eyes locked, then Mykhail tilted his head to one side and gave a disconsolate shrug. "What are you going to do?" he said quietly.

"Well . . ." Asher picked up the chair and gently sat down at the table again. "The first thing I'm going to do is listen."

Mykhail looked up, puzzled. "*Listen?*"

"I need to know for myself, Mykhail. I need you to tell me exactly what happened."

"And then what?"

"Look, I give you my word I won't go to the police or the newspapers. I just want to know the truth—how you ended up there."

Mykhail bowed his head and said nothing.

"Mykhail, we're brothers in all but blood. You have to tell me the truth."

"I . . . I . . ." Mykhail groaned and stood up. He stepped over to the sink, splashed his face with cold water a few times.

"Trying to cleanse your soul?" Asher said quietly.

Mykhail sat back down before replying. "You promise you won't tell the authorities?"

"Oh, Mykhail. That's not why I'm doing this. You were my best friend up until we parted in '36, and then again since '97, and you remain my best friend despite this. If it's important to you, I promise I won't do anything to get you arrested or put your name in the newspapers again. Apart from anything else I'd . . ."

Mykhail looked up at him, saw his lower jaw shaking a little.

"It's true," Asher continued. "I wouldn't want to see you locked up, and . . . I'd miss you."

Mykhail exhaled long and hard. "Thank you," he said. "So . . . I guess I owe you an explanation."

"Mykhail, you owe the world an explanation."

"Well, let me tell you—tell you the whole story. The complete truth."

"I'd be forever grateful. I only want to understand, nothing more."

Mykhail drew breath. "Everything I've told you up until I became incarcerated in the POW camp in Kiev is the truth. Now I'll tell you what really happened there, how I got out."

"That's all I want—everything you can remember."

"*Remember?*" He shook his head. "Believe me, Asher, it's a door I've kept firmly locked all these years. Keeping it locked has been harder than you could ever imagine, but I've always known what's lurking behind it, those awful memories scratching at the other side like a rabid dog." He covered his face for a few seconds with his hands, then sighed and said, "All right. This is what happened. The truth."

He swallowed half his apple juice in one gulp, took a few seconds to prepare himself, then started speaking again.

"I was offered a deal. I had no idea what it was, except that it would get me out of that wretched camp."

"A deal?"

"I only found out much later what the deal was. Does the word "Trawniki" mean anything to you?"

Asher nodded slowly. "Go on."

"I had very little choice, believe me. I was shunted around and told what to do. And I ended up at Treblinka."

"Treblinka. I see. And . . . what did you do there?"

"I . . . I looked after one of the engines."

"Engines?"

"The engines that produced the fumes."

Asher slowly slid both of his hands over his head. "Dear God," he breathed.

"You have to understand—"

"SHUT UP!"

Neither man said anything for some time. Eventually, Mykhail spoke slowly and quietly, as if his words could injure.

"I'm sure you know what that job entailed. And afterward, when they closed the place down and disbanded the Trawnikis, the men were largely free to wander the streets and make their own way as they saw fit. I walked for miles and hitched lifts, got casual labor in Berlin. I knew the story. I couldn't go back to Ukraine. Trawnikis were classified as traitors, and either executed or sent to the gulags. So I bought myself a new life here. I had no idea what had happened to my parents, and as horrible as it sounds, I tried my best to forget about them. Registering as Michael Peterson when I disembarked at New York helped with that."

Mykhail glanced at Asher once or twice, but couldn't look for long.

Asher cleared his throat. "Excuse me if I haven't fully listened to the rest of your lies."

"That was the truth," Mykhail said. "On my daughter's life."

"So, the truth is," Asher said, "that you collaborated with the Nazis."

"I collaborated *against the Russians.*"

"But that means you collaborated against the Jews too, surely?"

"Look. I would have died in that POW camp if I hadn't become a Trawniki, and I would have been shot if I'd refused to do as the other Trawnikis. You know it and I know it. It was the lesser of two evils. I thought it might lead to the overthrowing of the Russians—to Ukrainian independence."

"That's your defense?"

"Have you forgotten the Holodomor? What the Russians did?"

"That's hardly an excuse. And it's—"

"Do you know how many Ukrainians died in the Holodomor? Have you read up on it? It was easily a million or more. *A million or more*—systematically starved to death by Stalin in the early thirties." He prodded a crooked finger toward Asher and then to himself. "Our parents protected us, but it could so easily have been us, Asher—you and me and our families dying in the early thirties, long before Hitler did his worst."

"Like you say, that all happened a long time before Treblinka."

"It's still important, Asher. It's part of who I am, what motivated me. And . . . and there's something else you don't know."

"More lies?" Asher said, frowning. The frown softened. "I'm sorry. Go on."

"Soon after you left Dyovsta, when I was about fourteen, I asked Mama why I was an only child. She said she couldn't have any more children."

"And?"

"Years later, Papa told me the real reason. He spoke with tears in his eyes. After I was born, Mama put off having more children because of the hostilities with the Russians. She waited for as long as she could, then tried in the early thirties. She miscarried due to malnutrition—the Holodomor . . . that Russian abomination. So she tried again the next year, with the same results, and she was too traumatized to ever try again. The Russians made me an only child, Asher. *It was as if they killed my unborn siblings.* Think how that made me feel when I was a young man."

Asher scowled. "Okay, that's sad and horrible, but you think it excuses you siding with the Nazis?"

"You weren't in Ukraine at the time—when the Nazis invaded. If you sided with the Russians you joined the Red Army. If you sided with the Germans you joined the SS. If you wanted to be Ukrainian you were killed by either the Russians or the Nazis. The whole thing was a devil's mess."

"And have you conveniently forgotten Babi Yar? You were in Kiev at the time. You must have known. What was it? Over thirty thousand innocent Jews rounded up and shot dead in a few bloody hours of butchery by Hitler's henchmen?"

"Yes. I was in Kiev at the time. *In a POW camp.*"

"But you were there."

"And you weren't, Asher. *You weren't.* The world knows about Bergen-Belsen and Auschwitz, and not without good cause, but that POW camp was every bit as horrific—a disgusting, festering boil on the face of humanity. Starvation, disease, random beatings and shootings were all common, and the Nazis showed as much hatred for us as they did for any Jew. An ocean of men stretched over the horizon. In that and many other POW camps, millions of Ukrainians died, all with families and hopes for a normal life. So yes, I heard the rumors about Babi Yar. But do you honestly think that was important to me at the time? Me, rotting and diseased, living in a crowded field with hundreds of thousands of other rotting and diseased people?"

"And so you volunteered to kill people?"

"I had to take sides. Surely you can see I had to do that to survive. Yes, it sounds terrible in this day and age of plentiful food and shelter. But history doesn't know the future, Asher. *History doesn't know the future.* Context is everything. So it turned out I exchanged one form of hell for another. *I thought I was doing the right thing.*"

"The right thing for yourself?"

Mykhail nodded defiantly. "Of course for myself. Don't forget, you said you were a Totenjude—a Jew of death. I was there, remember. I know what you did. You helped kill too. Wasn't that self-preservation?"

Asher's voice dropped a little. His thin lips drew back to reveal gritted teeth. "There was a difference, Mykhail. I was ordered at gunpoint; you volunteered."

"You think I haven't wrestled with my memories over the years? You think my mind didn't spin around on a thousand sleepless nights, wondering whether I could have done anything different?"

"So you regret it?"

"That's not the point, goddammit! We both know who was really to blame—the people who had real power and real choice. The point is, I've suffered because of what I did. I still do suffer, and my poor daughter shares some of that suffering, even though she doesn't know it. But do you really think what I did was a free choice?"

"It depends. Knowing what you know now, do you still think you did the right thing?"

Mykhail shrugged and wiped his eyes. "Now?" He gave his head a slow shake. "Now I can't do anything about it."

Both men were silent for a few moments, neither looking at the other.

"Okay," Asher said eventually. "Yes, of course I can understand, to a point. But part of the reason I feel so bad is because you've been lying to me all this time."

"Well, I didn't tell you the *whole truth*."

"You lied about why you came to America. You couldn't go back to Russia or Ukraine because you would have been considered a traitor."

"I told you the truth. I could have stayed in Germany, but I came to America because I wanted something better for my life. I wanted to get away from the chaos of Europe. I assumed my family were all dead and wanted to do the best for myself—and for their memory."

"You never wanted to find out whether your parents survived the war?"

"Of course I did. But there was no way I could go back. And when I came to this country—well, I guess I forgot about that old Mykhail. I'm sure changing my name helped. It's a different life, and I'm a different person."

"Except, of course, that you're not, are you?" Asher stood up.

"What are you going to do?"

"I don't know."

"But you said you wouldn't tell the authorities. You promised."

"Oh, for God's sake, Mykhail. Will you quit with the self-preservation! I'm just disgusted with you, that's all. History is history, I know, but the worst thing, the *very worst thing*, was what you did to me only last month."

"Last month? What the hell are you talking about?"

"I was in hospital. You were by my bedside. I poured my heart out to you about Rina, told you how much I missed her all my life, how she could have become something special had she not been murdered. And you just sat there listening to me and nodding and telling me how terrible it all was. But all the time you were listening you knew that *you* were one of those sons of bitches who murdered her."

"You think it would have helped to tell you then?"

Then Asher sat back down and spoke through gritted teeth, jets of spittle coming out with his words. "It would have shown me a little *respect*! It would have shown my *sister* a little respect. Mykhail, I've been your friend all these years. We've shared some good times and you'll always be my brother in all but blood, and now I find . . . Oh, I just don't know how I can cope, but I don't think I'll ever be able to forgive you."

Mykhail's eyes turned glassy. He pursed his lips and gulped. "Asher, I'll do anything you want me to do. Please."

"Killing thousands of people—Jews or otherwise—is not something I find easy to forgive, regardless of the circumstances."

"Asher, I've explained what I did but I can't make excuses for it. You know if I could turn the clock back to that day in the POW camp, I'd like to be able to tell you I would have chosen to stay in the camp and rot. But . . ."

"But what?"

Mykhail let out a heavy sigh. "We both know I'd be lying if I said that. You're a friend and I'm being honest. I did what I needed to do to survive."

"And that's as close as you can come to apologizing? To admitting your guilt?"

"I'm . . . I'm sorry, but I'm afraid it is. You wanted the truth. That's the truth."

"And if people were to know about this? Your daughter? Your friends and neighbors?"

Mykhail's voice trembled. "Please don't destroy my life, Asher. I feel terrible about what I did. I hate myself at times for it, but what good would it do to admit everything publicly?"

"It would tell people the truth."

"Come on, Asher. You know that people wouldn't understand. How can anyone make a judgment about this from behind a desk? They'll make the same decision I would have done if I'd been sitting at a desk instead of rotting in a squalid POW camp."

Asher nervously rubbed his forehead and thought for a moment. "And that's your final word?"

"Well . . . yes, it is. I . . . I don't want to talk about it anymore."

Then Asher stood up again and glanced at the back door. "Very well."

"Very well, *what?*" Mykhail said. "What are you going to do?"

Chapter 32

Diane needed a few deep breaths. It had been a hard story to take in—one not only of her own father's part in the running of the Treblinka death camp, but of his subsequent lies and deceit. She stared absently across the table at Asher. Her mind was again back in that kitchen, witnessing the aftermath of her father's death. The smell of blood brought to her nose by the cool air, the stillness of her father's body at the table, the back door swinging so slowly she had to stare at it for a few seconds to tell that this was no freeze-frame but reality.

"Diane?" he said. "Are you all right?"

She took a hard swallow, and brought out a Kleenex to wipe away the tears she'd only just realized were wetting her cheeks.

"I won't go on," he said. "I think you can guess the rest."

"You . . . you went back and shot him."

"I signed a confession to that effect. Hardly seems polite to go back on it now."

"And you think he got what he deserved?"

Asher thought for a few seconds. "That depends on your views, I guess."

"On what, exactly?"

"What does and doesn't constitute a free choice. Your father said I played my own part in the murders at Treblinka, and he was right. He said he would almost certainly have perished in that POW camp had he not volunteered to be a Trawniki, and he was right."

"That sounds like a no."

"Did he deserve to die? No, I don't think he did. The vast majority of choices are free, but in this case?" He shook his head.

"So why did you kill him?"

"You know, Diane, I'm unable to answer that question truthfully. I just know that life's full of conundrums. If your father had rejected the choice of being a Trawniki, you wouldn't be sitting in front of me now."

Diane nodded. "I guess not. But if all you've told me is true—"

"Oh, it is," Asher said. "I might have lied to others, Diane, but I haven't lied to you. I've made that a kind of mission."

"But why didn't you just tell the police what Father did at Treblinka?"

"Because I promised him I wouldn't do that."

Diane opened her mouth to speak, but she couldn't find the words; as a conversation or argument, it was a dead end.

"I guess he was thinking of you," Asher continued. "Of the stigma or shame you might suffer if the story got out."

"I can see that. And what if I tell the police what you told me?"

"I'll deny it. I'll lie to them, Diane, but not you."

"Okay."

"And I hope you can move on with your life. I hope you can be happy with Brad."

"Thank you."

"Everyone deserves a little happiness, no matter how late in life. Tell me, are you going to move in with him?"

"I'm going to see my mother first. I don't know what after that."

"I know. All this must be a big shock."

"Quite a few big shocks."

Asher held his hands out flat on the table. "Well, that's it," he said. "I hope you got what you were after."

"I did."

"Good," Asher said, nodding thoughtfully. "Good. I have to go now."

Diane noticed pain on his face like she hadn't seen before, his jowls trembling, his frown casting a dark shadow over his eye sockets. He sniffed the tears away as the guard outside let him out, leaving Diane alone.

She called Brad, who picked her up. She didn't initiate a conversation all evening, and Brad didn't push her on the matter.

By daylight the next morning Diane had given up trying to sleep and was lying on the couch, her eyes shut but her mind firmly locked in the "on" position. Giving up trying to sleep must have done the trick, because then she managed to sleep in fits and starts, and was woken some hours later by the sound of the fridge shutting and the aroma from Brad's coffeemaker.

"I'm sorry," he said. "I was trying my best not to wake you."

"Oh, it's fine. I thought I was disturbing you in the night, so I figured I'd better come out here."

"I didn't notice, but you've got the bed to yourself now if you want to sleep more."

She shook her head. "No. I'll feel better for getting up. I'm restless and I don't think that's going to change. I'm sorry."

"Don't apologize. You've lost your father, and it'll take time to come to terms with it."

She glanced at him, and by the time she realized she was chewing her lip and grimacing, it was too late.

"What is it?" he said. "Is there something you're not telling me?"

"It's not that, Brad. It's not just that I've lost Father."

He eyed her quizzically. "It must be something pretty big to overshadow that." He gave her that brief window to reply, as he always did, before the politeness kicked in. "Look, you don't need to tell me if you don't want to."

"You know, I really do. I should have told you yesterday, and I can't keep it to myself any longer."

"Okay." He nodded—one of his serious nods. "Give me a minute to get us coffee."

Diane used that time to stretch the crick out of her neck and sit up. Soon they were next to each other on the couch, their hands clasped around steaming cups.

Diane went to speak, but only exhaled.

"Why not try saying it as it is?"

"Okay. I think Father was, uh . . ."

He waited. She didn't finish.

"You can tell me. Whatever it is, you can tell me."

"Well . . . okay . . . I'm not sure whether I told you at the time— it happened a couple years after we started dating—but Father was questioned by the authorities about war crimes."

"About *what?*" Brad almost spilled his coffee.

"Obviously I didn't tell you; it's not the kind of thing you go shouting about."

"Jeez. No, I guess not. But carry on."

"It was 1997. Some old guy said he recognized Father from one of the death camps—Treblinka, to be specific. He said Father helped operate the gas chambers there. Of course, the case came to nothing. Father said the allegations were the ramblings of a madman, that thousands of Ukrainians would have looked like him at that age, that he'd never been near the place in his life. And the cops—or whoever it was—obviously agreed, as they dismissed the allegations for lack of evidence. But some newspaper printed Father's picture, Asher saw it, and traced him. That was how they got back in contact."

"That was some coincidence. I never realized."

"Like I said, I probably chose not to tell you." Diane took a long breath. "Anyhow, earlier this year, Asher goes to Treblinka, sees a photo, suddenly goes along with this guy that I thought was a madman. He insists my father was there, that the allegations were true. I told him about the authorities dismissing the case, but he wasn't having it, said Father had admitted it to him."

Brad absentmindedly chewed on a nail for a few seconds. "That doesn't mean anything legally if he didn't get it on tape. But it would explain why Asher killed your father. It ties everything in so it all makes sense, because now we have a motive."

"It also means Father was a war criminal."

For a moment Brad stared, his face turning a shade lighter. He took a gulp before speaking. "Hey, I'm sorry, Diane. I . . . I wasn't thinking straight. It must be awful for you."

"It's no party, but I have to admit, it's like stubbing your toe after you've broken your leg."

"No wonder you hardly slept. He told you all that yesterday?"

"The day before. I didn't tell you at the time because I wasn't sure whether I believed him."

"And now?"

Diane huffed. "And now I'm starting to accept it. I trust Asher. And yes, I guess, stubbed toe or not, it makes me feel terrible to know what Father did."

"I totally get that. Is that why you . . . the question that night about the sins of the father?"

"That aspect kind of plays on my mind. I loved my father. I still do. He wasn't perfect, but he was good to me. It's hard to come to terms with."

Brad stood up and walked aimlessly around the room. "Your father? I mean . . . I thought I knew him too . . . but *this*?" He shook his head as though trying to discard his confusion and disbelief. "And you're telling me you feel some sort of guilt or blame?"

"I know it's stupid, but . . . well, yes, I do, if I listen to my heart. We're talking about my own father. I can't completely accept it. He was such a good man. He *seemed* such a good man."

Brad sat back down and held her hand. "Just listen to your head on this one, not your heart. None of this is your fault."

"I guess not. Thanks."

They leaned in and held each other, their lips touching, and for a few seconds their heads rested on each other's shoulders.

"I'm not sure it's my father's fault either."

Brad pulled away and frowned.

"No, really. Asher told me what happened. Father was just a pawn. He had very little real choice. One day I'll tell you. Not now."

"I . . . I don't know," Brad said. "I trust you, Diane. It's just that there's too much to take in. But I can understand it's complicated."

"To put it mildly," Diane said.

"So, where do we go from here?"

"There's nowhere we *can* go. I swore to Asher I wouldn't tell the authorities."

"Should you let that stop you?"

"Oh, I can't. It's Asher's story; it's up to him to tell the authorities if he wants to."

"Sure." Brad thought for a moment, his frown deepening. "I don't understand," he said after a pause for thought. "One minute I think I understand, the next minute I'm confused again. Why wouldn't Asher want such a thing to come out in the open? I mean, why should he care for your father so much, and at the same time want to kill him? It kind of makes sense, but equally makes no sense at all."

"I agree. It's a mess."

"Unless he wants to protect you."

"You mean, the publicity?"

"Oh, yes. If the story gets out, you'll have reporters and all sorts to cope with."

"You know, at this moment I really don't care."

"I get that. And I guess it solves one problem."

"What?"

"You said you found it hard to believe Asher murdered your father. This sort of solves that. We know he had a good enough reason to do it."

Diane nodded. "I guess he did."

Chapter 33

Three weeks had passed since Diane had listened to Asher's version of events, and she and Brad had discussed the story at length many times. What they hadn't discussed was where Diane was going to live. She'd arranged to visit her mother in Baltimore and stay there for a few weeks initially, and hadn't yet made a decision on what she was going to do after that. She told Brad again that she figured her mother had lost out due to her father's behavior, and was owed something.

Getting away from Pittsburgh was also starting to have an appeal. At first, when she'd come to accept Asher's story about her father, she was sure only she and Asher knew the truth. But every time there was a knock on the door and every time the phone rang there was a split second when she wondered whether she would meet someone who also knew. Details of her father's murder had been released to the newspapers, so she'd had journalists approach her about the story. That was bad enough, but Diane knew some were smart and very persistent; it was quite possible that one would investigate the case, dig deeper—specifically, into the 1997 charges—and put two and two together.

Each of those split seconds was a seed that germinated into a moment's thought that grew into a few seconds, enough for a conscious appraisal of the risks, and soon Diane could hear a little voice on her shoulder every time she was talking to strangers. The voice was asking, "Does this person know?" and the more she ignored it, the more it spoke up for itself.

She put it down to the stress of dealing with her father's estate. Yes, perhaps he was haunting her and perhaps it would all go away when the property was sold. The story of her father's death would certainly die down as more news was loaded onto the conveyor belt.

The practicalities were no less stressful. Diane had originally wanted little to do with the contents of the house, so had given the clearance firm instructions to remove everything, valuable or not. It had taken Brad to point out the obvious: that most of her own clothes and personal effects were still there. So she and Brad returned to Hartmann Way before the firm turned up. As it turned out, Diane couldn't bear to enter the house—not after the last time she'd been there and had stepped into a scene from a murder movie.

So Brad dutifully went inside and packed everything from her room into a few cardboard boxes. As he was loading them into the car, she asked him to return for a few other things, because she still wanted some reminders of her father. So he did, returning with a couple more boxes.

She'd extended her leave from work, and so, with a little time on her hands and on the other side of town from Hartmann Way, she found it easier to sort through the contents. She was doing just that the next day when the doorbell sounded.

"Diane Peterson?" the man at the door said.

Diane hesitated. "Who wants to know?"

The man took his baseball cap off and rubbed dirty sweat from his brow. "Big Steve's house clearance. We're doing your father's house on Hartmann Way." He pointed a thick thumb at the truck across the street.

"Oh, yes." Now Diane forced a smile. "Yes. I'm sorry. I've had reporters coming here ever since . . ."

His face cracked. He knew. It was understandable that he might have been curious. After all, he was emptying the very house where the event had taken place. He'd probably already loaded most of the contents into the truck; even the chair Diane's father had been sitting in when the bullet had trashed his brain and distributed a good proportion of it onto the opposing kitchen wall.

"Well, I'm no reporter," he said. "But we found this." He handed her an envelope. It was thick and obviously contained something more than paper. "I know you said to remove everything from the house, that you'd taken all you wanted, but this has your name on it. We found it underneath a kitchen cabinet."

Diane took the envelope. "Oh, it's probably not important, but it's kind of you all the same. Thank you."

"Part of the service." After a flat smile and a forefinger salute he turned and walked back to the truck.

Diane went inside, her fingers pressing into the envelope, feeling something rectangular and less than an inch thick, but also almost weightless.

Then something occurred to her that made her lay the envelope down very carefully on the hall table. She was the daughter of a man suspected of being a war criminal. Yes, the allegations might have been made four years ago and no charges were ever brought, but now her father had been murdered, what about those people who could put two and two together? Did her father have enemies from the past? And was the man she'd just seen really from Big Steve's? There were some very unforgiving people out there.

She took a few careful paces backward and swiftly spun herself into the living room. Her purse was on the coffee table. Good. For some reason—probably that yappy old dog her physician called insecurity— she'd kept the card with Detective Durwood's direct line.

She grabbed her purse, opened it, and ran her fingers around the little pocket on the inside.

There. Got it. Reading glasses too—get them. Three paces to the sideboard and she placed the card down next to the phone. Next to the bright red card with Big Steve's number on it.

Big Steve.

She thought for a moment. Was she being realistic here?

She called Big Steve. It got forwarded to his cell.

"It's Miss Peterson."

"Oh, hi, Miss Peterson. We'll be another two hours, I figure."

"No, it's not that. Did you send one of your men around here with an envelope?"

There was a long pause before he replied.

"Is that okay? We found it on the floor behind that big oak kitchen cabinet. It seemed the right thing to do, having your name on it and all."

Diane let out a calming sigh and secretly cursed her father.

"That's fine, Steve. I'm sorry I called. It's not a problem."

She put the phone down, letting it drop the last inch.

"Stupid, stupid, stupid," she muttered.

It was her father. He'd been on edge all his life. The doorbell had always made him fidget, and more often than not he would ask Diane to get it. She'd always put it down to laziness. Now she had other ideas. She loved him; he'd been a good father overall. She just didn't like the fact he'd passed his paranoia on to her.

Of course the man had been from Big Steve's. The goddamn truck had been across the street. If anyone knew the truth and had intentions of revenge, there were much easier ways to satisfy that urge.

But more importantly, her name on the envelope was written in her father's distinctive handwriting. She shook her head at her own stupidity. Then she headed back into the hallway, and within seconds the envelope was in two pieces, both fluttering to the floor.

She held the contents in the palm of her hand.

It was a cassette tape—one with her name scrawled on it in more of that spidery handwriting. Only in the last two or three years had the arthritis stopped him writing. He'd always joked that the son-of-a-bitch disease had more control over his fingers than he did. His daughter's name he could manage to write; a sentence, possibly; anything more was just not physically possible.

Diane went into the spare room, where she'd been sorting through the cardboard boxes representing her old life. She shifted two of them to get to the one she wanted. She'd given up telling her father to buy CDs: he always preferred his cassette tapes.

And here was his player. Which was also his recorder.

Fear of not knowing dried her throat to flypaper. She needed to hear it now.

Back into the living room, sit down, player on coffee table, slot the cassette in, press play, clench hands.

The tape hiss gave way to a cough, then a little breathless gasping. And then there were words, delivered with the trembling voice of a child about to take a beating. It was unmistakable. This was Father. It was Father in a frame of mind Diane had never known before, but it was unmistakably Father.

She listened, her eyes locked on to the tape player.

My dearest Diane. I've come a long way in my life, and had plenty of hard times. But leaving you this message is the hardest thing I've ever done. I wish I could tell you this to your face, but my stupid pride won't let me—just like my gnarled, useless fingers won't let me write it down. I'm sorry.

I did a lot of things in my previous life that I am ashamed of. I've told you my real name is Mykhail Petrenko, and that I was born and brought up in a small farming village in Ukraine.

That's true.

Something else is also true. I admit I'm a coward for not coming clean earlier. I kidded myself that I kept it secret for your sake, so that you could live a normal life. The truth is that I wanted to tell you years ago, but each time I pictured your face as you heard my words, and I couldn't bear to do it. I can't tell you to your face, but I can no longer keep the truth from you.

You'll remember four years ago some allegations were made against me. War crimes, they called them.

They were all true.

I was at Treblinka.

I operated an engine. I was a part of the machine—that death factory.

Even through this recorder, I can't bring myself to tell you any details. But I was there and took an active part in some horrible, inhuman acts.

I've done my best to lock those memories away for the sake of my sanity and your happiness, to pretend it all happened in a different life. I know I haven't been the best father to you; many times you've wanted to leave home, and I know I've stopped you. It's no excuse, but when your mother left me I felt the emptiness of a family eradicated by circumstances, and it seemed to take hold of my soul. In spite of my attempts to hide my feelings, I'm sure you know how I suffered in those months that followed, and I couldn't face the prospect of losing you too.

Apart from that, I think I managed to control myself well, to shut out those blood red memories and hide behind this confident shell of mine.

But my old friend Asher found me out, so I told him exactly what I did all those years ago. Understandably, he's very annoyed with me, and he's just left this house in a foul temper. He's promised not to turn me in, but I doubt he'll count himself as my friend now, and in a way that's worse punishment.

The phone has been ringing. I know it's him. He's prone to bouts of anger but at heart he's a good, gentle man with very strong principles. Please be kind to him, Diane; he's very upset. I know him well and I know why he's calling: he wants to forgive me for my involvement in those evil acts. He would do that for me, even though I don't deserve it.

I do, however, ask you to forgive me for what I am about to do.

Like Asher, you have a lot to forgive me for. I never could face the prospect of you disowning me, which probably explains why I screwed up your life just like I tried to screw up your mother's. I'm sorry. I never intended to do that. Guilt does that to people, it spreads the misery.

You've been a caring daughter, Diane—much more so than I deserve. I know you've made a lot of sacrifices over the years for my sake, so please remember that I will always love you. Over the coming months people will try to make you feel ashamed to be my daughter. Resist that. Believe me when I say that you have nothing to be ashamed of—absolutely nothing. My crimes were my own doing and nobody else's.

I've kept the lid on this for too long, and it's done too much damage, way more than I'm worth. But now the past has come back into my life, and I simply can't live with it.

I'm so sorry.

Chapter 34

Pittsburgh, July 2001

At the kitchen table of 38 Hartmann Way, Mykhail's finger dropped onto the stop button of his trusty old tape recorder, then shook uncontrollably as it moved along and did the same to the eject button. He'd already taken great trouble to scribble Diane's name on both the cassette and the envelope. That was good. That was foresight. He was shaking so much now that he would hardly be able to hold a pen, let alone use one.

And this was Mykhail Petrenko, not Michael Peterson. Asher had just reminded him of that fact—of the history of the man he really was. He was born Mykhail Petrenko, so it only seemed fitting that at this time he should become him once again. Fitting and truthful.

He took a sharp breath and slowly plucked the cassette from its holder. The cassette was shaking, the envelope was shaking. It was like threading a needle while sitting in a moving car. But by the fourth attempt it was in. He tried to lick the flap but there was no moisture on his tongue, so he reached across to his glass of apple juice, dipped his finger in it, and sealed the envelope shut. He placed the envelope in front of him, next to the tape recorder and his juice, and moved all three to one side—with a care that seemed perverse even to him—to where they would be safe. He glanced down at the remains of the glass Asher had smashed on the floor, then up and through the glass of the back door. That brush, balanced on the paint pot, which was balanced on the brick, was still waiting for him. Those three items might be the only things to miss him when he'd gone. Asher had almost kicked the thing over when he'd stormed out an hour earlier. That had left plenty of time for Mykhail to think, to come to terms with what he knew all along he needed to do. And Mykhail had decided, closing and locking the door for a little privacy, then composing himself before leaving a message for his one and only.

He reached for the gun. He stared at it for a moment. Strangely, he felt an element of peace, a kind he hadn't experienced in a long time.

He rested the muzzle of the gun on his temple.

He'd been in tears for the past half hour—which was so unlike him—but now there was an acceptance that it was all over.

Mykhail's closing thought was of lives being snuffed out in a different world. In a chamber. They screamed, they clawed, they clung on to hope that it wouldn't be the end. Mykhail didn't. He had lived his life.

That was something to be grateful for.

The tears stopped. The gasping too. He took a calming breath, then listened to the ringing of the phone. It was regular, like the cycle of life. Ringing, then silent and peaceful, ringing, then silent and peaceful, ringing, then silent and peaceful.

He pulled the trigger.

At the Pittsburgh bus depot, Asher Kogan was begging the phone to change its tune. Ringing, silent and peaceful, ringing, silent and peaceful, ringing, silent and peaceful.

Yes, when he'd seen that photograph of Mykhail at the Treblinka museum, his first thought had been that he never wanted to see his old friend again, that he was going to disown him.

But by the time he'd flown back home he knew that would never happen. That was because he needed answers. He'd spent hours struggling with his own sanity, trying to convince himself that somehow it wasn't Mykhail in that photograph, although he knew in his heart it was. He felt so betrayed, and needed to ask Mykhail how he justified what he'd taken part in—or, at the very least, whether he admitted it.

So as soon as he arrived home, he took the bus to Pittsburgh, and by the time he arrived he was ready for a fight. He was ready for Mykhail to deny, deny, deny.

He found Mykhail busy painting, but the painting stopped when Asher said he had something to say, and soon they were facing each other across the kitchen table. Asher struggled to contain his anger, but told Mykhail what he'd seen at Treblinka—the photograph.

Of course, Mykhail did deny, deny, deny for as long as he possibly could. Even when he said he didn't want to talk about it anymore, when Asher was about to leave, the two men continued arguing.

"You make me sick," Asher told him. "At first you deny, then you dismiss it like you stole something from the dollar store."

"Asher, I've explained till I'm—"

"That's what gets me the most. You betrayed me four years ago by lying to me, you betrayed me while I lay in hospital and you listened to me talking about my poor sister, and now you're betraying me all over again when you try to downplay the whole issue."

"I'm not downplaying it. Just explaining. Are you too dumb to tell the difference?"

"Dumb now, am I?"

"If you can't understand what I'm trying to say, then yes. I had no alternative. If I'd stayed in that POW camp I wouldn't be alive now, we wouldn't be having this conversation, and there would be no Diane. Yes. Yes, a thousand times, I did some terrible things, but so did you, Asher, so did you."

As Mykhail stood, Asher squared up to him.

"I didn't kill innocent people, Mykhail. *That's* the difference between us."

"Look, we can't agree, we'll *never* agree. But . . . what are you going to do?"

Asher stroked a palm across his sweaty forehead and wiped the moisture onto his shirt. He went to speak a couple of times, but nothing came of it.

"Please, Asher," Mykhail whispered hoarsely. "Please don't tell the authorities." He waited for a response, but there was none. "You'll destroy me in every way. Don't you think I've suffered enough?"

"You think you've suffered? You had a good job all your life."

"I hated my job. I hated the people I worked with."

"You got married."

"We hated each other."

"You told me the divorce was amicable."

"Oh, *Jesus Christ*, Asher. I was *lying*. It's what screwed-up sons of bitches like me do."

"You've still got Diane."

"She hates me too."

"You think so? Really?"

"I screwed up her life, and she's screwing up Brad's. Don't you get it, Asher? I hate myself. I loathe myself for what I did. I try to be logical and assess what happened by talking about choices, but the truth is that the fear and self-loathing always take over. Do you honestly think those things take sides? No. They screw up everyone in the end."

"I see." Asher nodded slowly. "So, after denying it and then downplaying it, now you turn it on yourself, like *you're* the victim." He took a long breath and looked his friend up and down, sneering. "God, you're an arrogant son of a bitch. It's as if the concepts of guilt and remorse are alien to you."

"It's not like that."

"It fits from where I'm standing."

"Well, you're wrong. Please. Listen." He motioned for them to sit back down, which they did.

"Asher, it's true I was like you say for most of my life. I tried to blank it out—to deny. I always told my wife and daughter that I couldn't talk about what happened to me during the war, that it was simply too horrible to go back over. They accepted that. But in my later years—and I'm talking about well before you came back on the scene—I came to accept that what I did was very wrong. And I've often wished that I stayed in that stinking POW camp, that I never set eyes on Treblinka—even if that meant I'd died there. Then it hit me that I'd actually thought that all along, but instead of admitting it I took it out on my wife and daughter. Instead of screwing up my own life by admitting what I'd done, I took it out on them and screwed up their lives, so I lost out anyway. Have you any idea how much I hate myself for all that?"

Asher gazed at Mykhail's face, peering into his sorrowful eyes, watching the tears trickle down his weather-worn skin. "I don't believe a word of it," he eventually said. "All you're doing is trying to save your own skin, just like you did all those years ago."

"No!" Mykhail screeched. "It's the truth!"

Asher stood and took a step back. He should have been pleased to see his best friend squirm after what he'd done. But it wasn't a pleasant sight. Not even one bit. And the worst thing was that he knew Mykhail was being honest. After all, he was contemplating a world in which Diane had never been born. Asher saw the truth in Mykhail's eyes; he would have known had he been faking it.

But now it was Asher's turn to be arrogant. He felt he could do nothing else.

Mykhail stood up too, stepping toward Asher, grabbing the lapels of his jacket. "You want me to beg?" he said, now sobbing freely. "Well, I'm begging. Please, Asher. If not for me, then for Diane. Please keep all this to yourself. *Please!*"

Anger smothered all thought in Asher's mind. "Mykhail Petrenko," he said, "I never want to see you again. We are no longer friends."

At that, Mykhail put his head in his hands. "Please, Asher," he said. "I've thought so much about this over the years that it's destroyed a part of me. The secrets, the deceit, the guilt. It's been a disease in remission, one I've always known could return one day." He looked up at Asher. "And today, all these years later, it has. You spring this on me and you expect me to have all the answers in a few pathetic minutes. Well, I've told you the truth. I can't say any more."

It was then that Asher cracked. He raged and shouted at Mykhail, standing up, pacing around the room, arms whirling, then sitting down again but still not allowing Mykhail to speak. Asher had never possessed much of a temper, but it was as if he'd been saving up what temper he had for those few minutes of telling Mykhail how evil and disgusting he was.

Again, Mykhail asked Asher to forgive him, and Asher told him to go to hell. Mykhail kept saying he was sorry, now red-faced and panting. He kept asking Asher to understand, to look at it from his point of view.

"I'll see you in hell first," Asher hissed. "Which is where you belong." Then he stumbled to the door, where he turned around and fired a final salvo. "I will never forgive you, Mykhail. You're no friend of mine and you never will be. I just hope I never see you again."

He left, leaving the door swinging behind him, and staggered to the end of the street, where he flagged a cab down. By the time the cab dropped him off at the bus depot he was starting to feel ill with the stress, and welcomed the chance to sit in the waiting room and recover as best he could. As he watched the motley selection of people passing by in front of him, he started wondering about their histories too—what dark secrets each of them might be hiding. After all, everyone is guilty of something; it's only a question of scale.

Those thoughts seemed to calm him down a little, and slowly, over the next hour, he started regretting so many of those things he'd said to Mykhail. He'd been unfair; Mykhail had denied this for most of his life, and now Asher was expecting instant and full disclosure and regret.

Asher had been at Treblinka too—he'd helped with the shepherding of those people into the gas chambers. It wasn't too far removed. Okay, so he hadn't volunteered: he'd been picked out and told what to do. But if he'd been given a choice would he have chosen to die instead? Nobody could ever be certain of such a thing.

Mykhail had said as much, and he had a point. There was a similarity, albeit with one important distinction: Asher never had a gun at Treblinka. If he had, he would like to think he would have used it on the guards. Mykhail, however, had been a Trawniki guard, as good as a soldier with access to guns. Would Asher have done the same as Mykhail had he been in his position? Would he really have stayed in the POW camp to take his chances there?

The more Asher thought on, the more confused he became.

Music blared from the speakers in the bus depot waiting room. Asher felt so bad he prayed for the volume to increase—increase so much it would hurt his ears. He just wanted to curl up in a corner and never come out again. At that moment, he wanted someone or something to take his life just to stop the cockroaches scurrying around his brain.

It was a long time since he'd had such destructive feelings.

He couldn't stop thinking about Mykhail. Should he forgive him? Would he want to consider them friends ever again? His mind was a sea of uncertainty about such things, but beyond that he was worried about his old friend. He hadn't looked at all well when Asher had stormed out.

That was when Asher decided to call Mykhail. He hadn't changed his mind. Oh no. He only wanted to be sure he was okay. He fumbled with change and willed his trembling fingers to dial.

There was no answer, only that interminable cycle: silent and peaceful, ringing, silent and peaceful, ringing, silent and peaceful. He hung on.

Yes, he should apologize for some of the horrible things he'd said to Mykhail—some of the worst things. Their friendship would never be the same again, but they'd been friends once, and Mykhail was another human being.

He double-checked the number and dialed again. Twice.

Still, Mykhail didn't pick up.

What if he *couldn't* pick up?

Asher slammed the phone down and cursed himself.

He left the depot and took a cab back to Hartmann Way.

Fifteen minutes later, Asher rushed from the cab to number 38, panting and coughing, taking no time to gather himself before he rang the doorbell, then hammered on it. There was no answer, so he went around the side of the house, past those kids who were still playing basketball.

He went through the gate into the backyard and approached the back door, next to the woodwork, where the pot of paint still rested on the brick, waiting patiently for Mykhail to continue. Asher's hand was raised, ready to bang on the glass, when he spotted Mykhail. He was sitting at the table, his head and shoulders slumped over. He was still and silent.

Asher shouted out to him and banged on the door, but he didn't move at all.

He cupped his hands against the glass and squinted to see better. On the table next to Mykhail there seemed to be a dark pool. And that object next to the pool, was it a handgun?

Oh no. Oh dear God, not this.

Asher turned, and his eyes settled on the brick under the pot of paint. He pulled it out, knocking over the pot, not caring about the spilled paint, then smashed the glass of the door. He reached inside and unlocked it, cutting his forearm on the glass in the process. He flinched, but it didn't warrant a second thought. A rattle of the doorknob and he was in, almost falling as he ran over and grabbed Mykhail by the shoulders.

For a second he was back at that wretched place again, seeing things no person should ever see, smelling that peculiar coppery saltiness nobody should smell. This figure—still warm, like the bodies he'd pulled from the chambers so many years before—was clearly no longer Mykhail, but something that used to be Mykhail. A crawling pool of blood surrounded the head, a spray dripped down the wall next to him. Each was peppered with fragments of bone and flesh.

Asher hugged the lifeless shoulders and called out Mykhail's name. Then his eyes settled on the pistol next to Mykhail's right hand. He picked it up and held it for a few moments, realizing he held a lot of the blame for this. They'd been through a lot together. Mykhail had always been the stronger of them, but now Asher had turned him into the weaker one. He checked the magazine of the gun. It was empty.

He glanced around, looking for bullets. Yes, that was what he deserved. He hunted, checking Mykhail's pockets and a few kitchen drawers. He found none.

And even if he'd found some, would he have had the nerve?

He started to feel physically sick at the thought, as if he was going to pass out. He returned to Mykhail's corpse. Below him, on the table, were Mykhail's glass of juice, his beloved tape player, and an envelope with a name scrawled upon it. In a rage, shouting to his God, Asher slammed his arm down and swung it to the side with so much force that the items flew across the kitchen, bouncing and crashing over the floor.

He shouted again, enraged all the more that there was nobody to listen. He staggered to the back door and stepped outside, where he took in a few lungfuls of fresh air and dropped the gun. Somehow he forced himself to walk on, although he sensed a disconnect between his head and his legs. One foot trod in the spilled paint as he went back around the house, passing the kids again, the nearest two of them giving him a look of fear and backing away. Again, Asher didn't care.

He flagged down a cab as soon as he reached the next street and jumped in. The driver was talkative and friendly at first, but that stopped as soon as he noticed the deep red blood on Asher's hands. Asher told him to go the bus depot and started wiping the blood off onto his jacket.

The driver asked Asher if he was okay, and was very quickly told to just shut up and drive on. At the depot Asher headed straight to the restroom to clean himself up.

The bus back to Detroit wasn't due in for another two hours, so he sat in the waiting room, huddled in a blur of regret and self-loathing. He drifted in and out of sleep, at times hardly aware of what was real and what was a product of his imagination. A glance at the bloodstains on his jacket told him he was trying to escape the horrible truth.

He knew exactly what he'd done. Okay, so Mykhail had done wrong all those years ago, but he was also Asher's friend, and between friends you understand and forgive, and Asher hadn't done that. He could never forgive the true Nazis—the masterminds, the planners, the drivers and motivators, those with cold minds who had instigated those terrible things he witnessed all those years ago.

But the people who were given little real choice?

Asher knew from his own experiences that the concept of free will was often a capricious one.

So, yes. He felt responsible for Mykhail's suicide. But he didn't take the gun and put it against Mykhail's head. When the trigger released the hammer, forcing the pellet of metal through his skull, it wasn't Asher's finger that had pulled the trigger. But everyone is guilty of something, and Asher had argued with him and badgered him so much it might as well have been he who had killed him.

Well before the bus bound for Detroit was due in, Asher had convinced himself he was to blame for Mykhail's death. So he went straight to the police station and told them he'd just killed a man. He told them Mykhail's address and exactly where and how the body lay. They held him while they checked everything out.

In time there was more: Mykhail's blood all over Asher, Asher's bloody fingerprints on the gun that was found outside the door, his own blood on the glass of the door, the paint on his shoes, the boys who had seen him running from the house with blood on his hands, the cab driver's account of a disturbed old man leaving blood on his seats.

The next day, Asher was charged. The day after that, he dictated and signed a confession.

As soon as he entered the cell he felt sure he'd done the right thing. He felt strangely at home; after all, this was as close as he could get to how his family had died, so in a sense he was closer to them. He felt at peace.

Chapter 35

Versions of the story got onto the TV and into the newspapers, but Diane—having been the one to initiate the review of the case by handing the tape to the police—was kept informed of new developments at each stage.

The police had originally taken Asher's confession at face value. Why wouldn't they? Tight budgets and stretched resources had met with a signed confession and clear forensic evidence, producing as clean a case as any. But on hearing and verifying the tape, they took a closer look at the evidence and timings, and interrogated Asher once more. He eventually broke down and admitted his confession had been false, that he'd gone back to the house, seen his friend's dead body slumped over the table, broken in, picked up the gun in a panic, and stumbled out in a fog of shock.

What with the legal formalities, it took a few days for Asher to be released from jail and taken back to his home in Detroit. Since then, Diane had talked with him on the phone a few times, initially with stilted results, but they were soon talking like old friends or even uncle and niece. In passing she'd told him she'd decided not to go stay with her mother in Baltimore, but to stay with Brad. They were, however, both going to spend some time with her mother.

A few days before leaving, while Diane and Brad were sitting down to eat, the phone rang. Asher asked Diane if he could call round the next day, said he had to see her about something. He apologized for the short notice, and told her it wouldn't be a regular thing. Diane, just a little confused as well as intrigued, told him that would be fine, that he was welcome to stop by, an invitation he accepted.

A few minutes later, after Diane had made arrangements and put the phone down, she and Brad carried on eating.

"Hey, I'm sorry," she said.

Brad looked puzzled. "For what?"

"Being presumptuous. It's your house."

"It's *our* house."

"It still feels wrong."

"You'll get used to it. And Asher's welcome here too. Any special reason for the visit?"

"I didn't ask, but he sounded nervous."

"Do you think you might ask him . . . you know?"

"Jeez. I don't think he'll want to talk about that, and I'm not sure I want to. Perhaps we should all just move on."

"Sure."

The next afternoon, while Diane was preparing a meal, she heard a cab pull up outside. She peeked outside and saw Asher's familiar stooped frame stepping out.

She opened the door before he got there. They embraced in the half-hearted, polite way politicians and dignitaries would, and went into the kitchen.

"I hope you don't mind me coming round," Asher said, rubbing his clean-shaven chin.

"Not at all."

"And Brad? I mean, I'll understand if you'd rather not stay in contact."

"Don't be silly," she said. "It's fine. It's all good. I'm really pleased to see you."

She made coffee and they sat opposite each other.

"How are you?" she asked.

"Just now? Tired."

"It's a long journey."

"Yes, it is. But it might just be the last time I do it."

"Really?" Diane's face dropped. "Asher, you know you'll always be welcome to visit. The fact that Father isn't with us . . . Well, you're welcome to visit, is the point. Like I said on the phone, I don't hold you responsible in any way."

"That's awfully kind of you, considering what happened. Have you had any . . . repercussions?"

"Repercussions?"

"I think they call it 'press intrusion.' People with nothing better to do than blame you for what your father was involved in."

Diane shook her head. "Nothing so far. But I'm good. I'm in a good place to cope with all that."

"I'm glad to hear it. Your father was right: you have absolutely nothing to be ashamed of."

"Thank you."

Asher leaned in and held her hand. "And I hope things work out for you and Brad."

"I have a feeling they will. I only wish I'd done it many years ago."

"I'm sure." Asher stared into space for a second, concentrating. "You know, Diane, there was something else your father told me when I confronted him that day, when he was trying to explain his actions. I didn't understand it at the time, but I do now. He said that sometimes circumstances stop us being the people we'd rather be."

"Yeah," Diane said. "Yeah, I get that."

They exchanged a smile, and each took a sip of coffee.

"You got rid of the beard," Diane said, nodding to his face.

He laughed. "First time I've seen my chin in thirty years."

"Suits you," Diane said.

"Thank you." Asher looked around the kitchen. "Nice place Brad has here."

"Well, it's kind of Brad and Diane's place now."

"Oh, yes. Of course. And I'm really pleased for you. I know how your father . . . well, I know what he was like."

"Yes."

Asher smiled again and said how nice the coffee was. It was then that Diane couldn't help herself. It hadn't been the kind of question to ask over the phone, but she got the impression it might well be her last chance to ask him face to face.

"Why did you do it, Asher?"

There. The question had been burning a hole, and now it was said. It was out there. A look of severe concentration cast a shadow over Asher's face. He froze, staring at her, then slowly and quietly said, "The confession?"

"I still don't understand. And I'd like to. If you don't mind."

Now he just looked bewildered. "I'm still not sure I can say. But I know I've felt guilty all my life, and that evening I felt guiltier than ever. I guess I still feel I was responsible for your father's death, even though I didn't pull the trigger. I was guilty in that respect."

"But you really weren't, Asher. It's only looking back that I can see Father was always on the edge like that anyway."

"Thank you. But I'm still sorry. I still miss him."

"I know. Me too."

"You realize if it hadn't been for him I wouldn't have met Izabella earlier this year?"

"I guess not."

"He paid for my vacation, and he persuaded me to return to Warsaw—for the wrong reasons, perhaps, but he persuaded me nonetheless."

"He was my father. I know he wasn't all bad."

"Of course not. I know that too." Asher stopped and took a long breath. "That brings me to the reason I'm here. I have to ask you something."

"Sure. What?"

"You see, when I saw Izabella in Warsaw we got on better than I ever could have dreamed of."

"You told me that already."

"No, I mean *really* well. It was uncanny—almost as if we'd been together all those years as a married couple. If anything, it was even more beautiful than it was when we knew each other during the war."

"I can believe that. You painted a pretty picture, I have to say."

"And I told her about my life up in Detroit, how I had friends I met regularly in the library—buddies, so I thought. Do you know that when I was in hospital not one of them came to see me? Not one. The only visitors I had were you and your father."

"No, I didn't know that. I'm sorry."

"You see, we told each other about everything. It felt so good for me. And then, on the day I left, when I thought it couldn't get any better, she sat me down and asked me to live with her permanently in Warsaw."

"Oh, Asher. That's really nice."

"Well, it should have been. I wanted to say yes to her. I wanted to say yes a thousand times. But I was too scared."

"I don't understand. Scared of what?"

Asher gave his chin a rub, pausing for thought, before continuing. "You see, I had this image in my mind. Izabella and I are married—have been married for fifty years. And we're happy, deliriously so. We have a lovely house, nicely decorated, clean and tidy, fresh flowers on the dining table. We go on vacation together, just the two of us now our children are all grown up. But we help out the children by giving advice, and we play with our grandchildren." He shrugged. "Schmaltzy, I know. But I couldn't get those thoughts and images out of my mind. I knew damn well that I'd spend my time with Izabella regretting the past, wishing to God we'd got together just after the war and enjoyed all those years together, had that family and the nice house and the vacations. All that regret, it would have made me angry. And that wouldn't have been fair on her."

Diane gave a thoughtful nod.

"The regretting, the longing for a past I never had—I just couldn't face it. I guess getting myself locked up meant I could avoid having to explain it to Izabella. It's only now I realize that. But I called her after I got released, explained it all to her. We talked for hours, just like we had in Warsaw, and with her help, I think I'm ready. She told me I can still have those thoughts of what might have been, and that in time I'll come to accept that the chance has gone. And she's right. I don't long for those things anymore. I *think* of them occasionally, but I don't *long* for them. I accept the chance has gone."

"You know something?" Diane said. "I completely get that."

Asher smiled softly, sadness in his eyes. "Somehow I thought you might."

"Well, good on you. And does that mean you're going?"

"Uh-huh. This is my farewell tour, and you have the only ticket."

"I'm so pleased for you, Asher. You deserve a little happiness."

"Thank you." He leaned in and whispered, "So do you."

"Okay, okay." She blushed.

"Anyway," he said. "I have a big favor to ask you."

"Sure. Anything."

"I'm an old man, Diane. You may have noticed. And despite what I just told you, I still have reservations about going. I know I love Izabella, but the thought of moving to a new house at my age—and moving *countries*—well, I can't help but be nervous. Would you promise me you and Brad will come visit us?"

Diane needed a gulp before replying. "You know, you've told me so much about Izabella, I'd really love to meet her."

"Oh, thank you, Diane. I was afraid I'd never see you again."

"Well, you will."

"Thank you."

Diane finished her coffee and stood. "We can keep talking, but I need to cook. How hungry are you?"

Early the next morning, Diane and Brad drove Asher into Pittsburgh—to the bus depot. Brad gave Asher a firm handshake, and Diane gave him a long hug—this time nothing like politicians or dignitaries, more like a close uncle and niece. Asher told Diane he'd be in touch about Warsaw, then they waved him off on his way back to Detroit.

"What did he mean by that?" Brad said as they walked to the mall.

"I'll tell you later. First, we need a present for Mother because we can't go empty-handed. Then we need breakfast."

"Well, okay. Aren't chocolates kind of compulsory for these occasions?"

Thirty minutes later, with a heart-shaped box of gourmet Belgian chocolates duly bought, they sat down to a late breakfast.

"So, did you two have a good time yesterday?" Brad said.

Diane nodded. "It was good. It was . . . worthwhile."

"Worthwhile? That's rather specific a word. He told you why he signed that confession?"

"Mmm . . . in a roundabout way. I think I know why."

"Really?"

"Yeah."

"That's good." Brad waited while she took a bite of hash brown. Then he waited while she took a sip of coffee. "Tell me at your leisure, won't you?" he said.

"I might. It's a long story and perhaps something only Asher and I understand. I think we have a bond."

"A bond. Right." He laughed. "Have it your way. Anyhow, what was that about Warsaw?"

"Well . . ." She showed him a comedy grin. "I have a couple favors to ask you."

He tutted.

"It's not what you think—definitely not what you think."

"I'll be the judge of that. Go on. Put me out of my misery."

"The Warsaw thing. You see, Asher's moving there to live with this Izabella I told you about."

"The woman he met during the war? You're kidding me!"

"They want to be together."

"Good for them. Jeez, Asher has a lot of years to make up for."

"He does. And, uh, I've promised we'll go visit them sometime. Is that okay?"

"A European vacation? I'd like nothing more."

"Well, that's both of us happy."

He smiled. "For sure."

They ate in silence for a minute or so.

"And the other thing?" Brad asked.

"Huh?"

"You said you had a *couple* favors to ask."

"Oh, yes. There was one other thing."

"Shoot."

"That question you asked me."

Brad frowned, trying to remember. "What question?"

"The one you asked me at the millennium celebrations."

He choked on his hash brown and coughed a few times before regaining his composure. "Oh," he said between coughs. "Oh, yeah. *That* question."

"It's time to start asking me again, this time with a little real purpose."

Brad swallowed, his face reddening. "Are you . . . are you serious?"

"Asher isn't the only one with a lot of years to make up for."

"Wow!" he said. Then he composed himself. "I'm sorry. I guess I should have something better to say after all these years together."

She shook her head. "*Wow's* good."

Brad said he'd call "that swanky French restaurant" to see if they had any tables free. Then they smiled and ate, and ate and smiled, words unnecessary.

Diane knew she would never stop missing her father—whatever his faults. But now she could see a brighter future for her and Brad, and also for Asher and Izabella.

Just like Asher, Diane knew she wouldn't waste another moment longing for a past she never had.

ACKNOWLEDGMENTS

This novel was a team effort, more so than anything else I've written. It also caused me untold grief, as it turned into a different tale quite a few times during its lengthy gestation period.

For its development during the early stages, thanks are due to Jill Worth, Delphine Cull, Sarah Manning, and Lee and Marcus of Frostbite Publishing. I'm also immensely grateful to Sammia Hamer and Victoria Pepe at Amazon Publishing for their unstinting belief in this story even when it wasn't quite right, Celine Kelly for her structural editing expertise, Gemma Wain for her copy-editing skills, and Ian Bahrami for his thorough proofreading. Special thanks are due to Maria for encouraging me to persevere, when I could easily have put the whole thing to one side.

ABOUT THE AUTHOR

Ray Kingfisher was born and bred in the Black Country in the UK, and now lives in Hampshire. He has published novels under various pen names, most notably Rachel Quinn, but also Ray Backley and Ray Fripp.

For more information on the author, please visit www.raykingfisher. com.